The French Girl's War

Karen,
Wishing you all the best!

Herb Williams-Dalgart

ISBN-13: 9781493570881
ISBN-10: 1493570889
Library of Congress Control Number: 2013920027
CreateSpace Independent Publishing Platform
North Charleston, South Carolina

Acclaim for The French Girl's War

"*The French Girl's War* is a novel of hope and determination that lights up a dark place in human history. A generous humanity fills the pages of this book. As readers, we can't help worrying about Sophie, yet with her fortitude and grit—and with the hope she inspires—we believe in her. We know she won't rest until goodness prevails."

—Paula Cizmar,
Award-winning playwright, author, and screenwriter

"Set early in World War II, this novel charms with its depictions of French village life and its vivid, quirky characters. But don't be misled. The ravages and cruelties of war come calling, forcing eighteen-year-old ingenue Sophie to abandon her dreams of an artistic life—and forging in her a new necessity for courage and fierceness. Sophie is the perfect heroine for the reader who loves to live, for a time, with greatness."

—Louella Nelson,
Best-selling author

To my darling, Maggie—your bravery is boundless. You married a writer without knowing what you were in for.

Acknowledgements

Like my protagonist, Sophie, I have been fortunate in my friends, family, and supporters, to whom I remain eternally grateful.

My mentors are numerous and diverse, but of particular importance are Paula Cizmar and Louella Nelson, both gifted writers, each impressive in what they know, generous in what they share, and immeasurable in how they inspire. Paula, you taught me how much can be done with just a few words, so long as they're the right ones; entire worlds can be built or toppled. Lou, you reminded me that our hearts can be felt, heard, smelled, seen, and tasted through language and that every moment should be an important one—a good lesson in writing as well as in life.

To my fellow writers' group members, I thank you for constantly helping me enjoy what is mistakenly thought of as a solitary endeavor, the act of writing. The process of bringing this story forward was daringly supported by talented writers, each with wonderful stories to tell: Beverly Plass, Brad Oatman, Tim Twombly, Fiona Farrell Ivey, Debby Gaal Silverberg, Mary Garliepp Myers, and my former group members—Blake Bullock, Dennis Phinney, Brenda Barrie, and Janet Simcic.

To the wonderful Benrey family of Mareil-Marly, France, I thank you for your friendship, generosity, and kind support in keeping my French references and names in line. We'll always have *profiteroles!*

To the historian and author, Ian Sumner, I send my thanks for your guidance in providing historical detail to my fictional tale, just enough to help me feel authentic but allowing for all the creative license I needed to tell Sophie's story.

To my parents, I thank you for your constant encouragement. I still learn so much from you alter kockers. And a particular thanks to my mother for suggesting I take typing back in high school. Sure came in handy!

To my remaining friends, family, and in-laws too numerous to mention, I am thankful for your love and support, most notably in the form of your forgiveness for the hours I spent writing rather than with you.

And most of all, I thank my dearest Maggie, Emily, and Ethan. You make me want to try harder, live better, learn more, and laugh loudly. You give me hope.

Chapter 1

The Envelope

Fall had come, and it made the goats angry. Sophie tried to sing "Au Clair de la Lune" to them, just as her father used to do when she was upset. However, today the animals could not be calmed, and she feared their milk would sour from their discontent.

In truth, Sophie hated the goats, and perhaps they hated her, too. Or maybe it was just their slotted eyes that gave this impression—permanently fixed to view her sideways. They saw Sophie like most people in Avoine saw her—not as a girl with dreams but as the Jewish farmer's daughter. The goat girl.

She emerged from the barn into the cool evening air, her goosefleshed forearms straining with the weight of the last bucket of goats' milk. She raised her face to the darkening sky and drew a breath to savor the scents of the river valley. The Loire's pungent smells and rumbling sounds reassured her that change was natural, inevitable. Tonight, things were going to change; she would see to it.

Sophie lifted her bucket haltingly through the gate, past the blackberries that choked the fence, past the chicken coops, to the cooling shed. She lowered her pail into the cooling box, next to the two others she'd already set there. Angry or not, the goats had been productive. Her father would be pleased.

Free of her cargo, she flexed her fingers to rid them of pain and closed the lid of the cooling box, against the protest of the rusted hinges. She left the shed to head to the chicken coop and stopped, reaching into her dress pocket for the envelope she'd received in yesterday's mail. She unfolded it and pressed it against a fencepost to smooth out the creases.

"*Université de Paris, La Sorbonne,*" she read to the rooster who'd poked his head through the pen. "This changes everything." She waved the envelope tauntingly at the cockeyed bird. "Soon I'll be through with you and those horrible goats."

As if in response, the rooster clucked quizzically, causing Sophie to giggle. She quickly remembered there was no time for play. Even with the milk taken and the animals penned for the night, she still needed to fix supper for her father. Only then could she have the discussion she'd been planning all day.

She stuffed the envelope back in her pocket. Ignoring the soreness in her legs, she sprinted over the weed-patched field to the house, up the creaking steps to the porch.

Sophie's father had already lit a lamp in the window of their humble farmhouse, clearly believing it would be dark by the time she completed her chores. As always, he'd underestimated her.

She strode through the front door, expecting to find him after another hard day plowing, sitting in his threadbare chair by the radio, listening to Alix Combelle's jazz or the latest boring speech from Prime Minister Daladier. Yet her father's chair was empty and the house was silent. With a look down the hall she confirmed he wasn't home.

Perfect, she thought. I can prepare supper and surprise him when he returns.

Before dawn, before her chores, she'd ridden her bicycle three kilometers to the only Jewish market near Avoine to retrieve her father's favorite: kosher lamb. It had cost her three month's savings and was a long journey to take before her usual routine of feeding the chickens, cleaning the pens, and milking the goats, but her labor would be worth it when her father came home and saw the feast she'd prepared.

Sophie hastened to the kitchen, eager to start, but knocked her toe into a large, wooden chest her father had mysteriously left out in the living room.

"Ow!" She wiggled her toe.

It took her a moment to recognize the chest, usually kept in the depths of the hall closet. It was rare for her father to take anything out of storage and more unusual for him to open his memory chest. The items it contained only served to remind him of Sophie's deceased mother, a topic of conversation her father always avoided.

Tonight, however, Sophie hoped the conversation would be pleasant. She would put her father in the best of moods, soften him with culinary pleasures, and care for him like a king—at least as much as their meager means would allow. That, she thought, is what it would take to convince him to let her leave for Paris by the month's end.

Dismissing its peculiar position, she pushed the chest next to her father's empty chair and moved to the kitchen. She opened the pantry door in search of their last bottle of red wine, a particularly good one, saved for a special occasion. They had no money to spend on such things, but the gift from Monsieur Marcoux, given at Purim, had languished in the dark cupboard long enough.

To her surprise, the bottle was gone. She searched the cabinet behind the sack of flour and below the sink where she kept the copper boiling pot, but couldn't find the wine.

Perhaps Papa's given it away...Whatever the case, it didn't matter. Her father would find ample pleasure in her lamb and parsnips.

From the kitchen drawer, she snatched her grandmother's linen tablecloth, and from the rack by the sink she retrieved the tall water glasses. She set the table, folded the napkins, turned on the gas, and lit the stove and oven. She then chopped the onions, warmed the bread, and readied herself for her big night.

Once the scents of broiled lamb, sizzling onions, and rosemary had filled the house, Sophie lit the fire in the hearth and turned on the radio to search for the jazz her father adored. Instead, all she found was news of Germany, how Hitler had begun closing Jewish businesses, treating Jews as criminals, moving people to ghettos. She knew enough to know that Germans couldn't be trusted—even now, so long after the Great War—and that they were no friends to Jews, but why would they want to send Jews to ghettos? The announcer said America's President Roosevelt had admonished the Germans and that Prime Minister Daladier predictably agreed. Whatever the issue, she thought, it didn't concern her here on the farm.

She turned the dial and finally found the bouncy trumpet of the American Louis Armstrong—one of her father's favorites. With the scene now set, the only thing missing was her father. She moved to the door and opened it to the evening air.

"Papa?" she called. "Dinner's ready."

Her father startled her when he leaned in from around the corner of the house, the open bottle of Purim wine clutched in his hand. He'd been outside the house all along.

"Smells good," he said softly.

His demeanor was curious, his gaze not quite meeting hers. As he drew nearer, she saw his eyes glossy with sadness. His breath was sour with wine and his shaggy black hair was tussled. He hadn't shaved and the stubble on his face, peppered gray, made him look tired. Not quite drunk, he seemed, haunted.

"Papa, what's wrong?"

He moved past her into the house. "Nothing, *ma chère.*"

"Were you crying?" she asked. "What's happened?" She rushed to follow him back into the house.

He blinked, sniffed the air, and offered a forced smile. "You've cooked lamb."

"Yes." She donned a grin, hoping to find some happy influence over him and change his mysterious mood. "Your favorite."

Her father pushed the door closed and took his seat at the table. He rubbed his shoulder, the one that gave him trouble when the weather got cold.

Sophie bustled back to the kitchen to retrieve the dish of lamb warming in the oven, one eye locked on her father, trying to decode his behavior. Using her frayed oven mitt, she carried the dish, bubbling with rosemary gravy, to the oak table and set it in front of him.

He leaned forward and breathed in the meal as if smelling her cooking for the first time. What was wrong with him?

Sophie took a seat and her father bowed his head. He half-heartedly mumbled the Hebrew *brucha* over the meal and then turned to her. "This is lovely."

"I wanted to surprise you. It's kosher."

Her father did not respond, instead surveying the food and the house around them. He seemed somehow displaced, more than could be attributed to the wine he'd consumed.

Rather than asking the reason for the fancy meal or where she could have scrounged the money to fund it, her father glanced to the window and stared into the shadow of dusk.

Perhaps the cause of his anxiety was buried in the memory chest he'd dragged out to the living room. Nothing in his behavior made sense.

"Papa," Sophie said. "What is it? What's wrong?"

He turned back to the lamb and parsnips without remark, as if he hadn't heard a word. He served Sophie and then himself, giving his attention to the food.

She reached into her pocket to stroke the tattered edge of the envelope, recalling the letter's final promise: with the proper secondary school transcripts, written recommendations from her teachers, and her father's permission, she could begin her art history courses by the end of the month. The scholarship from her school would cover the first semester's tuition. The rest would be up to her.

"Please, Papa...Tell me."

Her father put down his tarnished fork with a clink on the dish. He chewed quickly and wiped his mouth with the edge of the tablecloth, mistaking it for his napkin.

"Something has happened, Sophie," he said at last. "Something important."

She released the envelope in her pocket and moved her hand to the table, trying to keep her fingers from trembling. She'd never known her father to be this dramatic.

"The Germans," he said flatly. "They've invaded Poland." He took a breath. "Now, they appear to be on the move." He again turned to look outside as if he was sitting in Poland and the Germans were just outside the door.

Sophie had heard stories of the Great War, of how her grandfather had died defending France, fighting the Germans. She knew they took Austria last year, and then part of Czechoslovakia, but her father hadn't seemed troubled about it, so she gave it little thought. The radio had just said they were bothering the Jews in Germany, but she must've missed the part about Poland. Why would this so upset her father? They didn't know anyone there.

"Yes," she said trying to engage him. "I heard something on the news."

Her father reached into his pocket and pulled out a letter of his own, which he tossed onto the table as though folding a losing hand in a game of cards.

Sophie's heart raced in time with the frenetic Armstrong jazz from the radio. Had the university sent her father a letter as well? Had he learned of her plans before she could prepare him? Surely he'd think they couldn't afford La

Sorbonne, but Sophie would find work. She'd get a job at a *fromagerie* or help some family in exchange for room and board...

"Papa, I can explain. Paris is my dream, and you know I love art—"

"France is calling all able men to serve," he announced. Her father finally faced her, his sunken eyes now focused and precise implying he'd made his final point. Yet, if he had, that point was lost on Sophie.

"To serve?"

"To fight if this becomes a war, Sophie. That letter is from *l'Armée de Terre*. They're starting with those who've served before. Remember my service? I leave Friday."

"Friday?"

His meaning swirled into focus, and the room seemed to close in on her. He rose from the table and walked to the memory chest. He lifted the heavy lid with one hand and reached into the chest with his other, drawing out a folded stack of woolen clothes he then placed on his chair.

He pulled one garment free from the stack and turned to Sophie, letting the fabric unfurl in front of him as he held it to his shoulders. It was his uniform from his days as a young soldier.

"Do you think I'll still be handsome?" He offered a broken smile, attempting to change the mood. "Your mother used to think I was good looking in my uniform."

Sophie opened her mouth and hoped to hear herself say something convincing, something magical that would change everything, make it right. However, no sound came.

War? All she knew of war was that it had left her grandmother a widow and her own father fatherless—a pain topped, he had said, only by the loss of her mother on the day of Sophie's birth. Her father had served the army when he was a younger man in more peaceful times. What did he know about fighting a war?

"You can't go," she said at last. "You can't."

"There's no choice, *ma chère*. France needs me."

"I need you," she snapped back, already feeling like she'd lost him. "Who will run the farm? Who will care for me?" She realized that, only moments ago, she'd planned to leave the farm, leave her father, to tell him that he could hire a boy from the village and that he didn't need her at all. She'd planned to say pointedly, but with pride, that she didn't need him to care for her any longer—the very thing she was now claiming was so important.

"Your grandmother," he replied, tossing his uniform onto the chair. "You'll stay with her in Ville de Lemaire. It's all been arranged. We'll close the farm until I return."

"Return? How do you know you'll return?"

"I'll return," he pronounced, "because I said I'll return." He gathered the uniform from the chair and retreated to his bedroom, where he closed his door with a thud, his final words on the matter spoken.

Sophie reached into her pocket for the envelope from the university. Without removing the letter, she walked to the hearth, tore the envelope in two, and tossed the pieces into the fire, a fitting end, she thought, to both her dreams and the dinner her father hardly noticed.

The cold outside the farmhouse grew and the wind began to lick at the walls. Sophie scrubbed the dishes with extra vigor, uncertain if she was more angry or sad at the cruel irony of her circumstance. On the very day she'd been ready to reveal her secret dream, it was, instead, a secret fear she'd realized. Her father's letter, not hers, had set her destiny. Now, rather than preparing for her own adventure, she was preparing for abandonment; she was preparing for his death, which she knew would surely come.

This seemed to be her curse, to send those she loved to an untimely death. Her mother had died in childbirth, and Sophie had always felt she was the one responsible, even when her father had assured her otherwise.

"Your mother's frailty was not your fault," he'd said. "Nature took her, not you." Just as he'd done tonight, he'd made it clear: there was to be no debate about things he'd already decided. The truth of things was his alone to declare.

Nevertheless, Sophie held the belief that, if she'd been important enough, her mother would have found a way to live, and that it was she who was responsible. Now her father too was getting ready to leave her, to court death, choosing the dangers of war over her. Her need of him wasn't enough to keep him home, just as it hadn't been enough to keep her mother alive.

Paris would have changed everything. It would have made her an educated teacher of art, a cosmopolitan lady. The women of Paris, the ones in the magazines, were glamorous. They had opportunity, they had art, and they had love. Such women only brought joy to those around them. Such women would never bear a curse like hers, and none of them ever had to touch a goat.

Sophie wiped clean the last dinner plate, her anxiety rising like the storm outside. Was the whole world growing unsettled?

She tossed her rag aside, left the remaining pots upside down in the sink to dry, and retreated to the bathroom to gain some measure of composure. As she passed her father's room, she heard the familiar rumble of his snoring. The combination of wine and food had bested him, though Sophie still felt restless like the wind.

With a huff, she filled the bathroom basin with water from a ceramic pitcher and cleaned her face with a thin shard of foul-smelling soap. She employed the same angry vigor to her cheeks that she'd used to scrub the dinner plates, eager to clean away as much of this dreadful day as she could.

She dried herself with a crispy, line-dried towel, then, without bothering to change into her nightclothes, kicked off her muddy shoes and climbed into bed. With a final glance to the small Van Gogh postcard on her wall and Monet bookplate over her desk, she blew out her bedside candle. The artists of her dreams would have to wait.

The tree at her window, now animated by the angry breeze, clawed at the clapboards, determined to keep her from sleep. She closed her eyes, turned away from the window, and wished for the darkness to take her. She drew her knitted blanket to her ears and tried to ignore the ghoulish cacophony.

Just as she felt herself drifting, the wind unlatched a shutter in the front of the house, freeing it to beat against the window frame. In her half-dream state, she imagined it wasn't a shutter at all, but the French army, pounding on the door, demanding her father come with them. The wind's whistle became a wail, and the wail soon became a woman's scream—the cries of her mother, inexplicably alive, howling in grief, the way Sophie imagined her on the night she'd killed her, seventeen years ago.

The world was wrenching itself apart and Sophie knew, as she braced herself, that her curse wouldn't be so easily defeated after all.

Chapter 2

Friday's Rain

Just as Sophie feared, Friday had come too soon. Throughout the week, a cold and unrelenting rain had fallen as though the sky itself had felt her sorrow.

She'd spent the week packing what few belongings were worth keeping—the art books from her mother, her Van Gogh print depicting the artist's room at Arles, a few dresses and necessities, and the handful of photos and keepsakes her mother had left behind.

They'd sold the goats and chickens to Monsieur Marcoux. This was a feat of luck, according to her father. Half the men in town had tried to do the same, but Monsieur Marcoux, himself a Jew, had shown them favor, or perhaps pity.

Now, weary from lack of sleep and a profound sadness, Sophie stood beside the wagon in the shelter of the musty barn, warming her fingers under her arms. She wore her favorite blue dress to impress her father, although its ornate floral patterns were hidden beneath the thick black coat he'd insisted she wear. Again, his plans had supplanted hers.

Their gray horse, Plouf, stood unfazed in his stall, munching oats from a feedbag. He appeared calm, giving no care to Sophie, the sound of the rain, or the wagon and rigging that awaited him. To Plouf, it seemed this was just another drizzly morning.

Sophie tapped her frozen foot, waiting for her father as he raced around the farm in the rain, closing the house, inspecting its security one final time. They'd spent the predawn hours under the shelter of the barn, storing away household items in the rafters and loading the wagon with Sophie's necessities and food for the road. They'd covered the wagon with the stained tarp usually reserved for protecting their hay bales from weather such as this. Working together as they'd always done, they'd seen to all the needs of the farm and had spoken very little about their needs of one another.

She tried to convince herself she'd be fine without him. Given her original plans for La Sorbonne, one thing was supposed to have remained certain: her father would be here, at home, should things go wrong. He was supposed to be like the straw in the barn when she used to climb in the loft. If she happened to fall, it would be there to cushion her.

In fact, he'd always been there for her. He consoled her when the schoolchildren of Avoine had taunted her for being Jewish, when they pitied her for having no mother, or when they mocked her for being thinner than the mild-mannered, milk-fed Catholic farm girls of the valley. He praised Sophie's strength when others had teased her for being rough, told her she was beautiful even though she was all knees and elbows. Though no one would ever describe him as an emotional man, he always showed his love for her, even if he rarely said it in words.

Now, like her mother, he was leaving her, perhaps forever.

In a flurry of mud and rain, he dashed into the barn, raindrops beading off his coat. He shook his head and ran his hand through his wild hair to slick it back from his eyes. "Ready?"

"Yes," she lied, knowing he'd allow no other answer.

"It's nearly nine," he explained.

She nodded, knowing at nine o'clock the men would come for him, and joining them would be Maurice. Caretaker of the cemetery, Maurice often helped people in Avoine with odd jobs when his grave digging responsibilities would mercifully wane. This week, Sophie's father had bartered with Maurice to take her on the three-day journey to her grandmother's in exchange for their wagon and horse. Her father had told her they'd never find a buyer for a horse as old as Plouf anyway, and that they'd have to replace the aging wagon regardless upon his return. He said Maurice would treat Plouf with kindness—a better fate than the one usually reserved for old horses. Nevertheless, to Sophie this seemed too high a price for a transporting a girl, even if it was halfway across France.

"Let's get Plouf ready," her father said, cutting short her reverie.

"All right."

Glad for a chance to get circulation back to her toes, she followed him toward the horse's stall. As her father retrieved the wagon, she removed Plouf's feedbag and walked the horse to the center of the barn. She then fitted Plouf with his driving halter, breast strap, and tug. The horse brayed, suddenly eager for an adventure, still unmoved by her anxiety.

When her father returned, he pulled forward the wagon and reached for the horse's bridle. Plouf stomped his hoof, agitated at being strapped so abruptly. Her father patted the horse's speckled flank. "There, Plouf." His voice was gentle and calm. "Easy, now."

Sophie watched her father's movements and listened to his deep, reassuring voice. A longing for him, as if he'd already left, rose in her heart and gripped her.

"Will you write to me?" she asked, trying to sound as casual and unafraid as her father seemed.

"As often as I can." He smiled uneasily. "You should write me, too." He gave a tug on Plouf's reins to test his handiwork.

"Of course I will," Sophie swallowed.

Her father moved around the cart, crouching down to each wheel, seeming more concerned with the wagon than with Sophie.

Without warning, the rain stopped, and a silence washed over the barn. The quiet froze everything, punctuating the moment. She closed her eyes, took a calming breath, and let the stillness fill her.

She drew in the yeasty scent of the damp straw and the bouquet of remnant manure, felt the chill in the air, heard the beat of her heart and the hollow emptiness of the farm, now free of goats and chickens…Her every sense was raised like the gooseflesh on her legs until she was floating above her body, watching the scene from the sky. Colors, textures, and emotions locked into a single memory. A rich oil painting of the moment formed in her mind, framed there forever.

She opened her eyes just as her father removed his gloves. He stuffed them into his pockets and stepped away from the wagon, away from Sophie, toward the open barn door.

"Terrible weather…" he said. He massaged his shoulder against the pain.

"Does it hurt again?" Sophie asked. She liked to rub it for him on days like this, days when he'd worked the fields and the bad weather found its way into his bones.

"No." He let his hand fall to his side. "Not a bit."

Sophie strode forward, forgiving his lie, and slipped her cold palm into his, asserting her need to connect with him.

He turned to her, surprised by her gesture. He then smiled, laced his fingers between hers and, together, they stepped out into the bitter morning.

The clip-clop sounds of distant hooves traveled toward them from the road above, guided by the now-gentle wind, and Sophie knew their time together was coming to an end.

Her father stopped to draw a frosty breath, and Sophie did the same. He lifted his head to the cloudy sky and again, Sophie followed suit. She thought by mimicking his gestures, she might show him she was equal to their task ahead, or at least equal enough that he wouldn't worry for her as much as she would worry for him.

He returned his gaze from the sky. "There's one last thing," he said quietly. He withdrew his grasp, reached into his breast pocket, and removed a necklace— a simple silver chain that carried a small key. "I need you to keep this safe."

"A key?"

He held out the necklace, the key swaying before her. "It belonged to your mother."

"Mama?" Immediately, Sophie's mind raced. She thought she'd seen everything ever owned by her mother, read every art book she'd owned, viewed every photograph, heard every story...

"It fits a box I've kept with your *grand-mère*. It contains things that will... raise questions."

"What questions? What's in the box?"

"Please, Sophie. Take the key. Keep it safe. When I return, I promise we'll open the box together."

Sophie took the necklace, draped it over her head, and tucked the cold metal key beneath her clothing, close to her racing heart as if clutching her mother herself. A million questions begged to be asked, but her father's face told her this wasn't the time.

He grasped her hand, squeezed it hard.

"I love you," he said, tears welling in his eyes.

A stone formed in her throat. When was the last time he'd said he loved her, spoken it so simply and directly? She'd known it to be true—never doubted it—but hearing it declared felt like a cup of warm chocolate cream on this cold, wet day.

"I love you too," she stammered.

To hide her burst of tears, she gripped him around the waist and pressed her face to his chest. His wool coat scratched her frozen cheeks and resisted her tears just as it had resisted the rain, but still, she held him tight. They stood locked in their quiet embrace, rainclouds threatening to open again, another canvas painted in her mind.

Soon, the creaks and groans of the approaching wagon were too loud to ignore. The harsh breathing of the horses, the knock and splash of their hooves on the wet road echoed around them until she felt it was the Grim Reaper who was coming.

Plouf neighed, perhaps in anticipation of the journey or at hearing the sounds of other horses.

Sophie squeezed her eyes closed against the imposing world, trying one last time to wish it away, until her father's grip softened and she felt him touch her cheek. She opened her eyes to his face shining upon hers.

"It's time," he whispered.

At the roadside, forty meters up the path, a wagon pulled to a halt. Two black mares shook their heads, clouds rising from their nostrils. Crowded into the back of the wagon, a group of men sat hunched under gray blankets and drank from steaming tin cups. One man stepped out of the wagon into the mud, drew up his collar against the chill, and approached Sophie and her father. It was Maurice.

"Bonjour," the gravedigger said. His warm, white breath swirled around his words. His eyes were ice blue and his bottlebrush hair and mustache were dirty gray. The creases in his face spoke not just of his age, but of sadness. He looked at Sophie and then back to her father, seeming to recognize the anguish of the moment.

Her father released her to shake Maurice's hand. "Bonjour, Maurice."

"The horse?"

Sophie blanched at the man's bluntness.

"In the barn," her father replied. "He's hitched and ready."

Without further word, Maurice disappeared to retrieve Plouf and the wagon, giving Sophie's father a moment to pick up his rucksack and hoist it over his good shoulder.

Again, he touched Sophie's face, this time wiping away the rain and her tears with his calloused thumb. He lowered his hand and kissed her cheeks with fervor. He then took a step back, and looked at her for a long, lingering moment, as though painting a canvas of his own.

"*Au revoir, ma fille,*" he whispered.

Sophie released her lip from her teeth. "Be safe, Papa." This was not her wish, but her command.

He opened his mouth as if to reply, but said nothing. Instead, he gave a final nod and turned to the waiting men.

She watched him trudge through the mud, toss his sack to his new companions, and climb into the wagon. With a decisive "Ha!" the driver snapped the reins over the horses' backs and the wagon lurched forward.

Through her tears, she watched her father accept a tin cup from another man and then disappear, absorbed under the dark cover of a blanket. He'd become one of them, these men of war rolling into the fog…a final canvas in her mind.

As the wagon faded over the crest of the hill and out of sight, the wind grew and lightning split the sky, giving Sophie a start. Thunder shook, sending a rumble over the farm.

Through the echoing rain that followed, she thought she could hear her father singing, "Au Clair de la Lune" one last time. She filled her lungs with cool air in an attempt to settle her heart. When the freezing rain began to fall anew, she faced the gunmetal gray sky and welcomed the numbing cold it offered. This, she thought, is what it feels like to be alone.

Sophie retreated from the rain to the barn, where she found Maurice standing next to Plouf, murmuring into the horse's ear and stroking his blond mane. Oddly, Plouf had tilted his head and seemed to be listening to whatever it was Maurice was saying. It was clear from the man's familiarity with her horse, the gravedigger believed his compensation had already been provided. Plouf was now his.

"What are you doing?" asked Sophie.

"I'm explaining to Bernard how the journey will go."

"His name is not 'Bernard.'" Sophie marched in front of Maurice to rub the horse's head. "His name is Plouf."

"It's Bernard now." He gave a gentle tug on the horse's reins.

Sophie glowered. Maurice had been a decent man the few times she'd made his acquaintance. Of course, each of those times was in her father's presence, when Maurice had been hired to help on the farm. Now, his disposition toward Sophie had changed along with the circumstances of his employment. He'd taken advantage of their situation, commanded too high a price for his labor, and had received it.

"Are you ready to leave?" he asked.

"No. I have one last thing to do." She turned from the horse and strode out of the barn, back into the rain.

In fact, Sophie had nothing left to do, but felt compelled to cause Maurice some measure of inconvenience in return for his rudeness.

"Make it fast!" he called. "We have a long way to go before dark."

Sophie didn't reply, but instead ran toward the house, over the muddy clearing, through the puddles. Sheets of cold rain drifted over her, urged on by the pressing wind. With another crack of lightning and grumble of thunder, she dashed to the porch to a dry spot under the sloping roof.

She shivered and stomped her feet on the wood planks to rid her shoes of muck and her head of angry thoughts. The length of her dress was wet and mud-spattered, but she no longer cared. Instead, she wiped the rain from her face and looked at her front door, her attention drawn to the gleam coming from her family *mezuzah*, attached at an angle to the doorframe.

The thin box, wrought of metal, was the size of a cigar and had been painted with sapphire-blue Hebrew letters and braided with a golden trim. Less shiny than it once had been, the mezuzah remained where her father had affixed it on her fifth birthday, and still contained the traditional Hebrew parchment blessing that had protected their home these many years. Sophie wondered if the blessing would protect them now, even after they'd forsaken their house.

She recalled that day, watching her father fasten the cherished item to their door to replace the old one that had rusted in the river valley air. He'd lifted her onto his shoulders so she could be the first to view the blessing. Impulsively, she leaned over his mop of black hair and kissed the mezuzah, feeling the cold metal on her lips.

"*Très bien, ma grande!*" he'd called, tossing her, giggling, into the air. "Very good, my big girl!"

Now, surrounded by rain and clouds, she stood on her porch without him. She kissed two of her freezing fingers and pressed them to the mezuzah, hoping this would not be the last time she looked upon her door. She wished she could hear her father's cheers once again.

"Let's go!" called Maurice through the rain.

He now sat atop the wagon, parked in front of the house, holding the horse's reins. To Sophie's dismay, Plouf appeared cooperative, despite the thunder, the downpour, and the presence of a new master. Whatever the gravedigger had said to the horse, it appeared to have worked.

Maurice leaned down beneath the driver's bench and returned with a black umbrella, which he opened and waved over his head. "Now!"

She squinted in anger, pulled her gloves from her coat, and strode back through the mud to the wagon, spitting curses under her breath. She hoisted herself up onto the wagon with a single, swift leap, and sat decisively next to Maurice, just as he appeared ready to step down to help her.

He sat openmouthed, astonished at her feat. She replied to his awe with a triumphant smirk and faced the road.

"You're quite strong for a girl," he remarked.

"I'm quite strong for a boy, too."

The gravedigger frowned, mumbled something she couldn't hear, and handed her the umbrella. "Your job for the journey is to hold this over our heads."

She snatched the umbrella. "That's all?"

"That, and pray for the rain to stop." He turned to the horse and called "Yah," snapping Plouf to action.

Fuming and uncertain of the road ahead, she lifted the umbrella, struggling to keep it steady in the wind. The wagon rolled forward, away from her home and the life she knew.

If she was to pray for better weather, it would be for the horse's sake, not Maurice's, and in her prayers, the horse's name would still be Plouf.

Chapter 3

Maurice

Disheartened and angry, Sophie held the umbrella for the first three hours of their journey in silence, content to let the thunder and the persistent pummel of rain speak for her.

Maurice sat solemnly, his eyes fixed on the road. Aside from the occasional cough, he too kept quiet.

Sophie couldn't tell if he was irritated or antisocial. Either way, she was satisfied with their unspoken agreement not to converse. Silence suited him.

Plouf, on the other hand, seemed to enjoy the excursion. He tossed his head, shook his mane, and flicked his tongue in and out like a schoolchild catching raindrops. Even the lightning wasn't enough to dampen the horse's spirits.

Once the rain lifted, Sophie closed the umbrella and set it at her feet. She quietly fingered the key around her neck, pondering the secrets it might unlock and wondering why her father hadn't shared it with her until now. How could he have left her with such a puzzle and expect her to withhold her curiosity until his return? It seemed a cruelty she didn't deserve, and the thought only served to feed her foul mood.

Yet, in spite of her wet gloves, cold hands, and dark disposition, she chose not to complain. To do so would give Maurice some amount of satisfaction, which she was determined to deny him.

After a few hours, they approached a clearing and Maurice finally broke the peace. "I'm hungry," he announced. "It's time for a picnic." He steered Plouf off the road to stop in a dry patch of dirt under a hulking oak tree.

Although she wanted to disagree, Sophie was also hungry and figured Plouf was hungry, too. She jumped down, set the brake on the wagon, and retrieved a small sack of carrots she'd packed as a snack for the horse.

As she fed Plouf, Maurice dug into the wagon's keep under the canvas tarp and found the basket of food Sophie had prepared for the trip. He withdrew the basket and carried the food over to the tree.

Plouf happily munched the carrots, allowing Sophie to join the gravedigger under the oak where he leaned against the tree's wide trunk. Maurice used his pocketknife to open a can of kippers and carve a wedge of hard *Comté* she'd packed. The basket sat three meters beyond his feet where he'd seemingly tossed it.

"It's not much of a feast," Maurice declared when she approached, "but I suppose it'll have to do."

Sophie held her tongue.

"I think I saw a baguette in there," he called. "Why don't you fetch it?"

Smoldering, she snatched the basket and brought it back to the tree, counting her steps between clenched teeth to ease her anger. She too lowered herself against the dry trunk and plopped the basket between them to make a point. Shen then removed the baguette and held it out for him. "Here."

"Slice it," he commanded, chewing his kipper, oblivious to her irritation.

"Pardon me?"

Maurice swallowed and enunciated his words. "I said, slice it." He stuffed another pungent kipper into his mouth, its yellow oil dripping from his bushy mustache.

"Please," she seethed.

"Hmm?" Maurice looked up from his fish, puzzled.

"You say 'please' when you ask someone to do something for you," she raged. "Slice it, please." She withdrew a serrated bread knife from the basket and wagged it at him. "Or you could say, 'Would you please slice the baguette?' or 'Would you be so kind...' Don't you have any manners?"

Maurice raised his chin and narrowed his eyes. It was obvious he was not used to being spoken to this way, especially by a girl waving a knife.

Sophie eyed him back, waiting for his reply. This was not how she thought she'd make her inevitable stand against him, battling over manners, but she concluded this was as good a time as any.

After an enduring moment, locked in each other's gaze, Maurice slackened his shoulders, and looked away. "Forgive me," he muttered.

Maurice's apology gave her pause. He seemed remorseful, even sullen.

"It's fine," she replied, and began to slice the bread.

He eyed the clouds. "I live alone," he explained. "I have no children, no wife. I'm...not used to proper ways or proper people like you...I'm sorry."

Sophie piled fresh slices of bread into a hand towel and continued her work. She'd never been referred to as "proper" before, and now felt bad for having been curt with her companion. "I understand."

He looked back and forth between Sophie and the sky, appearing to search the clouds for more words to offer now that the door to conversation had opened. Each time he looked over, Sophie shifted her eyes back to her task.

"Are you afraid?" he asked, pointing a drooping kipper at her.

She stopped slicing. "Afraid of what?"

"Of war, of course—of what the Germans are doing." He swallowed his fish and wiped his hands on his trousers. "After saying good-bye to your father, you must be afraid."

Had Maurice asked this question an hour earlier, she would have offered some sarcastic reply. Instead, she looked up from the bread. His eyes were now wide, needful.

"Are you?" she asked in return. "Afraid, I mean?"

"Yes," he looked down to his liver-spotted hands, "but I'm too damned old to fight. I can still dig a grave, but no army would have me."

She cocked her head. "You'd prefer to fight?"

"Of course, girl. Wouldn't every man?" He shoved a wedge of cheese beneath his bushy mustache and chewed.

"You could die in a war," Sophie reasoned.

"Bah. You can die falling off a ladder. Believe me, I've seen it. Better to die fighting than to die some foolish way, or to sit around and let others die for you." He looked away. "Disgraceful."

For the first time since they'd left the farm, Sophie understood Maurice. It wasn't her impertinence that had put him in a foul mood, at least not entirely. Nor was it the food, the horse, or the weather. It was the possibility of war. He was more afraid to miss the fight than to die waiting.

He turned his eyes back to the clouds, looking more forlorn than before. Like her, Maurice wished for something he was denied. He too had been left behind. Perhaps Sophie wasn't the only one to carry a curse.

She gathered the sliced bread in her cloth, leaned over the picnic basket, and offered the slices to Maurice. "Here you are," she said. "Take what you like."

Maurice lifted a piece but stopped before stuffing it into his mouth. He smiled politely. "Thank you."

"You're welcome." Sophie grinned her approval, the chill of her hostility quickly melting away.

"So," he said, chewing, "you never said whether you were afraid."

She looked to the clouds Maurice had been studying.

"Yes," she answered. "I'm afraid," she took a slice of bread for herself, "but now I know I'm not alone."

As the wagon rolled over the muddy road, Sophie used her blanket like a cloak, pulling it over her ears to ward against the growing chill. She drew a deep breath, tasting the musk of wet earth and cork trees. The road no longer smelled like home.

After their short rest for lunch, Maurice's demeanor toward Sophie, and hers toward him, had changed. Now, instead of sporting a brooding silence, he hummed some popular tunes. When Sophie happened to recognize a song, like "Moonlight Serenade," she'd hum along.

Her chapped lips caused some of her hums to come out as trills. Each time this occurred, Maurice bellowed a laugh, the kind that comes from a person unused to making such a sound. His laughter so delighted her that, twice, she trilled on purpose, just to hear him roar. When the road finally flattened and the wagon's sounds had quieted, she attempted conversation.

"Did you know goats actually get angry when the weather changes, even when it gets better?"

"No, I didn't," Maurice replied.

"It's peculiar," she scoffed. "I don't like goats."

Maurice chuckled. "Me neither."

"Those eyes," she ranted, "I hate their eyes." She used her gloved index fingers to make horizontal lines in front of her face. "Staring. Always staring."

Maurice nodded. "Can't tell if they like you or hate you."

"Exactly!" She rolled her eyes. "Horrible."

Now buoyed by their common disdain for goats, she proceeded to list the further reasons why she felt goats were not to be trusted. "They eat garbage... Even the females have beards..."

Maurice would crack an occasional smile, but continued to focus on the road as she spoke.

When evening came and the sun had nearly set, Sophie ran out of disparaging things to say about goats. Instead, she grew weary of the cold.

"How much farther?" she asked with a shiver.

"Four kilometers, more or less."

"Where will we sleep?"

"My cousin, Narina's," he said with enthusiasm. "She lives alone and has plenty of room." A smirk transformed his face. "I'm sure she'll have a pot of onion soup and a fresh-baked baguette ready for us, too."

"Soup and a baguette?" Sophie gasped. The mention of hot food brought life to her frozen toes. "Why didn't you say so? Hurry!"

"As you wish."

He flicked the horse's reins and Plouf seemed happy to oblige.

"Narina's quite a talker," Maurice warned. "A lot like you."

"I didn't hear you complain."

"Perhaps you weren't listening."

Plouf brayed as if he too were in on the joke.

"I think our company will do her good," Maurice added. "Narina lost her husband, Berliose, a couple years back. Tuberculosis." He shook his head. "I'm her only family now."

"Do you see her often?"

"Not as often as I should."

"Is she nice?"

"As nice as they come. She's a bit older. Cared for me when I was young, after my mother passed. I guess you'd say Narina's like my second mother." The gravedigger looked to the road ahead.

Sophie intuitively moved her hand to her breast, pressed the key belonging to her own mother against her heart. She didn't know what it was like to have one mother, let alone a second. She counted Maurice lucky, in spite of his wistfulness at missing his cousin. Better, she thought, to have someone you don't see enough than to have no one at all.

"I think you'll like her," said Maurice.

"—and her soup," added Sophie, prompting another chuckle from the gravedigger.

Sophie was both relieved and excited when, at last, she saw the silhouette of Narina's house at the end of a clearing, standing against the purple and orange sky beneath the streaks of retreating clouds.

As the wagon drew near, she saw the home was small like her own, adorned with a well-tended garden, rows of vegetables, and a couple small fruit trees. A wrought-iron wind vane, shaped like a rooster, stood on the roof's crest and pointed east toward the rising moon. Fluted wood chimes rang from the eaves and blew in time to an empty rocking chair on the porch, nodding with the breeze.

Oddly, no lamp had been lit at the door and she saw no light through the window. This curiosity caught Maurice's attention as well. He pulled Plouf's reins abruptly and halted the wagon thirty meters from the house.

"Stay here," he said and handed the reins to Sophie.

"What's wrong?"

"There should be light. She was expecting us."

Before Sophie could ask what he meant, Maurice hopped down into the mud, reached under the wagon's tarp and removed a rifle. He loaded it and strode toward the house, pointing it at the door, each step quicker than his last.

Sophie's heart rose to her throat.

Maurice approached the front door and gave a hard knock. When no answer came, he turned the knob and stepped in, rifle first.

His haste into the darkened house caused Sophie's pulse to quicken. She leaned forward to listen for some clue as to what was happening, afraid she'd hear a gunshot. Instead, between the chime songs, she heard the twitter of night birds and the eerie click of insects among the trees.

Soon, the call of the woods fell silent and she heard a sound she'd never heard before—a sound that chilled her—the howl of an anguished man.

Before she realized she'd moved, Sophie stood in the doorway of Narina's house. She was out of breath, moonlight shining in behind her, her shoes caked with mud. Maurice knelt on the floor of the kitchen, the rifle beside him. A woman, who Sophie presumed was Narina, lay cradled in his arms. She was dressed in her nightclothes and appeared stiff and lifeless. A smell—a horrible odor like rotting onions and vomit—permeated the house and prompted Sophie to throw her hands over her nose and mouth.

"Her heart," Maurice wept. "The doctor warned of her heart."

Sophie's throat closed in a rush of panic and revulsion. She'd never seen a dead person, and looked away.

"I...I'm so sorry," she said, between shallow breaths. "What should we do?"

Maurice closed his eyes and sobbed, rocking Narina without replying. He finally stopped and gathered himself. When he opened his eyes again, he spoke with a soft composure.

"She's got no electricity. Light some lamps so we can see what we're doing. Then, go tend to Bern—" he paused, "I mean, go tend to Plouf. I'll bring Narina to her bed and we can make our plan."

Sophie dashed to complete her tasks, glad to have a place to focus her erratic thoughts. Maurice had proved, once again, to be something more than she'd expected. In the midst of his grief, he'd found the kindness to give Plouf back his name.

She searched the kitchen drawers until she found matches, which she used to light the oil lamps throughout the house. Overwhelmed by the reek of death, she opened some windows, deciding the chill was preferable to the smell.

Once the frosty autumn breeze had set through the house, she returned to the wagon, where she found Plouf in the garden, munching Narina's apples under the moonlight.

"No, Plouf!" she called, as if the horse had committed some blasphemy. She grabbed him by the bridle and hurried him to a hitching post at the other side of the house. Once there, she found a tin pail filled with rainwater. Plouf immediately began to drink. She tied the horse's reins to the post and patted him on the rump. "Stay here."

When she returned to the house, the air was colder but clearer than when she'd first entered. Animated by the wind, the cloth curtains now waved over the living room chairs like the arms of ghouls reaching in, drawn to the presence of death.

Maurice emerged from the bedroom. "If I had to guess, I'd say she passed three days ago, the day we spoke on the phone." His voice held both authority and sadness. "She died alone."

Sophie knew that, as a gravedigger, Maurice must have encountered more than his share of death, but surely nothing as personal as this.

"Should we call someone?" Sophie asked, trying to be helpful. "You said she had a phone?"

"The phone's at the general store, five kilometers north." He looked through the swaying curtains into the night. "No. Too much time has already passed." His eyes were wet. "At this hour, it's up to me to deal with what comes next."

"It's up to us," Sophie corrected, unsure what "it" was. "We're a team."

Maurice lowered his head, appearing honored by her offer.

"So, what do we do?" she pressed.

He raised his head and looked her in the eyes. "Narina wished to be cremated."

Sophie heard the words and realized what they implied. There was no priest, no hospital, no doctor—no one but them to carry out Narina's wishes.

"Cremated," she repeated. As a Jew, she had no experience, and even less comfort, with cremation. Jews were buried.

"She's already been dead for days," Maurice explained. "Besides, it's Friday. If we're going to get you to Ville de Lemaire by Sunday, we have to leave in the morning. This must be done tonight."

Sophie nodded to obscure the look of horror she knew had crossed her face. She would be willing to delay her trip to avoid this burden, but it was clear this was something Maurice felt obliged to do himself. Besides, she was committed now, and Maurice deserved her help. It was as simple as that.

"I can do this alone if you want," Maurice offered.

"No." Sophie swallowed, uncertain what her promise required but eager to get it over with. "What do I do?"

"Out back, beyond the clearing, is a log bench," he began. I'll bring Narina there." He stared blankly as if reading from a list. "We'll need kindling and splits. Can you chop wood?"

"Of course."

Maurice gave a half smile. "As much as any boy, right?"

"Right."

"Then chop as much as you can. I'll dress her and bring kerosene from the shed."

"Kerosene?"

"We need the fire as hot as we can get it," he declared. "A body doesn't burn easily."

Sophie dropped the blanket full of wood and kindling next to the log bench at the edge of the mossy clearing. She ran her hand across her brow to wipe away the cold perspiration.

Maurice leaned over the bench where his cousin now rested, her arms crossed over her chest. He attempted to arrange her hair, moving errant strands away from her ear and back again. He stood, studied her, and shook his head. "I can't remember how she wore it."

Sophie placed a hand on his shoulder. "May I?"

Maurice nodded.

She took a breath, her heart lurching. She exhaled steam into the frozen night and knelt beside the bench. She had never been this close to a dead person. Losing a goat, a hen, a cat—these things were part of life on the farm, easy to rationalize and explain as part of the natural order of things. Losing a person seemed different, out of step with reason. The death of a person disturbed the fabric of everything, like cutting a hole from the center of a blanket.

She thought of her father, off with *l'Armée de Terre*. Would he end up like Narina, cared for in death by a stranger? Would he too be cut from her blanket as her mother had been?

Sophie removed her gloves and took another breath for courage as she leaned closer to Maurice's cousin.

Wrinkles radiated around Narina's eyes and lips, "smile lines," her grandmother would call them. Narina appeared to be in her late sixties, her hair long and gray, streaked with stubborn strands of brown. Sophie moved the wavy locks away from the woman's face and tucked them behind her ears, arranging her hair the way she would if she'd been Narina. Once satisfied, Sophie withdrew her hand, inadvertently brushing Narina's cheek, and was startled by the coldness of the woman's skin, a stark contrast to the warm smile that remained on her face. Narina reminded Sophie of the *Mona Lisa*, content and yet somehow mischievous, strong, yet vulnerable.

Sophie rose, turned to Maurice, and shrugged quizzically.

"Yes," he said. "That's her." He stepped toward his cousin and opened his mouth as if to say something, then closed it again. He looked to Sophie. "I've dug a hundred graves," he said, "heard prayers of all types. Now, I can't recall a single one." His voice quaked with emotion. "Can I ask…Would you say a prayer for her?"

Sophie froze. She didn't know any Catholic prayers and never had occasion to learn any Hebrew prayers for the dead. Sophie and her father could hardly be considered observant Jews. They rarely attended synagogue except at holidays like Purim. The temple was ten kilometers away in Vouvray. They didn't keep kosher, and often worked on the Sabbath. Sophie's father had explained long ago that God makes allowances for families such as theirs, offers forgiveness for farm families with no mothers and little means. So long as goodness was in their hearts, he'd explained, God would show them favor.

She'd always figured their lack of religious obedience was more a product of her father's skepticism than this well-reasoned philosophy. Now, faced with the need to pull a prayer out of thin air, she wished they'd been to temple more.

The expression on her face must have conveyed something unintended to Maurice because he quickly added, "A Jewish prayer would be fine." He lowered his head and closed his eyes.

It seemed she had no choice.

She mirrored his somber gestures and, letting her instincts take over, began to recite the Hebrew prayer to give thanks for the day's bread—her father's daily *brucha*, the prayer she knew best. It was foolish, she knew. However, it was a baguette they'd expected when they found Narina and this was the only prayer she could recall.

"*Barukh ata Adonai Eloheinu melekh ha-olam, ha-motzi lehem min ha-aretz.* Amen."

"Amen," Maurice repeated, his voice thick with anguish.

Sophie felt a strange combination of respect and humiliation. It now occurred to her that she could have recited the *Shema*—the simple prayer to God, or the *Kaddish*—the mourner's prayer, prayers she would have remembered immediately had she been a better Jew.

When she opened her eyes, she saw Maurice had begun setting the kindling and logs around his cousin, sliding some beneath her back and laying them over her body. Sophie pulled her gloves back on and stepped over to help, relieved at the chance to be useful, placing sticks and wood splits around the bench. Soon, Narina was covered with branches and wood, as if the forest itself had begun to claim her as its own.

The wind had died having chased away the clouds, offering a silence to their work. Maurice retrieved the large, spouted kerosene can. With his brow furrowed, he poured liberal amounts of the fluid over the kindling, around the bench, and over Narina, until the smells of the fuel swirled through the chill.

The kerosene flowed over the branches and onto Narina's face and body, soaking into the dress Maurice had picked for her. Sophie half expected Narina to leap up, annoyed at being doused with fuel, but Maurice's cousin stayed peaceful and unmoving, smiling.

"Step back, child," Maurice said.

Sophie took several strides backward, choosing not to challenge his characterization of her as a child, instead rubbing her arms against the cold that had found its way into her coat.

Maurice withdrew a small box of matches from his pocket. He leaned over his cousin one last time, whispered something Sophie couldn't hear, struck a match, and cupped his hand around the flame. He let the match fall, and stepped back just as the funeral pyre erupted in a boom of flame.

Sophie raised her arm to protect her face and eyes from the searing blast, but stayed in place to show respect. Maurice walked back to stand next to her, facing the flames that rose like fiery songbirds, freed from an invisible cage. Tears shone on his wet cheeks and reflected the growing blaze.

"Thank you," he said over the crackle of the fire.

Sophie hooked her arm through his, a gesture he seemed ready to accept.

The fire snapped and spat as it consumed the gravedigger's cousin, the hot pops and hisses releasing Narina's flesh from her bones. Sophie held her breath against the sickly sweet burning smell, suppressing her instinct to flee, clutching to Maurice and to her duty. Soon, the smell of burnt flesh was replaced by the spice of the glowing oak cinders that peppered the hot black air.

The fire roiled over the branches and licked the sky. It seemed the elements themselves were conspiring in a secret dance to welcome Narina's spirit into the breast of oblivion.

As the wind lifted Narina's soul into the frozen night, Sophie heard, laced within the crackle of flames, the ring of Narina's chimes, playing a tranquil song—the sound of a smile.

Chapter 4

Deserters

They had stayed by the funeral pyre until the flames died and the ashes smoldered, leaving them shivering in the bitter cold. Well into the night, Maurice had completed the grim task of collecting Narina's ashes, which had mixed with wood cinders and bone fragments too willful to be consumed by the fire. He'd used a dust brush from the pantry to sweep his cousin's warm remains into an empty cookie tin, which he sealed with a lid and tucked into a burlap sack until a time when he could find a vase fitting her dignity.

Too weary to contemplate death any further, Sophie now entered the house to close the windows, tend the hearth, cast off the chill, and prepare for sleep. Uncertain of the hour, she staggered to the guest bed and drifted off, lulled into slumber by memories of flames and Narina's enchanting song.

After what seemed more like minutes than hours, she awoke to the sound of Maurice chatting to Plouf outside her window. Bleary-eyed, she stood from the bed, drew back the curtain, and blinked with surprise at the daylight that shone in.

Maurice turned from Plouf and faced Sophie through the glass. "Bonjour."

"What time is it?" she croaked, pushing her dark tangled hair from her face.

"After nine," he replied. "I only woke half an hour ago myself." As her vision adjusted, she saw him smirk. "We're quite a lazy pair."

She thought staying up all night to cremate a person hardly counted as laziness, but she appreciated his attempt at humor. Survivors of a dark night, they needed a moment like this.

"I'll fetch water from the well," he said.

"I'll cook breakfast," she countered. Her grumbling stomach reminded her that they'd never eaten the dinner of soup and bread they'd expected.

As the gravedigger set off with a pail, Sophie tied back the curtains to let the sun in more fully. She found a brush on the bedside table and ran it through her uncooperative curls. She visited the outhouse and then, realizing she still smelled of smoke, rinsed her hands and arms in a stream of freezing water from the pump. She proceeded to the kitchen to dry herself. There, she discovered eggs and cheese in a small icebox, stale croissants in a basket, a bowl of berries, and a well-stocked cupboard filled with cans and jars, more than enough to cull together a reasonable breakfast.

With care and speed, she prepared a meal of sweet *chèvre*, fried eggs, thumb-sized raspberries, croissants resurrected with *crème de marrons*, and a pressed pot of fragrant coffee. A feast, to be sure, in honor of Narina.

When Maurice entered the kitchen, he closed his eyes and breathed deeply, an action that would have been unthinkable last night when the smell of the house was intolerable.

They ate voraciously, and between bites, Maurice said, "We need to make up time on the road," he spread more marmalade over the crusty tip of his croissant, "and Plouf agrees."

"Plouf said this to you?"

"More or less," he replied, chewing.

Sophie ate with haste, but savored every bite. It wasn't the onion soup or fresh baked bread she'd hoped for last night, but it satisfied her empty stomach. As soon as she'd cleaned her yolk from her plate with a remnant of her bread, she took the dirty plates to the sink. "I'll wash the dishes and we can go."

"Take what you can from the icebox and cupboards," Maurice said. "It'll spoil here otherwise."

Sadness slipped back into his voice and a melancholy washed over his features. With Narina gone, he would now be more alone than ever. It was a curse Sophie understood.

"Once I've delivered you to your grandmother's, I think I'll return," he said, interrupting her thoughts.

"Return here? To live?" She tried to imagine Maurice tending a garden.

"I feel Narina in this place," he explained. He moved his gaze around the kitchen to the small living room. "I like that feeling."

Sophie nodded. "Me, too."

"Well," he said, gulping his last drop of coffee from his mug, "enough daydreaming."

They cleaned up, filled a few sacks and boxes with canned beans, jars of peaches, a few root vegetables, the remaining hunk of *chèvre*, two bottles of red wine, and some utensils and pans suitable for the trip. Once they'd loaded the wagon and Sophie had taken her seat on the bench, Maurice gave one final walk around the house but lingered at the empty rocking chair on the porch.

He approached the chair, turned it to face the path they would take, nudged it so it would rock by itself, and then climbed into the wagon. He drew a breath and, with three clicks of his tongue, directed Plouf back to the road.

Sophie looked to the bleak sky and to the menacing clouds gathering overhead. "Those clouds don't look good," she remarked, opening the possibility for conversation.

Maurice didn't reply. Instead, he sat at the reins, alone with his private thoughts, clearly a changed man.

Plouf, however, snorted and trotted down the frozen mud road, conveying his prior enthusiasm if not his obliviousness to all that had transpired here in this place of life and death.

The path from Narina's soon disappeared behind them and the road to Sophie's grandmother's unfurled ahead. Once the road flattened and the wagon's creaking silenced, Sophie heard the distant sounds of Narina's chimes, one last time. The song drew forward an unexpected mix of feelings about death: fear and sadness blended with peace and tranquility, memories of flame and frost, conflicting feelings that seemed part of a larger puzzle just beyond her ability to solve.

It was then she realized that this journey had not just changed things for Maurice.

The ruddy road led them east, through slender beech trees lined like soldiers heading to war. Sophie imagined her father marching in uniform, rifle over his shoulder, his trademark scowl on his face as he angled into battle in Poland. She hoped his courage and his tenacity would keep him safe, but she feared for him nonetheless. She rubbed her mother's key for luck, a wish for her father as much as for herself.

The sky now filled with rainclouds and threatened to unleash another downpour like the day before. The air that filled Sophie's lungs did not calm her. It merely hastened the sense of foreboding that had floated in with the fog.

"It's freezing," she muttered, shivering under her blanket.

"It's hard to believe it's still fall," Maurice replied, at last breaking his silence. He blew steam into the air. "This weather's taking its toll."

Even Plouf seemed affected by the chill, braying and huffing, slowing his pace when the road opened to a meadow of tall, dead grass.

As the terrain sloped down, the road split in two. One road headed east through the lilting reeds, the other curved north into a dense forest of black walnut and cork. A wooden post stood at the fork and marked the eastern road "Troyes," and the northern road "Paris."

"Paris!" cried Sophie, the chill in her bones replaced by visions of La Sorbonne. "Are we going through Paris? Oh, Maurice!"

"No," the gravedigger announced. He pointed at the sign. "We'll head toward Troyes and turn north down the line."

"Can't we go through Paris?" She imagined the city's artful archways, the Eiffel Tower, the impeccable gardens she'd seen only in pictures, the art from her mother's books…and the university of her dreams.

"Didn't you hear me, child?" he growled. "I said no."

Her cheeks grew hot with anger. "Why not?"

"Because," he snapped, halting the wagon, "sometimes you just do what you're told." He sounded like the old Maurice from the start of their journey, the one she didn't like.

She folded her arms and turned from him in a huff.

"You're damned stubborn, you know?" Maurice spat.

"You're the stubborn one."

"Look, child, the road to Paris can be dangerous, and I'm not fond of the place." He glanced toward the signpost. "There's no point in going there, not when there's another way."

"I just want to see La Sorbonne," she pleaded, trying not to sound like a petulant child. "We could take a quick look. That's all. Can't we do that?"

He closed his eyes and rubbed his temple, the frustration clear on his face. She stared at him, willing him to change his mind.

When he opened his eyes, she fixed her gaze on him, searching for some sign of compassion. "Please?"

"Fine," he sighed. He held up his index finger. "One night, but we're off at dawn. You understand?"

Sophie threw her arms around him. "Thank you!"

"Don't thank me," he grumbled, shirking free from her grip. "You don't know a thing about Paris."

The muddy northern road cut through crowds of walnut trees with branches laced like clasped fingers into a canopy overhead. The moist path bred mounds of clover, tufts of lichens, and knobby mushrooms. Fallen walnuts cracked and crunched beneath the wagon's wheels, tempting Plouf to dip his head to munch a few of the delicacies, but Maurice's firm grip on the horse's reins kept them moving.

The air had grown thick and primordial, smelling of rot. The obscured sky, now darker than before, robbed them of what little comfort the afternoon sun had offered. This sudden change in their environment caused Sophie's stomach to tighten and she began to wonder at the wisdom of her demands.

Seeming to read her mind, Maurice snapped the reins to urge Plouf to move more quickly. "We'll find a public house near the Seine," Maurice said. "Your father gave me a satchel of francs for lodging and food."

Sophie nodded, distracted by the caws of magpies roosting in the trees and the putrid smells of the musty wood. For some reason, she imagined this was what Poland smelled like.

An hour into the depths of the forest, they were startled to see two men with rucksacks at the side of the road, striding toward them on foot, pointing at them as they approached. The first man, the shorter and fatter of the two, raised his arms, and waved for them to stop.

Maurice straightened his posture and set his jaw, a tension crossing his face, prompting a sudden fear in Sophie's gut.

"Ho, there!" called the short man.

Maurice halted the wagon and Plouf stomped and blew. Both men were unshaven and unkempt, wearing what appeared to be ragged, muddy soldier's uniforms. The squat man had a potbelly and wore a rumpled cap, tilted back to expose his large forehead.

"Ho!" he called again.

The second man, tall and thin, wore no cap at all, his large ears red from the cold. His craning neck bore a bulging Adam's apple and his lips were meaty. He dropped his rucksack and shuffled toward them behind his fat counterpart, walking with a pronounced limp.

"*Bonjour, mes amis*," called the short man.

"Bonjour," said Maurice without enthusiasm.

"May I say you're a blessing for the weary?" The fat man's voice was practiced and measured like a tonics salesman. He lowered his rucksack and flipped off his cap, revealing a mop of oily hair. "We haven't seen a soul on this road for days. No cars, no wagons…" He smiled disarmingly.

As the fat man spoke, the thin man eyed their wagon and then looked at Sophie. His stare made her skin prickle and she wondered just where Maurice had stashed his rifle.

"Looks like you're heading in the other direction," called Maurice, "and we've got an appointment in Paris." He'd lost his congenial tone.

"Ah, Paris," replied the short man, replacing his cap. His casual tone seemed designed to slow Maurice's urgency. The man sauntered over, and Plouf tossed his head and huffed as the man came near. "What's your business in the city, may I ask?"

"No, you may not," Maurice snapped.

The tall, limping man hobbled around them, circling the wagon. Sophie grasped Maurice's arm.

Maurice turned to the tall soldier. "You there. What do you think you're doing?"

"I like your wagon," the thin man replied slowly.

"You can admire it from over there." Maurice pointed at the opposite side of the road.

"You misunderstand us, sir," the squat man interjected. "We're just simple men, interested in the passing of strangers."

"We have no time to chat about your interests. Excuse us." Maurice grasped Plouf's reins to set the cart in motion. Before they could move, the short man raised his hands to Plouf's snout and snatched the horse's bridle, pulling Plouf's head down, halting the wagon.

"Ho, horse. Ho!"

In the same instant, the tall man withdrew a rifle from his pant leg. In a fluid motion, he flipped the firearm around, pointed it in the air, and pulled the trigger.

The loud crack of his shot sent a flock of magpies to the sky, screaming their protest, a shock running through Sophie.

Plouf jumped and reared, rocking against his bit.

Sophie grasped the bench with both hands to keep from falling. "Ah!"

Maurice yanked the reins to gain control, but to no avail. The fat man had Plouf in hand.

"There, there, horse," the man said. "Easy."

"What do you think you're doing?" barked Maurice.

"I could ask you the same, monsieur." His smile shone like the glint of a dagger. "We've shown you nothing but courtesy, and yet you tried to run us down."

"Courtesy? It's not a courtesy to fire a gun near a man's horse."

"On that point, you're correct," the fat man said. He turned to his lurking companion. "Pierre, that was discourteous. Make note. Never fire a gun near a man's horse."

The skinny Pierre chortled a smoky laugh.

"There's a war brewing," said Maurice looking over the fat man's uniform. "Shouldn't you be reporting to your unit?"

Sophie feared Maurice's anger was putting them in further danger. "Maurice, please. Let's just go."

The fat man lost his smile. "Perhaps, monsieur, you could spare some food, some wine from your wagon?"

Pierre, cured of his limp since the production of his rifle, stepped forward and raised his smoking gun. He aimed at Sophie.

"And a kiss."

Sophie shifted closer on the bench to Maurice, disgust creeping up her throat.

"We can spare a day's rations," replied Maurice, "No more." He squinted in defiance. "You'll take what we give you and be on your way."

"No..." The portly man ran his forefinger along the wagon and approached them. "We'll take your cart and your horse. Then *you* can be on *your* way."

"What about the girl, Henri?" interrupted Pierre. He licked his thick lips, keeping his rifle fixed on her. "I'd like to keep the girl, too."

Sophie's mouth fell open, her steamy breath rising into the frosty air.

"All right, Pierre," said Henri. He toyed with a button on his uniform. "The girl, too."

Sophie's heart lurched, like a machine missing a cog. Before she could speak, Maurice stood from the bench.

"You won't touch her," he snapped.

"Now, now," replied Henri. "No need for hysterics." He strolled back and stroked Plouf's snout, examining the horse's tug and bridle with curiosity. He then returned Maurice's stare. "The girl will be in good care, monsieur. You have my word. Pierre is a gentleman. We're both gentlemen."

Pierre smiled his agreement, baring his yellow teeth like a dog.

"Gentlemen don't desert the army," Maurice snarled.

"What did you say?" Henri's syrupy voice was now serious; Pierre raised his shotgun.

Sophie looked to the wagon, realizing she had no way to retrieve Maurice's rifle beneath the canvas.

"Gentlemen don't harass strangers," the gravedigger railed. "They surely don't force themselves on young girls. What kind of cowards are you?"

A vessel in Henri's temple pulsed to prominence and his face grew red. "Enough, old man!" He spun to Pierre. "Shoot him!"

"Wait!" cried Sophie, jumping in front of Maurice, half-expecting the bullets to fly. "I'll come with you."

Henri's scowl softened. "Smart girl."

Pierre lowered his barrel.

"Child." Maurice gripped her shoulders. "What are you doing?"

Sophie wasn't sure what she was doing, she had no plan at all, yet one thing was certain: Maurice would die if she did nothing.

"I'm not a child," she replied, expecting to see anger in Maurice's face. Instead, she saw desperation. Fear. She quelled her nerves and quieted her voice. "I'll be fine."

Before Maurice could challenge her further, before she could formulate a coherent plan and convince herself of her own safety, the improbable sound of a woman's distant laugh broke the tension.

The two deserters perked.

"Quiet!" called Henri. He raised his hand to his ear and turned his head to the woods.

The feminine laugh was followed by the clank of another horse's rigging and the creak of carriage wheels, announcing the approach of another party.

Sophie's suffocating fear was replaced by a moment of hope.

Henri turned to Pierre and gave an urgent nod.

Pierre slipped the rifle back down his trousers just as the new travelers came into view.

An ornate carriage painted red and white sped toward them, pulled by a hulking, black horse. Its driver, a young man in a gray wool coat, sat atop the carriage. Again, the laughter of a woman warmed the frozen air.

"Let us leave," Maurice blurted to Henri as the new carriage approached. "You can still do the right thing."

"Sit down." Henri pointed a fat finger at Maurice and approached him. "One word and Pierre will shoot you both."

Pierre patted his hip in warning.

Sophie gritted her teeth, trying to figure some plan of escape. Maurice scanned the ground. He too seemed to be weighing their options.

The approaching carriage pulled to a halt next to them, its black horse offering a loud snort. The driver appeared to be in his late twenties with a pleasant face and round glasses. His hair was brown and parted down the middle. His long felt coat and white gloves seemed too nice for someone accustomed to driving a carriage, even an ornamental one such as his.

"Bonjour." He gave them a tentative smile.

"Bonjour, monsieur!" Henri employed the same seductive tone he'd used earlier with Maurice. He stepped away from Plouf and ambled toward the carriage, grinning to the driver. *"Comment allez-vous?"*

The bespectacled driver tilted his head in suspicion. Something in Henri's overzealous demeanor seemed to stir the man's curiosity, just as it had earlier stirred Sophie's distrust. The driver dropped his smile. "What have we here?"

"A simple roadside dispute." The squat Henri cleared his throat. "Nothing of concern, I assure you."

The driver removed his glasses to scan the scene.

Sophie attempted to remain calm, afraid to take action that would prompt her captors to violence, yet fearful this may be their only chance of escape. When the driver's eyes met hers she gave a quick, furtive look toward Henri and back toward Pierre, raising her eyebrow in warning.

If the driver recognized Sophie's signal, his face did not betray it. He put his glasses back on and turned to Henri with a grin of satisfaction. "Well, then," he began, "perhaps we should just be on our way."

Suddenly, the carriage door swung open, releasing into the putrid forest air the pleasant smell of rose water. From the darkness of the compartment, a woman emerged.

She was dressed in a ruffled red frock and coat with a fur shawl draped over her shoulders. Her flaxen hair was wavy and hung in tresses, held in place with two mother-of-pearl combs. Her lips were red, her cheeks pink. She looked like the women in magazines Sophie admired.

However, in spite of her striking beauty, she seemed unfazed by the rot and stench of the forest around her.

"Why have we stopped, Etienne?" she asked indignantly.

The man at the reins climbed down from his perch and approached the woman.

"It appears, sister, that these people are resolving a dispute."

"A dispute?" She eyed them all more intently.

"A simple roadside dispute, mademoiselle," Henri proclaimed. "Truly of no concern."

Her eyes widened and a knowing look washed over her flawless face. "Sir, a dispute is always a thing of concern, and is rarely simple." Her words were carefully pronounced for dramatic effect, like those of an actress. "May I ask the issue?"

"Colette," interrupted her driver. "This gentleman feels they can resolve their problems without our interference. Besides, we need to get to Paris to return this horrible carriage."

"Brother," Her voice sounded commanding, "are you saying this is like that time in Lyon?"

Etienne looked at her intently. "I believe so."

"Well," she announced, "I agree we should leave now, just like we did then."

Sophie's pulse pounded so hard she felt it in her ears.

The driver grinned. "Wise as always, dear sister."

Sophie wanted to call out for help, but feared to do so would doom them all.

"Yes, indeed," parroted Henri. "Off you go to Paris." He motioned with open hands down the road. "Bon voyage."

"Au revoir," chimed Pierre, matching Henri's disingenuous tone.

Etienne held the door for Colette. "Bonjour," she called, and with a smile and a ceremonial wave, she disappeared back into the carriage.

Sophie locked eyes with Maurice, sensing in his face that he too saw this fleeting moment may be their last chance at freedom. As she readied herself to call out for help, Etienne turned back from the carriage door to face the road. To Sophie's surprise, he held a pistol, which he pointed at Pierre. Over his shoulder from the open carriage window, a rifle barrel appeared aimed at Henri.

"We're not fools," called Colette, holding the rifle. "Arms up where we can see them."

"What's this?" Henri grew flush with surprise.

"You may wear soldiers' uniforms," Colette replied, "but you're thieves—deserters—and you've got these poor people at your mercy."

Etienne caught Sophie's look and winked at her from behind his spectacles.

"Mademoiselle," Henri pleaded, "I assure you—"

Etienne cocked his pistol. "No talking. Your voice is maddening."

Sophie smiled. Since Henri had first opened his mouth, she too had wanted him to stop talking, but she didn't have a gun to make it so.

"This is all a misunderstanding." Henri raised his hands in surrender and took a step backward toward the wagon.

At the same moment, Sophie glimpsed Pierre, who was now reaching into his trousers for his rifle. "Stop!" she cried.

Startled, Etienne fired his pistol. The shot whizzed between Sophie and Pierre. Pierre stepped back and threw his arms up, dropping his rifle into the mud. "Don't shoot!"

At the snap of Etienne's pistol, Henri drew a knife from his jacket and, with a sudden gesture, slashed Plouf's tug. The horse reared again and when he did, his bellyband and harness came undone, apparently loosened by Henri when no one had been looking. The horse was free of his rigging.

"Plouf!" called Maurice. The gravedigger struggled to regain his balance.

It was too late. Henri had moved with surprising alacrity to the horse's side, gripped Plouf's mane and bridle in his plump fists, and hoisted himself onto the horse's flank.

"Stop!" Sophie screamed, but Henri held fast.

Etienne fired a wild shot into a tree, missing Henri and giving the horse more reason to run.

With a whinny, Plouf tossed aside his riggings and galloped away with his rider before anyone could stop him, disappearing into the murky woods.

Chapter 5

Things Left Behind

From within the passenger compartment of the red carriage, Sophie pressed her face against the cold window, enduring as a penance the icy sting that grew in her forehead and nose. She watched the waning sunlight dance like a jester across the barren branches of the cork trees, mocking her as it retreated beyond sight. She closed her eyes and listened to the rhythm of the carriage wheels, wishing she could fall asleep.

"What's wrong, dumpling?" asked Colette from the darkness of the compartment.

Sophie remained silent.

"Surely, you don't feel sorry for that skinny thief we left in the woods. Even his partner abandoned him." Colette leaned closer to Sophie in an obvious attempt to confirm she was awake, but Sophie kept her face to the window. "We took the brute's shotgun. We owe him nothing after what he tried to do to you and Monsieur Maurice. Etienne and I came across such thieves in Lyon, two horrid men robbing a grocer. We left them without their pants! I'll tell you, we had no regrets there either."

Sophie was in no mood to talk, instead trying to decipher the murmurs of Maurice's conversation from above on the carriage bench. Maurice had chosen to ride beside Etienne atop the carriage, but Sophie could guess at the content of his private conversation. She knew why her companion might have chosen not to sit with her.

Plouf was gone along with half their supplies, left behind with the wagon they were forced to abandon, all because of her; all because the allure of Paris had been too strong. She held on to dreams like a little girl when the world needed her to behave like a woman, and so it was that her curse could persist.

Sophie lowered her lids and imagined her home in Avoine, a fire in the hearth and her father singing "Au Clair de la Lune." What would she give now, just to hear him sing one verse?

Colette sighed. "All right, dumpling. We can just sit quietly."

They rode in silence for another hour until Sophie felt the wagon slow. Through the window, she saw they'd entered a small village and stopped at a tavern painted blue. Sounds of laughter and the clinking of glasses rose from the tavern and reminded her that life for others was not as miserable as it was for her.

"We'll rest here," Etienne called to his passengers, "just long enough to water the horse and have a bite of food."

Colette placed her hand on Sophie's shoulder. "Let's stretch our legs, shall we?"

Sophie sat back from the window, a cold numbness in her face. Colette lit a small lantern, just as Sophie turned to her.

"Oh, dear!" Colette cried at the sight of Sophie. She set down the lantern on the compartment floor and raised a manicured hand to Sophie's face, running her warm thumb along Sophie's forehead.

Instinctively, Sophie pulled away, unused to be touched so intimately.

"I'm not going to hurt you. I just want to help." Colette tilted her head with empathy. "You're as pink as a ham hock, and your hair...Tsk, tsk, tsk..."

Colette ignored Sophie's fidgety discomfort and moved the curls from Sophie's eyes. She then reached into a large bag at her feet and withdrew a gold-trimmed tortoise-shell compact that glistened in the lantern light. "This should fix you." She flipped it open with her thumb, dabbed a pink velvety puff with white powder, and gently blotted Sophie's face.

"Hmmm..."

Colette snatched a powder brush from her mysterious bag and stroked its cool, soft hairs over Sophie's reluctant cheeks to smooth the powder.

"There," she said with a gleaming smile. She grabbed Sophie's cold hand. "Beautiful."

Out of courtesy, Sophie gave a nod of appreciation but truly didn't care how she looked, wishing instead she could close her eyes and wake to find this whole journey had been a bad dream.

Colette returned the items to her bag, grabbed the lantern, and pushed open the carriage door. She snatched Sophie's hand. "Come, dumpling."

They stepped into the icy dusk to find Etienne by the horse. He adjusted the mare's riggings and stroked the horse's hind, reminding Sophie that Plouf was somewhere out there in the company of a deserter, lost forever.

Colette brought the lantern over and hung it on the carriage to help Etienne see. "Are you and the horse friends, now?" she asked him.

Etienne turned to Colette with a smirk. "Her backside is oddly reminiscent of yours."

Colette swatted Etienne and laughed. "Show some respect."

Etienne chortled, but Sophie could find no humor today. Instead, she turned to see Maurice standing at the side of the road, hands on his hips, leaning back and stretching his spine. He paid no attention to anyone, including Sophie.

Colette appeared to notice Sophie's awkwardness with Maurice and changed the subject. "Etienne, how long until we get to Paris?"

"An hour," he replied. "Maybe two. I don't know." He peered over his glasses. "I'm used to traveling by automobile."

Colette faced Sophie. "You hear, dumpling? Soft linens and a warm house await us. Don't worry. Madame Lefavre will be happy to have you."

At Colette's words, Maurice spun to face her, his eyes wide like the new moon. "What did you say?"

Startled by his tone, Colette shot a look to Etienne and then back to Maurice. "I said I'm eager to reach Paris."

He strode to Colette. "The name." He took her by the wrist. "What was the name?"

"Monsieur Maurice!" warned Etienne.

"The name was Madame Lefavre," Colette replied calmly. She raised her eyebrow. "Josephine Lefavre. My employer."

Maurice released Colette and scowled. He then set his jaw, clenched his fists, and huffed off toward the tavern.

After he disappeared through the tavern door, Etienne turned to Sophie. "Does he know Madame Lefavre?"

"I don't know." Sophie had never heard the name.

"Don't be fools," Colette said. "Of course he knows her. Didn't you see his face?" She smiled. "There's a story there." She snatched up the lengths of her ruffled dress and shuffled after Maurice.

"Perhaps he wishes to be left alone!" Etienne called after her.

Sophie silently agreed.

"Nonsense," replied Colette without stopping. "No one wants to be alone."

As she strode off, Etienne shrugged his shoulders. "My sister is a woman of her own mind," he said to Sophie. "I'm a bit concerned."

"I don't think Maurice would harm her."

Etienne grinned. "It's Maurice I'm concerned about."

Sophie half smiled, still unable to laugh.

"Let's tie the horse and join them," Etienne said. "I think we could all use a bite and something warm to drink."

Sophie knew no drink could warm her tonight—and whoever this Josephine Lefavre was, it was clear she was only going to make things worse.

The tavern air was thick with scents of alcohol and tobacco. Snappy music rang out from a player piano and a fire crackled in the hearth, reminding Sophie of all that Maurice had already endured. A string of lights winked over the bar to the patrons below, yet it was the bawdy laughter and the bursts of profanity that caught Sophie's attention. This was not a tavern like the few in Avoine.

"Perhaps you should wait outside," said Etienne over the music.

Sophie pretended not to hear him and used the moment to scan the room and the people around her as if viewing the artwork of some new painter. She judged most of the patrons to be villagers, people like her. Only these people seemed happy.

After a lively crescendo, the song from the piano ended, causing a lull in the tavern's volume.

"There." Etienne pointed to the bar. "I see them."

Seated on a stool at the end of the large oak bar was Maurice. He scowled over a glass mug filled with beer, twice the size of his fist, and looked as miserable as Sophie felt. On the stool next to him sat Mademoiselle Colette. Seeming impervious to Maurice's foul mood, she talked without pause, her arms waving to accompany her words. A glass of red wine sat in front of her, untouched.

"Oh dear," said Etienne with a grin in his eyes. "I think your friend needs to be rescued again."

Colette turned and spotted Sophie, waving her over. "Dumpling!" she called. "Come tell Maurice what you think."

Maurice's response was to take a deep swig from his mug, emptying it of its contents.

"What I think?" Sophie asked as she arrived at Maurice's side.

"Your chaperone wants us to leave him at the edge of Paris," Colette announced. "Apparently, he doesn't wish to accept our hospitality."

Sophie's heart fell.

Maurice faced Sophie and sighed. "You can stay there if you like," he explained. "I'll find a place to sleep and collect you in the morning."

"Nonsense!" said Colette. "Etienne, tell him that's nonsense."

"She's right," Etienne replied flatly. "By the time we arrive in Paris no one else will have you."

"There," Colette snapped. "I'd hoped you'd hear the wisdom of a woman, but if it's a man's voice you need, now you have it. The same advice I gave you." She reached for her wine and drank half of it in one gulp, as if celebrating victory.

The barkeep, an aging bald man with laughter in his eyes, replaced Maurice's empty mug with a full one. When he spied Colette, the man offered her a broad grin and, without asking if she wished it, handed her another glass of wine.

"Oh, aren't you a dear?" Colette's gracious appreciation sounded rehearsed.

Sophie had no doubt Colette was the recipient of many complimentary glasses of wine. In the golden tavern light, her beauty made her stand out like a shiny new franc in a handful of change. Sophie saw others were gazing at Colette as well, but if Colette was aware of her admirers, she didn't reveal it.

"I don't care what time it'll be," grumbled Maurice. "I can sleep in a park."

"A park?" Colette slammed her glass, nearly breaking it. "You'll be robbed and accosted, or freeze to death! What's wrong with you? What trouble do you have with Madame Lefavre that you'd rather die alone in a park?"

At the name "Lefavre," Maurice bristled.

Colette grabbed Sophie's hand. "He talks nonsense!"

Sophie saw Maurice was in no mood for Colette's assault and replied, "Can you leave us alone for a moment?"

Colette peered into Sophie's eyes and smiled. "All right, dumpling. See what you can do." She stepped off the stool, swung her dress with flair and accompanied Etienne toward the large fireplace. Heads turned as she passed.

Once Colette and Etienne were out of earshot, Sophie climbed the stool by Maurice. "They saved our lives."

"Then you can stay with them if that's what you want." Maurice stared into his mug.

Sophie placed her hand on her necklace and clutched her mother's key to steady her nerves. "Maurice...I...I'm sorry." Her throat squeezed closed and raised the pitch of her voice. "I'm so sorry."

The gravedigger looked up from his beer. "Sorry?"

"It's all my fault." Tears slid down Sophie's face. "I lost Plouf. I lost the wagon. I've ruined everything, all because I had to see Paris."

Maurice's demeanor softened and he faced her. "Child, I chose to take the path to Paris."

"Only after I insisted...I forced you."

"Forced me?" Maurice frowned. "You overestimate yourself." He gulped his drink and ran his sleeve across his bushy mustache. "You only gave me the excuse I needed. I came this way because I'd hoped..."

"Hoped what?"

He lowered his voice like a man ashamed. "I hoped to see Fifi."

"Madame Lefavre?"

"When I knew her, she was called Josephine Devereux...Fifi. She was engaged to Benedict Lefavre. I suppose that was the problem." He finished his beer and again tapped the bar.

"You loved her?"

He scowled. "A woman like that can't be loved. I know that now."

The barkeep returned and replaced Maurice's mug with another, froth slopping over the top.

"Anyone can be loved," Sophie retorted, trying not to sound defiant.

Maurice turned and gestured with his chin toward the hearth. "You see your friend over there?"

She spied Colette chatting with a crowd by the fire.

"Yes…"

"Fifi was like her, but even more beautiful in her day."

The way he said "beautiful" sounded more like an accusation than a compliment.

Sophie had never felt beautiful, but had always hoped that someday, someone would find her to be so. She couldn't fathom how beauty could be bad.

Maurice peered at Sophie as she puzzled over his pronouncement. "Child, don't you know what she is?"

"Of course," Sophie said, meeting his eye. "She's an actress."

"An actress!" he laughed. "Yes, that's mostly what she is."

Maurice was mocking her, but she couldn't understand why. She folded her arms.

At her anger, Maurice leaned forward. "Child, that woman is a prostitute."

The player piano suddenly roared to life, its phantom keys pounding out another jumpy tune. Sophie's heart leapt, though she was unsure if it was from the startling music or the startling news. How could a woman of such strong opinions and compassion—of such poise and beauty—be a prostitute?

She looked again at Colette. A group of men had now formed around her, clapping to the music, encouraging Colette to dance. Sophie never had such male attention; she wouldn't have known what to do with it.

Colette stepped forward, obligingly, a smile crossing her face. She swung her dress to and fro, stomping to the beat of the music. The lamplight amplified the gleam in her eyes. Sophie watched the bounce of Colette's hair, the shine of her smile, the frill of her waving dress.

"Why?" Sophie asked aloud, turning back to Maurice.

He leaned closer next to her ear, to be heard over the music and cheering. "Everyone's reason is different. Fifi was an orphan. It was a matter of survival, or so she said."

"Now she's married to Benedict Lefavre?"

Maurice drew back. "Yes." Sophie could tell this was the part of his story he didn't wish to discuss.

When the music ended and Colette took her bows, something had shifted—something inside Sophie. She knew at that moment, her life on the farm had kept her from understanding many things about the way the world worked. The farm, Avoine, her very existence, all suddenly seemed small. Now, all she wanted was some measure of understanding...and forgiveness.

She turned back to Maurice. "If you were looking for an excuse to see Madame Lefavre," she began, "Colette is it. Why change your mind now?"

Maurice's voice grew soft. "You said you just wanted to have a look at Paris. A quick glimpse of the university. That's what I wanted, a glimpse to see if Fifi was happy."

"You don't want to speak to her?"

"There's nothing left to say."

"There's always something to say."

Maurice looked into Sophie's eyes. "A man's heart is not like a woman's. It can only break once, child. That's all it can stand."

Even with her limited experience, Sophie knew what Maurice meant. She'd seen such heartbreak in her father the few times he'd talked about her mother. He'd told Sophie once that he carried on because Sophie had needed him to carry on. To be needed, her father said, was the key to surviving heartbreak.

That's all he'd ever said about his feelings.

She touched Maurice's sleeve. "I need you."

Maurice scrutinized her.

"I can't go to Paris alone, and I can't sleep in a park," she urged.

The gravedigger scowled. "I'm sure you'll be—"

"No," Sophie interrupted. "You promised my father. You promised me."

"Child, I—"

Sophie held up her hand. "If Madame Lefavre—if Fifi is married then the matter is closed. You don't have to speak to her at all, do you?"

Maurice lifted his head in consideration.

"In fact," Sophie added, "I'm sure Mademoiselle Colette will be happy to do all the talking for you. Haven't you been listening? She's worse than me. She doesn't stop."

Maurice squinted, pondering Sophie's words.

"It's simple," Sophie declared. "We'll accept their offer, quietly go to bed, and wake early to fetch our wagon. You'll have your glimpse and protect me all at once. You don't have to say a word to Madame Lefavre."

Before Maurice could respond, Colette and Etienne returned to the bar.

"Whew, I'm exhausted," Colette said. She perched herself on the last empty stool next to Sophie, snatched a bar towel from the counter, and dabbed away the beads of moisture from the nape of her neck. "I confess, I do love to dance."

Etienne stood next to her. "I can't keep up, so I don't even try."

"Well?" Colette asked after catching her breath. "Do we have an agreement?"

Sophie stared at Maurice, still uncertain of his answer.

He reached for his drink, gulped the remaining beer without stopping and slammed the mug, empty, back on the bar. "All right," he said. "You win."

Colette smiled, her red lips parting to reveal her gleaming, perfect white teeth. "Of course." She winked at Sophie. "I always win."

Chapter 6

Paris

The carriage emerged from the forest under a milky blanket of stars, the road opening to a meadow like a gasp of fresh air. Nevertheless, Sophie felt trapped.

While Maurice had returned to the carriage roost to brood next to Etienne, Sophie had rejoined Colette in the passenger compartment, uncertain how to feel now that she'd learned Colette was a prostitute. If Sophie had been at home, she would have retreated to the barn and whispered her thoughts to Plouf, or run to the banks of the river where she'd have climbed a tree and thrown sticks into the Loire to watch nature sort things out. Now, trapped in the carriage, Sophie could only pull her blanket around her and move close to the copper bed warmer she'd filled with coals from the Taverne Bleue, working to keep her distance from the woman she no longer understood.

To preserve their dwindling lamp oil, Colette had dimmed the lantern and set it on the floor between her feet.

"So," Colette said, cutting the cold silence. "Your friend Maurice can be quite stubborn."

Sophie sighed, but said nothing.

"What's the matter, dumpling? Are you still upset? I thought you'd cleared the air with him."

The compassion in Colette's voice, at first endearing, now seemed insincere in light of the evening's revelation. Sophie squinted at Colette through the flickering amber light. "I know what you are."

Colette leaned back into the shadows. "What am I?"

Sophie couldn't voice the word on her lips, so instead let her silence speak her disapproval.

The way Colette had handled a gun, the way she'd spoken to the deserters, the way she'd powdered Sophie's cheeks, even the way she'd danced at the tavern—all these things conveyed a sense of confidence, of self-reliance, of pride and empathy that Sophie admired and respected. Colette had proven every bit as smart, strong, and formidable as the men around her, giving Sophie a sense of hope for her own future as a woman in Paris. The fact that Colette was a prostitute, however, diminished her in Sophie's mind, and with Colette's descent, so went Sophie's hopes for herself.

They both sat mute, the darkness growing between them. Finally, Colette replied, "I'm sorry to disappoint you, *ma chérie*."

"Why?" Sophie grumbled. "Why do you disgrace yourself?"

"Disgrace myself?"

"How could a woman like you—a clever woman—give herself to men?"

At first, Colette did not respond, leaving Sophie to believe her insult had ended the conversation. At last Colette said, "When I first got to Paris, I was very much like you: a young girl from the farm with a heart full of dreams and a mind of my own. I too thought I had the world figured." She sat straight. "I was wrong. I learned quickly I had no business going to Paris alone."

Sophie wondered if this was an accusation, but heard the humility in Colette's voice.

"For months, I was hungry…always hungry," Colette sighed. "I accepted charity from the few people who took pity on me and stole from those who didn't. Mind you, I'm not proud of that. Stealing is wrong; about that, there's no debate."

Colette looked away for a moment, seeming to gather her thoughts in the flickering lantern light. When her attention returned, her voice was softer.

"Paris is quite a city," she breathed. "So beautiful, but lonely, generous in what it gives but cruel in what it takes."

Sophie leaned forward to listen.

"You see, dumpling, Paris is a woman. A beautiful, generous, but sometimes heartless woman."

The carriage hit a rough patch of road and the lantern shook, its flame casting wild shadows. Both Sophie and Colette stuck out their feet to steady the lamp between them.

"After months of begging," Colette continued, "I met a man, a gentleman with a handsome mustache and a tall hat. He was like no one I'd ever seen, at least not in my village."

Colette's voice fell to a whisper and Sophie strained to hear her.

"He found me dirty, starving and alone by a bridge over the Seine. I'm sure I was quite a sight." Colette gave an uncomfortable laugh, pushing her hair clip farther into her wavy locks. "Instead of judging me, this man showed me kindness. He bought me a warm meal and took me to a house, a *maison close*, where he introduced me to girls like me, alone with only their dreams. That man was Benedict Lefavre."

"Lefavre?" Sophie couldn't disguise her interest in the man Maurice had mentioned earlier, the husband of his former lover. "What was he like?"

"I don't really know. That night was the only time I ever met him, but I remember it distinctly. He told me I had something I didn't realize I had. He said I had power."

Colette raised her head and closed her eyes.

"He told me Paris was filled with men who would desire me for my beauty and, should I choose to give it, would pay me handsomely and end my hunger."

"What did you say?"

"I was afraid, of course. I knew what he meant. I'd only been with someone that way once before, a boy from my village. I didn't love him and decided long before coming to Paris that I would never be with another man I didn't love. Whether you believe it, I wasn't eager to give myself over like that."

"So why did you?"

"Monsieur Lefavre saw me struggle with my choice. He told me others in the maison had struggled with his offer as well, yet each had prevailed, he said, just as he knew I would. He said I had one decision to make, to get past a single, stubborn, incorrect belief that our virtue rests solely in our actions, in how we behave."

Sophie worked over Colette's words. "I thought virtue *is* about how we behave."

Colette pressed her hand to her breast. "Lefavre told me our virtue is in our hearts. How we behave, he said, is something else."

"I don't understand."

"Let me ask you this: Your father is off to defend Poland from the Germans. Is that right?"

"Yes…"

"In battle, if your father shoots a German, is he a murderer?"

"Certainly not."

"Ah. You say that with conviction, and I don't disagree. He'd be a hero if you ask me. Now, what if he meets that same German in the street and shoots him while strolling down the Champs-Élysées? The German is no less dead, but the act—the very same act—is now murder, *n'est-ce pas?*"

"I suppose."

"The virtue, then, is in our hearts: the action—the same, how we think of it—different. Lefavre told me to think of my actions as separate from my beliefs."

Sophie remained unconvinced. "How could you be with a man you don't love and still believe you've kept your virtue?"

Colette's voice got smaller, like a girl's. "I didn't say I believed it, dumpling. I said Lefavre told me to believe it." Colette sighed. "I just learned to live with it."

Sophie swallowed against the lump forming in her throat.

Colette leaned closer. "Let me tell you something I've never told a soul, not even my brother." She lowered her voice to a whisper. "I knew if I was to survive, I'd have to be like Paris; Paris the woman—eager to give, but willing to take. Strong and generous, but at times, heartless."

"Heartless?"

"I learned to make men love me without returning their love. Play to their vanity…Oh, yes, men are vain—more than women, believe me." Colette drew a long breath. "I learned to free my body, but keep my heart. That I held, and still hold, for someone special…someone I have yet to meet."

"When you meet him, don't you fear he'll judge you for what you've done?"

Colette opened her eyes and leaned back into the shadows. "For him to be special, for him to be the right man for me, he'll have to understand and forgive me."

When the road curved and the moonlight shined into the carriage, Sophie saw moist lines had formed on Colette's otherwise perfect face. Her powdered cheeks were now lined with tear tracks like rivers on a map, her beauty interrupted.

Sophie tried to collect her thoughts as if she were chasing chickens in a pen. It was not common for her to speak so philosophically with others, let alone another woman. On some level, she enjoyed it. However, this talk of virtue and danger gave her pause. How would she handle the complexities of the world outside Avoine?

Colette reached over the lantern and clutched Sophie's hand. "We get older, dumpling. When that happens, we stop thinking we can change things and accept them the way they are. That's why it's important to make good choices—the right choices—from the start."

Sophie felt a surge of emotions: sympathy for the woman she thought flawless only hours ago, and guilt for having judged her harshly. Above all, Sophie felt a pressing fear that if Paris could undo a woman like Colette, it might crush a girl like her.

"I'm sorry," said Sophie. "I shouldn't have been so rude to you."

"Oh, my dear." Colette squeezed Sophie's hand. "I can see you're a smart girl. You're right to be wary of people like me." She withdrew her grasp to run a knuckle under each moist eye, gathering her mascara tears. "My life is not for everyone, though it does afford me greater freedom than most. But you, dumpling...I can tell," Colette smiled, "your life is meant for greater things."

Sophie returned the smile, warming again to Colette's friendship.

"So tell me," Colette threw back her head with feigned composure, "what is it you dream of?"

The warmth and rhythm of the rumbling carriage was hypnotic. After Sophie had revealed her dream of La Sorbonne, Colette had explained that this fancy carriage was part of another dream of sorts, a fantasy concocted by her client in Troyes, a well-to-do man with penchant for all things regal.

Colette was asked to play the part of the visiting *Comtesse d'Almonde* and her client, the part of the fictitious *Comté d'Egnont*. Etienne was the reluctant carriage driver, but that was no pretense. He plainly would have preferred to take a car.

Unable to fathom the purpose of such an elaborate game, Sophie's bewilderment only added to her exhaustion and she decided to rest her eyes. Colette too had succumbed to fatigue and now slept against the carriage compartment.

Sophie moved closer to the bed warmer and lay against a tapestry cushion on the soft seat. Just as she pulled the blanket around her and drifted toward slumber, the carriage slowed to a stop. She vaguely heard someone climb down from the perch. When the door squeaked open and the cold night air rushed in, she was stirred to rise.

"Come, child," said Maurice abruptly.

"What's wrong?" Sophie whispered, trying not to wake Colette. However, Maurice had already turned away and climbed back up to the perch.

She half-consciously gathered her blanket and slid past Colette, who gave a sleepy grin from where she lay on her seat, lost in a dream.

Sophie stepped out of the compartment and into the brisk night, closing the carriage door behind her. She worried that Maurice was going to tell her she was on her own, that he'd reconsidered his plan and was withdrawing his promise to continue with her to Paris. Of course, she wouldn't blame him. What reason did he now have to accompany her further? She'd brought the man nothing but misfortune. No one was safe from her curse.

She draped the blanket over her shoulder, gripped the rails and climbed to the driver's bench, ready to receive her news. There, she found Etienne still smiling, and Maurice, inscrutable. The men moved to make room for her.

"Sit," commanded Maurice.

Sophie huddled under cover to ward off the chill, sat down, and braced herself for Maurice's pronouncement.

Etienne cracked the reins and the mare leapt forward. Sophie felt bad for the poor horse, now pulling twice as many passengers and possessions as she'd started with. She wondered if Plouf was all right, pained at the reminder that she even brought bad luck to the horses.

The carriage ascended a hill, but the mare didn't falter. Instead, she let out a whinny, quickening her pace.

"What's wrong?" Sophie repeated.

"Shhh," said Etienne, answering. "You'll see."

Sophie's fear and impatience didn't last. Once the carriage crested the hill, she saw why she'd been called.

Laid before her, beyond the slope of the hill, was a brilliant tapestry of colored lights, blinking against the inky black canvas of night. It was a city, seeming to float in the sky like the kingdom of God.

"Paris," said Maurice. "You said you dreamed of it, and so there you have it."

Sophie had seen pictures of Paris in magazines and books, saw the city in a newsreel at the start of a Charlie Chaplin motion picture, but nothing had prepared her for the feeling the city now evoked, a feeling beyond words.

It moved as something alive, bathed in an otherworldly glow. Automobiles bounced down boulevards like blood coursing through veins. Colorful billboard lights encircled advertisements for cigarettes like winking eyes filled with electricity. The Eiffel Tower stood tall and mothered over her Parisian children, casting her shadow over the boats that bobbed in the river Seine arching through the city like a smile. The city's lights seemed to be France's answer to the silent questions posed by the stars.

"You see?" Etienne laughed, elbowing Maurice. "I told you she'd gasp."

Sophie broke her trance and turned to the men, realizing the carriage had stopped. Maurice stared at her, his eyes glistening, an uncharacteristic grin on his face. His teeth were like a regimen of war-weary soldiers, some broken, some missing altogether. It was a smile she had not yet seen.

"Are you mocking me?" she managed.

Maurice looked away, down to the city. "Your face just now, seeing Paris for the first time..." he turned back to her, "It reminded me why I came here so many years ago."

Sophie squinted. "Why was that?"

"Same reason as you." He swallowed. "Dreams, child. I came because I had dreams." His eyes fixed on her. "It's why I return now."

A warm sensation blossomed inside her, a peace offered by her companion that felt like forgiveness.

Etienne gave out a loud, "Ha!" and flipped the reins, prompting the mare to step forward and draw them down the hill. "Madame Lefavre's is just over the bridge."

At the mention of the name, Sophie looked to Maurice, whose smile faded. His dreams may have returned, but it was clear his anxiety had not diminished.

In spite of the thrill, Sophie too felt anxious. If Paris were going to break Maurice's heart once again, the blame would be squarely hers and no one else's. There was no pretending otherwise.

She unraveled her blanket and stood to stretch it out behind her, but before Maurice could caution her to take her seat, she draped her blanket around them both, letting Maurice share its warmth. She knew this expression of familiarity would make him uncomfortable, but she didn't care.

She truly did need him after all.

Chapter 7

Shadow and Light

It was near midnight when the carriage rolled across a steel arch bridge, traversing the Seine into Paris en route to Madame Lefavre's. From Sophie's post on the carriage bench, the Eiffel Tower now seemed ever-present, soaring higher and more nobly than the buildings around it, its dramatic beauty leaving her breathless.

Etienne had announced he'd taken a slight detour, just to enjoy the Parisian flavor. From the way he watched Sophie, she saw he was more amused by the way her jaw kept dropping than he was with the city that had seduced her so completely.

In spite of the hour, Paris was busy, its thoroughfares frenetic with black automobiles racing to and fro like kitchen bugs after a lamp's been lit. The city's wild energy was as exciting as it was alarming.

"This is wonderful!" Sophie exclaimed.

"It's no place for a carriage," grumbled Maurice, eyeing the speeding traffic of cars.

"Of course, of course," Etienne chuckled. "I was thinking only of the girl." He made a clicking noise with his tongue and yanked the reins to change course.

As they passed the Tower, Sophie spied its rising iron latticework, delicate like lace and yet strong enough to carry the spire since the World's Fair, fifty years ago. The closer she got, the more the Tower's stance seemed to widen, curving like the hips of a lady. It turned out Gustave Eiffel was not the engineer Sophie thought him to be. He was an artist. Like Colette, he too had seen that Paris was a woman.

They rolled down the boulevard, past the *fromageries* and *boulangeries* that had closed for the night, past hat shops and watchmakers'. Sophie listened to the frenzied melodies of cabaret jazz and car horns woven through the raucous laughter rising from bars and cafés. Petrol fumes and cigarette smoke mixed with women's perfume and the salty-sweet aroma of roasted nuts. All these sensations created an atmosphere Sophie decided could only be produced by a city—this city.

She lifted her head toward the gargoyles that stared down from stone buildings. Paris, it seemed, worked on levels, with as many captivating sights up high as there were on the street.

Sophie snapped her attention back to the boulevard when a shiny black car with sloping fenders roared around the corner, directly in front of them. She clenched her teeth, swallowed a breath, gripped the bench, and braced for a crash.

In an instant, the car swerved and missed them, its shocking horn masking the profanity shouted by its driver, a crazy-eyed man in a felt hat and scarf.

Etienne gripped the reins as the car flew by, but the horse only snorted, tossed its head, and stayed the course.

"*Stupide!*" Maurice cursed, his fist raised at the fleeting automobile. He spun back to Etienne. "You have a plan?"

It had become clear that Etienne couldn't maneuver through the center of town any longer, even for Sophie's amusement.

"Of course. Nothing to fear." Etienne adjusted his glasses, pulled the reins, and turned the carriage east, past Les Invalides, the elaborate domed building Sophie recognized as the final resting place of the Emperor Napoleon. She gathered her nerves and again faced the city as they rolled along its streets, colorful signs noting their departure from l'avenue la Motte Picquet.

Well-dressed men and fur-coated women walked down the avenue, arm in arm against the cold night air. Sophie had never seen such people—people with long, clean coats or fancy hats tilted with attitude, people like the man walking his dog, the size of a rat. She watched as these people passed street dwellers huddled around a barrel fire, ignoring their plight.

She wondered what her father would say if he saw these wealthy people, hustling about the city so late at night with nothing important to do. Clearly, no one in Paris had goats to milk or chickens to feed in the morning, and none seemed to have been called, as her father had, by *l'Armée de Terre*.

Again, the carriage crossed the river to a road that passed the famed Jardin des Tuileries, where Sophie saw a couple embracing, lovers swooning beneath manicured trees.

It was clear how Paris could amplify a person's feelings, especially feelings of love. She wondered if she too might someday lose herself in the eyes of a handsome man who would embrace her, love her perfectly in the geometry of such a garden.

She scanned the streets and pondered how far she was from *l'Université*. She turned to Etienne.

"How far are we from La Sorbonne?"

"We're a bit to the west. Do you know someone there?"

Sophie looked to the road. "No, I was just wondering."

A cold gust of air brought the unexpected smell of sewage down the boulevard, ripping Sophie from her fantasy, back to the reality of her circumstance. Dreams were for later, she thought. The Germans had seen to that.

The sounds of cabarets and the danger of the occasional speeding car soon faded behind them, replaced by the whispering hiss of the glowing gas lamps that urged them down the cobbled road of a residential street. As they entered a quiet neighborhood, the horse's shoes sent echoes between the narrow brownstones. The air smelled of warm coal, though Sophie felt a chill return to her bones.

"How much farther?" she asked Etienne.

It was Maurice who replied, "Not far." He peered ahead as if lost in a trance.

Sophie had forgotten that Maurice also knew where to find Madame Lefavre's. In her excitement, distracted by her lost dreams, Sophie had managed to ignore the growing tension in her companion. Josephine Lefavre was moments away and surely Maurice was dwelling on dreams of his own.

"I'll go in first," offered Sophie. "I can see if she's awake, figure her mood, and tell you when it's safe to come in."

Maurice moved his head, but stopped just short of meeting Sophie's eyes. "That would be fine."

"Halloooo?" sang Colette, now obviously awake in the compartment below. "Aren't we there?"

"Soon, sister, soon," answered Etienne, rolling his eyes. "Only a block."

"My foot fell asleep and my toes are cold."

"Of course, sister," he called. Etienne smiled at his shivering companions who had braved the night air without complaint. "You poor dear."

Sophie giggled. Even Maurice managed a smile.

Moments later, Etienne hauled back on the reins. "*Nous sommes arrivés!* We've arrived!"

Beside them, surrounded by a waist-high, wrought-iron gate, a stately clapboard *lupanar* rose three stories into the night sky. It was bright white with etched-glass windows and a series of pipes lining its exterior, painted to match the clapboard. Wispy smoke rose from the chimneys and electric lamplight glowed dimly in the upstairs windows. The place seemed inviting and pleasant, not at all as Sophie had imagined.

"Maurice and I will collect your things and tend to the horse," Etienne said. "You go in with Colette. She'll explain everything to Madame Lefavre."

Sophie stepped free from her blanket, leaving it with Maurice as he sat, unmoving. She reached over and grasped his cold hand. "Don't worry," she whispered, though she knew he wouldn't listen.

Maurice nodded, lost in thought, unfazed by her words.

She released his hand and took a breath, knowing it was time for her to act. She climbed backward down to meet Colette, who had just stepped out of the carriage. Colette had reapplied her makeup and now looked as perfect as when they'd first met in the forest. Sophie followed Colette's gaze to the maison.

"It looks nice," said Sophie, as much to comfort herself as to seek Colette's reassurance.

"Yes," Colette agreed. "It's a good place. It's home."

Sophie inhaled the cold, foreign air. What would her father say if he were to learn about her journey to a Parisian brothel, so far off the path he'd prescribed? How would he judge her choices—her insistence on coming to the city, the selfishness that had brought Maurice loss and disappointment?

Here at Madame Lefavre's doorstep, Sophie had one chance to make things right.

Colette looped her arm through Sophie's. "Relax, dumpling. Relax."

Sophie realized she was frowning, contemplating how she might help Maurice face the woman he both loved and feared. "I just want to make a good impression, that's all."

"You will. Trust me." Colette led her to the door and reached for the knob.

Sophie grabbed Colette's hand. "Please don't mention Maurice to her. At least not yet. I promised him I'd make sure things were all right with Madame Lefavre first. I think he's nervous. He's not sure he even wants to speak with her."

Colette grinned, a softness in her face. "All right, dumpling. No mention of Monsieur Maurice."

With a twist of the beveled glass knob, Colette gave the door a gentle push. They entered a small, but well-appointed parlor; the smells of burning wax and perfume wafting in the warm air.

Candles glowed on tables throughout the parlor and a series of tea lights winked and glistened on the mantel. The hearth's fire was waning, its logs spitting their demise.

Sophie put her gloves in her coat pockets and rubbed her hands together to warm them.

Lamps with colored shades infused the room with tinted light, giving a sense of movement to the framed photographs of elegant women hanging on the walls. Sophie wondered if the women in the photos, like Colette, had each sacrificed their virtue at the urging of Benedict Lefavre.

This place was opulent, not the unseemly refuge of iniquity she'd expected. Rather, the place felt friendly, protected, with the tender allure of a home.

The parlor's glow momentarily faded, replaced by a bright gleam that flooded from the kitchen when Madame Lefavre opened the door and entered.

"Colette!" she sang. "At last!"

Dressed in a fringed purple Japanese kimono, Madame Lefavre greeted Colette with open arms. The golden threads of her hanging sleeves shimmered in the firelight like the spread wings of an angel. The two women clutched hands and kissed opposite cheeks with zeal, sisters in their splendor.

"Madame."

Madame Lefavre's beauty seemed more natural than Colette's, relying less on makeup. She was just as Maurice had described. Her brown hair was pulled back, its soft color joined by a gray streak that cascaded down her shoulder like a frothy country brook. Her eyes were deep brown, her cheeks round and healthy. Slight creases around her eyes and mouth gave hints of her age, or perhaps sadness, but the glow of her skin still sang of tenacious youth. Her full bosom made her matronly, but her long legs, exposed below the length of her kimono, were strong and shapely.

Madame Lefavre turned her infectious smile toward Sophie. "Who have we here?" She seemed to evaluate Sophie, her outline, height, size, shape, clothing...

"I'm Sophie from...the Loire Valley." She chose not to reveal the name of her town, Avoine, for fear Madame Lefavre might know the town as the place Maurice lived. Sophie's heart began to patter harder, half from excitement, half from inexplicable fear.

"Sophie from the Loire Valley," Madame Lefavre repeated slowly, and then leaned in to kiss her cheeks, which Sophie hesitantly accepted. This close, she thought Madame Lefavre smelled like lilacs and nutmeg.

Colette stepped over and hung her arm over Sophie like an old friend. "Etienne and I found Sophie and her brave chaperone in the woods. Poor dears were being robbed."

"Robbed? *Mon Dieu!*" Madame Lefavre touched her hand to her breast, and looked Sophie over more closely as a market patron would survey an apple for bruises. "Are you hurt?"

"Colette saved us," Sophie replied. "The thieves left our wagon but took our horse."

"We couldn't abandon them, so we brought them here."

"Of course, of course!" Madame Lefavre stepped back from Sophie and squinted at her with a renewed interest. "Lovely...Quite lovely. Darling girl." Madame Lefavre touched Sophie's shoulder and glanced around the parlor. "Where is this brave chaperone you speak of?"

Unready for how she might broach the subject of Maurice, Sophie felt her voice leave her.

"He's helping Etienne feed the horse," Colette offered. "I'm sure he'll be along."

Grateful for Colette's fast response, Sophie shot her a knowing grin.

"Well," Madame Lefavre sighed, "you must be cold and ready to freshen up. "May I show you around, maybe draw you a bath?"

A hot bath sounded tempting to Sophie, just the thing for which her cold flesh longed. However, the idea of bathing in a lupanar made her uncomfortable. It was hard enough to imagine sleeping here. Then she remembered Maurice. She had a mission to accomplish, a favor to return, a promise to keep, no matter her discomfort, and Madame Lefavre's offer had the potential to give Sophie the time she needed—time to speak privately, set the scene for Maurice and get Madame away from the parlor should Maurice enter unexpectedly.

"Oh, yes, a bath!" Sophie replied too eagerly. Catching herself, she added, "Though I don't want to be any trouble."

Madame Lefavre beamed. "No trouble at all, darling. There are two things I've learned in life and here they are: women have always had it harder than men, and there is very little that ails us that a warm bath can't make better."

Colette gave an affirmative nod.

"We have indoor plumbing and hot water all year," Madame Lefavre continued. "If that's trouble then I don't know what's become of France." She laughed a girlish laugh and took Sophie by the hand. "Oh, dear. Your hand is cold. Let's see to that bath right now. Colette, darling, take her coat, won't you?"

Colette obliged and hung Sophie's coat on a brass coatrack by the door.

"I've started a pot of tea, just brewing," Madame chimed to Colette. "Help yourself, if you don't mind." She turned to Sophie. "Shall we?"

Madame Lefavre led Sophie up the stairs. As they ascended, Sophie glanced down to Colette who gave a wink of assurance, but in the last day, Sophie had learned to be wary of Colette's judgment and felt assured of nothing. For now, she was on her own.

Chapter 8

The Truth about Monsieur Lefavre

"We have nine rooms and four bathrooms," explained Madame Lefavre, lifting large, fluffy towels from a cabinet at the top of the stairs. "Quite a place, don't you think?"

"Yes," agreed Sophie. She worked to hide the trepidation in her voice. "It's like a castle."

Madame Lefavre chortled, walking further down the dimly lit hallway. She moved swiftly and spoke nearly as fast. "Well, not much of a castle. You won't find servants here. We take care of our own."

On their way to the bath, they passed two bedrooms with doors on opposite sides of the hall. Sophie heard laughter—a man's and a woman's—coming from behind one of the doors, even though the lights were out. Madame Lefavre said nothing, but turned to Sophie and raised an eyebrow. It seemed Madame counted on Sophie to understand just where she was and what happened here behind closed doors.

In spite of the welcoming warmth and kindness of this home, Sophie knew it was also a place of business, a business she did not approve of. Like the parlor, the whole maison, even Madame Lefavre herself, seemed filled with both darkness and light.

Madame flipped a switch on the wall, illuminating the bathroom at the hall's end. Electricity was still a marvel to Sophie, like Paris itself, working by rules she didn't comprehend.

The bathroom was expansive, larger than Sophie's living room, and equipped with a hulking oak vanity, a cushioned stool, and a gilded mirror that hung on the wall. Near the door, aside a porcelain toilet, stood a carved sink with a wide washbasin, deep enough to carry a pair of men's boots. This was nothing like the outhouse at her farm, and it truly seemed a wonder.

However, across the room sat the piece that left Sophie in awe: an enormous claw-footed copper tub.

"Is that a bath?"

"Yes, my dear."

"It's big enough for three people!"

Madame Lefavre only smiled.

Sophie recalled her small tub at home, the one she'd fill with well water, boiled in kettles. She had no faucets there, no ornate mirrors. Her best hope at home was that the water would be free of silt.

At the foot of the copper tub rose a tall, three-paneled dressing screen. Each panel was made of colorful fabric like the silk of Madame Lefavre's kimono, set with images of cranes and tiger lilies, hand-stitched with golden thread.

A stone pedestal stood beside the bath, topped by a silver tray, and upon the tray sat a variety of colored bottles, long glass vials, a snuffbox, candles, and a small book of matches.

"My favorite room in the maison," pronounced Madame Lefavre. She leaned over the tub and twisted the polished knobs. "Hot or warm?"

"However you think," said Sophie, trying to sound gracious.

"Hot," Madame replied. "It's good for the skin." Once the flow of water had started, Madame Lefavre turned to Sophie. "Now, let's see." She scanned Sophie up and down, spun her around by her shoulders, and leaned over her head to smell her hair.

Sophie clenched her fists, trying not to flinch at the inspection. "I'm sorry," Sophie peeped. "I'm sure I don't smell very good. We've been traveling."

"I'm just trying to decide your scents, dear. The ones that are right for you."

"My scents?"

Madame Lefavre raised her head. "In all my years, I've learned two things: women are stronger than men in all ways that matter, and we each have scents that are right for us, and only us."

Sophie enjoyed Madame's "two things" and quickly understood why Maurice had found Madame so enchanting.

"Honey and lavender," Madame said at last. "I'm sure those scents are yours." She turned to the tray on the pedestal and lifted an amber bottle to the light. She drew the stopper and tilted the container over the bath until golden globs fell liberally into the water. The air grew warm with the aroma of honey.

Next, Madame retrieved a thin glass vial with a cork top. "Lavender oil," she announced, "from Provence." She pulled the cork with a "pop" and added three drops. Soon, the room filled with a fragrance that made Sophie's eyes close with delight.

"Ah, yes," remarked Madame, seeming pleased by Sophie's reaction. "I'm never wrong. Two scents for everyone—something sweet and something secret. All things in two."

"Yes, I understand," said Sophie, transfixed.

"Care to guess my scents?"

"Lilacs and nutmeg," Sophie replied. "I knew the moment I met you."

"Well done, my dear." Madame Lefavre grinned. "Well done, indeed. You have the gift, same as me."

Oh, no, thought Sophie, emerging from her trance. I'm not like you at all. In fact, she'd never met anyone like Madame Lefavre, anyone who'd been so able to read her needs, yet raise her defenses, so giving with compliments and free with hospitality but so inexplicably intimidating.

Madame Lefavre sighed. "Now, off with that dirty dress."

Sophie's stomach knotted. She'd never been naked in front of another person and was unaccustomed to sharing her bathroom while bathing. Without a word, Sophie reached to the vanity for a bath sheet and stepped behind the dressing screen.

"A shy one, I see," Madame laughed. "Very well."

Embarrassed, but happily obscured by the silk-covered panels, Sophie unbuttoned her favorite blue dress. She removed the silver chain from around her neck, kissed her mother's key like the mezuzah at her door, and tucked it in her shoe. She then pulled her arms free of her dress, stepped out of her underclothes, and piled her garments neatly at her cold, bare feet.

For Maurice, she told herself. For Maurice.

She wrapped herself in the bath sheet and stepped out from behind the screen.

Madame Lefavre turned the faucets to stop the water and, without a word, glided to the vanity where she retrieved a golden hairbrush before turning to Sophie.

"A Chinese brush," Madame announced. "A noble gift from a visiting dignitary whose name I must never say."

"A dignitary?" asked Sophie, working to steady her voice against her mounting discomfort.

"Oh, I'm only joking," laughed Madame Lefavre. "This was a gift from the grocer, Monsieur Declerc. He must have saved his francs for a month just to buy it. Such a lovely man. We get no dignitaries here, my dear. I just like to pretend."

It occurred to Sophie that Madame's joke was intended to help Sophie relax, just like the bath, the honey, and the lavender. She scolded herself for appearing so unnerved. Focus, she thought. She recalled how Colette spoke of setting aside her heart, separating her actions from her values.

Madame Lefavre moved closer and gestured with the brush to the tub. "Your bath awaits, mademoiselle."

Still wrapped in her bath sheet, Sophie stepped into the hot water, her flesh prickling, the water saturating her towel. She held her breath and released the corner of the sheet, spreading it in front of her naked body to obscure herself from Madame Lefavre's view. She exhaled and lowered herself into the tub, letting the towel sink over her in the bath like a blanket.

The warmth of the scented water cut straight to her bones and absolved her of the chill she'd felt for the last two days. She sank against the slope of the tub, the water enveloping her like a womb. Despite her fear, despite her vulnerability, she closed her eyes and let her mind drift, let herself enjoy this single exquisite moment as if she were all alone.

She inhaled the air, thick with honey and lavender, which intermingled like night and day at dusk, elements meant to be joined. Madame was right. These were her scents.

Sophie dunked her head, soaked her hair until she was fully infused with the rich, clean aromas of the bath. Once she re-emerged, she was surprised to see that Madame had retrieved the cushioned stool and had taken a seat beside her.

"May I brush your hair?"

"All right…of course." Sophie squeezed her hair dry and let it fall. She gathered the sunken towel around her as she sat in the water.

With daunting familiarity, Madame ran Sophie's hair between her fingers like a tailor examining fabric. "You have a natural wave, my dear."

"It's curly and I hate it," Sophie replied, allowing conversation. "I can never seem to make it go the way I like."

"How do you like it?" Madame ran the brush through her damp locks.

"I guess I don't really know…but not how it is."

"My darling Sophie from Loire," Madame cleared her throat "there are two things in this life I know and precisely two: we can't choose who we love and we can't choose our hair."

"Yes," said Sophie feeling churlish, "but we can change our hair."

"And, my dear," Madame smirked, "we can change who we love."

The two shared a giggle at their own cleverness. From Madame's grin and the flash of her eyes, it was clear she was pleased with Sophie's attempt to match her wit. To her surprise, Sophie was pleased to have made Madame laugh.

Warmed by the bath, protected by her towel, and buoyed by Madame's generosity, Sophie felt a rising sense of comfort…of boldness. This talk of love had given her the moment she needed.

"Where is Monsieur Lefavre?" Sophie ventured.

Madame stopped brushing Sophie's hair and grew silent for a moment. She sat unmoving, and Sophie feared she'd spoken out of turn.

Then with a soft, controlled tone the Madame replied, "What do you know of Monsieur Lefavre?"

Sophie steadied her voice. "Nothing, really. Only what Colette told me."

"Colette speaks of things she doesn't understand," Madame chided and returned to brushing Sophie's hair. It was the first terse thing Madame had said.

Sophie curled her toes beneath the swirling hot water but clung to her newfound courage and worked to appear unfazed.

"You said you could change who you love. I only thought that meant you no longer loved Monsieur Lefavre…"

Sophie glanced as casually as she could toward the mirror to spy Madame Lefavre's reaction, hopeful to see her plan work. She braced herself, desperate to hear Madame utter the name "Maurice."

Instead, Madame Lefavre remained focused on the rhythm of brushing, her thoughts imperceptible on her face. At last, she sighed, expanding her already large bosom, and looked at Sophie. She seemed to calculate her, judge her, and assess her sincerity. To Sophie's relief, Madame smiled.

"Your question," she replied, "is fair." She stopped brushing. "I like you, Sophie from Loire, so I'll tell you something. I'll tell you the truth about Monsieur Lefavre."

"The truth?"

Madame returned to brushing. "Monsieur Lefavre was a man of many gifts. When I first arrived in Paris, he was the one who convinced me to come here, just as he did many of the others who call this place their home."

Sophie recalled Colette's story in the carriage. It seemed improbable to Sophie that a woman as self-assured as Madame Lefavre could have also been manipulated by such a man.

"Above everything, the monsieur was a shrewd businessman," Madame continued. "He had dreams of wealth, of richness and privilege. He wanted to assure his future just as I did. So, on my twenty-fourth birthday he came to me with a proposal that changed my life, a proposal of marriage."

"So, you did love him once."

"Not so fast, my dear. My story isn't through. The monsieur offered marriage, but not from any feelings of love—at least not a love for me. He told me plainly that he wished to leave this maison and begin a new business in Brussels. Banking, as I recall."

Sophie couldn't imagine such a man sitting behind a desk in a bank. Then again, she could hardly imagine such a man at all.

"The problem," Madame Lefavre added, "was that he had established a fine reputation here in Paris, and a regular clientele. He didn't want to leave that behind. His offer of marriage was an offer of partnership. He had no children, no family, and so he had no choice. As long as someone carried the Lefavre name, the Lefavre maison could exist without him here."

"Wouldn't people know he'd gone?"

"People were used to Monsieur Lefavre's comings and goings. Those who would take advantage of a woman—even a woman with money—would think twice when dealing with the wife of a man they respected, a woman who carried his name."

Respect was something Sophie struggled to muster for anyone in this unseemly profession. Nevertheless, Madame's story intrigued her.

"Women run businesses all the time these days," Sophie countered. "Why did you need the monsieur's name for that?"

"Ah, my dear. Your head is strong, so much like mine, but you must understand the rules were different for a maison close, at least back then. Women haven't always had the privileges they now enjoy. Our arrangement was simply good business. It allowed Monsieur Lefavre to leave Paris, and gave me both money and control of my own destiny." Madame stopped brushing Sophie's hair and leaned in to meet her puzzled look. "Offers like that don't come along every day for a young woman."

Madame must have seen the confusion on Sophie's face because she added, "Offers such as that assure a woman's future and allow her to be certain of a reliable income. That's rare these days." She spoke more emphatically. "I'm speaking of independence, my dear."

The Madame set the brush on the silver tray and reached to touch Sophie's cheek. "I'm making you an offer, Sophie from Loire: the same offer made to me and to Colette after me. Come work in the Lefavre maison. Your future will be certain and your income assured."

Sophie's chin dropped to the bath water.

Madame Lefavre stood from the stool and extended her arms wide, her golden wings spread. "Join us, and you can take a bath like this every day." She smiled broadly. "Rich and happy. All things in twos, my dear. Remember, we take care of our own."

"What?" In spite of the bath's warmth, Sophie felt a chill rush through her long, awkward limbs. She clutched the towel and scrambled to get it around her naked, submerged body. "How…how could you suggest—?"

Before Madame Lefavre could respond, Sophie stood, sending waves of water spilling over the edges of the copper tub like the banks of the Loire when it too grew overwhelmed.

"How could you think—?" Sophie's voice faltered. "I—I'm not that kind of person. I'm just a girl."

Madame Lefavre seemed genuinely taken aback. "I meant no offense, my dear. I simply thought—"

"No!" Sophie screamed. She didn't want to hear another word. All she wanted was to transport herself home, back to her father's side, before the Armée de Terre had taken him.

She tried to step out of the tall bath to flee, but her towel had tangled itself around her knees. Before she could collect herself, she tumbled over the tub's edge and hit the tile floor with a painful, wet slap.

"Oh, my dear!" Madame called. "Are you all right?" She leaned down to lift Sophie from the wet floor like a fish monger retrieving a fish, fallen from his bucket.

"Stay away from me!" bellowed Sophie, yanking her bare arm from Madame's grasp. "I can't imagine how Maurice could love someone like you!"

The moment the words fled Sophie's angry lips, she realized her error.

"Maurice?" Madame Lefavre rose. "Did you say Maurice?"

Sophie fumbled to secure her towel and stood. "I...I meant—"

The bathroom door flew open and Colette dashed in, half out of breath. "*Mon Dieu!* Why are you yelling? What's wrong?"

Madame Lefavre spun to face Colette. "This young lady you brought me...she's not a recruit?"

Colette looked to Sophie who stood dripping, her wet towel clinging to her trembling flesh.

"Good heavens, no, Madame. She's my guest, a girl needing a place for the night."

Madame Lefavre raised her head toward her colleague and narrowed her eyes. "You were not clear on that point." She enunciated each word like an accusation. "I offered her work here, much to her offense."

Colette bowed her head. "Forgive me, Madame."

"It's this young lady's forgiveness you require, not mine."

Madame faced Sophie. "I meant you only the greatest respect, my dear."

Sophie didn't respond except to pull her towel more closely around her dripping, naked body.

Madame pursed her lips as someone who'd tasted something sour. "Now," she turned back to Colette, "where is Maurice?"

Colette flashed a wide-eyed look to Sophie, surprised to hear Maurice's name come from Madame's mouth. Sophie said nothing. She'd already said too much.

"Yes," Madame replied, answering Colette's confusion. "I know Maurice is her chaperone—" she turned back to Sophie, "or have I gotten that wrong, too?"

Sophie recalled Madame Lefavre saying she was never wrong and knew this moment was not a pleasant one for her, either. With a voice lacking any enthusiasm, Sophie answered, "He's with Etienne. He's waiting for me to..."

"To what?" asked Madame. "To soften me up?"

Sophie lifted her eyes. "I suppose."

Madame crossed the bathroom to the dressing screen, where she retrieved another dry bath sheet and offered it to Sophie. "You must think me a terrible person. For that, I'm sorry, but please know this. I have nothing but fondness for that man." She looked Sophie in the eye. "He's very lucky to have a friend like you."

Sophie took the dry towel without responding and retreated behind the dressing screen. She wanted to accept Madame's apology and forgive the misunderstanding, to make sense of all that had happened. The truth was she still didn't understand how good people could knowingly do bad things. She couldn't reconcile how people so generous and kind could be the same people who practiced prostitution for the love of the comforts it brought. She feared she'd never understand the world, at least not the world of Paris.

She worked over her confusion as she wiped herself dry, donned her underclothes, and replaced her mother's key around her neck. However, her contemplation was interrupted when a dress suddenly appeared, draped over the screen. It was yellow with floral patterns woven into its fabric. White stitching traced the hem and held generous lengths of delicate lace.

"From the finest seamstress in all of France," Madame explained. "A gift for you, and please don't argue."

Sophie stared at the dress, drawn by its beauty. She raised a hand to touch it and found it as soft as it was beautiful, but she couldn't help but wonder the price. Would accepting the dress mean accepting this place and these people?

"Madame—"

"I don't expect your forgiveness," Madame said, seeming to hear Sophie's thoughts. "The dress is yours and yours alone. Let's just leave it at that."

Before Sophie could reply, the click of Madame's heels on the tile announced her departure. There would be no protest.

Sophie ran her fingers along the fabric, inadvertently causing the garment to fall upon her, into her arms. She clutched the dress and pressed the gentle cotton to her face, thinking it was the finest thing she'd ever handled, finer than her blue dress, which now lay wet and rumpled at her feet. She lifted the yellow dress to the light and pondered whether it was safe to call it her own. She stepped into it, slid her arms through the sleeves, and hooked it together behind her back.

She peered from behind the screen to view the dress in the mirror. However, when she emerged, she found Colette kneeling on the floor, using a thick towel to mop up the water Sophie had spilled from the tub.

"I offended Madame," Colette murmured. "I don't know if she'll ever forgive me."

"It's not your fault." Sophie placed her hand on Colette's shoulder. "I'm sure her anger will pass."

Colette looked up through glossy eyes as if to respond, but halted and, instead, offered a gleaming smile. "You look…beautiful."

Sophie turned to the mirror and saw herself, as if for the first time, a stranger in yellow. This dress fit her in every way. It made her gangly limbs less long, made her slender form seem elegant. She looked older, more composed, no longer the goat girl of Avoine. When she saw her face she was surprised to see a smile.

She looked back to ask Colette about the maker of this wonderful dress, but Colette was no longer engaged in Sophie's joy. Instead, she was gathering Sophie's damp clothes into a large bamboo basket.

"I'll wash these tonight and hang them to dry," Colette said. She picked up Sophie's muddy blue dress, spotted with soil from her adventure in the woods—the dress that was, until today, her favorite.

Sophie looked down at the yellow frock that now embraced her so perfectly. How would her father feel if he were to learn she was being waited on by people such as Colette and Madame Lefavre, people offering her new favorite dresses?

"Please, don't," Sophie urged. "I can wash those myself."

"I think Madame would expect this of me." Colette's frown dared a different view.

"All right," Sophie conceded, "but maybe I can help."

Colette gave a noncommittal sigh and carried the basket out of the bathroom. Sophie followed down a long hallway toward one of the bedrooms where Colette gestured with her elbow toward the open door. "I've prepared your bed with fresh linen and put a night dress on your chair. You'll sleep well."

"Sleep?" Sophie's brief nap in the carriage and the drama in the bathroom had filled her with new energy, and she couldn't imagine taking off the fine dress she'd just put on.

"Oh, dumpling, you must be tired," Colette laughed, a warm flash of her earlier self, shining through her somberness. "This has been a trying time for all of us."

The truth of Colette's words wasn't lost on Sophie. She'd left her childhood home, said good-bye to her father, helped cremate Maurice's cousin, and nearly died in the woods at the hands of thieves. On top of it all, her father had left her with her mother's key and a mystery she hoped to unlock.

Colette was right. It had been at trying time.

Nevertheless, as tired as she was, Sophie desperately wished to learn how Maurice was getting on with Madame Lefavre. She feared the broken heart he said he couldn't bear again was unavoidable now that Sophie had bungled their plan. Madame was probably confronting him right now.

"It's late," said Colette, interrupting her thoughts, "and I'm sure Maurice will be fine without you."

Sophie gave a single, reluctant nod, uncertain what she could do. More importantly, she wondered what she *should* do. She remembered her father once told her that she had all the right energy for all the wrong things. He'd said this to her when she'd first expressed an interest in art, when she told him she thought she might someday work at a gallery or museum like her mother had done. His harsh response had made her cry, caused her to dream in secret.

Now, in this matter with Maurice, her father's words haunted her. Maybe she had done enough; maybe she needed to leave Maurice alone.

"All right," Sophie replied to Colette, trying not to sound defeated.

"When you wake, we'll discuss your plans. We'll send word to your grandmother, tell her that you're fine and eager to see her."

"I'd like that," said Sophie.

"Then I'll see you in the morning, dumpling. *Bonne nuit.*"

"*Bonne nuit.*"

Sophie closed the door and, seeing the steel key protruding from the keyhole, turned it to engage the lock. She had not forgotten where she was and would have no more misunderstandings of her desired profession tonight.

The bedroom appeared well-furnished, with the same conveniences she'd seen throughout the house. A cherry wood nightstand with contoured legs stood next to the bed. A small electric lamp with a stained-glass shade sat upon it, shining like happiness, mocking her.

The bed was covered with a blanket and was large enough for her to sleep sideways. Wide feather pillows leaned against the cherry headboard, promising to cushion her weary head, calling her to slumber.

She reluctantly removed her yellow dress and hung it on the mirror above the dressing table. From the chair, she took the cotton nightdress Colette had left and slipped it on, releasing into the air the scents of honey and lavender that clung to her skin and hair, the comforting scents she'd accepted as her own.

She climbed into the bed, slid beneath the warm sheets, mingled her slender legs together like a country cricket, and drew in the bed's soothing softness. The day had been confusing and upsetting, but this bed was already putting her at ease.

She leaned over and pulled the chain of the lamp to quiet the light, placed her head on one of the pillows, reached to her necklace to clutch her mother's key, and closed her eyes.

However, just as she began to succumb to her exhaustion, voices rose from the parlor below through a grate in the floor beside the bed. The first voice, a woman's, was Madame Lefavre's, the other, the unmistakable grumble of Maurice. Sophie opened her eyes, her fatigue vanquished by overwhelming curiosity. This was a conversation she had to hear.

Chapter 9

Conversations in the Parlor

Sophie pulled herself from the sheets, threw two pillows to the floor and lay upon them, leaning her ear to the floor grate to hear the conversation from the parlor more clearly.

"—implying I'm old?" Madame Lefavre's voice rang through the metal vent, angry and accusing.

"You forget, I know you." Maurice retorted in a loud voice filled with gravel. "I know you think of your future."

"My future? Don't you see? My future is here."

"Nonsense!" Maurice snapped. "Your past is here. You choose your future—where it will be, who it will be with."

Madame did not respond.

Sophie's heart pounded. This conversation, if one could call it that, was not going well. She kept her breathing shallow, fearful that any sound from her room would alert them to her presence. She clutched a pillow and wished she could see their faces, read their expressions.

"You're beautiful," Maurice finally said, a new tenderness in his voice. "More beautiful than I remember."

"Maurice—"

"But I see something different in your eyes now. It's the same thing I've seen in my own eyes. You're lonely."

"I'm not lonely."

"You can't lie to me, Fifi." Maurice let his words hang in the air, lingering like the lavender on Sophie's skin. At last he added, "You don't have to be lonely. If you love me, you have a choice."

Sophie was surprised to hear Maurice utter the words of his heart so plainly. She imagined the gravedigger's blue eyes, his bottle-brush mustache, his crooked teeth. She remembered his lips, dripping with oil from his kippers. He seemed an unlikely match for a woman of Madame Lefavre's beauty and sophistication. Yet, his feelings were clear. He'd been vulnerable with Madame, honest and open, even when she'd discouraged him. That made him daring. How could Madame refuse such a man?

"Or," he continued, "are you afraid?"

"Afraid?" Madame's anger was palpable. "Surely, if you know me as you say, you know I fear nothing." Madame's voice was breathy and untamed. "Has it occurred to you I don't love you enough to throw everything away? Everything I've worked for?"

"Yes," Maurice said softly. "It has occurred to me." He cleared his throat. "That's what's kept me away for so long."

"Then, why now? Why, Maurice?"

Sophie heard tears in Madame Lefavre's voice. She was transformed—no longer the strong, controlled businesswoman who offered Sophie a place at her *bordel*. She sounded like a girl, a confused and desperate girl.

"Narina died," replied Maurice. "Remember her, my cousin in the country? She died alone, the kindest woman with no one to love her." Maurice's voice caught on his emotion, but he pressed on. "I can't die like she died. Not when there may still be some chance of happiness...for us both."

Sophie could only imagine what it took from a man so awkward and irritable to confess his love for someone.

"That girl, Sophie...She has dreams," Maurice said. "Remember when we had dreams?"

Sophie cringed at hearing her name, but Madame Lefavre did not respond.

"*Ma chère*," Maurice said, now more gently. "You can be in love and be afraid. Both can exist together." He was now surprisingly steady and focused. "Love and fear. All things in twos, *n'est-ce pas?* Just as you say? Isn't that life?"

She recalled Maurice's words: "A man's heart is not like a woman's. It can only break once." She bit her lip, suddenly conscious of the tears that had formed in her eyes. She hung on to the silence, desperate for Madame's reply. Could the same woman break a man's heart twice?

"I'm tired," Madame sighed. "You've overwhelmed me, Maurice, and I must rest."

Maurice did not reply, and without so much as a *"Bonne nuit,"* Madame's shoes clicked on the parlor floor, announcing her departure.

Rest? thought Sophie. She hadn't answered him! How could she end the conversation there?

Maurice grumbled something Sophie couldn't make out and then all words ceased, folded into the smooth darkness like a love letter written and stuffed into a drawer.

Sophie closed her eyes, releasing her tears to her cheeks. She squeezed her pillow, squeezed it as though she might wrest from it the acceptance Maurice desired, the acceptance he deserved. It seemed she too had something at stake.

No matter how she felt about Madame Lefavre's profession, she knew Maurice loved the woman and she could not disapprove of love. He'd confessed his dream, and if his dreams could come true, then why not hers?

"The finest bed in all of Paris and you prefer the floor?"

Sophie opened her eyes to the sight of Madame Lefavre's high-heeled shoes, green and polished, reflecting the morning sunlight that shone through the curtains. Pillows remained scattered around the floor.

Sophie sat up, sleepy and perplexed.

Madame stood hovering, a vision of beauty with a smirk of bemusement across her face. She leaned over her expansive bosom. "I suppose conversations from the parlor are more easily heard from down there by the vent." Madame offered Sophie her hand.

Ashamed, Sophie took Madame's hand and stood, remembering the conversation on which she had eavesdropped last night.

"I—I'm sorry," Sophie stammered.

"*C'est bien, ma chérie.*" Madame glided to the window and drew the sheer muslin curtains back to let the day enter the room. "Knowing you heard the conversation last night makes what I have to ask you much easier."

"Me?"

Madame stepped to the dressing table and turned the chair to face Sophie. "Sit a moment…please."

Sophie sat in the chair, moved her tangled hair from her face, and pulled herself together as Madame circled and faced her. She took Sophie's hand and squatted in front of her. "I find myself in need of advice, my dear. It's… difficult." Madame looked away. "I'm sorry," she sighed. "I'm usually the one who gives advice."

"It's okay," said Sophie, eager to sound helpful after being caught on the floor and after her outburst in the bathroom.

"What I must ask, I can only ask one person in the world," Madame fixed her eyes on Sophie, "and that person is you."

A knot formed in Sophie's throat.

"Is he still a good man?" Madame breathed.

Sophie opened her mouth but Madame interrupted.

"I know you'll say Maurice is a good man. That's surely why you've endured your time here. What I mean is, is he a *good* man? Does he keep his promises? Is he kind? Can I trust him?"

The litany of questions, so simple and erratic, startled Sophie. This woman, a worldly woman who knew people's hearts better than most, was asking her, a girl, about a man.

"I don't understand," said Sophie. "You've known Maurice longer than I have. Don't you know?"

Madame sighed. "Maurice was my first. You understand that?"

Sophie nodded.

"So much time has passed." Madame looked away. "There have been many others, but none like him. None who've made me feel the things I feel for him, even still."

Maurice could not have been the most handsome man Madame had ever met, nor could he have been the best-spoken. However, Madame must have seen the courage, the honesty others could not.

"I'm not sure I trust myself anymore," Madame muttered. "I surely know what a man desires, but I fear I've lost my ability to know a man's true heart. Maurice speaks of loneliness, as if this were a good reason to love someone."

Sophie shifted in her chair, uncomfortable at seeing this well-postured woman so unraveled.

Madame stood. "You must understand, my dear. Loneliness rarely leads us to the right decisions. Many men—married for years—find they're lonely. Most people don't approve of the decisions lonely men make when they come here."

Sophie looked down, ashamed her judgment was so easily perceived.

"Maurice was right. I too am lonely. Now, we're both making choices based on one of the worst feelings there is, and I need to know," she turned back to Sophie, "is he still a good man—the man I fell in love with so long ago?"

Madame's eyes were clear and honest, as vulnerable and desperate as her words, as vulnerable as the words Maurice had spoken in the parlor.

"He *is* a good man," Sophie answered, taking Madame's hand. "He's brave for being here when he didn't want to come, for telling you his feelings after carrying them inside for so long."

Madame closed her eyes as if absorbing Sophie's words into her flesh like the heat of a hearth fire.

Sophie leaned forward. "I saw him cry when his cousin died, but he was strong when he was the only one to cremate her."

Madame bit her lip, stayed silent.

"He's been good to me when I've been rude to him," Sophie added, "and he stayed with me when I gave him plenty of reasons to leave. He may be stubborn, Madame, but he came to you, knowing his heart may break forever, and not because he's lonely, but because of what he feels for you. Because he *is* a good man, a brave man with dreams—a man who loves you more than anything."

Madame Lefavre released Sophie's hand and turned away, as if in a trance. She walked to the window and fingered the curtain, moving her gaze to Paris.

"Then my heart can still be trusted," she said, seemingly more to herself than to Sophie. After a moment, Madame turned back. "Now, I'm afraid it may be too late."

"Too late? Why?"

"Maurice left this morning. He took Etienne's horse to find your wagon in the woods and return to Avoine."

"No!"

"He left money for Etienne's mare and left you a sack of francs with instructions to buy a train ticket to your grandmother's." Madame withdrew a slip of paper from her dress pocket. "It's all explained in his note. He's through with us both."

"No," Sophie repeated, standing from the chair. Once again, her curse had robbed her of someone she'd cared for.

"He's stubborn, just as you said," replied Madame.

"I can't believe he left so quickly, that he took Etienne's horse. He didn't even say good-bye." A hard knot formed in Sophie's throat.

Madame spun to Sophie, her eyes flashing with a new resolve. "Yes. Yes, he did leave quickly." Madame smiled. "My dear, you've given me an idea."

"What do you mean?"

She lifted her head. "There are two things I know, and perhaps, today, these are the most important two things of all: a stubborn man is no match for a stubborn woman, and a horse is no match for a car."

Sophie returned the smile. "How can I help?"

"Get dressed. Gather your things. There's work to be done."

Madame hastened out the bedroom door and into the hall. "Wake up, ladies! Wake up!" She clapped her hands. "Down in the parlor in five minutes! *Dépêchons! Rapidement!*"

Another bedroom door flew open and a man appeared. He clutched his trousers by the waist, one leg submerged in his pants, the other leg bare save a long black sock.

"What is she saying?"

A thin blonde in a black bustier came into view behind him, one of her bare breasts showing. "Madame is saying our evening has come to an end, *mon cher.*"

Sophie watched with some shock, and then amusement until her eyes locked with the man's, a sudden panic rushing through her as though she were a voyeur caught in the act. Before she could retreat to her room, the man harrumphed and slammed his door closed.

Sophie rushed back to her bureau to collect her new yellow dress and clean underclothes and then dashed to the bathroom hoping to avoid seeing anything else unsavory. She washed her face, brushed her hair and got dressed, listening to the sounds of men saying their adieus and racing out of the maison.

Sophie put on her shoes and suddenly realized they did not match her new dress in either color or condition. Before this adventure, she couldn't have cared less whether her clothes were clean or whether her shoes matched her dress. Somehow, things were different now. Nevertheless, she had no choice. These shoes would have to do.

She folded and returned the nightdress to the bed she'd never slept in and hurried downstairs to the parlor. There, she found several women she didn't recognize, each in various states of undress, some in what appeared to be their underclothes. One woman, a redhead with a short bob, wore men's pajamas. Another, a tall brunette with cherry-red lips, donned a lace dressing gown, a matching corset, and high-heeled shoes. None of these women seemed surprised or embarrassed when Sophie descended the stairs, her cheeks warm with her own discomfort.

At the end of a velvet chaise sat Colette. She held a subtle grin, but still seemed to lack the enthusiasm and glow she'd had when Sophie first met her, only yesterday.

Colette now wore a green dress, modest when compared to her red dress of the previous day or to the clothing of her colleagues. However, she remained beautiful and smiled more broadly when Sophie entered the parlor.

"Dumpling!" she motioned with her hands. "Come, come. Madame has called a meeting."

Sophie sat beside Colette, but before she could tell her what had transpired, Madame strode in from the adjacent room.

"Gather, ladies, gather," Madame announced. She now wore bifocals, which she quickly removed and secreted into a pocket of her dress. She carried a stack of papers. "I have an important announcement to make and I'm afraid there's little time to spare."

The ladies, who'd been nonchalant moments before, suddenly began to chatter.

"Have we been robbed?" one asked.

"Is it the *gendarme* again?" The woman in the bob scowled.

"Is someone ill?" asked another.

"No, no," said Madame.

"Is it the Germans?"

The ladies booed and hissed, some uttering profane responses. Sophie had never heard some of the words used.

"Dears, dears." Madame Lefavre raised her open hand to the room as if gathering the room's rising angst. "Don't be grim. The news I share is all good." She turned to face the chaise. "Colette, my dear, please stand."

Colette squeezed Sophie's hand and then rose, mystified. Sophie wanted to stand at her side, still feeling guilty for the chiding Colette had received last night. Nevertheless, she stayed seated, uncertain what Madame had to say.

"Colette, darling, I've treated you unfairly. You've been a loyal friend and an excellent example to these splendid women. Quite simply, you've deserved better than I've offered you. I hope this will show you my true feelings."

Madame lifted her stack of papers in the air.

"What is that?" asked Colette.

"The deed to this home and my agreement with Monsieur Lefavre," said Madame with intentional flair.

The ladies gasped and the chatter began anew.

Colette placed her hand on her breast as if she were keeping her heart from leaping out. "The maison?"

"Along with the business accounts of the Lefavre trust, established to keep this house open as long as the matron sees fit. Now, my dear, that matron is you." Madame handed the papers to her protégé.

Colette's jaw fell, as did her tears. "I don't understand."

Madame Lefavre put her palm under Colette's elbow. "My journey here has come to an end, my friend. Today, a new journey begins for us both." She turned to Sophie. "We have this magnificent young lady to thank for it."

As the ladies stared at her, Sophie shifted on the chaise, the velvet fabric unable to steady her.

"Who is she?" asked the lady in the pajamas.

"This is the angel, Sophie. She's shown us that dreams can prevail if we are willing to let them," Madame beamed.

Sophie chewed her lip, unsure how, or if, she should respond.

"Oh, Madame," called Colette, more comfortable with this unfolding drama than Sophie. "This is all more than I deserve, and surely more than I can manage."

"Nonsense," Madame retorted. "You have power. You all have power. Use it."

"What of Monsieur Lefavre?" Colette asked. "Will he approve?"

"I approve, and that's all that's required."

Colette nodded, seeming only half-convinced of her good fortune.

Madame Lefavre then faced the women of the maison. "Remember, dears, no woman remains here whose heart is not filled with a dream." She moved her hand to Colette's cheek and smiled. "Your Madame will see to that."

After a moment, Madame Lefavre cleared her throat. "Mademoiselle Colette, before I take my leave I have but two favors to ask you."

Colette seemed to lose her breath. "You leave today?"

The ladies again grew unruly, ranting in their disbelief.

"I leave now, this very instant. As I said, there's little time to spare."

"Then, please Madame, what favors can I grant?"

"First, I need Etienne to drive me back to where you found Sophie and Maurice, back to the woods where they left their wagon."

Colette spun to the crowd of women. "Lillian, go wake Etienne and tell him to collect Madame's car." She clucked with her tongue. "*Allez!*"

An auburn-haired woman in a fur-fringed, sheer housedress dashed out through the kitchen. Sophie couldn't imagine wearing such a thing, let alone wearing it to fetch a man.

Colette turned back. "The other favor, Madame?"

"A special one, indeed. I need you to accompany our dear Sophie and her belongings to the station. Her train leaves in forty minutes."

Sophie leapt to her feet, ready to protest. She wanted to join Madame on her trip to the woods, to see Maurice's face when Madame confessed her love, though she realized almost instantly that such a moment did not belong to her. She had only met Madame yesterday, had only come to feel warmly for Maurice the day before.

Madame turned to Sophie. "Is something wrong, dear?"

The ladies of the Lefavre lupanar all seemed perplexed, if not by the turn of events, then by Sophie's curious connection to Madame Lefavre. Surely, they had a greater claim to Madame's attention than Sophie.

"No, Madame. I'm just...happy for you."

87

Sophie reached for her mother's key, instinctively drawn to the maternal comfort it offered. Her father had given her simple instructions to go to Ville de Lemaire, to her grandmother, to await his return. Why was it so hard for her to do as she was told?

Madame placed a reassuring hand on Sophie's shoulder and raised her head to the room. "Ladies, I must take my leave, but I must also say my good-byes to Sophie privately."

"Oh, Madame!" a woman cried.

"No tears. No tears. I promise to write each of you a proper au revoir very soon." She scanned the room and smiled. "Now, please excuse us."

Among the protests, Madame extracted herself from her flock, grabbed her coat and Sophie's from the rack, and led Sophie through the throng of dutiful women, out into the cool Paris morning.

The ladies called their farewells to Madame, to which she replied only, "Au revoir, my dears. Au revoir."

The sunlight momentary blinded Sophie, but once she focused through the haze, the street appeared different than it had when she'd arrived last night. Even the maison now seemed simple, unassuming, like every other house on the block. She wondered if the neighbors had any idea what drama took place here.

"I must share something with you before I leave you in Colette's care," Madame whispered, slipping on her coat. "Another secret about Monsieur Lefavre."

Sophie perked. "Yes?" She donned her coat as well.

Madame leaned in conspiratorially. "I received a telegram six months ago with sad news. The monsieur died in Brussels."

"Oh, no!"

"I haven't told a soul—remember, it's helpful for people to believe there is a monsieur. You must keep the secret."

"Of course," said Sophie. "It's just sad to hear."

"Very sad, indeed," Madame lowered her head, "but there's more. With no living heirs, he apparently had one documented family member and business partner to speak of…me."

"What does that mean?" Thoughts raced through Sophie's mind like the traffic of Paris.

"Providence, my dear. I'm free to marry who I like, and I now have a considerable nest egg to keep me comfortable."

"That's wonderful…" Sophie tried to reason it out in her mind. "Isn't it?"

Madame lifted her eyes to the sky. "That depends on fate, I suppose, and a grumbling man I never stopped loving." She shook her head back to the moment. "Ah, forgive me. There's something more."

From the pocket of her coat, Madame removed a small, beaded purse. She pressed it into Sophie's palm. "It's a small amount to be sure, but something for your journey."

Sophie stood agape. "Madame, I can't—"

"You can and you will."

"Madame…"

"I sent a telegram to Ville de Lemaire as Maurice instructed. Your grandmother is expecting your train this afternoon."

"Madame, I don't know how to thank you."

The former matron of the maison touched Sophie's face and, surprisingly, Sophie no longer felt the fear or anxiety Madame had inspired the night before. She only felt warmth.

"You don't need to thank me, dear girl. You already have."

Sophie smiled just as a black car came around. It squealed to a stop and Etienne leapt out, his hair disheveled from being roused only minutes before. "Madame, your car is ready."

"*Merci*, Etienne. Merci. I've had no time to pack and will send for my things later. This morning, we travel light."

"Very good." Etienne seemed relieved he didn't have to lift any trunks or play the part of a carriage driver, at least not today.

He turned to Sophie. "I hear this is good-bye, mademoiselle. I hope our paths cross again someday, but not amongst thieves."

"I hope that, too."

Etienne bowed ceremonially. "*Très bien.*"

Interrupting her brother's gallantry, Colette strode out of the maison. She now wore a broad hat and scarf that matched her green dress. "Madame, is it time?"

"I'm afraid so, my dear."

"Oh, I shall miss you desperately." Colette reached forward to Madame, arms open. The two shared kisses and one final embrace, costars in life's theater.

When the long embrace ended, Madame sighed. "Colette, my dear, there's one more thing."

Colette cocked her head. "Just one? I thought all things came in twos."

"Times have changed," Madame replied, flashing Sophie a quick look. "One is sometimes all it takes."

Sophie grinned, though she remained uncomfortable with all this attention.

"Very well," said Colette. "Name your one thing."

"Live a good life," Madame commanded. "Live the life of your dreams, the life you deserve."

Colette's eyes welled and, for once, she fell speechless.

Etienne took his cue and opened the car door for Madame Lefavre to take her seat.

"Bon voyage," called Sophie. "Be safe."

Madame removed a handkerchief from her sleeve and wiped a tear from her eye. "And you, dear girl. And you."

Then, with a roar of the engine, and two toots of the horn, Madame Lefavre waved good-bye and flew into fate's waiting arms.

Chapter 10

Adieu

Colette sniffed back her tears, straightened the bodice of her dress, and lifted her chin as if collecting her composure.

"Well, dumpling," she breathed. "My first act as Madame is to bring you to your train. Are you ready?"

Inspired by the women who'd shown her such kindness, Sophie replied, "There are two things I know, Madame, and I learned them both from you."

"Two things?"

"Women are always ready for anything, and anything is precisely what might happen."

"Smart girl."

As Sophie grinned with pride, a black taxi sped forward and stopped in a swirl of exhaust, parking where Madame Lefavre's car had been moments before. The driver, a tall man with a sharp jaw and cap, stepped free of the car and approached.

"Mademoiselle Colette," he said with a pinch of his brim. "You called for a taxi?"

"Indeed, Rémy." Colette stepped forward and gripped his arm. "You're sweet to be so prompt."

Rémy blushed at the flirtatious tone Colette had adopted.

"This is my charge, Sophie," Colette said, placing her arm around Sophie's shoulders. "I'll be accompanying her to the station, *tout de suite*. Be a dear and collect her things, won't you? There's a wooden chest and bag of clean clothes in the parlor."

"Of course, mademoiselle."

Rémy dashed off with the urgency of a man willing to do anything for a beautiful woman.

Colette led Sophie to the taxi, where they took their seats. "There's nothing more exciting than waving to a train from the platform," Colette proclaimed.

As Colette pulled the taxi door closed, Sophie grew more anxious. "Do you think I'll ever return to Paris?"

"Everyone returns to Paris, dumpling." Colette fixed a look upon her. "What about La Sorbonne? Surely you haven't given up your dream of *l'Université?*"

Sophie looked out the window. With all that had occurred, she'd never seen La Sorbonne, and now she was rushing to leave the city. It seemed her dreams would never come true.

Rémy quickly returned and loaded the trunk with Sophie's belongings. He jumped into the taxi, proclaimed, "Gare de Lyon!" and then threw the car into gear. They sped away from the curb, leaving the white maison in a cloud of smoke.

"Rémy?" asked Colette, her eyes still fixed on Sophie.

"Yes, mademoiselle?"

"Sophie's train leaves in less than thirty minutes. Do we have time to drive by La Sorbonne?"

Sophie spun back from the window, excitement stealing her breath.

"Mademoiselle," Rémy said with concern, "La Sorbonne is on the other side of the river."

"Would an extra couple francs help?" Colette reached to her purse.

He sighed. "Petrol fuel is rationed, mademoiselle."

It seemed to Sophie that Rémy was less uncertain than he was unwilling. She looked to her own small purse, her gift from Madame Lefavre, and opened the latch. Several franc notes were folded over, accompanied by a handful of coins.

She smiled. "An extra *ten* francs, then," blurted Sophie. "Please hurry."

Colette's mouth fell open.

"Ten francs?" laughed Rémy.

Before Sophie could respond, Rémy wrenched the wheel and whirled the taxi down a side street, causing Colette and Sophie to slide, hip to hip, along the smooth taxi seat.

"It would be our preference to make it there alive," called Colette, grasping the seat to remain steady.

"As you wish!" Rémy maneuvered them onto a thoroughfare.

Colette leaned to Sophie and whispered, "Dumpling, when you negotiate, you never start with your final offer."

"Ten francs wasn't my final offer."

Colette tossed her head back in laughter. "Oh, Rémy," she announced, "I shall miss this girl dearly."

Rémy looked to his rearview mirror, angled toward his passengers. "Ten francs? I'll miss her too!"

Sophie turned back to the window, watching the fleeting streets roll by. The buildings, dark and hulking last night, seemed more inviting and ornate in the daylight. It appeared careful consideration had been given to their design; many were flanked with wrought iron, some featured etched stone and carvings with no apparent function except to offer beauty. This, she thought, was the generosity of Paris—art was everywhere.

The streets were even busier this morning than they'd been when she'd arrived, but the people walking along the boulevards seemed no more aware of the wild energy around them than Sophie would have been of the bees that flitted through the air in Avoine. They were simply used to it.

"There," Rémy announced. "On the right."

Sophie moved her attention from the curious pedestrians to the shadow that fell upon them.

Rémy stopped the car. "I can't park long," he warned.

Sophie hardly heard him. There before her, just as it had appeared in the watermark of her acceptance letter, stood the silhouette of La Sorbonne.

The dome and steeple of the university pointed toward the sky, seeming to invoke God's attention. Statues of scholars stood in alcoves, built into the face of La Sorbonne's central building. Classic columns flanked a wooden door, an invitation to step into its alluring history. Students strode across the wide lawn carrying armfuls of books, and a few stood in front of easels, painting. Courtyard trees, made barren by the fall, reached their branches to the sky like arms heralding the wisdom that was created there. Sophie absorbed all she saw, feeling the call of destiny, the nearness of her dream.

"It's quite something," said Colette, narrating Sophie's thoughts. "Perhaps you should stay."

"Stay?" Sophie's heart seemed to halt. "My grandmother's waiting for me."

"Surely she would understand why a smart girl would want to stay at a place like this."

Stay? Sophie's mind grappled with the possibility. She now had some money, thanks to Madame Lefavre. Even if it wasn't much, she could offer it as partial payment for her fees to supplement her small scholarship, and then work to assure the rest, just as her letter from the dean had suggested. Perhaps she could stay with Colette, maybe work around the maison. Of course, her work would be to cook or clean, and nothing else. She would be clear on that...

It could work, she thought. Her dream could come true.

"What do you think, dumpling? Should we stop here?"

Rémy stared in the mirror, awaiting Sophie's answer.

She thought of her father, recalled their final moments in the barn, days ago. She didn't need to wonder what he'd think. He'd asked her to join her grandmother. That was the plan, even if it wasn't her own.

She reached to her chest, keenly aware of her mother's key against her beating heart, reminded of the questions that needed answering, questions that couldn't be answered at La Sorbonne.

She suddenly knew that, for her dreams to truly come true, it had to be her father who brought her to La Sorbonne, who kissed her on the head and gave her his blessing. It was his blessing, and not this place, that was her fondest dream.

"To the station, Rémy," Sophie managed with a crack in her voice. She faced Colette. "Everyone returns to Paris, right?"

"Oh, yes, dumpling." Colette clutched Sophie's hand. "Everyone."

As the taxi pulled away from La Sorbonne and onto Boulevard Saint Michel, Sophie's tears fell. Now, more than ever, she wished to be assured of her father's safety. She wanted to know with certainty that both he and her dream would live, and that curses like hers could die.

The taxi barreled toward Gare de Lyon station, weaving through a rabble of other black automobiles. Car horns and police whistles sounded off in a cacophony around them, the perfect accompaniment to the chaos of the moment. Sophie squeezed Colette's hand, at once thrilled and terrified. This is how Sophie would remember Paris: wild and unpredictable, as beautiful as it was dangerous. All things in twos.

Rémy's eyes darted to the rearview mirror. "Which platform, mademoiselle?"

"Platform three," Colette replied, "but Sophie's ticket is waiting at the ticket window. Would you mind, Rémy?"

"What about mademoiselle's luggage?"

"I can manage," offered Sophie.

Colette smiled. "Such a modern girl, this one. It's all right, Rémy, we'll handle her things."

Once at the curb, Rémy set the brake, flipped open the trunk of the car, and abandoned his passengers with his taxi, sprinting through the station around the crowds toward the ticket booth.

As Colette opened the taxi door, Sophie saw Gare de Lyon. The station was enormous, hundreds of meters wide with a dozen long tracks and boxy metal trains flanked by platforms. Throngs of people swarmed like bugs, buzzing and humming in hordes, some standing, some running to catch trains, but only a few sitting on benches. Some appeared to be commuters in business suits, others like foreigners on a sojourn, burdened with children, luggage, animals, or groceries. Beggars held cans for change, but were largely ignored. A large clock hung overhead in the center of the station, like time itself started and stopped here at this depot. Steam and smoke swirled around.

Sophie spied a large man in a wooly overcoat calling to a thin lady in a feathered hat, carrying a poodle. Another woman pushed a baby in a pram, cooing at him as she walked. Four young soldiers laughed at something, prodding each other in fun. It was as if every corner of France had sent a representative. There were more people in one place than she'd ever seen.

Stepping from the taxi, she inhaled the station's smells of tobacco and peppermint, coal smoke and wet wool, scents which drew a colorful portrait in her mind.

"We must hurry, dumpling."

Sophie thrust herself back to the moment and joined Colette at the open trunk. Before they could decide how to manage Sophie's belongings, a lanky, uniformed platform agent strode over, rolling a luggage trolley behind him.

"Bonjour, mesdemoiselles. May I help you?"

Colette donned the same alluring grin she adopted each time a man arrived. "What a gentleman!" Colette announced. "Forgive us, monsieur. We're very late."

"Which train, mademoiselle?" the man smiled.

"The ten-thirty train to Ville de Lemaire."

He squinted at a brass watch attached by a chain to his hip pocket. "Ten twenty-five. They've just called final boarding."

"Final boarding?" Sophie's stomach fell.

Madame Lefavre had already sent word to her grandmother of her new plans, told her Sophie would be arriving by train today. Sophie imagined her grandmother, cane in hand, hobbling across Ville de Lemaire to fetch her at the station, only to find her missing.

"Have I missed the train?"

The man shook his head. "Not yet, but you must hurry."

Colette stepped closer to the man. "Monsieur, our driver has just gone for my friend's ticket."

"No ticket?" He shook his head and Sophie's fear grew. "With no ticket—"

"Please, monsieur." Colette stepped even closer and squeezed the agent's forearm. "Can't you help us?"

The man stared into Colette's sparkling eyes, reached to his breast pocket, removed a whistle, turned his head, and blew.

At the loud *thweeeeeeeet* Sophie covered her ears.

"That should hold the train, but only for a moment."

Suddenly, Rémy burst from the crowd, red-faced and out of breath, waiving Sophie's ticket like a prize.

"Rémy!" Colette laughed. "You're a darling."

Between frantic breaths, Rémy replied, "The least…I could do…for ten francs!"

Reminded of the fee, Sophie placed the franc notes in Rémy's trembling hand and took her ticket. "My hero!"

The platform agent loaded his trolley with Sophie's things and said, "Follow me, *s'il vous plaît. Rapidement!*"

Colette turned to Rémy. "Will you wait?"

Sweating and breathless, Rémy hunched over and waived them on in agreement. Sophie worried he'd retch.

"Thank you, Rémy." Colette kissed his cheek and rushed to link arms with Sophie, hurrying after the platform agent who pushed the trolley five strides ahead.

They dodged scurrying people, weaved against the flow of the crowd. Racing toward platform number three, Sophie glimpsed the blur of women embracing soldiers, Parisian businessmen striding to their trains, and children waving to departing fathers. She couldn't help but wonder how her own father was faring.

"Dumpling!" said Colette, withdrawing her arm from Sophie's. "I almost forgot!"

Maintaining their hurried pace after the agent, Colette managed to reach into her purse and produce an envelope with Sophie's name scrawled across the front. "From Monsieur Maurice," she huffed. "He left it with your things."

Sophie took it with a pang of anxiety and longing, reminded that her friend, the gravedigger, had left in despair, unaware that Madame Lefavre would follow.

"Thank you, Mademoiselle Colette. Thank you for saving me."

"Oh, dumpling…"

"Platform three," the agent announced, stopping the trolley.

Strung before them like charms on a chain were the passenger cars of the train to Ville de Lemaire. "Your belongings will be in the baggage car." The conductor handed Sophie a claim ticket. "*Bonne journée.*"

Sophie's pounding heart filled with an odd blend of dread and excitement as her belongings vanished into the baggage car.

Hooooooooooot! The call of the engine's steam whistle filled the station urging her to board.

Sophie embraced Colette, held her tight.

"Mademoiselle!" called the platform agent, clearly irritated with Sophie. "Your train is departing!"

A cough of dark smoke bellowed from the engine.

Sophie withdrew from Colette's embrace and ran to the train, turning her tear-wet face toward Colette one last time.

"Au revoir!" Sophie called.

"Au revoir, dumpling!" Emotion caught Colette's final words. With her head held high, she blew a kiss, basking in the moment she proclaimed would be so exciting: saying good-bye from the platform.

Sophie turned to the train, wiped away her tears and climbed the steps to the passenger compartment where a conductor smiled and reached for her ticket. He furrowed his brow.

"Mademoiselle?" He cocked his head at her ticket.

"Yes?" Sophie hadn't looked at her ticket and feared that Rémy had made some mistake.

"This is the wrong car. You're in first class."

"First class?" Madame Lefavre's generosity seemed to know no limit.

The conductor raised Sophie's ticket above his head and grinned. "No fear, mademoiselle," he said, "Follow me."

She trailed the conductor through a passenger car, crowded with commuters and budget travelers. Small seats were arranged with some facing forward and others facing one another on opposite sides of small metal tables. People were crammed in, elbow to elbow, but appeared unfazed by the close quarters—quarters that reminded Sophie of the pens in which she'd kept the goats.

Toward the front of the car, she passed a jumble of children, jumping like stray cats from seat to seat, climbing over their beleaguered mother. Their restlessness made her recall her first and only other train ride she'd taken when she was eight. Her father had purchased tickets for them to travel through the Loire Valley to view the castles. He'd saved for months, just to give her the experience of a train ride, the thrill of one day's indulgence. Unlike these children, Sophie had remained on her best behavior in spite of her excitement. Her father had expected it. Then, just as now, she was determined to make him proud, to prove herself worthy of his sacrifice.

In the next passenger car, in a seat to the right of the aisle, Sophie noticed a mustached man, squinting through his wire-framed glasses at his newspaper, *Le Petit Parisien.* The man was ignoring the prattle of the slender woman in the round hat who sat across from him. As Sophie passed, she spied the headline: "Germans Tighten Grip on Warsaw."

She tensed at the reminder of the danger her father might be facing. How wrong it felt that he might be traveling into battle even as she was traveling first class to safety. She hoped her grandmother had already received word from him so she could be assured of his welfare.

The floorboards rumbled and the train began to move. She steadied herself, bit her lip, and tried to adopt Madame Lefavre's position that life's fondest moments may still lie ahead.

The conductor led her into yet another passenger car where she was immediately affronted by the sour stench of liquor. Young soldiers, some of whom she'd seen laughing on the platform, were now piled into a space hardly large enough to fit the eighteen or twenty of them. They were raucous and unruly, far worse than the children in the last car.

As she shuffled through on the heels of the conductor, the volume of the soldiers' laughter and the crassness of their language grew until one turned and saw her pass. *Fweee-weeet*, he whistled through his gapped teeth.

The car fell quiet as the sweaty, drunken soldiers paused to watch her walk by.

Sophie stopped, frozen. The yellow dress, which made her feel so beautiful this morning, now made her feel like a beacon for all the wrong attention. A young and particularly drunk soldier climbed over two rows of seats to reach her.

"Bonjour," he slurred, and then grabbed her by the arm. "You like a man in uniform?" He angled his head as if trying to get her into focus.

Three paces ahead, the conductor turned back to the soldier. "Monsieur, please let the mademoiselle pass."

The scene reminded Sophie of the Taverne Bleue, when Colette had enthralled the room of villagers, dancing, smiling, and teasing them. Colette knew how to control a crowd such as this. Even Madame Lefavre had shown she could bring a group of unruly people to attention. Both women had charisma, control, and Sophie thought they could easily manage this situation.

"What do you say, mademoiselle?" urged the drunken soldier, gripping her more forcefully. "What do you say to a soldier who would ask for a kiss before facing death?"

Sophie squared her shoulders and lifted the soldier's hand from her arm. "I'd have two things to say, monsieur—"

The other soldiers leaned forward to hear.

"I'd say a man never knows when it's his time to die, and a kiss from me could be the very thing that kills him."

The men burst into laughter. One swatted the soldier who'd approached Sophie, and then tousled his hair. The soldier turned and shoved his assailant playfully, falling back over seats into a drunken pile, beginning the raucousness anew.

The conductor smirked and touched Sophie's shoulder. "Shall we?" He motioned to the door.

She hurried after him knowing this was no place for a respectable girl in a clean dress to linger. Once free of the crowd, she breathed her relief, eager to find her seat and collect her nerves.

"Here you are, mademoiselle." The conductor opened the final door and motioned to a private compartment on his left. "First class."

Sophie gasped. Unlike the crowded quarters of the other cars, first class was spacious and elegant. Daylight beamed in from the fleeting station, reflecting off the polished wood panels. Four small windows formed a portrait of the cityscape outside, and an aluminum vase, bolted to the wall, carried a single white rose, its bloom as large as a cabbage. Two upholstered benches faced one another, silently implying that this space was meant for more than one person.

"Bonne journée, mademoiselle."

Sophie turned to the conductor who smiled, but didn't leave. She quickly realized why he remained, reached to her purse for a franc, and handed it to him.

"Thank you for your help."

The conductor grinned. "*Pardon*, mademoiselle, but I don't think you needed my help." The man winked and then exited the compartment, allowing the door to slide closed.

Sophie took her seat and stared at the empty bench across from her. Despite her relief at catching the train, her victory over the drunken soldiers, and the luxury of first class, she now felt a profound emptiness.

The train shook and creaked as it gained momentum, the hum of the Gare de Lyon station still buzzing in her head. Yet, the hum no longer held the thrill of Paris. Rather, it felt like a warning, and with each rhythmic clack of the train, her anxiety grew.

The rail yards and cityscape fled the portrait windows, replaced by warehouses at the edge of the city, then by tenements and coal-charred factories. Eager for something familiar, Sophie recalled her envelope from Maurice. She removed it from her pocket and ripped open the flap. She unfolded the note, releasing the scents of lilacs and nutmeg into the compartment. Evidently Maurice had used Madame's scented paper from the maison. Sophie read his scribbled words.

Sophie,

You're a stubborn girl. The wagon and horse belonged to me and I take the blame for losing them. You owe me nothing. Enough about that.

You're as strong as any boy, true, but still a girl, so I've asked Fifi to get you to Ville de Lemaire safely. I hope you understand why I had to leave. Old fools need things spelled out, and now I have it, plain and simple: Fifi no longer loves me, or maybe never did.

Et bien. I'll return to Narina's house for a fresh start. Come for a visit when you can.

I have no regrets and no more unanswered questions, thanks to you. Stay well, child.

Maurice

This journey had been hard on him, riddled with death, loss, and disappointment. These were feelings Sophie knew well. She also knew how wrong he was and grinned at the thought of the surprise on his ragged face when Madame Lefavre embraced him and finally confessed her love. How happy he'd be to be wrong!

Nevertheless, these thoughts offered Sophie only a moment's respite. The absence of her friend and her wish to be with him amplified her growing unease. Again, she turned away from the empty bench to the window. Farm roads went by, seeming to lead to nowhere, and once the farmland passed, she saw only open fields of grass blowing in a silent breeze. No more haphazard automobiles. No more artful architecture. No music. No beauty. Soon, even the clack of the locomotive went quiet in her head, leaving nothing but silent apprehension.

Then it struck her. Like her mother, her father, and now Maurice—Paris had left her.

Chapter 11

Ville de Lemaire

A cold fog crawled through the forest and over the tufted battlefield, illuminated by the relic moon. Sophie stepped slowly, squinting into the bright mist, mud sucking at her shoes, begging her not to move. The scene resembled the monochrome photos of the Ardennes from her old school geography book, but no photo could convey the cold, stench, or fear that now gripped her like the mud.

As she crept forward, she was careful not to step on the bodies of the soldiers that littered the ground, souls released to the swirling mist. Her heart beat like a battle drum, terror rushing through her veins. She clutched her mother's key on the cold chain around her neck and wished for courage.

Her father, striding three paces ahead, suddenly turned to her. His helmet and uniform were splattered with mud, his face unshaven. He looked tired, but held a fire in his eyes she'd never seen. He pressed his forefinger to his lips and nodded.

Sophie nodded back, but didn't understand. Why were they here?

He moved like the fog and Sophie followed through the thickening haze as she did when wading the murky Seine back home. It was only at her father's side that she'd feel safe.

He halted, froze his stance, and raised his rifle.

A quiet panic ran down her spine, gooseflesh on her neck rising. Oddly, the key in her hand became illuminated.

Then, a click.

Her father fingered the trigger, aimed into the vapor, and let out an explosive shot.

Sophie screamed.

Thweeeeeeeeee!

The whistle of the locomotive woke her, announcing the train's approach to the Ville de Lemaire station.

Sophie sat up from where she'd fallen asleep on the cushioned bench and blinked away the afternoon haze spilling into the train's first class compartment. Her erratic pulse fought her efforts to calm herself, the fog of her dream still commanding her thoughts. As the train slowed, she took a deep breath, half-expecting to taste the cold air of the muddy Ardennes. Just as in her dream, she held the key in her hand, warm and moist from sweat, still hanging from its chain. However, this key did not glow.

She licked her dry lips, released her key to her breast and turned to the window to get her bearings. On the hillside, opposite the provincial station, she spotted a vineyard, its rows of vines now empty of their fruit, no doubt taken during last month's harvest. The barren branches looked like skeletal children, arms outstretched, clutching one another by the wrists in an act of solidarity, facing the tracks, facing Sophie.

"Mademoiselle?"

Sophie turned, startled by the entrance of a conductor—a different man from the one who'd led her to her to first class.

"We've arrived. Ville de Lemaire station."

She nodded her understanding and rose from the bench. Her grandmother would be waiting. "My luggage," said Sophie, finding her composure. "The baggage car?"

"Of course. Follow me."

More eager than ever to see her grandmother, Sophie stepped off the train to join the throng of other passengers moving to collect their bags. Once at the baggage car, she handed the conductor the slip she'd been given in Paris.

"A wooden chest with an iron lock and a bag of clothes," she urged.

"Oui, mademoiselle." With Sophie's claim ticket in hand, the conductor disappeared, leaving Sophie to wait.

The small, provincial station of Ville de Lemaire was missing the businessmen and well-dressed women of Gare de Lyon. Instead, this depot seemed to serve shopkeepers and farm families. There was, however, one thing Ville de Lemaire now shared with the station in Paris: soldiers.

Even here, young soldiers clutched their wives, clung to their children and kissed the cheeks of their families with noticeable desperation. It raised the same feelings as those she felt with her father in their barn in Avoine: fear that saying good-bye might mean saying good-bye for good.

She had only been to Ville de Lemaire once as a child, and her memories of the place were incomplete, drawn from the feelings of a child rather than from the perceptions of a young adult. Nevertheless, the village was warm and familiar. It brought thoughts of vanilla and lace, matzo ball soup, and *tarte aux pommes*. Ville de Lemaire was not so much a village as it was a person. It was her grandmother.

Sophie scanned the station for silver heads in the crowd, for the short bob her grandmother wore, or the wool hat she donned when the chill set in. Though only in her sixties, her grandmother used a cane, the result of rheumatism in her hip. "God's reminder," her grandmother once said, "not to take myself too seriously."

For several moments, Sophie saw no sign of her until, from behind a crowd of soldiers, her grandmother appeared. Her hair was still in a bob, but whiter than when Sophie had last seen her at Passover in Avoine five years ago. She wore her favorite burgundy coat and seemed to favor her cane more than Sophie remembered. The old woman hobbled forward and scanned the passengers. Her careworn features lighted when she spotted Sophie, a smile pressing away the creases.

"Sophie!" Her grandmother waved.

Sophie rushed forward and threw her arms around her grandmother with more enthusiasm than she had intended, nearly knocking the poor woman over. "Grand-mère!"

"Oh, my dear child!" Her grandmother leaned on her cane for balance against Sophie's vigorous, loving, assault. She smelled of vanilla. "It's all right."

"Grand-mère," Sophie managed again, and then burst into tears. It felt like she'd completed some sort of race for which her grandmother was the reward.

"There, there, angel." Drawing her close, her grandmother patted her back. "We're together now."

Sophie released her grandmother and stepped back to view her, desperate to replace her anxiety with the sight of the woman who'd always loved her.

Somehow today her grandmother seemed smaller. Of course Sophie was just twelve when she'd last seen her, and smaller herself.

Her grandmother returned the look, glancing Sophie over and smiling. "Yellow," she said, noting Sophie's dress. "Your mother's favorite color."

"It was?" Sophie dared not tell her grandmother the dress was a gift from the madame of a Parisian maison.

"You're so tall and thin, like her. I saw you standing by the train and, child, I thought for a moment..." She bit her lip. "Well, I'm so happy you're here."

Sophie gripped her grandmother by the hand. "Have you heard from Papa?"

"Yes," her grandmother released her hand, "but, *chère*, the news is not good."

Sophie's heart fell. "Is he hurt?"

"No, no, dear..."

Just then, the conductor returned with a service dolly, stacked with Sophie's memory chest and bag. "You have a car, mademoiselle?"

"I have a taxi waiting," replied her grandmother, taking charge. "Just at the curb."

"Very good, madame."

As they followed the conductor, her grandmother again took Sophie by the hand. "Let's go home, child." She kissed Sophie's fingers and looked her in the eye. "I think you'd better read your father's telegram for yourself."

Sophie stood by the sofa in her grandmother's tiny apartment, fingering the key around her neck, waiting as her grandmother dug in her black leather purse for some coins to offer the taxi driver.

In spite her frown, her grandmother thanked the man for carrying up Sophie's belongings and closed the door behind him. "I remember when a man would help a woman for free," she muttered, moving with her cane toward the kitchen.

"May I see Papa's telegram, Grand-mère?"

Her grandmother halted and raised her chin. "What about my tarte aux pommes? I thought you'd be hungry after your trip."

Sophie became aware of the warm smells of her grandmother's baking that somehow she'd neglected to notice. The aroma of baked apples and allspice hung in the air, but her favorite treat was not enough to distract her from news of her father.

"Later, Grand-mère."

"All right," her grandmother conceded. "All right."

She shuffled across her small living room to pick up the telegram, which leaned against the table lamp on her small writing desk. "It's not much." She handed it to Sophie and motioned to the loveseat. "Sit, my dear."

Sophie scrambled to read, lowering herself onto the sofa.

Dearest ones STOP Arrived Paris but off to another base tomorrow STOP Because I am expert with rifle I was chosen for special assignment STOP Postal service suspended last letter for a while STOP

Sophie's throat tightened. She figured the only thing worse than her father's absence would be his silence.

Pray we stop Germans soon STOP Love you both STOP Gérard

Signing "Gérard" rather than "Papa" conveyed to Sophie his note was meant more for her grandmother than for her. This realization only compounded her anxiety. He still saw her as a child.

"See?" her grandmother sighed from behind her. "It's not much." She seemed to speak more to herself than to Sophie. "He couldn't even say when he'd write again."

Sophie stared at the telegram. Her father was first to battle simply because he could fire a rifle; a punishment rendered because he'd confessed his skill with a gun. It'd been years since he'd shot at anything besides a pheasant or a quail. Why didn't they ask, instead, if any of the men had children? Shouldn't that have mattered more?

"Well, then," her grandmother clutched her cane and stood, putting clear punctuation on the moment, "since you're not hungry, let's unpack your things."

She wondered why her grandmother was so quick to dismiss even this paltry news from her father. Surely she felt something.

Sophie lifted her memory chest and followed her grandmother to the back bedroom where her grandmother had kept an extra bed, baskets of spun wool, and knitting needles.

"Forgive the dusty old yarn," her grandmother said, sliding open the closet. "I rely on my old lady friends to do the knitting. The kitchen was always my place." She walked with her cane to the other side of the bed to smooth out the comforter.

Sophie unlatched the chest and began to lift articles of clothing into the dresser. How could her grandmother feel nothing?

"Aren't you worried about Papa?"

Her grandmother rose from her work on the bed.

"You think I'm not worried?" Her tone was terse and direct, a tone she'd never before taken with Sophie.

"You don't seem to be."

"Child!"

"Papa may die and you just want to talk about yarn and tartes! You don't even care!"

Her grandmother stepped back.

"You pretend there's no danger," Sophie charged, "but there is. He's using guns and facing Germans and can't even tell us where he's going, and you don't care."

"Hold your tongue," hissed her grandmother. "How could you think such a thing? I lost a husband to war. Have you forgotten your grandfather?"

Sophie had never met her grandfather, but had certainly not forgotten how he'd died.

"The man I loved was killed by the Germans," her grandmother railed, her lip trembling. "I'll be damned if I lose my son the same way—"

Her grandmother staggered under the stress and Sophie leapt to steady her, feeling her own anger become regret.

"I—I'm sorry, Grand-mère. Please…I'm sorry."

Tears welled in her grandmother's eyes, making her look even older than she was. "When the men go away," she sobbed, "the women cook. We keep the house; we pray…pray we've given them something to return for, given them reason to live."

Embarrassed by her disrespect and insensitivity, Sophie fought back her own tears. She maneuvered her grandmother to the end of the bed to sit.

"I know you care," Sophie whispered. "I should never have said you didn't—"

"No, no, my angel. Forgive me." Her grandmother wiped her tears and sighed. "I've broken my promise to your father. I thought I could be strong for you. I told him I wouldn't cry."

"You are strong," said Sophie. She then recalled Maurice's comforting words to Madame Lefavre when she too had faced a fear for which she was unprepared. "I mean, you can be strong and still be afraid, right? Both can be true, can't they?"

Her grandmother swallowed, looked at Sophie, and reached a hand to her face.

"Oh, my child," she said with surprise. "When did you become a woman?"

Sophie held her grandmother's hands, feeling less like a woman than a child. "Let's have some of that tarte you baked. I'm starving."

"Of course you are, dear." Her grandmother smiled, wiped her tears, and shifted to the edge of the bed, but as she stood, a knock echoed from the front door.

"I'll get it." Sophie jumped up, eager now to be a helpful granddaughter and to put this episode behind them. She dashed through the living room and opened the door to a squat woman with hair woven like spun sugar, smelling of hair wax. The woman grinned, her false teeth shifting beneath her painted lips. She squinted up through her thick glasses.

"You must be Sophie," the woman said with a commanding German accent.

"Ilsa!" Sophie's grandmother walked in from the bedroom. "Come in, dear. Come in."

The German woman waddled in past Sophie to the dining table, obviously familiar with her grandmother's apartment. She gave her grandmother a kiss on each cheek, removed her coat, handed it to Sophie, and took a seat at the head of the table, sitting with authority.

"This is Madame Bavard," explained Sophie's grandmother.

The woman turned to Sophie. "I'd love some tea."

"Oh…of course." Sophie gave a look to her grandmother, unsure how to manage the demands of their guest.

"One sugar, light cream, and please, no vanilla," Madame Bavard rolled her eyes. "Your grandmother is overly fond of vanilla. I am not."

"Madame Bavard has particular tastes," her grandmother explained. "Let me help you."

"Standards, Etta. I have standards. I'd hold my sponge cake to your tarte any day."

Sophie's grandmother sighed. It seemed these old ladies had had this conversation before.

Sophie hung Madame Bavard's coat on the rack and lit the stove to start the tea.

"I was just getting ready to serve my tarte, Ilsa," said her grandmother, "but I suppose you wouldn't care for any. It's surely not your famous sponge cake."

"Let's not squabble," said Madame Bavard, "I'm sure you worked very hard. "Why don't you just give me a small slice?"

Sophie's grandmother joined her in the kitchen and leaned in to whisper, "Her sponge cake is made with real sponges."

Sophie covered her mouth to refrain from laughing.

"I have news, Etta," Madame Bavard called from the table. "And a lot of it."

"News, dear?"

Madame Bavard patted her hairdo, pretending to seem nonchalant when it was clear she was bursting with her tale. "News from Germany and from right here in our neighborhood."

"Germany?" Sophie couldn't help her curiosity, especially after her father's letter.

"Yes, dear. Germany. Born there and lived in Dusseldorf for thirty years. Of course now, I'm very French."

The kettle sang its promise of hot water and Sophie quickly prepared Madame Bavard's tea, eager for the woman's story. She carried over the cup and saucer, followed by her grandmother with the glorious tarte. They joined their guest at the table.

Before Madame Bavard spoke another word, she took a long, slow slurp of tea.

"Come, Ilsa," said Sophie's grandmother as she set the table with plates and silverware. "The news."

"Well," Madame Bavard swallowed, savoring both the tea and the anticipation she caused. "My youngest cousin, Ingrid, and her husband, Karl, were thrown out of their home in Berlin, sent to a neighborhood only for Jews. Evicted from their apartment with no notice!" She set down her teacup and wiped her mouth with a napkin, her eyes fixed on Sophie and her grandmother. "Soldiers came. Pushed them out with the heels of their guns."

"Guns?" Sophie's grandmother placed her hand on her breast.

"There are posters all over Germany," Madame Bavard continued. "No Jews can have a business or even live in the towns. They have to wear stars on their clothes to brand themselves. Karl had to close his watch shop. How will they live if Karl can't work? For all I know, the soldiers are helping themselves to the watches."

"Why do the Germans do this to their own people?" asked Sophie.

"Because Adolph Hitler hates the Jews." Madame Bavard's pronouncement sounded like a newspaper headline or the title of a newsreel. "Hitler won't be happy until all of Europe is free of us, every last one."

Though obviously a shameless gossip, Madame Bavard seemed upset and Sophie couldn't help but feel upset as well.

"I thought Hitler was after Poland," Sophie answered, recalling what she'd heard on the radio in Avoine. "What's his quarrel with Jews?"

"A man in need of a target always finds one," Sophie's grandmother interjected, giving Madame Bavard a moment to collect herself. "Hitler is a desperate, angry man."

"I have to agree," said Madame Bavard with a sigh. "Things haven't been good for any Germans, but especially Jews. Ingrid hasn't had two Reichsmarks to rub together for years. Hitler is only looking to blame someone for Germany's troubles besides himself."

"Why the Jews?" Sophie repeated.

"We always find ourselves at the wrong end of a spear," said Madame Bavard. "Pharaohs or dictators. Read your history, dear. They always pick us."

Sophie still wasn't sure she'd had her answer, but her grandmother seemed to sense her distress and placed a hand on her shoulder.

"Let's speak of other things, Ilsa. I think we've had enough of Germany today. You said you had news of the neighborhood? Tell us."

Madame Bavard swallowed her tea, leaving a layer of pink lipstick on the cup to match the stamp she'd left on her napkin. "Of course." She adjusted her false teeth with her tongue and her eyes flashed a new control. "Have you heard about our new neighbor"—her tone became conspiratorial and she leaned forward— "the artist, Lévèque?"

At the word "artist" Sophie's interest in Germany dissolved. "An artist? Here?"

"Blind artist," Madame Bavard added, "if you believe the rumors. I do not."

"A blind artist!" Sophie couldn't imagine such a thing.

"I, for one, think it's questionable. Who's ever heard of an artist who can't see?"

"I've talked with him," retorted Sophie's grandmother, serving her guest a slice of tarte, "yesterday as I was preparing for Sophie's visit. We chatted downstairs. He's a lovely man and I assure you, he's blind. I saw one of his paintings and must say the man is an excellent artist, nevertheless."

"Well," said Madame Bavard before swallowing another gulp of tea. "That remains to be seen." She scooped a bite of the tarte into her mouth.

"It *has* been seen," snapped Sophie's grandmother.

Madame Bavard chewed her tarte, seeming impervious to her host's irritation. She then sipped more tea.

"What's he like?" asked Sophie.

"Quite polite," answered her grandmother, "and his art—"

"I'll tell you what he's like." Madame Bavard placed her cup on its saucer with a clink, snatching back the conversation. "Last Wednesday night, quite late, I was up with my arthritis. Very painful, you know." She dabbed her mouth with her napkin. "I happened to glance out my window and saw him waving his arms, barking directions to a suspicious boy, moving furniture into the flat downstairs—"

Sophie's grandmother scoffed. "That 'suspicious boy' is his assistant, the orphan, Felipe." A vein in Sophie's grandmother's temple grew more prominent.

"—in the dark of night," Madame Bavard ranted, ignoring Sophie's grandmother. "Imagine such a thing, moving furniture at that hour?" She faced Sophie, clearly sensing an eager audience. "Very curious, don't you agree?"

"Curious or not, Monsieur Lévèque is a nice man." Sophie's grandmother was terse. "He said he likes my tarte aux pommes."

"He's thin and probably very hungry. I'm sure he'd be grateful for any food."

"*Any food?*"

"Tarte aux pommes is my favorite," offered Sophie, hoping to cut the tension between the old ladies.

"I mean, how can a man make an honest living painting? Especially a blind man? What do you suppose he's really doing?"

Sophie's grandmother stood from the table and tossed her napkin onto her chair. "Ilsa, Sophie is tired from her journey. We need to give her some rest."

Sophie tried not to smile at the battle before her, lest she undermine her grandmother's tactics.

"Oh," Madame Bavard gave a longing look to her half-eaten slice of tarte and then looked up. "Of course, my dear." She rose and offered Sophie her hand. "It was my pleasure to meet you."

Sophie stood from her chair and took Madame Bavard's hand. "The pleasure was mine."

Madame Bavard looked over the tops of her glasses. "Your grandmother's right, child. You do look tired." She shuffled back to the door. "*Bonsoir*, Etta," she called. "Next time, I'll bring sponge cake."

"How delightful that will be." Sophie's grandmother handed Madame Bavard her coat. "*Bonsoir*, Ilsa."

After their guest had departed, Sophie's grandmother closed the door and leaned against it. "That woman has a big mouth," she explained, "but she's a loyal friend, even if she makes horrible sponge cake."

Sophie laughed, but it wasn't Madame Bavard who'd captured her imagination. She began to collect the dishes.

"Grand-mère?"

"Yes, my dear?"

"What more can you tell me about Monsieur Lévèque?"

Chapter 12

Monsieur Lévèque

The morning sun had brought a shift in the weather, making the storage shed stifling and stuffy. Sophie fanned herself with a cloth, recalling how the chill of Ville de Lemaire had bothered her when she'd first arrived in the fall. Now, with the advent of spring and the cooler months a fading memory, it was the heat she found bothersome.

She'd risen early and spent half an hour in this shed, wrestling her grandmother's old bicycle free from piles of blankets and splintered milk crates. She then spent two hours inflating the tires with the hand pump and cleaning the bike to make it suitable for riding. Spider webs in the spokes and basket reminded her of the dark corners of her Avoine farmhouse, and how much she missed her father, from whom no letter or telegram had come since the first one in September, warning of his silence.

"Aren't you afraid of spiders?" asked Céline, a ten-year-old neighborhood girl. She hovered over Sophie, leaning on the doorframe of the shed, twirling her blond locks with her fingers.

"No," smiled Sophie. "Spiders don't scare me."

What did scare her was the thought of her father, alone, in battle. She'd had the dream again—the one she'd had on the train months ago, with her father charging into the fog of battle. She prayed for his safety every night and continued to write him letters, but news from the radio said Germany and Russia were splitting Poland down the middle, and such thoughts only raised her anxiety and fear.

However, it wasn't Sophie's angst about the war or her need for a bicycle that had brought her to the storage room. It was her mother's mysterious box—the one reportedly under her grandmother's care, the box that matched the key she still wore around her neck.

Though her father had asked her to wait for his return to open it, the box's allure had proven more than she could ignore. She thought if she found the box in the course of other mundane tasks such as this one, she could ask her grandmother about it, maybe even open it. In light of her father's prolonged absence, Sophie reasoned he would forgive this disobedience. And if he didn't, she'd welcome his rebuke, if only to hear his voice.

She'd searched the apartment high and low and found nothing. That's when she'd learned of the shed. Now, after hours of looking, it appeared the box wasn't in the shed, either.

"You have to be afraid," Céline explained. "Girls hate spiders."

Sophie pulled a cobweb from her clothes. "Not this girl."

"You're very strange." Céline squinted, reminding Sophie of her goats in Avoine and the way they viewed her with suspicion.

"I've been told that." She fitted the bicycle chain onto the teeth of the cog and squirted it with oil from a can.

"My sister, Héloise, says you're Jewish."

"Well, she's right," said Sophie, applying more oil. "I'm Jewish." She recalled Héloise was about her age and that the butcher's daughters had also lost their mother when they were young. It was at their father's *boucherie*, on the shop's radio that Sophie had first heard Russia was carving off its own part of Poland, like one of the roasts hanging in the *boucherie* window. According to the news, the world seemed ready for war. Of course it was her father who was actually doing the fighting.

"Héloise says it's because you're Jewish that you and your grandmother can't eat cheese." Céline folded her arms.

"We *can* eat cheese," Sophie corrected, "just not with meat."

"Why not?"

"Because it isn't kosher."

The girl furrowed her brow. "What *do* Jews eat?"

Sophie sighed, unsure if her exasperation came from her failure to find her mother's box, her anger with the Germans, or her frustration with Céline's persistent interrogation. She frowned and wiggled her oily fingers at the young girl. "We eat spiders."

"Huh?" Céline stopped leaning on the door frame.

"And for dessert we eat little girls who ask too many questions," Sophie cackled. "Delicious!"

Eyes wide, Céline took a step back, turned, and ran.

Smiling her satisfaction, Sophie scrubbed her hands in a bucket of soapy water and dried them with a clean rag. She then wheeled the bike into the alleyway and closed the shed door.

From the alley, she called to the upstairs apartment. "I'm going to the market, Grand-mère!"

Her grandmother leaned out the open kitchen window. "Don't forget vanilla," she called down. "I'm making *hamantaschen.*"

Tonight their plan was to eat heartily to celebrate Purim, Sophie's favorite holiday. Back in Avoine, Purim was one of the few Jewish holidays she and her father celebrated, and one of the only times of year they actually went to temple. She'd always enjoyed the delicious *hamantaschen* cookies and the rabbi's stories of brave Esther who, according to legend, had risked her life to stop evil Haman, the king's advisor, from exterminating the Jews of ancient Persia. It was Esther's bravery and selflessness that made her a hero. With all that was happening to Jews now, Sophie couldn't help but think Purim was the perfect holiday.

"One baguette, a chicken, and a bottle of vanilla," her grandmother recited. "We've got the rest."

"Très bien, Grand-mère." Sophie confirmed her small purse was still in her pocket. She'd chosen to spend the money Madame Lefavre had given her to help her grand-mère buy groceries, and a nice Purim dinner was just the thing to ease her anxiety.

She gave her grandmother a wave, leapt onto the bike, and pedaled down the cobblestone road, maneuvering the bouncing cycle around the apartment building. However, Sophie slowed as she passed the flat of the artist, Lévèque.

Ever since the gossiping Madame Bavard had revealed the artist's presence to her, Sophie had seen neither the artist nor his art, despite her constant efforts to do so. His supply of empty easels, buckets, and blank canvases on his porch had been moved to and fro, apparently at night, as if he were intentionally avoiding public scrutiny. She began to wonder if the artist was a phantom or some antisocial hermit. Perhaps Madame Bavard was right to be skeptical of him…

As Sophie rolled toward the village, her thoughts of the reclusive artist were displaced by thoughts of Ville de Lemaire's village square. The square held the village's most popular shops. However, with a war on and all of Europe short of money, business had been slow. Some of the shops were closed and boarded. With most of the men now off to join the mounting conflict with the Germans, few people in the village were left, and those who stayed had little money for shopping. Most, like her grandmother, had to scrape from their pensions just to pay rent.

Sophie dismounted and walked her bike to the sidewalk. In the distance, up on the hill, the château Lemaire rose among its vineyards like a guardian watching over the village. It was at the Lemaire vineyards most of the remaining townspeople worked, and the Lemaire champagne, like lifeblood, had kept the village thriving for over a hundred years. It seemed an irony that few people in Ville de Lemaire could actually afford a bottle.

She leaned her bike against a wall and began shopping. First, she collected a flakey baguette from Monsieur DeGarde—the best bread she'd ever tasted. Of course, no sooner did she have the warm loaf than she craved some cheese from Madame Lalonde's shop next door.

"Like the feet of angels!" Madame Lalonde would say of her fragrant *tomme*, but, as Sophie had explained to Céline, cheese would not be part of her Purim meal.

Sophie tried to ignore her desire for cheese and, instead, dashed to Madame Geneviève's *chocolaterie*. When she entered the shop, the familiar ring of the bell on the door set her mouth to moisten even before the aroma of warm chocolate had reached her.

"Bonjour, Sophie," Madame Geneviève sang from behind the counter. "Would you like to try a chocolate buttercream? They've just cooled." The tiny woman lifted a silver tray with a dozen dark mounds the size of grapes, arranged on a lace *napperon*.

"I've come for a bottle of vanilla," said Sophie. "My grandmother's cooking tonight."

"I didn't ask what you were shopping for," replied Madame Geneviève with a smile. "I asked if you'd like a chocolate."

It was too much for Sophie to resist. "Well, perhaps one."

She accepted the buttercream chocolate with fervor, yet savored each bite. She tasted the brown sugar and the Tahitian vanilla, the only kind her grandmother would buy, found only here at Madame Geneviève's.

"Sophie, you eat with the enthusiasm of a fat woman," Madame Geneviève pronounced with glee. "Yet, somehow, you stay so thin. You must have another."

"Oh, Madame, I can't. I'll spoil my dinner."

"I suppose thin is the fashion now, anyway, at least in Paris." Sophie detected what sounded like disdain in Madame Geneviève's voice when she mentioned Paris. "In Ville de Lemaire, not so many girls are thin like you."

Sophie winced at yet another reminder of how different she was from the other young women here, and it wasn't just Céline and Madame Geneviève who thought it. Even her grandmother had remarked on how dissimilar Sophie was to the local young ladies, implying Sophie differed in more ways than just her looks.

In school, Sophie had been told she didn't fit in—too headstrong for a girl of her pedigree. When asked by her teacher what sort of man a stubborn girl might expect to marry, she'd replied, "The type that will listen to reason, if such a man exists."

She'd been scolded for her impertinence and continued to be teased by the schoolchildren for being different—a skinny, Jewish, motherless goat farmer. She'd hoped those days of ostracism were over, but even here in Ville de Lemaire, it seemed she was still the goat girl of Avoine.

Madame Geneviève must have seen some pitiable look on her face because, along with Sophie's purchase, she wrapped four chocolates free of charge.

At last, Sophie walked to the Van Hoden *boucherie*, albeit with less enthusiasm than she'd had when visiting the other shops. Despite her need for a chicken, this morning's interaction with the butcher's daughter, Céline, had made her uneager to visit the shop where she might encounter Céline's older sister, Héloise, whom Sophie found even more annoying.

During Sophie's first visit to the village, her grandmother had assured her that Ville de Lemaire welcomed newcomers with kindness, especially at times like these, with half the town serving its country. However, when they'd entered the *boucherie* that day, Héloise had greeted Sophie with a scowl and said, "Who are you?"

"I'm Sophie," she'd explained.

Rather than the warm welcome her grandmother had promised, Héloise turned up her nose and retreated to the back room.

Now, Sophie entered the butcher shop and, to her relief, saw only Monsieur Van Hoden, the butcher. He stood over the counter, balancing a flank of beef on his shoulder, readying it for carving.

"Hello, Sophie!" he called out. Monsieur Van Hoden was a barrel-chested bald man with thick arms, his cheeks blemished with broken vessels, perhaps from too much time in a freezer. He looked more like a wrestler to Sophie than a butcher. Nevertheless, he welcomed her with a warmth and kindness his daughters lacked, a courtesy that stood in contrast to the blood on his apron. "What brings you in today?"

"I return for one of your kosher chickens."

Before the butcher could reply, Héloise slipped into the shop from the back room, a rush of cool air accompanying her. The young woman's long blond hair was pulled tight, rolled into a bun, unlike her sister's curly locks. Her lips were puckered as though a lemon candy were melting under her tongue.

"Oh, it's you," she said flatly when she spotted Sophie. "Where's your grandmother today?"

"At home, cooking," Sophie replied cheerily. She pretended not to notice Héloise's frostiness.

"How large a chicken?" asked Monsieur Van Hoden.

"Large enough for two hungry ladies. We're celebrating Purim."

Héloise scoffed, which drew the attention of her father. "Héloise, is there something you need?"

"No, father."

"Then prepare a kosher chicken and wrap the giblets, with our compliments." He smiled at Sophie. "For your gravy."

"Merci, monsieur." She tried to not seem overly pleased at seeing the butcher chide his daughter.

"Happy Purim," he said, and returned to the freezer leaving his daughter to run the shop.

Sophie busied herself with the latch on her coin purse, unhappy to be left alone with Héloise.

Nevertheless, Héloise complied with her father's request and, to Sophie's surprise, proved adept at packaging the bird and its giblets.

"Anything else?" she asked like a dare, pushing the wrapped chicken across the counter.

"No. This is fine. Thank you." She handed her franc note to Héloise, who took the money, keeping her eyes fixed on Sophie.

"Did you tell my sister this morning you would eat her?"

Sophie recalled Céline's interrogation in the shed and regretted being so surly with the younger girl.

"Yes," Sophie admitted. "I'm afraid so."

In response, Héloise punched a key on the register, released the drawer with the sound of a bell, inserted the franc from Sophie, and gave her coins in change.

"I guess it wasn't very nice of me," Sophie added.

Héloise closed the drawer. "Of course it wasn't nice," she smirked. "That's what made it funny."

Sophie frowned her confusion. "I guess so."

"Wish I'd thought of it. Céline can be such a pest."

"Well…I meant no harm."

Héloise stared back. "Enjoy your chicken."

"Thank you." Sophie pocketed her change and hastened back to her bicycle, perplexed. She laid the wrapped chicken in the basket with the other groceries and rode toward home.

Somehow, her chat with Héloise felt like a victory, but she couldn't figure why. Perhaps it was because Héloise had admitted Sophie was funny, and maybe even half compliments could still be considered compliments from someone like Héloise.

Thoughts of the village square and her encounter at the *boucherie* were soon replaced by dreams of roast chicken and *hamantaschen*, drawing Sophie's attention away from the bumpy cobblestone to the Purim feast that awaited her. In her reverie, she pedaled toward home, and just as she moved her eyes back to the curving road, she spotted a man tilting a bucket into the street only a meter in front of her.

"Aagh!" She squeezed the handbrake like a vice, expecting to hit the man or find herself in a tangle of spokes and chicken. However, at the sound of her squealing brakes, the man leapt back, narrowly escaping collision.

Sophie bounced to a halt, steadying her feet on the road.

"Oh, monsieur," she gulped. "I'm so sorry."

"Why sorry?" the man said, regaining his footing.

"Because I nearly hit you, of course!"

When the man stepped forward into the sunlight, Sophie glimpsed a hint of yellow paint in his long hair. He was tall, lean, and appeared to be in his early twenties. He had a solid jaw, smooth and clean-shaven, and was undeniably handsome.

"Entirely my fault," he said. "I'm the one standing in the street where bicycles ought to be. I should be the one apologizing." He smiled, his clouded pupils aimed somewhere over Sophie's shoulder.

"Oh," she exclaimed, noticing his eyes.

"Yes, it's true." He appeared to recognize the surprise in her voice. "I'm blind." His leaky bucket dripped diluted, sweet-smelling paint and thinner onto his worn leather shoes. "At least mostly so."

"Monsieur Lévèque," Sophie grinned.

"Again, true... You know me?"

"Yes," she replied. "I mean—no. I'm Sophie. Sophie Claveaux."

Lévèque inhaled the air between them as though drawing her in. Her heart pounded, which she attributed to her lingering panic from their near-accident, yet something in this moment felt intimate, exciting.

"Sophie," he repeated. He set his bucket down, wiped his palms on his trousers, and offered her his hand. "Pleased to meet you."

She shook his hand and noticed both the strength and softness of his grip—the touch of an artist, the first she'd ever met. It felt electric.

When it seemed like she'd lingered too long in his grasp, she added, "My grandmother lives just there." She pointed upstairs, but realized with embarrassment her gesture was meaningless to the blind man.

"Above my flat," Lévèque replied. "Of course. Madame Claveaux's your grandmother."

"That's right." Her heart still raced.

"She's lovely," Lévèque smiled. "A gifted pastry chef." He patted his stomach. "I adore her tarte aux pommes."

"She'd tell you her secret is vanilla."

"I think having an enthusiastic recipient helps, too."

Sophie laughed. "Oh, yes!"

"She says you've moved here from the Loire Valley."

"Yes, from Avoine. My father—"

"Off to war," Lévèque sighed with sympathy. "Your grandmother told me. Terrible times."

Sophie looked to the ground, unready to discuss her father's predicament with anyone.

"I'm sure your presence in Ville de Lemaire is a comfort to her," the artist offered. "You can care for her while your father's away."

"I think the arrangement is for her to care for me."

Lévèque smiled. "Perhaps you care for each other."

"She tells me you're an excellent painter, monsieur." Sophie hoped her interest might prompt Lévèque to show her some of his paintings.

"Right now, I'm only an excellent exterminator."

"Exterminator?"

"My brushes," he said, crouching down to collect his overturned bucket. "I rinse the paint and dump the mixture into the gutters. The solution I use to keep the color; it kills the rats. I'm glad they're not art critics." He grinned and stood, now carrying his bucket full of wet brushes.

"Sad for the rats," Sophie said, attempting to match his cleverness.

"Very sad, but your grandmother says she no longer worries for her tartes cooling in the window." He chuckled. "If I can't sell a painting, at least I can perform this public service." He lowered his head, his long hair falling into his eyes.

"I like you, Monsieur Lévèque." She was surprised by her own proclamation.

"Because I kill your rats?"

"No, because you're kind to my grandmother."

"You're sure it's genuine?" he teased. "Perhaps I'm just after her tarte aux pommes."

"Either way!" Sophie felt a sudden flush of warmth rise in her cheeks, afraid she'd somehow embarrassed herself.

Lévèque raised his bucket. "I must ask you to forgive me once again," he said. "I'm off to kill more rats."

"Bonjour," said Sophie.

"Bonjour." He gave a brief nod and walked back to his flat. Even without a blind man's walking stick, he seemed to know where he was going, navigating back from the gutters using the toe of his sodden shoe to guide his way.

How wrong she'd been about Lévèque. He was clearly not the antisocial hermit she'd imagined, nor the recluse Madame Bavard had described. He loved her grandmother's cooking. He was witty and charming, misunderstood, different from everyone else because he looked different, acted different...wasn't from here. He was different as she was, and maybe that was why she liked him.

She smiled. In her heart she suddenly felt it. She'd finally met a man of reason.

Chapter 13

Purim Dinner

The giblet broth bubbled and sputtered from neglect.

"Sophie, the gravy!" her grandmother called from the buffet, attuned to the proper sounds of a kitchen.

Perched on a stool by the stove, Sophie had abandoned the one duty she'd been given. Instead of stirring the giblets, she had been fingering the key on the chain around her neck, staring out the window at the empty birdhouse in the neighbor's garden below.

"I'm sorry, Grand-mère."

"You've been in a daze ever since you returned from the square." Her grandmother stepped over and used the spoon from the counter to stir the thickening gravy. "Is something wrong?"

How could Sophie explain that a blind artist had captured her imagination from a single encounter? How could she confess her longing for La Sorbonne, and for anyone who might speak to her of the art she loved? Her grandmother would find her dreams impractical and unrealistic, foolish and unreasonable, just like her father would have done.

No, now was not the time. Like the neighbor's empty birdhouse, Sophie's dreams would have to wait.

"Nothing's wrong, Grand-mère. I just like to daydream."

"Well, a nice meal should bring you to back to yourself." Her grandmother handed her the spoon and began to place clean silverware beside each dinner plate. As the old woman set the table, she raised her nose to the air to sniff the scents of roast chicken and onions. "Smells good."

Sophie resumed stirring the gravy and glanced over to see her grandmother had set three places at the table. "Is Madame Bavard joining us?" She didn't conceal the disappointment in her voice.

"Didn't I tell you? I invited Monsieur Lévèque."

Sophie shot to her feet. "Monsieur Lévèque?"

"While you were shopping, the poor man came by to ask for a can of beans. How could I send him away with beans when I knew this—" she waved her hands around the room, "the smell of Purim dinner, would drift down to his flat?"

Lévèque hadn't mentioned the dinner arrangements when she'd met him in the street. Now, Sophie imagined herself staring at him over the table, losing herself in his cloudy eyes. One glimpse of Sophie gazing at the artist and her grandmother would easily discern her fascination with him and, perhaps, her secret dreams.

"That's nice of you," said Sophie, trying to sound casual. "I'm sure Monsieur Lévèque would like a hot meal." She turned away, back to the saucepan to gather herself.

"He'll be here shortly, dear. Why don't you go change?"

Sophie was still wearing the old dress she'd worn shopping, the one she wore to clean the bicycle.

"Oh, I suppose I should."

She strolled to her room and closed the door. Once alone, she raced to her closet to find the yellow dress she'd received from Madame Lefavre. She knew Lévèque couldn't see the dress, but she hoped her grandmother might comment in his presence about how beautiful it looked.

She stepped to the bureau drawer and removed a folded handkerchief embroidered with yellow roses. Tucked inside the soft cloth were two corked vials Sophie had discovered among her things, scents Madame Lefavre had secreted into her coat pocket the day she left Paris. The first contained lavender oil and the second, honey water, the scents Madame named as Sophie's own.

She delicately applied them in equal parts to her throat and behind each ear, hoping the artist's habit of sniffing the air would cause him to notice. The thought of drawing his interest gave her a brief thrill, but the feeling was soon replaced by a rush of fear that he'd think her too forward.

After a deep breath to quiet her nerves, she pulled back her hair and tied it with a ribbon. She slipped on a clean pair of flat shoes and returned to the dining room, just as Monsieur Lévèque knocked.

Her grandmother opened the door to reveal the young artist, holding a bouquet of flowers in one hand and a wrapped package in the other. His clothes were clean and his long hair, now free of paint, was neatly combed.

"*Bonsoir*, Monsieur Lévèque." Her grandmother greeted him with a kiss to each of his cheeks. "Please come in."

He thrust forward a fist full of yawning irises and lilies, their stems wrapped in waxed paper. "For Sophie," he said, "with my apology for our near mishap in the street."

"Oh, my!" replied her grandmother.

Sophie stepped forward. "Merci, monsieur. They're beautiful, but it was my fault. My grandmother will tell you I have a habit of daydreaming."

"A wonderful habit," he countered, "and the source of all art. It's how we fight the darkness."

Sophie raised the flowers to her nose, using the blooms to shield from her grandmother the redness she felt warm her face.

"For my gracious hostess," Lévèque handed the package to her grandmother, "a small canvas. Though, may I ask you to wait and open it after the meal?"

"Certainly, monsieur, but why?"

"From the wonderful smells, I fear my artistry with a canvas won't compare to yours in the kitchen."

"Oh, nonsense," her grandmother protested with a smile. She placed the wrapped canvas on the desk. "Please, come in. May I take you to your seat?"

The artist raised his elbow, which Sophie's grandmother took to lead him to his chair, switching her cane to her other hand.

As he'd done in the street, the artist used his toe to guide his way. When he reached his chair, he turned it out from the table and sat. "Thank you."

Sophie watched with admiration. In spite of his blindness, Lévèque seemed quite capable of navigating new places, and knew how to navigate her grandmother.

"Why don't you get those flowers in some water?" her grandmother called. "I'll serve dinner."

Sophie turned from Lévèque to the kitchen, where she placed the blooms in a vase and added water from the tap.

"The food smells delicious," Lévèque said. "You're kind to take pity on me."

"Purim dinner," her grandmother announced. "Welcoming guests to the table is a holiday tradition."

"Purim?" the artist asked. "You're Jewish?"

"Yes." The hesitation in her grandmother's voice told Sophie they shared the same sudden fear, that the artist held some prejudice against Jews.

Lévèque grinned. "My mother was Jewish. I haven't had Purim dinner since she died. Ten years."

Her grand-mère smiled and joined Sophie in the kitchen to retrieve the tureen of giblet gravy. "Then I can only hope this meal will honor her."

Sophie felt relief at learning Lévèque was a Jew, but felt further kinship at the news that he too had lost his mother. More ways they were different from others; more ways they were alike.

She placed the vase of flowers on the buffet.

"May I help you, Grand-mère?"

"You may not. It's a cook's privilege to serve. Sit, child."

Sophie took her seat across from Lévèque, careful to keep her eyes on her grandmother, who'd set her cane against the wall to present her serving platter. Pieces of roast chicken sat on a bed of sizzling carrots, onions, and potatoes, which her grandmother had tumbled with broth and rosemary.

She first served Monsieur Lévèque, who requested that Sophie's grandmother name the items and their locations on his plate as she filled it.

"Chicken," she began, "at nine o'clock." She placed a slice on the left side of his dish. "Potatoes, onions, and carrots at six o'clock, giblet gravy at three…and a slice of baguette at twelve."

The artist licked his lips.

"And to drink," she added, "water on your left and a glass of red wine to your right." She set a napkin in his lap.

Gripping his fork, Lévèque poked each portion on his plate, confirming where each item sat. "Merci, Madame. It all smells miraculous."

Once both Sophie and her grandmother had filled their own plates, the artist asked, "May I say the *brucha?*"

"Please," her grandmother answered.

Once his prayer was complete, his grace seemed to vanish, allowing his enthusiastic appetite to reveal itself. He stuffed himself with such abandon, Sophie had to look away to stifle a laugh. She noticed her grandmother smile as well, appearing proud at the zealous response her cooking had inspired.

The trio gleefully consumed the feast before them as the sun set. Between bites, Lévèque spoke of his fondness for the spring, but made no mention of Sophie's scents of lavender and honey. It further occurred to her that her grandmother had made no mention of her dress, either. The evening had failed to produce the connection for which Sophie had hoped.

After an hour of eating, her grandmother served hot, black tea with vanilla to accompany her *hamantaschen*, inspiring the artist, once again, to lavish her with compliments.

"A masterpiece, Madame. Truly a meal worthy of the finest restaurants in Paris."

"Oh, monsieur," her grandmother blushed.

Tired, or perhaps jealous, of the pleasantries Lévèque aimed at her grandmother, Sophie's curiosity for more details of the artist's personal life overcame her, particularly now that he evoked Paris.

"Monsieur," she began, "Madame Bavard says she's seen you out in the street nearly every night. May I ask why?"

"Sophie!" her grandmother scolded. "Don't be rude."

The artist finished his final bite, used a napkin to wipe apricot jam and pastry crumbs from his lip, and sat back from the table. "No, no," he chewed. "That's not a rude question. Neighbors have a right to know why people mill around their neighborhood at night."

"No, they don't," her grandmother countered, looking crossly at Sophie. "Neighbors should mind their own business."

"You presume offense where there is none, Madame Claveaux."

Sophie smirked in victory and raised an eyebrow at her grandmother, who responded by rolling her eyes.

"I must say, however, I'd rather not answer Sophie's question." Lévèque set down his tea cup and turned to Sophie. "I'd rather show her."

"Show me?" Sophie felt her voice waiver.

"Yes," said Lévèque. "I can tell by the coolness of the room the sun's gone down and darkness has settled in. The time's perfect to cure you of your curiosity." He turned his hazy eyes toward the head of the table. "With your grandmother's permission, of course."

"You surely have it, monsieur, and if you can cure her of her bad manners, I'd be grateful for that too."

"Grand-mère!"

"I'll do the washing up." Her grandmother stood, leaned on her cane, and began collecting the plates.

Lévèque rose from his chair. "May I help?"

"Certainly not. Just go before it's too late."

The young artist again held out his elbow and this time offered it to Sophie. "*S'il vous plaît?*"

Sophie stood, her voice lost somewhere in her throat. She walked around the table and nervously took Lévèque's arm to lead him toward the door.

"We won't be long," called the artist.

"*Bonne journée,*" called Sophie's grandmother over the sound of running water.

Once through the door, Lévèque withdrew his elbow from Sophie's hand. "Ready?"

"Yes." She closed the door behind her.

To her surprise, Lévèque moved swiftly and without her help down the stairs to the cobbled street below.

"Follow me," he called in an urgent whisper.

Sophie trailed behind, finding it hard to keep up with the artist who now moved with unexpected certainty. Seeing him stride so ably, Sophie began to doubt his blindness, feeling like Madame Bavard in her skepticism.

"This way," he said, turning down an alley.

"Where are we going?"

"Trust me," Lévèque called, and rounded the corner.

Had he been any other man, she would have insisted on knowing where they were going before taking another step, or would have refused to follow, but as he continued to demonstrate, Lévèque wasn't like other men.

The ever-narrowing alleys opened at last to a quiet cul-de-sac, lined with vaulting apartments. The street was cobbled with smooth river stones, and at the end of street was a well-manicured garden courtyard, an unlikely haven in this forgotten part of town.

She approached the garden and noticed it was flanked by a hedge of fragrant, night-blooming jasmine, yet the most striking feature of the garden stood at the end of a path that cut through the hedge. A white-latticed gazebo stood under the darkening sky. Its beauty caused Sophie to gasp aloud.

"Yes," Lévèque whispered. "I know."

This time, it was the blind man who took Sophie's elbow. He led her to the gazebo where they sat on the structure's clapboard bench. The artist released her, raised his nose to the floral air, and inhaled.

"Jasmine," Sophie said, mesmerized.

"Yes."

"How did you find this place?"

Lévèque faced her, the rising moon reflecting in his eyes. "At night, when the moon is full and the contrasts are sharper"—he turned to her—"I see more."

"You can see?" The mist in each of the artist's blue eyes emphasized the improbability of his claim.

"I can make out shapes," he said, "silhouettes, differences between dark and light."

"Contrasts," she proclaimed.

"Yes." He returned his gaze to the sky. "It isn't full sight," he said with disappointment, "but bright light in the midst of darkness, like the moonlight, can be enough to guide me...inspire me."

Sophie heard both humility and sincerity in his voice.

"Sometimes I even see color, at least in my mind." He scanned the gazebo as if making out its details. He ran his fingers across its latticework. "Some places exude light and color, special places like this."

"That's remarkable." Sophie tried to imagine what colors would look like if they existed only in someone's mind. What would a color be if it couldn't be seen?

"There are people," he added, now more softly, "whose voices, whose presence, create colors for me too."

"People? Which people?"

"Well...you, for instance."

"I create color for you?" Sophie's heart raced.

"Yes. From the moment we met in the street."

"What color am I?"

"The color I like most." Lévèque smiled. "Blue."

Warmth rushed through her limbs at the thought of being connected to the artist, of being named his favorite color, and she didn't know what to say. Sitting in her yellow dress, she thought maybe he would have said "yellow." It seemed Lévèque saw her differently than she saw herself.

"Blue," she repeated.

For a few moments, they sat quietly under the moon until Lévèque broke the silence. "Ville de Lemaire comes alive at night, don't you think? It's noisy."

"Noisy?" she laughed. "You must be kidding. No place is quieter than this."

Lévèque angled his head. "Not even Avoine?"

She recalled the summer nights at home in the valley, when the frogs would offer their throaty songs or when night birds would praise the darkness with their incessant hooting. Even when the creatures of the forest were quiet, the bubbling flow of the Loire could always be heard.

"Yes," she said. "Avoine is loud compared to this."

Lévèque chuckled. "This place is very loud. Close your eyes and listen."

"You're joking."

"Please?"

Sophie played along and lowered her lids. "Okay."

"Shhh," the artist's voice returned to a faint whisper. "No more talking. Just listen." After a moment of smothering silence he asked, "What do you hear?"

"Nothing," she giggled. "I told you, Ville de Lemaire's quiet."

Lévèque moved his hand to her forearm. His grasp was gentle, but firm. "You're not trying very hard," he said. "Now, don't open your eyes."

The bare skin of her arm tingled beneath his grasp, but she clenched her eyes shut. "Okay."

"Now," he began, "listen farther. Pretend you have no sight to rely on whatsoever. Your ears are your eyes, your hands. Let them reach out. Listen across the courtyard."

He released her, allowing her to focus. She imagined her senses amplified, a glowing ribbon emerging from her ears reaching for sounds, like a kite tail stretching over the courtyard, licking the stones in the road.

"Now, farther, through the alley, to the street."

"That's far."

"Shhh!" he scolded in a playful whisper. "Just listen."

She stifled her laughter and imagined the sound ribbon unfurling from her mind, reaching out, weaving through the streets of Ville de Lemaire.

"Now…past the street and into town."

At a distance, Sophie heard the hollow clunk of a tin can hitting the street, and then the mew of a cat…

"A can?" asked Lévèque, successfully reading her thoughts.

"Yes," she replied, "and a cat."

"Good."

Some place beyond, she heard soft music…jazz…then, the click of a gramophone needle as it hit the scratch of the record it played, over and over. *Click. Click.*

"Music?" Lévèque queried.

"Scratched record," Sophie replied.

"Excellent!"

Sophie opened her eyes to face the artist. He was smiling broadly, gazing at her as though the clouds in his eyes weren't really there.

She realized she was smiling too, and clutched the key on her neck.

"Ville de Lemaire has four courtyards like this one," he explained. "One on each side of town. This one's my favorite. There's a park near the school with a swing that squeaks. Three streets up from ours, a man named Pierre and his wife Arianne argue about his drinking. They throw things."

Sophie laughed.

"This is what concerns Madame Bavard," Lévèque said. "This is why I'm out all night and how I found this courtyard. I move in the darkness under the full moon to learn the lay of the town. Once I memorize the streets, they're easier to travel without a walking stick during the day. Your grandmother seems resigned to using to her cane, but I've never liked them."

"You're quite clever, Monsieur Lévèque."

"No," he replied. "I trust the world to teach me, and the world has never let me down."

Sophie wished she shared Lévèque's view of the world. It seemed to her, the world had done nothing but let her down. It had killed her mother, stolen her father, and dashed her dreams of studying in Paris. It didn't guide her to places that inspired her. It led her away from them. Her curse had made her a pariah to those she loved. She didn't trust the world as Lévèque did; she refused to trust it. The world had betrayed her too many times.

"What's wrong?" he asked, sensing the change in her mood.

She drew in the cool air, not wanting to share her dark feelings with the artist. "You're the jasmine," she replied, the words jumping to her lips.

"The jasmine?"

"Yes." The idea began to form more fully. "You take in the night; you open under the moon, just like the jasmine."

Lévèque sat back. "Ah-ha!" His laughter echoed through the courtyard. "You've proven my suspicions."

"Suspicions?"

"You think in pictures," he beamed. "Like an artist."

The moment froze. No one had ever claimed to know how she thought, nor had anyone seemed to care. No one, until Lévèque.

"I'm hardly an artist," she replied. "The only thing I've ever painted is a barn."

"You have art here"—the artist tapped his chest—"the only place it counts."

A sleeping pride awoke within her. Could it be that someone believed in her—believed, as she did, that art was part of her, buried in her heart? Comforted by his words, emboldened by the powerful moon, Sophie was ready to trust Lévèque. She took a breath.

"I plan to study art," she revealed. "It's my dream."

She watched Lévèque intently, scanned his face in the moonlight for some reaction. A warmth—something between fear and joy—washed over her.

He nodded. "Studying art is a noble endeavor."

"You think it's silly."

"Of course I don't." His tone changed and he leaned toward her. "Studying is a worthy act. I'm just more inclined to play the game than to watch from the sidelines."

"My grandmother cooks," she countered, "and I like to eat. What would cooking be if there was no one to enjoy it?"

Lévèque smiled at her challenge. "Art isn't like food. It doesn't require consumption by others," he said. "Art nourishes the artist himself."

"I believe that too," Sophie said, thrilled at the movement to more intellectual conversation, "but I think for art to live, artists need art lovers."

"Lovers?"

Sophie grew warm. "Of course. How could an artist buy his canvases, his brushes, his paint, unless someone loved his art? Someone has to buy his paintings."

"You make a good point."

"When artists cut off their ears or die, someone has to remind the world of their brilliance."

"I see you've done a bit of studying already."

Sophie closed her eyes, and uttered her biggest secret aloud: "I've been accepted to study at La Sorbonne," she said. "I'm supposed to be in Paris right now."

She opened her eyes, her words hanging in the air.

Lévèque grew quiet. His face went dark and his features blended with the shadows. After a moment's cold silence, he stood from the bench.

"We should go," he announced. "I wouldn't want your grandmother to worry." Without waiting for Sophie, he stepped out of the gazebo, into the street.

"Monsieur?"

He continued across the cul-de-sac, ignoring her.

She raced after him. "Monsieur Lévèque?" She grabbed his arm. "Is something wrong?"

He turned to face her, his sightless eyes shooting a look over her shoulder. "La Sorbonne is not the place you think," he said tersely. "It's no place for anyone who cares about art."

Anger rose in her chest, offense at his tone replacing her confusion. She released his arm. "You're wrong," she snapped. "It's an honor to be accepted there."

She suddenly regretted sharing her secret, revealing her dreams, allowing herself to be vulnerable.

"The people at La Sorbonne know nothing," he spat, now angry. "It's a place for senseless bureaucrats."

"What's wrong with you? La Sorbonne is the finest institution in France!"

"If you think that, then I was wrong about you." The moon's light flashed across the artist's twisting mouth. "You're nothing but a foolish girl."

He turned to the alley and strode back the way they'd come.

As he marched away, Sophie's anger with him grew. Where was his reason now? She chewed her lip and fought back tears, but rather than remaining alone in the darkness, she followed him, keeping her distance.

Lévèque cocked his head around each narrow turn, appearing to listen for her footsteps. Still, she trailed behind. When he reached his apartment, the artist stopped as if he would say something more. Instead, he keyed himself into his flat and closed his door without a word.

"Bah!" Sophie shouted at his door, knowing he'd hear her. "Bah!"

She climbed the stairs to her grandmother's apartment, stomping in anger with each step, struggling to hold back tears.

Why should I even care what he says about La Sorbonne? Why should he matter?

Sophie walked in to find her grandmother sitting on the sofa, staring at the wall above the buffet.

"I think it's love," her grandmother announced.

"What?" Sophie pushed the door closed, her pulse still throbbing.

"This curious painting." Her grandmother squinted at Lévèque's small canvas which she'd unwrapped, per his instructions. She had hung it on the wall while Sophie was out. "The gift Monsieur Lévèque brought to dinner... He's painted a symbol, don't you see? I think it's love."

The framed square canvas, hardly bigger than a serving dish, was crafted in the Impressionistic style. It featured a dark blue backdrop, deep like velvet. The focus of the piece was a white circle in the upper center of the canvas: the moon, glowing with a yellow halo in the inky darkness. Below the luminescent moon, Lévèque had painted a white lattice fence rising behind a lush green hedge. From the midst of the dark leaves, a single flower opened to the moon as if inspired to bloom.

The painting was nothing short of brilliant. Each delicate brush stroke seemed to carry intent, a color, a thought. Just like the place it commemorated, the canvas took Sophie's breath away, slowed her pulse, calmed her rage.

"It's just a courtyard," Sophie explained, struggling to keep the pain out of her voice, trying to reconcile the brilliance of the work with the obstinacy of its creator. "It's where he took me tonight."

"This place is here in Ville de Lemaire?"

"It's where he goes at night. It's where he sees."

Her grandmother looked perplexed. "What are you talking about, dear? Monsieur Lévèque is blind."

"Yes," Sophie frowned. "Yes, he is."

Chapter 14

A Brief Visit

S ophie lay awake in bed, haunted by Lévèque's words.

You're nothing but a foolish girl.

He'd been cruel and hurtful, yet she couldn't help but wonder herself: *was* she a fool to cling to her dreams of La Sorbonne? It was unthinkable that an artist as brilliant as Lévèque could dismiss La Sorbonne so plainly—could dismiss her. Yet, he had. Whatever his quarrel with La Sorbonne, that quarrel now included Sophie.

She rose from her sheets and tucked her toes into her worn cloth slippers. From the dresser chair, she lifted her robe and jammed her arms through the sleeves, convinced that tonight sleep was not possible. Guided by the blue glow of twilight that beamed through the living room window, she made her way to the sofa where she sat and faced Lévèque's canvas.

His moon, though bright and inspiring, glared at her, persistent, accusing. It gripped her, as Lévèque himself had done in the gazebo, urged her to listen, to perceive things beyond herself. His canvas spoke to her as directly as he had.

Abandon your hopes.

How could he be right when she felt so deeply he was wrong?

Follow your dreams.

Where was the truth? How could she both abandon her hopes and follow her dreams? Even Madame Lefavre's alchemy couldn't combine these two opposing thoughts.

She closed her eyes. The Purim meal, Lévèque's kindness, the alleys, the sounds of the village, his touch, his anger…all created strong but confusing feelings. He was handsome, enigmatic, gifted, and yet he'd turned so callous, so cold, the moment she mentioned the university.

Trapped between his painting and the blue glow from the window, Sophie knew she couldn't escape the moon any more than she could escape her confusing feelings for the man who had transformed her in a single night, the artist who'd taken her heart.

Three raps on the door startled Sophie awake.

She lifted her head from the arm of the loveseat, her face tingling with the indentations the fabric had impressed upon her.

Three more raps brought her grandmother in from her bedroom, leaning on her cane.

"Good heavens. Who's calling so early?" She hastily buttoned her housecoat and looked to Sophie in surprise. "Angel? What are you doing on the sofa?"

"I couldn't sleep." Sophie squinted in the morning light that seemed to refute her words.

"Well, gather yourself, dear. Someone's at the door."

Sophie pushed her fingers through her matted hair and drew her robe around her. Could it be Lévèque, coming to apologize?

Her grandmother unlatched the lock and drew open the door. Two men stood, haloed by the morning sunlight, each in a brown military uniform. One man was broad and full-faced, his breast pockets covered with medals. The other was younger and thin, his uniform hanging on his spindly frame.

"Madame Claveaux?" the broader man asked.

At the sound of the man's words, Sophie's grandmother gasped, dropped her cane and staggered, but the man was fast and caught her before she fell.

"Grand-mère!" Sophie ran over and, with the help of the large uniformed man, guided her grandmother to a chair at the kitchen table.

"Get her some water!" Sophie cried, barking orders as if she, too, was in the military.

The thin, younger soldier, complied, closing the door and then dashing to the kitchen.

Sophie used a napkin from the table to fan her grandmother. "Grand-mère? Are you all right?"

"Yes." Her grandmother's eyes fluttered and she took a calming breath. "Yes, child."

The young soldier placed a glass in front of Sophie's grandmother, but she did not drink. Instead, she turned to the older soldier.

"Just tell me. Is he dead?"

A rush of nausea overcame Sophie. "Dead?" In her haste to help her grandmother, the implication of soldiers' presence hadn't set in.

"Madame, please. May we sit a moment?" The older soldier's voice was soft, calming. It seemed was gifted in having such conversations.

Her grandmother gave a nod and both men took their seats. Sophie remained standing, her trembling hand finding her grandmother's shoulder. It seemed her curse had found her once again.

"You are the family of Sous-Lieutenant Gérard Claveaux?"

"Yes, yes. Please monsieur, what's happened to my son?"

"Forgive me, Madame. The news is...uncertain."

"Uncertain?" Sophie couldn't help but sound panicked. "How could it be uncertain?"

"My name is Capitaine Edourd Netoine," the decorated soldier began, "and this is Aspirant Michel Fontaine."

The junior officer shifted in his chair, awkward and uncomfortable.

Sophie's grand-mère leaned forward. "Yes, yes."

"What I need to share should be considered secret."

"Please, monsieur, get to your point."

The captain took a breath. "Your son was sent on a reconnaissance mission to lead a small squad into Luxembourg, near the border with Germany and Belgium."

"Luxembourg?" Sophie was surprised to learn her father was so close. She'd thought he'd gone to Poland.

"What's happened?" her grandmother repeated, impatience clear in her tone.

Sophie squeezed her grandmother's shoulder, unsure if she was offering assurance or seeking it.

"Eleven days ago," Netoine continued, "the Sous-Lieutenant's squad was ambushed in a skirmish that took the lives of three of his men. Nine escaped and returned to their camp unharmed, thanks to your son."

Sophie bit her lip at the details of the danger her father had faced.

Young Fontaine sat forward and swallowed before speaking. "He saved my life, Madame. I was one of those men."

Sophie stared at Fontaine. This young man, hardly older than she, had seen her father, thought him a hero. He carried her father in his recent memory—the way he'd last looked, the words he'd last spoken...Sophie wanted to reach out like Lévèque had taught her, perceive the man's thoughts, his experiences. She wanted to see her father as this man did. She wanted what he had.

"He was very brave," the young soldier added. "He knew better than anyone how to use his weapon..." His voice trailed, his statement punctuated by a sniffle from Sophie's grandmother.

"Please," said Sophie. "Just tell us what happened."

"Sous-Lieutenant Claveaux saved this man's life," the captain continued, "and the lives of eight others by keeping the enemy at bay."

"Then what's uncertain?" her grandmother pleaded, her voice cracking with fear and impatience. "Where's Gérard?"

"That's just it, Madame. Your son is missing."

The word buzzed like a swarm of bees ready to strike.

"How could he be missing?" Sophie snapped. "You said he was in Luxembourg."

"We encountered Germans in Luxembourg, apparently on a secret reconnaissance mission of their own. Most of the French military is expecting to fight the Great War again, facing the Germans along the Maginot line. Some of us, your father included, aren't so certain. It was prudence that brought us north. German soldiers in Luxembourg might mean—"

"—they may attack France from the north instead," Sophie interrupted.

Netoine nodded. "Perhaps. We suspect they are in Belgium as well, examining their options. They seem to be one step ahead."

"Has no one gone back for him?" her grandmother asked. "Is there no one looking for my son?"

Netoine looked to Fontaine and then back to Sophie's grandmother. "We've shared detailed activities of the French military with you, Madame—information about your son that might help us find him. The German movements demand our attention throughout the region. We cannot afford to commit forces in the search for one man. You must understand."

"Well, I don't understand," Sophie asserted.

Netoine drew a breath. "In battle, mademoiselle, some soldiers are wounded or captured and can't return. Others fall too far behind enemy lines to retrieve." His voice fell. "Sometimes," the captain looked to his soldier and back to Sophie, "sometimes, they choose not to return."

"Choose?" Her grandmother's voice echoed. "Choose?"

"My father would never do that." Sophie recalled the two horrible men that she and Maurice had encountered in the woods outside Paris—deserters who'd stolen her horse at gunpoint—and the scorn she had for such men. "My father's no deserter."

Captain Netoine was stoic. "We don't judge, mademoiselle. We explain the possibilities." He looked to her grandmother. "No matter the circumstance, we pray for your son's safety and for his return."

After his words dissolved, Netoine rose from the table. It seemed his questions were complete, as were his answers. Fontaine followed, but Sophie's grandmother didn't budge.

"France is thankful to you both." He pulled a card from his pocket, laid it on the table in front of her grandmother. "If permitted, we'll search for your son. You have my word. If we hear news of him, we'll contact you." He narrowed his eyes. "Please...we ask you to do the same."

Sophie's grandmother looked away, down at the card.

The captain gestured to his soldier. The two grasped their hats and marched toward the door, their mission accomplished.

Sophie followed, and just as they opened the door, she reached for Netoine's arm. "*Mon capitaine?*"

"Yes, mademoiselle?"

She raised her chin. "He's alive." She wasn't sure if she was telling Netoine or asking him. "I feel it."

The captain squinted, seeming to consider his words carefully. "Anything is possible." He then nodded to Fontaine and the two men left.

Sophie closed the door and turned to see that her grandmother had left the room.

"Grand-mère?"

She walked to the back of the apartment to find her grandmother's bedroom door closed. She touched it, unsure if she should call out again, knock, or try the knob. Instead, she moved, stunned and uncertain, to her own room where she lay on her bed to stare at the ceiling.

Her father fought the enemy in Luxembourg, near the border with Germany. That's what the captain had said. Were the Germans nearer to France than anyone knew? How could Netoine search for her father if he were captured? Sophie couldn't make sense of any of this.

Instead, she imagined herself in Avoine alongside her father in the barn on the rainy morning he'd left. She recalled the series of canvases she'd created, moments captured in her mind: the frozen silence when the rain had quieted, the key he'd given her with the promise of her mother's secrets, his assurance that he'd write, and his final loving embrace…however, none of these memories calmed her. None gave her any answers. All she wanted was to hear the sound of her father singing "Au Clair de la Lune" and to hold his hand again, to feel his warmth and use it to ward off the curse that seemed determined to take everything she had.

Chapter 15

Sitting Shiva

The morning sun shone in, drawing Sophie from her bed. In spite of the brightness of the room, a darkness had worked its way into her bones during the night and possessed her. She brushed her hair and methodically put on a dress, shoes, and a hair ribbon. She drifted like a phantom to the loveseat, weary and forlorn, disconnected from her own movements. She reached for the key that hung from her necklace and silently implored her dead mother for reassurance, for feeling—any feeling at all.

These thoughts were interrupted when her grandmother tottered in on her cane. She was grim-faced yet walked with an air of purpose, a woman possessed with clarity. In her free arm, she cradled a stack of sheets, towels, and blankets.

"Help me, my angel," she commanded.

Sophie rose and joined her, confused. She lifted the linens from her grandmother's possession. "What are these for?"

"We must sit *shiva* for your father," she explained.

"Shiva?"

"We need to cover the windows and mirrors." She moved across the living room. "Let's start with the kitchen."

"Shiva?" she repeated. The word brought memories of old Madame Marcoux's death in Avoine last year when her daughters sat shiva. They'd lit a candle according to the Jewish tradition, sat on cushions rather than chairs, and gave up nearly all normal activities as if they too had died. The usually beautiful girls had shrouded themselves in black, were unable to wash, wear makeup, or even cook. The ancient Jewish ritual had created as much anxiety for the family as the death it was supposed to honor. Nevertheless, all those rules about how to behave, all those Jewish traditions, had done nothing to ease the grief of poor Monsieur Marcoux. He'd stayed in his room for a month and was never the same.

Hearing the name of the ritual spoken aloud raised Sophie's own anxiety. "Shiva?" she repeated. "Papa's not dead. You heard those men say so. He's missing."

"Oh, my darling." Her grandmother faced her. "Those words were meant to comfort us. They told me the same thing about your *grand-père*." She shook her head. "He wasn't missing."

"No!" Sophie dropped the sheets and blankets to the floor, her pulse thumping in anger. "It's not the same."

"My child, you're just making this more difficult." She moved forward as if to embrace her, but Sophie stepped back.

"How could you?" She turned from her grandmother and raced to the door, threw it open before the old woman could respond.

Sophie sprinted down the stairs, struggling to breathe, wishing she could sprout wings and fly.

Shiva?

She reached the foot of the stairs with nowhere to go, and sat with a thud. Rage and fear brought a sour bile to her throat, heat to her flesh.

Was she wrong to want her family to be safe? Was her wish for her father's well-being enough to trigger her horrid curse? Was she naïve to think that she could dream, even for a moment?

She buried her face her hands as if she could keep the frantic tears from falling with her palms, but to no avail.

"Sophie?"

She raised her head and, through hot tears, saw Lévèque.

"Oh, monsieur!" she cried.

Puzzled by her disposition, his voice softened. "What's wrong? What's happened?"

She found no strength for words, hardly enough to stand. Instead, she sobbed.

With a tenderness she would not have guessed him capable after their last encounter, he squatted down to her and whispered. "Come," he said. "Come with me."

His arm around her waist, the artist drew Sophie off the stair and led her down the path to his door. Along his doorframe, Sophie noticed his *mezuzah*, reflecting the morning light, offering a sense of familiarity and comfort.

He twisted the knob and guided her in.

Lévèque's curtains were closed, his apartment dark. Through her tears, she made out traces of furniture, two covered easels, books stacked in one corner of the room, several chairs and a dining table.

"Sit at the table," he said. "I'll make us some tea."

She ran her sleeve across her eyes and tried to pull herself from her nightmare.

"Do you take vanilla, like your grandmother?"

Sophie set her jaw. "I'm not like my grandmother."

"Forgive me." Lévèque paused, perplexed. "Perhaps just sugar." He lit the stove, started the kettle, and collected cups and saucers from his cupboard, all with a nimbleness that continued to impress her.

"Pardon my apartment," he said. "I have very few guests. Please, feel free to turn on a light or open the curtains."

Sophie calmed her nerves and scanned the dim room. She spotted a table lamp but decided she liked it better just the way it was. "The dark is fine."

"As you know, I rarely use the light," he remarked.

Sophie recalled Lévèque's use of contrasts which he'd revealed on their evening walk. She remembered his touch...their argument.

Lévèque seemed to recall the same thing.

"Sophie, forgive me for my behavior. I was abrupt and impolite with you. You didn't deserve that." When she didn't respond, he added, "Is that why you're upset?"

"No, that's not it. It's not you."

"An argument with your grandmother, then?" He added tea satchels to the cups.

"It's my father," Sophie managed. "He's...missing."

Lévèque grew silent, but the silence was soon broken by the whistle of the kettle.

Lévèque turned off the burner and poured the crackling water over the tea while keeping one hand near each cup as he filled it. He seemed to judge the water level by the heat.

Without a word, he placed the steaming cups on a tray alongside a bowl of cubed sugar and a glass plate full of raisin brioche and biscuits. He brought the tray over, set it on the table between them, and took a seat.

"I'm so sorry," he said at last.

"My grandmother is ready to call him dead. She wants to sit shiva."

Lévèque lifted his teacup to his lips.

"He's alive," Sophie added, "and you don't mourn the living."

Lévèque was quiet, but his continued silence only upset her more.

"Please, monsieur. What are you thinking? Tell me I'm not foolish to think my father's alive."

"You're not foolish." Lévèque hung his head. "I was wrong to say you were."

"Tell me it's wrong to sit shiva. Tell me he's alive."

Sophie knew she sounded like a desperate child, but she no longer cared. Today, for her father, she was a child.

"Hope isn't foolish," the artist said at last, "but I also think your grandmother's shiva is not for your father." He set down his tea and reached across the table to take her hands. His touch was steady, his fingers warm from his teacup. "I think the shiva is for your grandmother. She can't bear the lack of news, so she's acting in the only way she knows how. She does what she remembers. She remembers how to sit shiva."

The warmth of Lévèque's hands and the wisdom of his words comforted her. Still, she felt unprepared to accept her grandmother's actions.

"I can't pretend my father's dead, monsieur. Not even for her. Not when I know he's alive."

"Then don't." The artist squeezed Sophie's hands more firmly. "Don't pretend anything. Just allow. Allow your grandmother this one thing. Let her sit shiva and ask only that she allow you to keep hope. Give those gifts to each other."

Sophie closed her eyes and imagined Lévèque's painted moon glowing within her, unfurling the jasmine in her darkened heart and giving her hope instead of accusing her of foolishness, filling her dreams instead of destroying them.

Sitting with him, feeling his touch, hearing his words, it truly did feel as if everything would be okay.

She opened her eyes. "May I sit here, with you, monsieur? I mean, just for a while?"

"Of course," said Lévèque. "As long as you like." He gave a crooked smile. "But, may I ask one thing?"

"Yes, of course."

"Stop calling me 'monsieur.' I can't be much older than you." He cocked his head. "My friends call me Jean-Claude."

"Jean-Claude," she repeated, and drank her cooling tea in one gulp.

The artist nodded his satisfaction. "More tea?"

"No, thank you."

"Would you like to talk about your father? It might help."

"I think I'd rather talk about something else."

"All right."

"How about your art?" she said. "May I see your canvases?"

Lévèque paused and Sophie expected him to decline.

"Certainly," he said, perhaps out of pity. He stood and moved to one of his easels positioned in the corner of the room.

She placed her teacup on the table and followed him.

"Why don't you turn on a light?" Lévèque said.

She reached to a small lamp and pulled the knotted string. Brightness filled the room, and it became clear how well-organized he was. Each piece of furniture had been arranged to allow for clear walkways. The books she'd noticed stacked near the door were riddled with bumps: Braille-embossed covers. Aside from the rug he had placed under the dining table, the wooden floors were clean and uncovered, presumably to allow Lévèque to move without tripping, to use his toe to navigate just as he'd done in her grandmother's apartment and in the street.

Lévèque lifted the drape from his easel and dropped the cloth to the floor.

"I painted this for a patron in Lyon," he explained, "but Felipe, the boy who helps me, hasn't framed it."

The painting, nearly a meter wide and half a meter tall, absorbed the light from the room to fuel the painting's breathtaking beauty. The canvas featured a marsh of tall grass with angling reeds, bending in an almost palpable breeze. The blue sky was streaked with thin clouds, and sunlight bathed the scene in a warm, delicate radiance.

"It's beautiful!" she proclaimed.

"Please," he shook his head, "you don't need to—"

"It *is* beautiful," she insisted. "The color's so bright."

"It's the solution I add to my oils," he explained. "It strengthens the hue, sets the paint."

"The solution that kills our rats?"

"Yes," he laughed. "You remember my brush bucket." He wagged his finger. "Stay clear of the gutters."

"I will." She smiled, pondering the irony that something that could make such beauty could also cause death.

The artist stepped to the second easel and removed the drape to reveal a portrait of an empty street winding through apartments that rose on either side. Shadow and light played off the Impressionist shutters, the bricks, and the cobblestones. Flowers leaned over balconies, yearning for attention.

Sophie immediately recognized the image. "Our street!"

"Yes. Or at least my view of it."

She moved closer to the picture to investigate his work. "Raised, broken strokes," she announced. "Like Van Gogh."

"Van Gogh? Now I know you're being insincere."

"No, monsieur...I mean, no, Jean-Claude. It's your gift. You must know that."

He hung his head. "You're kind to say so."

"It's not a kindness," she protested. "You're very good. I've studied the masters." She fought the urge to touch the canvas. "You use small strokes of white to show light, like Monet." She pointed to the canvas. "You favor yellows and blues, like Van Gogh, and here—" so close to his canvas she could smell the paint, "these shutters remind me of Caillebotte's *Vue Toits, Effet de Neige*. It's incredible."

"Caillebotte?" he scoffed. "I can't create his realism." He shook his head. "Once Impressionism falls out of fashion, my career is over."

"Nonsense."

Still, Sophie marveled at the beauty captured by a man who could hardly see. His gift seemed nothing short of miraculous.

The artist walked back to the dining area to retrieve the empty teacups and plates, placing them, clinking, onto his tray.

"Let me help you," Sophie called.

"No need," he replied, and carried the tray to the kitchen.

She took a breath. "May I ask you something?"

"Of course." He began to rinse the dishes in the sink.

"Why don't you paint people?"

Lévèque lifted his gaze and a frown transformed his face. He turned off the water, abandoned the dishes, and wiped his wet hands with a towel.

He gestured toward the sofa. "Sit down." His voice held a peculiar decisiveness. "Sit down and I'll tell you."

She sat on his sofa, fearful she may have again triggered the artist's mysterious anger.

He walked to the opposite side of the room, to a closet she'd failed to notice, and removed a small canvas. He took his seat on the chair across from her, placed the canvas at his feet, and shot a look over her shoulder.

"As a student of art, you know the human figure is difficult to draw, even for an accomplished artist. Bright light—contrasts—can only reveal so much of my subject. I can't always rely on the shadows."

Lévèque leaned down to the small picture, and then turned it to face Sophie. It featured four green apples stacked in a ruddy iron bowl set on a wooden table.

"It's lovely," Sophie remarked.

"First semester project. My professor at La Sorbonne said it was one of the finest still-life pieces he'd seen."

"La Sorbonne?" The pain of their conflict rippled through her memory. "I thought—"

"It took me a month to complete," he continued, ignoring her query, "but I didn't spend that month painting. I spent most of that time handling each apple, touching it until I knew every curve, every dimple. Only then was I prepared to paint." He set the canvas back at his feet. "After that, it took me two days."

Sophie fell silent, hoping his story would reveal more about La Sorbonne.

"After the apples, our next assignment was to paint a flower. I chose the lily. More delicate to touch, but I employed the same method and received high marks. I was told it was even better than the apples. I gave that one to my aunt in Aix-en-Provence."

Lévèque shifted in his chair. "It wasn't long before we were assigned a figure. A woman. They brought in a model, asked us to portray the curve of her body, the texture of her skin." He sighed. "To do this, I knew I had to ask an indelicate question."

Sophie gathered his meaning immediately. "You needed to touch her, like the apples and the lily."

He nodded. "An indecent request. Unheard of. Yet, when she learned I was blind and heard about how I worked, she made the offer before I could even ask."

Lévèque looked away and Sophie completed his thought. "You accepted."

"Yes, and she assured me the faculty had already consented. Nevertheless, I suggested the master or other students be present in the studio to satisfy any concerns about propriety."

"What happened?"

"She was…remarkable. Beautiful." He closed his eyes. "I should have seen it coming."

"Seen what?"

He opened his eyes. "We fell in love."

Sophie swallowed, forcing down an inexplicable discomfort at hearing Jean-Claude had loved someone.

He leaned back and turned his blind eyes to the ceiling. "We began to meet outside class, beyond the oversight of others, sometimes painting, sometimes…" He drifted into silence.

Sophie cleared her throat to regain the artist's attention. "Did you finish the painting, the one of her?"

He blinked back to the conversation and faced her once again. "It was the only piece I've ever thought was good."

Her intrigue mounted. "May I see it?"

Lévèque's jaw tightened and his voice grew strained. "My professor, the master, found out I was seeing the girl outside class. He denied he had any knowledge of our arrangement. He knew how I worked and became furious. He insisted I'd seduced her, that I'd forced myself on her."

Sophie grew outraged on Lévèque's behalf but held her tongue.

"The professor wouldn't listen," Lévèque added. "He wouldn't believe we were in love." The artist clenched his hands into fists, appearing both eager to tell his story and pained at hearing himself tell it. "He didn't believe the painting was mine, said it was too precise to have been created by a blind man." Lévèque furrowed his brow. "I'd been painting since I was seven, before going blind at twelve. I was no fraud, and he knew better."

"What did you do?"

"We argued...we both had a temper." Lévèque shook his head. "Before I knew it, he'd driven his foot through my canvas, crushed my work beyond repair."

"No!" Sophie's own anguish mixed with the artist's. It was clear she would be unable to escape such feelings today.

Lévèque again leaned back in his chair, his voice less steady than before. "My professor was angry, and maybe rightly so. I came to learn the permission the girl told me she'd received from the faculty had never been granted—she'd never even asked for it." His voice fell to a whisper. "She lied to me."

"Why would she lie?"

"The professor was her uncle. She knew he'd find out—posed for me to make him angry, to show him he couldn't control her. She'd orchestrated the whole thing just to make him mad. She used me."

Sophie covered her mouth to stifle her shock, thankful the artist couldn't see the look she knew crossed her face.

Lévèque picked up the picture of the apples and stood. "I was asked to leave La Sorbonne." He returned to the closet. "I haven't drawn another person since. Landscapes and villages. Flowers and moons. That's what I paint."

Sophie now understood his reaction at her mention of La Sorbonne, his angry response when she'd argued it was a place to be respected. She wished she hadn't pressed her point, and feared Lévèque now faulted her for her belief.

"I'm...sorry," Sophie offered.

"I've never told that story to anyone."

She stared at him, felt his pain as if it were her own: dreams broken, hopes denied. It was a pain she knew well. He was alone and desperate for a connection.

Compelled by a clarity she couldn't place, she stood from the sofa and walked to the artist. When she reached him, she took his hand, placed it on her face, pressed it against her cheek and held it there.

"Paint me," she said, breaking his trance.

"Sophie," he whispered.

"Don't talk." Her heart pounded fiercely. "Just do it."

He opened his mouth as if to protest, but she stopped him. "I need this, Jean-Claude. Draw my face for my father, a canvas for when he returns."

The artist sat motionless, gray spots of blindness obscuring the warm blue of his eyes, storm clouds in an otherwise clear sky. When he said nothing, she feared she'd failed to convince him.

She released his hand and lowered her arms, expecting him to snatch back his hand from her face and scold her as foolish girl once again. However, Lévèque's hand remained just where she'd placed it upon her cheek. His blind eyes stayed fixed on her, locked in the moment. At last, he nodded.

"Very well."

He moved back to his easel and Sophie followed, perplexed when he dropped to his knees. He walked his fingers along the dark floorboards and traced the edges of a large square panel until he found a groove, carved into the floor, which he used to lift a creaking plank. With the plank set aside, Sophie saw it: a set of steps leading to a dark room beneath Jean-Claude's apartment.

"My studio," he whispered, and, with no further explanation, descended the steps into darkness.

Sophie drew a breath and held it, thrilled and afraid. She stepped down after him as though submerging herself in the Seine at night, her skin tingling as she arrived in the cool subterranean studio. Once there, she inhaled the air, thick with scents of oil paint and thinner.

Lévèque reached for a place in the center of the ceiling and pulled a beaded chain, giving life to a bare bulb that hung over the room. The staggering brightness sent shadows everywhere, contrasts sure to guide his art.

On the floor lay a white bed sheet, spattered with dried layers of colorful paint speaking of the artist's constant work. However, it was a blank canvas that sat on the easel beneath the bulb.

Lévèque silently walked to a sofa pressed against a far wall to retrieve a wooden chair that sat at its side. He brought the chair next to the easel, and turned to Sophie.

She took her seat on the chair, watching him wheel a large wooden cart onto the sheet, close to the canvas. The cart had been meticulously arranged with baskets and drawers, each filled with tubes and cans of oil paint, copper pots holding brushes, emptied bean tins now bursting with charcoal pencils, and small apothecary jars filled with a thick, translucent liquid.

He ran his hands over the cart like a conjurer, orienting himself to the position of its contents. From a tin, he retrieved a black charcoal pencil and returned to Sophie.

Without a word of direction, she knew what to do. She reached for his empty hand and, again, placed it upon her face.

This time, to her surprise, the artist's hand trembled. She felt his pulse in his fingers and understood he both wanted this and feared it as much as she did.

She shut her eyes and attempted, as she had before, to use senses other than sight to build a deeper awareness of the space around her. She held her breath as the artist's hand grew steady against her face.

The scratch of his charcoal revealed he'd connected with his canvas, joining her to his art. He glided his thumb along Sophie's cheek to her eyelids, over the curl of her lashes and across the bridge of her nose, learning her features.

Her skin thrilled to his touch, gooseflesh rippling along her arms, down her back. She tried not to shiver as Lévèque's hand moved with growing familiarity along her jaw and over her lips. It seemed his hand belonged there, upon her, that it had always traced the contour of her face, her mouth. She fought the urge to part her lips, to taste his fingers, to experience the flavor of his art as it was being made. Instead, she focused on the sounds around her, hearing the artist sketch more fervently now, sensing that Lévèque too was giving himself to the moment.

With each breath, she felt absorbed by him, translated by him into the language of his art, recreated in the echoes of his pencil—traces on his canvas matching the movement of his hand on her skin.

Although he was using a black pencil, she imagined her fears overtaken by color. Each scratch of his charcoal, each gentle caress of his hand on her skin, brought forward a new color in her mind, recrafting the portrait of doom she'd begun. Yellow painted over the gray soldiers who had marched into her home and delivered empty news. Green obliterated the black of shiva and her grandmother's bold dismissal of her father. Red vanquished the Germans, their planes, and their guns. Yet it was blue, Jean-Claude's favorite blue, that eased her anguish, warmed her, and filled her with courage.

His tenderness, these colors, these feelings, washed over her and calmed her like the warm water of Madame Lefavre's enormous copper bath. They blended like the oils from Madame's vials, creating, through some magic, a feeling she could not name, but one she could only share with Jean-Claude.

Lévèque moved his hand from her chin to her throat. When he brushed against the open neck of her blouse, however, his movements slowed. His hand continued to the back of Sophie's neck, to the hair she'd tucked behind her ear. She leaned her head forward, allowing him to bury his hand deep against her scalp, to lift her locks free, to run his fingers through her curls and set them loose to sway against her skin.

With each passing moment, she felt a deeper connection to Lévèque. The mood was undeniably intimate, and although the artist's touch was limited to her face, her hair, and her neck, she felt the effects of this intimacy throughout her body. She knew he must have felt something too, as the sounds of his charcoal took on a new rhythm: the beat of her heart.

Each pulse, each pencil scratch, transported her beyond the studio, away from France, away from war and the unknown fate of her father, to a place that glowed in shades of blue under the light of Lévèque's luminous moon. This place smelled of honey and lavender, her scents, a safe place where she could be herself alone with Jean-Claude.

As if hearing her thoughts, Lévèque quieted his charcoal. He stopped his movements and withdrew his hand.

In the sudden silence, she opened her eyes to find the artist's gaze locked on hers. His familiar square jaw, his crooked mouth, and those stormy blue eyes were all she could see—all she wanted to see.

She rose from the chair, but this time it was Sophie who touched the artist's face. She pulled him closer and, without a word, kissed him.

His lips were soft, his breath warm. He dropped his pencil to the floor, placed his hand on the small of her back and pulled her toward him, their hearts beating against one another. His strength, his passion—she felt them even more completely in his embrace, in his kiss, than she had in his touch.

Just as their feelings seemed to find expression, the artist stopped and stepped back.

"I can't," he whispered, and turned his head.

"What's wrong?"

"Your grief... Your father... You're not thinking this through. You're only here because you're upset."

"No," she said, "That may be why I came, but not why I stayed."

Lévèque turned and strode up the steps, into his apartment.

"Jean-Claude?" Sophie followed.

He hastened to his front door and pulled it open to the daylight. "You must leave," he said. "I'm sorry."

She wanted to argue, to make him understand that grief was not what drew her to him. However, from his posture, she saw that nothing she could say or do would sway him.

She understood after his story of La Sorbonne, his reaction was not about her, but about him. He'd learned to fear the intimacy they'd just shared. It reminded him of something wrong. For her, it was the only thing that ever felt right.

She walked to the door, but before she stepped through, she turned to him and whispered, "Thank you, Jean-Claude."

He held his head down and didn't respond, but she didn't need him to. She knew he cared for her, and for today, that was all she needed.

Chapter 16

The Rabbi Getzman

Sophie sat on her grandmother's loveseat, the apartment darkened by the sheets that still hung over the windows. She stared at Lévèque's painting over the buffet with one thought repeating in her mind: two weeks was long enough.

She'd taken Jean-Claude's advice and informed her grandmother she would not oppose shiva so long as her grandmother wouldn't expect her to grieve. Her grandmother seemed angry at first, but finally agreed. Since then, they'd hardly spoken, leaving one another alone in an uneasy alliance.

Sophie's acceptance of this arrangement, however, was based on her knowledge that shiva only lasted a week. Yet, for nearly fourteen days now, she'd obediently left the cooking for the evenings, left the sheets on the windows and towels on the mirrors, fighting the daily temptation to turn on the lights. Now, her patience was faltering.

Shiva required this dark isolation to keep those grieving from the distractions of the outside world, but the outside world was constantly on Sophie's mind. The radio, which she'd been secretly listening to in her bedroom for the last few days, had offered no comfort. Both Denmark and Norway had been invaded, the Germans had more planes than anyone could count, and Paul Reynaud had replaced Édouard Daladier as prime minister of France. Maybe the Americans would join the fray and help—at least that's what the newsman had said. Commentators worried for the safety of France, but reported that, with the Maginot Line refortified, there seemed little chance the Germans would dare challenge them. However, this news told her nothing of her father and offered no relief to her growing anxiety.

To combat her unease at home, she'd turned to a different obsession. Over the last several nights, she had again searched the apartment high and low for her mother's mysterious box. The key on her neck was calling her, urging her toward a fate she couldn't name. She'd ventured twice into her grandmother's bedroom after the old woman had nodded off on the couch. She'd searched the closet, peered under the bed, and rifled through her grandmother's dresser drawers. Nothing.

Now, after two weeks, she had to admit: it wasn't the war, her missing father, the mystery of her mother, or her grandmother's endless shiva that most occupied her thoughts. It was that remarkable kiss with Jean-Claude Lévèque. As with Madame Geneviève's chocolates, Sophie desired another and another…

She'd decided to stay away from Lévèque, long enough so he could no longer blame her amorous desires on misplaced grief, but wasn't two weeks enough? She was desperate to see him, to know if he longed for her as much as she longed for him.

"His work really does brighten the room—even this one." To Sophie's surprise, her grandmother stared over her shoulder, gazing at the moon on the wall, an unexpected smile on her face. "Monsieur Lévèque has a gift."

Sophie hoped her grandmother's change of mood meant her prolonged shiva was ending. "Maybe I'll see Jean-Claude today," Sophie ventured.

"Jean-Claude?" her grandmother repeated, a curious tone in her voice.

"I plan to go to town, to collect some things for dinner. I thought I might offer to pick up his groceries, too."

A peculiar look crossed her grandmother's face. "I suppose we could use some groceries."

"All right, then." Sophie answered. "I'll go now."

She rose, smiled at her grandmother, and retreated to the shadows of her room. She changed from her nightgown into an embroidered blouse, cotton skirt, and shoes, picturing Jean-Claude's face as she dressed.

In the bathroom, she pushed back a corner of the towel that hung in front of the mirror. She squinted at her dim reflection, ran a brush through her hair to tame her curls, and let the towel fall back in place.

"I won't be long, Grand-mère." Without waiting for a reply, she gave her grandmother's cheeks two quick kisses and dashed out the door, blinking into the bright light of the late morning.

She raced down the steps and rounded the corner, already imagining the taste of Lévèque on her lips. She strode to his apartment and knocked on his door, but to her disappointment, no answer came. She knocked again loudly, wondering if he was in his basement studio. Surely, before noon, he could be expected to be home.

"If you're looking for the blind man, he's not there."

Sophie turned to find Héloise, the butcher's older daughter standing behind her, her expression typically inscrutable, her blond hair pulled up in her signature bun.

"So it seems," Sophie replied.

At Héloise's side stood Céline, appearing to find protection in her big sister's shadow. Céline sneered, reminding Sophie that she'd threatened to eat Céline the last time the girl had been impolite with her.

"You like the blind man?" asked Céline.

"We're friends."

"Is he your boyfriend?"

Sophie turned pleadingly to Héloise. She hoped, after their last encounter at the butcher shop, that Héloise had become more sympathetic to Sophie, that she might reprimand Céline for asking such questions. Yet, Héloise stood silent, arms crossed, a thin eyebrow arched in judgment. It seemed she also wanted an answer.

"That's none of your business," Sophie snapped.

Héloise shot a look to her sister. "That means he *is* her boyfriend. Otherwise, she would've just said no."

Sophie rolled her eyes. "Don't you two have some place to be?"

"We just delivered a pork roast to Madame de Paul," answered Céline, twirling her curls. "You can't have pork."

"That's right." Sophie remained irritated by Céline's fascination with Jews.

"If you're looking for the blind man," Héloise interrupted, "we saw him with that orphan boy, Felipe, walking into town."

Sophie couldn't tell if Héloise was trying to be helpful or just matter-of-fact. She wasn't as direct or expressive as Céline, and Sophie decided this was Héloise's way of maintaining control over situations. She kept people guessing.

"And your shoes don't match." Céline rocked on the balls of her feet, stifling a laugh.

Sophie looked down and realized to her horror that, in her haste to leave the dark apartment, she'd grabbed two unmatched shoes. Another reason to hate shiva.

"He won't mind your shoes," Héloise added. "He's blind."

Sophie scowled. "I wasn't coming to visit Monsieur Lévèque."

"Then why were you knocking on his door?" Héloise tilted her head.

"I came to see if he needed something from town," she said, trying to sound nonchalant. Then, because it was the last place these girls would ever go, she added with flair, "I'm on my way to see the rabbi." That detail, she thought, would perplex the girls, satisfy their fascination with Jews, and send them on their way.

"The rabbi?" Céline smiled. "Rabbi Getzman?"

"Yes." Sophie had forgotten the name of the rabbi her grandmother said had given her the silver *Kaddish* cup in the cupboard, but she assumed Ville de Lemaire couldn't support more than one rabbi. "Getzman. That's him."

"Perfect," said Héloise. She raised the paper sack she carried. "Father asked us to deliver these kosher lamb chops to the rabbi. We can walk there together."

Sophie nearly swallowed her tongue. She looked at Céline's proud smile and knew her plan had failed. There was no avoiding the sisters now. "Fine," she grumbled. "Let's go."

As the unlikely trio strolled, the sisters gossiped about Madame Bavard's ridiculous hats and the clothes she knitted for her poodle. However, rather than participate in the discussion, Sophie grew increasingly anxious. Thanks to her inept lie, she'd have to find some pretense for visiting Getzman.

She'd really only known one rabbi in her life—the one in Avoine who'd led High Holiday services, the same horrible man who'd sat shiva with the Marcoux family when Madame Marcoux had died. The young rabbi, Rabbi Lipson, was a scholar from Orléans who was nicely groomed, spoke with precision, and used every opportunity to decry the dirty farm life of Avoine.

Sophie hated him.

Upon Madame Marcoux's death, Sophie and her father had brought a kettle of soup to the Marcoux house to pay their respects. While her father had spoken privately with Monsieur Marcoux, Rabbi Lipson had taken Sophie aside and told her he was happy to see her, commenting that he'd only ever seen her at holiday events and not at regular services. It seemed he'd been keeping track of such things.

Before she could find some clever excuse for her failure to attend temple, Lipson had explained with a wide grin that her visit was fortuitous and that he needed her help.

"You can be a good example to the Marcoux girls, you see?"

"Example?"

"You've also lost your mother." The rabbi's tone had implied this should have already occurred to her. "Why not sit with the girls, befriend them, help them through this pain?"

Sophie had never known her own mother, and didn't feel like her loss was the same as the Marcoux's. Besides, she hardly knew the girls. When Sophie shared this perspective with the rabbi, he'd grown stern and looked unrelentingly into her eyes.

"Don't you know the tale of Esther?"

"Of course," Sophie scoffed, recalling her Purim parties at the temple. "I love *hamantaschen*."

The rabbi had turned red and barked, "Purim isn't about cookies. It's about sacrifice. I'm talking about sacrifice like Esther's. She risked her life to save the Jews." He'd peered at her. "Don't you keep the Sabbath holy?"

"Sometimes."

"Don't you say the prayer for the bread, the wine?"

"Usually."

Just as the rabbi had appeared ready to explode, he leaned back in the Marcoux's living room chair, took a deep breath, and shook his head. "Never mind."

Sophie knew she'd confirmed the rabbi's suspicions. The goat girl was a lost cause.

Now, faced with the prospect of another rabbi's judgment, she feared Getzman would share Lipson's opinion of her. Could she handle another rabbi looking into her eyes and finding nothing but *hamantaschen*?

"Where are you going?" called Héloise. "The temple's down here."

Sophie stopped and turned to find Héloise and her little sister standing ten paces behind, facing a side street.

"Sorry. I was just daydreaming."

To her surprise, Héloise smiled. "I like to daydream too."

She imagined Héloise's daydreams would likely include carving up some animal for her father's *boucherie*, but rather than comment, she simply strode back to join the girls.

Together they walked down the paved street through the oldest part of town, between faded brick buildings with flaking mortar. There were clothes-lines overhead, shirts and pants swaying in the late morning breeze. Somewhere in an apartment above, a radio newscaster spoke over the rattling sounds of recorded gunfire, the hum of planes, and the boom of warfare. Her pulse rose with each blast. After a moment, the radio sounds of war were replaced by the blessed relief of static as someone changed the channel, and then by the bouncy trumpet of American Glenn Miller's "In the Mood."

Just as the street began to turn and the music started to fade, the girls stopped at a tall wooden door. It marked the entrance to a narrow building, sandwiched between an aromatic *boulangerie* and a boarded up dress shop.

"Here," Céline said, clearly puzzled by Sophie's lack of recognition.

It would have been easy for anyone to miss this temple if one didn't know to look for the Hebrew letters carved high over the door or notice the mezuzah bolted to the doorframe.

Héloise pushed open the door, its rusty hinges announcing their arrival. Inside, the temple seemed larger than it appeared on the outside. The dimly lit chamber had high ceilings and smelled of burnt wax and a distant, aromatic broth. Its walls were lined with wooden shelves holding dwindling candles, assisted in their duty by a few dingy lights that hung on cords from the ceiling. Rows of cushioned benches lined the floors; prayer books were arranged neatly on each seat. There was room for maybe thirty people, if Ville de Lemaire even had that many Jews.

On a platform in the back of the temple stood a podium, but it was the large cabinet beside it that drew Sophie's attention most—an ark for the Torah. The two-meter-tall, cherry wood cabinet presided over the room, its polished doors inlaid with painted glass depicting opposite sides of a large blue Star of David. The center of the star held a colorful image of the Ten Commandments, which seemed to hold all the light from the room, its beauty reminding Sophie of Jean-Claude's art.

"Ah, ladies!" A short, hunched man with a wiry gray beard and an unkempt mustache shuffled in from the shadows. He wore ragged bedroom slippers, black trousers, and a black silk yarmulke, which barely covered his bald spot. "Your timing is perfect."

He stopped and attempted to stuff an errant shirttail into his pants while fighting with his uncooperative suspenders. Sophie had to stifle a laugh.

"Forgive me," he proclaimed with a boyish grin. "Been in the kitchen. Completely lost track of time." In spite of the tangles of his beard, the rabbi's face was bright, youthful.

"Kosher lamb chops." Héloise held up her paper sack. "Salted as you like."

"*Très bien*, Héloise. Just in time for my lunch." He took the sack and held it as a treasure. "I see you've brought little Céline and…who is this?" He turned to Sophie.

"This is Sophie," Héloise said with her signature lack of emotion. "She needs to speak with you, so we invited her too."

"Is that so?" he grinned, viewing her more closely.

Sophie swallowed and looked at the man who stood hardly as tall as she did. To her relief, there was unmistakable kindness in his eyes, not the judgment she'd feared.

"Yes, Rabbi," Sophie managed. "It's…a personal matter." She turned to Céline who glowered.

"Very well, very well," the rabbi replied, "but may we speak in the kitchen? I have a few things cooking." The rabbi crammed his hand into his pocket, drew out a few franc notes, and handed them to Héloise. "Thank your father for me, eh?"

"Merci, Rabbi." Héloise folded the money in her fist and offered a polite curtsy. "Come, Céline."

"What about Sophie?" the young girl whined.

"I said, come." Héloise pulled her little sister toward the door, thwarting Céline's struggle to stay.

Once the Van Hoden girls had left, the rabbi nodded to the back of the temple. "This way."

In spite of Getzman's friendly demeanor, Sophie fought back a growing nervousness with each step, regretful she'd ever mentioned the rabbi to the girls. She recalled Narina's funeral pyre, when her lack of religious faith had led her to recite the prayer for bread instead of the *Kaddish*. Maurice hadn't noticed, but she couldn't get away with such a faux pas in the presence of a rabbi.

She followed Getzman around the platform to a door in the corner of the temple. As he pushed it open, the smell of broth and onions intensified, helping ease her apprehension. She'd always found Jewish food, rather than Jewish prayer, comforting.

"You like to cook?" asked Getzman.

"Oh, yes." She followed him into his kitchen, the counters stacked high with bowls and sticky measuring spoons. Pots boiled on the stovetop, and the sink carried a tower of dishes, poised to fall. Flour seemed to have exploded everywhere. "My grandmother has taught me a lot about cooking."

"Your grandmother?"

"Etta Claveaux."

"Etta!" Getzman exclaimed. "Of course, of course. You're *that* Sophie. Have a seat, have a seat." He pulled out one of the two chairs at the kitchen table, revealing a seat speckled with flour. He turned to the stove.

Sophie brushed the flour off the seat and clapped it from her hands before sitting. "You've heard of me?"

"Etta spoke of you just before Rosh Hashanah." He turned a knob on his stove to lower the flame beneath his pot of broth. "She told me months ago you were coming to live with her. Of course, I haven't seen either of you at services...I've been meaning to pay you a visit."

It seemed Sophie wasn't the only one negligent in her temple attendance. "I'm sorry, Rabbi. It's not that we haven't wanted to come. It's just that we've been quite busy."

The rabbi opened the oven and reached in with a match, igniting the gas with a *whoosh*. He turned to the cupboard in search of a dish. "Busy, busy," he replied enigmatically, and Sophie feared she'd disappointed yet another rabbi. Getzman dashed from cupboard to cupboard until he found some cooking oil. "I never seem to put things back where I found them."

Lost in his cooking, the rabbi drizzled the oil into a baking dish, used a wooden spoon to scoop the cleaned vegetables from his colander, sprinkled the concoction with ground pepper, and laid the salted lamb chops carefully in the middle, murmuring over the dish as if performing some Jewish ritual. He covered the dish with a glass lid, placed it in the oven, and twisted the timer dial.

Sophie thought he should have added some *herbes de Provence* but remained quiet about it.

The rabbi closed the oven and turned back to scan the kitchen. "Where was I?" When he spotted Sophie, he added, "Oh, right, Etta. Such a lady. Quite devoted, eh? Your father, have we heard from him yet? Is he well?"

She took a breath. "That's why I'm here, Rabbi. He's missing."

Sophie hadn't consciously decided to raise this issue, but it seemed the rabbi's kind demeanor and the comforting scents of his kitchen had brought it out.

The brightness in the man's eyes dimmed and he nodded solemnly. "I see."

"My grandmother's been sitting shiva for two weeks, but I don't want to sit shiva." Speaking her thoughts aloud brought back the pang of her grandmother's betrayal. "Not when I know my father's alive."

Getzman pulled out the second chair. It was also covered with flour, but he sat on it anyway. He reached to Sophie and cupped her hands in his. "Of course, my dear. Of course."

The magic aroma of the broth and the unexpected friendliness of the Rabbi seemed to open a floodgate in Sophie.

"How can she sit shiva, Rabbi? My father isn't dead and I think—" she stopped to swallow the pain, "I think it's horrible that she believes he is."

The rabbi fell silent. He lowered his head as though the action might draw an answer to his mind. After a moment he looked up.

"You wish to hold onto hope; your grandmother wishes to conduct the ritual of death. You see these as opposites."

"They *are* opposite. A person can't be dead and alive."

"Ah, but 'dead or alive' wasn't your question, was it?"

"It wasn't?"

"No, it wasn't." Getzman released Sophie's hands. "You're not asking me if your father is alive, are you? Because that, I can't answer." He cleared his throat. "Your question seemed to be whether Etta's response or yours was correct."

"Yes."

"Well, you must first ask yourself why that matters."

Sophie considered her reply, but only for a moment. "It matters because… because if he's alive, it's wrong to mourn him. He needs us to hope."

"What happens if we mourn the living?"

Getzman's question hung in the kitchen air, more palpable than his broth, stirring Sophie's irritation. "We don't mourn the living."

The rabbi looked into her eyes. "You're angry."

"Of course I'm angry!" Her outburst reverberated through the kitchen and she feared it was loud enough to topple the dishes in his sink. "To mourn means we let go, and—"

"—and if we let go, we lose them." His pronouncement stung and they each sat still for a moment. "That's what you think," the rabbi continued, "and I can see why you'd think that. If we use our prayers to help others, the corollary could be—if we stop praying, or accept the worst, we harm others. Is that what you believe?"

"Yes." Her voice came out as a whisper.

The rabbi leaned closer. "You think your grandmother is letting go while you're trying to hold on, pushing your father to death while you're pulling him to life. A tug-of-war, eh?"

"Yes." Tears began to blur her vision.

Getzman leaned back in his floured chair and softened his voice. He seemed to be a practiced philosopher and an able counselor. "Your grandmother's actions are behaviors, my dear, not beliefs. These aren't the same things."

"Her behavior shows what she believes. She believes my father is dead."

"Does she?" Getzman cocked his head like a curious dog.

Sophie wiped her eyes. "That's what I've been telling you. She's covered the windows and mirrors with towels. She's not cooking, hasn't left the house at all…Two weeks of shiva."

"What have you been doing?"

"Nothing!" She cringed at the force of her voice and tried again, softly, "I've been doing nothing."

"You've been doing something, certainly…What have you been doing while she's been home?"

Sophie didn't want to say she'd kissed a blind artist, daydreamed of his face, his touch…

"I've been doing the cooking, the shopping, the laundry."

"Going about your daily business. Busy with the chores."

"Yes."

"Ah, but these are rituals too, eh? Behaviors. Not beliefs. When people have no answers, they turn to their rituals. You turn to yours; your grandmother turns to hers."

Getzman's words reminded Sophie of Lévèque's advice—that she should simply allow her grandmother to sit shiva.

"What you both believe lies underneath all that," the rabbi added, "and here's the important part:" he lifted a finger to the air, "what we truly believe may not match how we behave." He gave Sophie a wink, as though he'd conveyed the point she was meant to understand…and suddenly, she thought she did—it was the lesson of Paris. It was the lesson of Monsieur Lefavre to Colette and the other ladies of the maison, that one's actions were not the same as one's beliefs.

All things in twos, even contradictory things. Hadn't Madame Lefavre taught her this? Hadn't Colette proven it true, just by being a heartless, yet loving woman, like the city itself?

Sophie's whole diversion through Paris seemed riddled with contrasts and contradictions. Yet, somehow, these blended and worked in harmony, just as Getzman's beliefs and behaviors. Like honey and lavender.

"Are you saying my grandmother is sitting shiva but doesn't actually believe my father is dead?"

"I'm her rabbi and her friend." Getzman lifted his chin. "If she believed her son had died, she'd have asked me to recite the *Kaddish*—the mourner's prayer—just as I did for her husband, your grandfather. She'd have followed shiva rules for a week, not two. And I don't think I'm arrogant or presumptuous to think she would have invited me over. These are Jewish traditions that she knows well."

Sophie's mind raced, her thoughts as cluttered as the rabbi's kitchen.

"Two weeks of shiva is unusual," Getzman added, "though it could be dismissed as the act of a deeply mournful person, but, my dear," he pointed again to the air, "there can only be one reason your grandmother didn't ask me to recite the *Kaddish*. She doesn't believe your father is dead."

The timer on the oven buzzed and Getzman smiled.

"Time to turn the lamb."

Sophie smiled, her anguish dissolving, a huge burden lifted. She realized, or at least finally admitted to herself, that her grandmother's opinion mattered; she needed her to have hope. "Oh, rabbi, how can I thank you?"

"Well," he donned a pair of padded floral oven mittens and walked to the stove, "maybe you can answer a question for me." He opened the oven to attend to the sizzling lamb, then seemed to realize he was missing something. He scanned the kitchen counter.

"A question for me?" Sophie stood, walked to the counter and handed him the slotted spoon.

"About that key on your neck." He took the spoon and used it to rearrange the lamb. "Does it fit the box your grandmother gave me?"

The small kitchen suddenly seemed to collapse on her with the unexpected revelation. "You have the box?" She clutched her key in her trembling hand.

The rabbi replaced the lid on the dish, set the spoon back on the counter, closed the oven, and faced her.

"Your grandmother brought it to me when you came to Ville de Lemaire, asked me to hold it until the key arrived." He removed his gloves and set them on the table. "Today you arrived here at the temple with that key around your neck. I thought it was the reason you came, not to ask me about shiva."

Her knees felt weak and she reached for the chair to keep her balance. "Please, Rabbi." She swallowed against the stone in her throat. "Show me the box."

Chapter 17

The Box of Secrets

Sophie raced back through the old part of town, the scent of the rabbi's broth lingering on her clothes. As she rounded each corner, she shot a look over her shoulder to assure the Van Hoden girls weren't waiting to pounce. She wanted solitude, a quiet place to be alone with the item that had vexed her since she'd left Avoine—her mother's mysterious box.

This day had brought nothing but surprises. She'd asked the rabbi questions to help her decipher her grandmother, to understand better the way to handle the fate of her father. Yet it was the secret of her mother she now held against her breast.

No larger than her hand, the box was carved from oak and was smooth to the touch. Its lid was inlaid with a painted porcelain tile, adorned with fleur-de-lis in blue and gold. She had chosen not to open it in front of Getzman, both out of her desire to disguise its importance and because she wanted that moment to herself. She'd declined his offer of lunch in spite of the food's miraculous aroma, explaining her haste as an eagerness to return to her grandmother. It was a lie the rabbi had accepted with a wide grin and a zealous embrace.

"We'll see you at services," he'd said.

"Of course," she'd replied, but this was no lie. She thought she owed him that much, this rabbi who hadn't judged her.

Now, free of his imposing kindness, Sophie had to find a place, a private place, to open the box.

"It contains things that will raise questions," her father had said, explaining under the shelter of the wet barn that they would open the box together upon his return from the war. Sophie had intended to honor his plan, but she was eager for news, any news, and this box was the very thing she needed. It was a message from her father about her mother, his voice trapped in the box like a message in a bottle. She knew she was breaking a promise, but she figured he'd understand her curiosity, her desperation... and forgive her.

Sophie took a breath, scanned her surroundings, realizing she'd wandered off the path home. The calm, quiet air infused with jasmine immediately told her where her heart had led her. She was standing in Lévèque's courtyard and his miraculous gazebo, the place she'd learned to see beyond senses. It was just the seclusion she needed.

She dashed to the latticed shelter to take a seat and placed the treasure on her lap. She unlatched her necklace to free the key from its chain. She then found the keyhole and, with a flick of her shaking wrist, opened the box.

The stale air that escaped the box invoked the same mystery as the art books she favored from her school's library, and yet the box contained only three items: a yellowing newspaper clipping, a photograph, and a letter tied with ribbon.

The clipping was a thumb's length tall and several centimeters wide, carrying a headline and a date, five months to the day after Sophie's birth. The headline read: "Woman's Body Found near River."

She set the clipping back in the box and reached for the photograph. It was a picture of her mother sitting on a porch swing, smiling. She was looking down at a baby—Sophie, several months old—lying in her lap, smiling back.

A wave of confusion washed over her, almost causing Sophie to faint. How could this be? Her mother had died during childbirth. How could such a picture exist?

Desperate for answers, Sophie snatched the last item—the letter. It was folded into a square and secured with a yellow ribbon, which she hurried to untie. The letter was crisp with age and crackled as she unfolded it.

My darling Gérard,

Why can't I be content? These thoughts of destruction are unbearable and I lack your strength to face them.

Since our dear Sophie was born, my despair has grown, my hold on this earth slipping. Life surrounds me and yet all I think of is death.

Doctor Lapointe's medicines make me weak, too tired to fight, and so I've stopped taking them. Nothing has worked, mon chéri, *and I fear nothing will.*

Last night I awoke standing over Sophie, a kitchen knife in my hand. Oh, Gérard. What if I had not woken?

I see now there is only one way to stop this, to find relief, to protect you both. . . Know, mon chéri, *that I adore you and our Sophie. It is for you both I say adieu. Adieu. Adieu.*

Yours,
Vivienne

She folded her mother's letter slowly. Tears slid over her cheeks, her lip trembling. She tied the yellow ribbon with care, working to assure the aged note remained safe, driven by a sudden need to protect the box and everything it held. With the newspaper clipping, photograph, and letter secured, she lowered the lid as if closing a coffin, locked the box, and returned the key to the chain on her neck, wishing she could return all things to the way they were.

Half-stunned, she rose from the bench, bit her lip to steady it, and struggled to piece together what she'd learned. Her mother had survived childbirth, had known Sophie, had written that she'd loved her; yet her mother was driven by some madness to harm her. The mysterious headline that accompanied the letter seemed to imply it was her mother whose body was found, that it was her despair that led her to die on the banks of the river. She had taken her own life instead of Sophie's.

Her father had assured her that her mother's death wasn't her fault. "Childbirth is always a risk to the mother," he'd said. "Sometimes women die; it's not the fault of the child, only the weakness of the woman's body. Nature took your mother."

Sophie had tried to accept this—her father would never allow a discussion to the contrary—but she'd always feared it was her own curse that had caused her mother's death. Now, she had proof. Despair brought on by Sophie's birth had driven her mother to death. Nature was innocent after all. It was Sophie who'd killed her, and no one—not her father nor her grandmother—had been honest with her. The goat girl was the bringer of death.

A new anger rose like a phoenix, filled Sophie's mind and her limbs with fire, forced her to walk, to leave the seclusion of the gazebo. Her pace increased until she found herself running, flying to Lévèque's as she cradled the box.

She pounded on the artist's door, the fury at her family's betrayal contained in her fist. After a moment, the door opened, but it was not Lévèque who answered.

"Yes?"

A thin boy, younger than Sophie, stood before her. He was small and sinewy, olive-skinned and curly-haired. He seemed to notice she was a girl and puffed up his chest. "Can I help you?" His voice had miraculously deepened.

"You must be Felipe," Sophie said, her anger momentarily easing. She recalled Héloïse saying she'd seen the orphan boy with Lévèque earlier that morning.

"Do I know you?"

"I'm Sophie. I live upstairs."

The boy smiled with apparent recognition. "Oh, Sophie." His voice returned to a more youthful pitch.

"Is he here?" she asked, peeking into the artist's flat.

"He's busy."

"It's important. I must speak with him."

"Monsieur left instructions for me to tell you he's busy."

"To tell *me*? Sophie?"

The boy frowned. "Those were his instructions. To tell you…if you came."

How could Lévèque still be distant? It had been two weeks since their kiss. Surely he was ready to face her again, to discuss the abrupt end to their amorous encounter. Sophie wondered if his temper had, again, bested him. What if he had used these past days to become resentful toward her, as he'd become toward the other woman who'd sat for him? Sophie's indignation returned at what felt like yet another betrayal.

"Fine," she spat. "Let him be busy."

Felipe seemed confused by Sophie's anger but didn't pursue it further. "Au revoir," he said, and closed the door.

She took a deep breath and turned to the street. Could no one face her with honesty? Could no one be trusted?

Sophie felt the smoothness of the box in her hand, rubbed it like a river stone, and understood its message. Like her mother, she was left to the clawing of her own erratic thoughts, left to fight her demons alone.

She strode around the building, took the stairs two at a time, and then threw the door open.

Her grandmother sat in the shiva-dark apartment, leaning forward on the loveseat, staring at Lévèque's canvas moon as if listening to it. At Sophie's dramatic entrance, her grandmother spun to face her.

"My dear, what's wrong? Has something happened?"

Sophie drew a hasty breath from the dim room, and tried to contain her rage. She closed the door, walked in, and set the box on the table in front of her grandmother.

The elder woman stared at the box, a clear recognition on her face. "I see."

"Why?" Sophie hissed in a whisper. "Why did you lie to me?"

Her grandmother stared at the box as if in a trance. "Yes," she said after a long moment. "I suppose it's time." She pointed to the spot on the loveseat next to her. "Sit down, my angel."

Uncertain if she was willing to let her fury subside, Sophie gritted her teeth and took a seat.

"Do you know the meaning of the *Chai*—the Jewish symbol?" her grandmother asked. She reached beneath the collar of her blouse and withdrew a small necklace. Pinched between her fingers she held the Hebrew letters—the *Chet* and the *Yod*—wrought in a silver charm, attached to the necklace. She held it up for Sophie to see.

"Yes," Sophie replied. "Papa wears one, too. He says it means 'life.'"

"The cornerstone of Jewish belief," her grandmother added. "Chai is the gift God gives us when we're born and the one thing he asks us to care for until we die—life." She turned her eyes back to the box on the table. "Your mother—" her voice waivered, "that became a hard task for her."

Sophie recalled her mother's final words, lamenting her thin grasp on the earth, the despair she'd felt.

"It happens sometimes to women who bear children." Her grandmother's voice softened. "A dark curse even doctors don't understand."

When her grandmother used the word "curse," Sophie's heart sank. She was the curse. Unlike the doctors, Sophie understood.

"For women like your mother, feelings become confused when the child comes. They don't share the full joy of motherhood, but instead forget their gift. They forget to cherish life and the love it represents…They lose themselves to darkness."

Sophie's anger had now been supplanted by guilt, and yet she still felt the sting of her family's betrayal. "Why didn't you tell me?"

"My dear, some believe a suicide is a sin, a refusal of God's gift, a denial of life itself."

Suicide…the word bounced around in Sophie's head like a silk moth trapped in a jar.

"The rabbi that sat with us assured us your mother's death was forgiven for its circumstance, that Judaism allows for such tragedies. However, not everyone shared his belief, not even other rabbis. Even today, such a death can bring shame on an already grieving family."

Sophie swallowed. "That's horrible."

"Your papa chose to call her death an accident, to sit shiva without shame, to ask others to honor her, not to judge her or pity her. He saw the gifts in her life she couldn't see for herself."

"Why didn't he tell me?"

"How does someone tell a girl such a thing?"

"I'm eighteen in a month, Grand-mère. I'm not a girl."

"Not anymore. So I see." Her grandmother gave her a tentative smile and grasped her hand. "You must understand some secrets are easier to keep than they are to speak."

Yes, Sophie thought. I do understand.

Her grandmother pointed to Sophie's necklace. "When you arrived in Ville de Lemaire, that key on your neck, I knew what it was. I saw you wanted answers, but it didn't seem right to share your mother's secret without your father."

Sophie lifted her chain over her head and placed it in her lap. She stared at the key, feeling a pang of remorse at opening the box without her father, stealing from him his chance to explain it all in the way he had intended. Perhaps she was still a petulant girl after all.

Her grand-mère looked again to the box. "Rabbi Getzman was kind enough to take the box from me. I knew if I kept it here with me, a clever girl like you would find it." She looked into Sophie's eyes. "I should have realized you'd find it anyway."

Sophie didn't want to confess that it was entirely by accident, and not through cleverness, that she'd come upon the box. The Van Hoden girls were the ones to credit. Instead, she wanted more answers.

"How did it happen, Grand-mère? How did she...die?"

"You were five months old, asleep in your crib," her grandmother sighed. "Your father was on his way home from town. As far as we could tell, your mother put you to bed, walked to the river with a rope, and climbed a tree." Her grandmother swallowed. "They searched through the night until they found her, a kilometer from the farm. The note was in the box she left for your father under his pillow."

Sophie exhaled, realizing she'd been holding her breath. How many times had she climbed the trees by the farm, tossed sticks into the river while lounging on a bough, letting nature ease her fears and entertain her dreams? Now, it all seemed macabre, the idea of dreaming in the same place her mother had taken her life.

"In her picture," Sophie said, "the one I found in the box, she was smiling at me when I was a baby. She looked happy."

"Oh, my darling," her grandmother cried, "she was happy...at least sometimes."

"Do you think she loved me," Sophie choked, "like her letter said?"

Her grandmother leaned forward and embraced Sophie. "I *know* she did, my angel. She loved you more than her own life."

Her grandmother's words, her emphatic hold on her, did not offer comfort. Rather, they only served to deepen her anguish. Was she destined to bring loss and death to her grandmother, and her father too? Perhaps it was Jean-Claude's keen senses that inspired him to push her away, to fear for his own life—and who could blame him?

Her grandmother peered at her. "What's the matter, angel? Tell me what you're thinking."

"Everything ends," Sophie wept, her anger now replaced by a sense of doom. "Everything can be taken away. Especially the good things."

"Oh, my dear. My dear. Let's not speak that way."

She felt nauseous and upset all at once, felt as if she'd finally swallowed a pill she'd resisted her whole life. "Is he dead?" Sophie gasped between sobs. "Is Papa really gone?"

Have I killed him, too?

Her grandmother withdrew her embrace, but clutched Sophie's hands, stared at her as if reading her. "No." Her voice was stronger than it had been in days. "No," she repeated. "I refuse to think that."

Sophie wiped her face. "Then the rabbi understood. You think there's hope?"

The old woman raised her head. "You were right, child. Right all along. If there's one man that can survive this godforsaken war, it's your father." Her eyes widened and she seemed surprised to hear her own words. "Yes," her grand-mère confirmed, "I do think there's hope. There's always hope as long as we continue to cherish life. As long as we have love. I was wrong to call for shiva."

Sophie cleared her mind, tried to ease her aching heart and accept her grandmother's words. Something inside her did feel hope, still embraced it, in spite of the day's terrible revelations, in spite of her guilt.

"Take this." Her grandmother lifted the chain that carried the Chai and draped it over Sophie's head, replacing her key. The charm eased its way down the necklace to find its place at Sophie's breast. "A reminder of your gifts...A reminder to place life above all else."

A knot hardened in Sophie's throat. She looked first at the key that sat on her lap, the one that had unlocked her curse. She then touched the Chai that adorned her neck, a new hope for life. Which was her fate?

Her grandmother wiped away tears and reached for her cane. She stood from the loveseat and turned to Sophie. "Well," she huffed, "don't just sit there. Let's take those sheets off the windows and get cooking. We've got a tarte to make."

After indulging in a dinner of tarte aux pommes and vanilla tea, Sophie felt the darkness of the last two weeks ease, owing in part to the windows that were now free from their sheets, and in part to her grandmother's newfound energy. She shared stories of Sophie's father, embellishing his moments of bravery and laughing at tales of his foolhardiness, some of which Sophie had never heard. It was just the diversion she needed.

Sophie learned with perverse joy that, as a boy, her father had been bitten on his rear end by a goat. "He walked funny for a month," her grandmother chuckled. "Your grand-père teased him, saying he should have become a Christian and turned the other cheek." Her chuckle grew to a howl.

"No wonder Papa makes me care for the goats," Sophie laughed. "He hates them more than I do!"

"Oh, dear!" Her grandmother used a napkin to wipe her tears of laughter.

"What about his shoulder?" Sophie asked. "He's never explained why it hurts all the time."

Her grandmother poked the remnant crumbs of the tarte with her finger and licked them off. "He's never told you?"

"No," Sophie replied. "He just makes me rub it at night when the weather's cold. Says it's an old injury. I always figured he hurt it in the service."

"Your father hurt that shoulder the night he met your mother."

Sophie's stomach fluttered with anticipation. It was rare she heard tales of her parents' courtship, and tonight she longed for such a story more than ever. "Tell me!"

"Well," her grandmother began, "your father saw your mother at a spring dance and quite fancied her, but she was there with another boy...What was his name?" Her grandmother looked to the ceiling as though the boy's name might be written there.

"It's not important, Grand-mère. Get on with it!"

Her grandmother smiled. "All right, dear. All right." She leaned forward. "Your mother walked away from the dance with this boy to a neighbor's barn." She lowered her voice conspiratorially. "I think she intended to kiss him."

Sophie giggled. "Grand-mère!"

"Your father, as impulsive as he is, followed them and snuck behind the barn—to do what? I have no idea."

Sophie had never thought of her father as impulsive. Rather, he seemed deliberate, conservative, and untrusting of dreams, at least hers.

Her grandmother chortled. "Somehow, your father climbed up the back of that barn and into the hay loft. The boy with your mother sat on a bale and held her hand. Then, just as that boy leaned in to kiss her, your father lost his footing and fell from the loft, straight into your mother's lap!"

Her grandmother slapped the table and they burst into uproarious laughter.

"No!"

"It's true." Her grand-mère shook her head and chuckled. "The way your mother told the story, it was that very fall that made her love your father. It took his shoulder three months to heal and, as you know, it never did heal right. But he didn't mind. He said it was a fair price for winning Vivienne."

Sophie wished she could rub her father's shoulder tonight, just like she did at home.

Her grandmother stood. "Thank you for indulging me in these stories, my dear. I love talking about your father, but I'm thoroughly exhausted."

"Of course. Get some rest, Grand-mère. We can talk more tomorrow."

Sophie retrieved her grandmother's cane and handed it to her, kissing her on both cheeks, grateful they'd reconciled.

Once her grandmother had retreated to bed, and the sounds of her shuffling were replaced by the old woman's snores, Sophie sat on the sofa, alone once again with her thoughts.

She pulled a blanket from the edge of the sofa, wrapped it around herself, and turned to face Lévèque's bright canvas moon.

The story of her parents' romance reminded her how badly she'd left things with Jean-Claude. He was a man of many gifts, but also a man with a past, a man with an unrefined passion, a man with fears of his own. Like her, Lévèque had a temper, was prone to drawing quick conclusions, had lost his mother, and harbored a heart that had known pain and loss; yet these familiar traits only made her care for him more.

She laid her head on the fringed sofa pillow, closed her eyes, and recalled Madame Lefavre, struggling with similar thoughts about Maurice. Madame had wondered if, in spite of the gravedigger's harsh exterior, he carried within him a heart that was worth loving. Was he a good man? A man she could love? A man worth the risk?

Now, Sophie had to ask herself the same question about Lévèque. Is he a good man, and, knowing his flaws, could she love a man like that?

Perhaps her love for him, a life with him, would break the curse. She fingered the Chai that had replaced her mother's key. Yes, she thought. She could love a man like that, believed she already did—and tomorrow, she would tell him.

Chapter 18

The Dark Parade

Sophie awoke disoriented, the dim light of dawn bathing the living room, washing away the shiva. Once again, she'd fallen asleep in her day clothes to awake on the sofa under the complex stare of Lévèque's canvas. The sight of it reminded her—today she hoped to set things straight with him, to confess her love and embrace her life, to break her curse.

Before she could rise, a loud rumble startled her, like tractors from the farm, but a fleet of them, groaning as if in some mechanical pain. She dashed to the window where she could see only rolling clouds in the dawn sky. Yet, across the distance and over the countryside, past the farmhouses and the mills, a deep grinding noise pierced the morning, growing louder as if approaching quickly. She raced to her bedroom to grab a sweater, even as the disturbance intensified.

Her grandmother hobbled out of her bedroom, threading her arms into the sleeves of her housecoat and leaning on her cane.

"What's happening, child?"

"I don't know."

Sophie strode to the door and opened it to the bleak morning. She focused her eyes over the meadow, straining to find the source of the noise.

There, cutting between the trees some hectares away, was a line of black vehicles—tanks—moving in and out view, heading toward Ville de Lemaire. They lumbered along the wooded path like a herd of rhinoceros and seemed equally out of place in the French countryside.

"*Les militaires?*" her grandmother asked, squinting.

Sophie thrilled at the sudden thought that her father might be returning, bringing with him the troops he'd fought to protect, a procession befitting a hero.

The dark hulls of the muddy tanks absorbed the morning sunlight. Automobiles and a string of large canopied trucks followed, seemingly designed to carry soldiers. The convoy suddenly left the dirt road, climbed into the small grove, and smashed over the tall grass and wildflowers, the tanks churning black smoke into the birdless sky.

The smell of motor oil rode the morning wind and reached Sophie just as she scrutinized the line of machines, in search of her father.

Then she spotted it. At the front of the dark parade was a sight that took her breath away: a large crimson flag bearing the swastika.

As if in response to her horror, Madame Bavard cried out from her apartment across the road.

"*Les Allemands!*" Madame Bavard leaned out her window, her hair in curlers. "The Germans!" Her poodle began barking in fits.

The armored vehicles drew closer, their rattling engines seeming responsible for pumping the blood faster through Sophie's veins. Murmurs rose from the houses and flats. People ran, home to home, knocking on doors to awaken their neighbors.

Lévèque raced into the street at the foot of the stairs, tucking his shirt into his rumpled trousers. It seemed he, like Sophie, had fallen asleep before making it to bed.

"Jean-Claude!" she cried.

"Sophie!" He spun to face her. "What's happening?"

She descended the steps and then stopped halfway. The sight of him and the reminder of her wish to confess her love added a layer of emotion to her panic.

"The Germans have come!" she shouted over the rumble. "They're driving tanks through the meadow!" She realized that Captaine Netoine and her father had been right. The Germans were coming from the north.

"Come down!" he called. "Bring your grandmother!"

Without wasting a moment, she dashed up the steps, but her grandmother was no longer standing there. Sophie ran into the apartment where she found her, crouched on the floor, in front of the lower kitchen cupboards, throwing cans into a rucksack.

"During the Great War, we needed cans!" Her voice was unsteady, her hands trembling.

The gnashing metallic sounds of the tanks now filled the air.

"Not now, Grand-mère! You must come."

Without further protest, her grandmother allowed Sophie to pull her up. She grabbed her cane and the half-filled sack of food and they scurried out the door, down the stairs to Lévèque's apartment, uncertain what magic the artist could perform in the face of such advancing evil.

When they arrived, Lévèque's door was open and, as they entered his home, they found him kneeling on the floor with his back to them.

"What are you doing?" exclaimed Sophie. "We have to run!"

"No," Lévèque said without turning. "There isn't time. You must hide."

With his intuitive artist's fingers, Lévèque once again traced the floorboards to find the handle of the floor plank permitting access to his basement studio. He pulled it open and then rose from the floor.

"Hide here," he commanded. "I'll cover this panel with a rug."

"You'll do what?"

"For two people, you'll find four days' rations—five if you're thrifty, but you mustn't raise lights or make noises, no matter what you hear."

"Two people?" her grandmother asked. "What about you? Aren't you hiding?"

"No."

Sophie's throat tightened with horror. "Why? Where will you go?"

"I've made a terrible mistake. Yesterday, I asked Felipe to send you away so I could finish painting."

Sophie recalled the pain of his dismissal, delivered at his door by the young Felipe.

"When I was through, it was Felipe I sent away," Lévèque hung his head, "to allow us time alone. I had planned to speak with you last night, to apologize," he sighed, "but I lost courage."

"Felipe?" her grandmother asked, ignoring Lévèque's remark about being alone with Sophie. "The orphan boy?"

"He helps with my chores. Some days, I allow him to stay here." Jean-Claude turned his blind eyes to Sophie. "Last night, I paid him to stay away. Now…" His voice trailed off with emotion.

"It's too dangerous for you," Sophie said, releasing the artist from further explanation. "You can't go."

"I agree," her grandmother declared. "It's reckless and—forgive me, monsieur—you can't see."

Sophie knew, in spite of his blindness, Lévèque had used the light of the moon to learn the lay of the town. Nevertheless, her grandmother's point was fair. A blind man, even an adept one like Lévèque, would be no match for a dozen tanks and a troop of soldiers—a procession that now thundered down a nearby street.

Lévèque frowned. "Felipe's alone with no protection, Madame, and it's my fault. I must find him and bring him back."

"Where's Felipe gone?" Sophie couldn't hide the desperation in her voice.

"I sent him to stay at the temple."

"That's halfway across the village," her grandmother implored. "It's crazy."

"The temple—" Sophie had a sudden fear for her new friend, Rabbi Getzman, knowing how Germans were targeting Jews. "It's too dangerous."

As if to make her point, the rumbling in the village grew so loud, Lévèque's windows began to tremble in their panes.

"I won't rest until Felipe is safe," snapped Lévèque, not answering their concerns. "Now, quickly. Go. Remember, no sounds. No lights."

Sophie's grandmother let out an audible huff of frustration and clutched Sophie's arm. There seemed to be no convincing Monsieur Lévèque.

Unable to gather the frayed strands of her thoughts into a tidy knot, Sophie reluctantly followed the artist's directions. She pulled her grandmother closer and helped her descend the steps into Jean-Claude's studio.

Once at the foot of the steps beneath the floor, she surveyed the space where she'd sat for Lévèque a few nights before, taking a quick inventory: two chairs, a small couch, his paint cart with supplies, a wash basin, a pitcher, a spouted barrel of water, a table carrying three wide candles and a box of matches. Her eyes moved to the corner where she saw, facing the wall, Lévèque's easel—the one she presumed carried the same canvas he'd begun on their last night together.

Sophie turned back, climbed up a step and reached for him.

"Jean-Claude..."

Lévèque looked down from his apartment with a longing in his eyes, his blind stare missing her precise location.

"Yes?"

She moved up another step and reached for his cheek just as she had done on that wonderful night they'd shared.

"Return to me," she whispered. "Be safe."

Lévèque lowered his lids and nodded as if the canvas of the moment were too full to warrant another stroke.

He then took a step back, letting Sophie's hand fall. He lifted the panel from the floor and lowered it into place, giving her one last glimpse of him, a last portrait to cling to as he shut her away.

With the plank returned, only a single beam of morning sunshine pierced the dark basement from his apartment above. However, as Lévèque rolled out a rug over the floorboards, that last light was stolen and everything went cold.

She drew a long breath and turned to face the studio. "Grand-mère?" she whispered through the darkness.

"On the couch."

"The candles and matches next to you, can you reach them?"

"Yes, but you heard Monsieur Lévèque—"

"Please, Grand-mère, I need to see something."

With a sigh, her grandmother complied, striking a match against the matchbox. A sudden flash settled into a flame and she lit one of the candles. "There." She peered at Sophie through the winking flame. "What do you need to see?"

Sophie stepped over, lifted the candle from her grandmother without a word, and carried it to the corner of the room, where she'd spotted Lévèque's easel facing the wall. Using her free hand, she turned the easel on its wheels to reveal Lévèque's portrait of her, now complete.

He had recreated her in the Impressionist style using thousands of broken brush strokes, each a variant shade of blue. Her lips were parted in a half smile, the length of her neck exposed, her hair pulled over her ear, her eyes closed in bliss—a perfect impressionistic account of her magical night with Jean-Claude.

It seemed the image was meant to be viewed this way, surrounded by darkness, illuminated by an intimate flame, seen, perhaps, the way Lévèque saw her, in the color she created in his mind.

"*Mon Dieu*," her grandmother exclaimed, now standing next to Sophie. "He loves you."

Sophie broke her trance, now aware of her racing pulse and the tears on her cheeks. "What?"

"I may be an old woman, *ma chère*, but I'm no fool." The flickering light caught a glint in her grandmother's eyes. "Monsieur Lévèque loves you."

Before Sophie could gain her composure, before she could respond, the moment was shattered by the rattle of gunfire somewhere above.

The *rat-a-tat* sounds on the street sent echoes overhead, noises Sophie knew from the broadcasts of the war, sounds that now warned of danger. She grabbed her grandmother's arm, rushed back to the sofa, and blew out the candle, placing it on the floor. As they sat in the darkness, she clasped her grandmother's hand, working to allay her fears and stay calm.

Once again, she closed her eyes. Using Lévèque's technique for heightening her perceptions, she reached out for the sounds to gain some detail of what was happening outside fearing as much for the artist as for herself and her grandmother. She listened past the rattling windows, past the chatter of guns, beyond the cries of the villagers dashing through the streets, until she heard something even more unsettling than the sounds of gunfire. The growling voices of men, rough and course, bellowed in German as they drew near. She opened her eyes and turned to her grandmother. "They're here."

Her grandmother swallowed audibly.

The reverberation of tank engines and automobiles grew, replacing the thoughts in Sophie's mind until it felt as though the windows in Lévèque's apartment would shatter. Finally, when the walls of the building seemed ready to crumble, the noises stopped.

It was as if someone had lifted the gramophone needle off a record. Gone were the tank sounds, the cries of the villagers, the gunfire, the bellowing. Sophie strained to hear even a subtle noise past the throbbing in her head, but no sound came. A silent pressure built in her ears until a deafening crash sounded out.

Someone had broken into Lévèque's apartment.

Her grandmother squeezed her hand tighter, both of them stifling any sound that might betray them. Sophie tried to quiet the trembling in her legs for fear it would only make her grandmother more afraid.

Men barked to one another as they clamored through Lévèque's apartment, knocking items over, breaking them. The thud of heavy boots pounded on the floorboards and sent echoes into the studio. Dust fell from the basement ceiling. One man called, *"Nichts. Keiner da,"* and another called out, *"Nichts. . .Nichts."*

Sophie didn't understand German. The language always seemed angry to her, absent the music and poetry of French. Today, this seemed truer than ever. When the voices faded, she heard dishes break, a loud huff and again, silence. The rumble of the vehicles returned, but moments later those too faded. Whatever damage they'd done, the Germans had left Lévèque's.

"Grâce à Dieu," her grandmother said, at last letting go a breath. "Monsieur Lévèque saved our lives."

"I want to look," Sophie whispered.

"It's not safe, child. We must wait."

Her grandmother was right, and Sophie struggled to tame the nagging desire to know what was happening above.

Minutes passed, then an hour, and then more. They didn't speak, instead listening for any sound that might reveal the state of the village. The lack of noise and conversation permitted Sophie's darker thoughts to take root, visions of what horrible fate might befall Jean-Claude. What unspeakable things could happen to a blind man alone in a village overrun by Nazis? What would Nazis do to such a man, especially one who was a Jew?

Her grandmother rubbed her arm, perhaps sensing Sophie's mounting tension. "Don't fear, *ma chérie*," she whispered. "Lévèque's clever. He'll find Felipe."

Her grand-mère's words were of no comfort. What if Sophie had missed her only chance to confess to Jean-Claude what she held in her heart? Could love unspoken be love at all? Without embracing love, would she ever break her curse?

Unable to contain herself any longer, Sophie stood from the couch, reached to the matches and lit one, the smell of burnt phosphorous rising in the air. "Forgive me, Grand-mère," she said. "I can't sit a moment longer."

Her grandmother looked first to the ground, then up through the match light Sophie. "My child, he told us to wait. It's too dangerous."

"You saw his painting, Grand-mère. You said he loved me."

Her grandmother looked back to the floor, clearly conflicted.

"Don't you see?" Sophie cried. "I love him too."

Anguish washed over her grandmother's face. "I know. Of course, I know."

Sophie blew the match cold before the flame reached her fingers and took her grandmother's hand. "Every minute that passes may be the minute he needs me. How can I feel safe when I know he isn't? I have to go."

Her grandmother kissed Sophie's hands, then kissed them again. "I'm afraid."

"I am too, Grand-mère. But that's not important. Life is important. You taught me that." Sophie recalled the Chai that now rested against her skin. "Once I find Jean-Claude, we'll both return."

Her grandmother gave a rattling sigh. "Promise me."

"With all my heart," whispered Sophie.

Without allowing her grandmother another moment to protest, she moved through the darkness with outstretched arms, groping to find her way to the stairs. She climbed to the top and pushed on the floor plank above her head. To her surprise, she was only able to lift the board a few inches. The rug Lévêque had strewn over the panel remained.

Slowly, she slid her hand through the space and managed to flip the rug back enough to allow a beam of sunlight into the studio. The sudden brightness startled her.

"Steady!" her grandmother whispered.

Sophie blinked away her momentary blindness, regained her footing, and attempted again to move the plank. It appeared a piece of furniture in the sitting room had fallen on top of the rug and panel, blocking her exit.

She turned to her grandmother. "Your cane? May I borrow it a moment?"

The old woman stood, squinted into the new light and handed it to Sophie. "Are you sure no one's about?"

"I'm only sure of what must be done."

Her grandmother gave a hesitant nod. "Be careful."

Sophie slipped the cane through the opening and used it to maneuver the plank, clearing ample space through which to climb. She handed the cane back to her grandmother. "Promise me you'll stay here, Grand-mère."

"I will."

"Then I'll see you soon." Sophie smiled.

"Just be careful." Her grandmother's cheeks were wet with tears.

Without further word, Sophie hoisted herself out of the studio and into Lévèque's apartment, her heart protesting her actions. She flipped the rug back to obscure the panel and turned to the room around her.

As her vision cleared, she was shocked by the sight of tumbled furniture and debris. The artist's home, once perfect and organized, was now in shambles. His front door had been rent from its hinges, allowing in a cool breeze. His kitchen reminded her of the rabbi's kitchen, but the mess, the broken door, and the splintered furniture did not affect her as profoundly as what she saw in the middle of the room. Lévèque's beautiful canvases, taken from their easels, lay in a heap, torn and slashed, damaged beyond repair.

Her determination to find Lévèque overtook her. She clenched her teeth, set aside her fear, and climbed over the broken furniture to reach his empty doorway.

She craned her neck around the doorpost. Judging from the sun, it was now late afternoon. The street was empty of people and eerily quiet. Wooden shutters lay in the street. Broken glass was everywhere. Crushed bicycles in the gutters bore the footprint the tanks had left. If the Nazis were anything, they were thorough.

Sophie glanced up the stairs to her grandmother's apartment to see their home did not escape the Germans. Their doorpost was cracked, the mezuzah on the door missing, replaced by a wide gash as if a bear had clawed away any mark that a Jewish family lived there. Perhaps it was Lévèque's mezuzah that had drawn destruction to his door as well.

Her grandmother was right. Lévèque had saved their lives.

Sophie gripped the Chai that hung on the chain around her neck, pulled it over her head, and kissed its cool surface. Life was all that remained. Life was what now called to her. She walked the steps to their broken door and hung the chain on the door handle as if to replace the mezuzah that had been destroyed, a quiet victory over the Germans. Life would prevail; she would see to it.

Sophie turned to the street, to her hope for Lévèque's safety. Once certain she could move freely, she dashed down the steps and across the road to the alley behind Madame Bavard's building. The old woman's dog was no longer barking.

Sophie shook away the thought and crept among the shadows to the next building and the next, angling toward the town center, searching for some sign of Jean-Claude.

If he was seeking Felipe at the temple on any other day, he'd head straight through town, a path he surely knew from his evening jaunts under the moonlight. Today, however, Lévèque would have understood he'd be stopped if he took that route. The long path, the one unlikely to be traveled by the Germans, and the one he likely knew the least, was behind the blacksmith's shop and around past Madame Lalonde's *fromagerie*. That, she thought, was the route her man of reason would take.

Assured of her thinking, Sophie rounded the alley to be affronted by the unmistakable aroma of cheese. "Like the feet of angels," she recalled Madame Lalonde saying. "The smell of heaven." If Sophie were Lévèque, this smell would be an excellent guide. Luck seemed to be favoring her.

However, when she got to the *fromagerie*, she saw why the aroma was so strong from so far away. The back door had been left open to the alley.

She entered with care and noticed the front window had been shattered and that *clochettes* of goat cheese, wheels of Gruyère, and wedges of Comté were melting and sweating in the afternoon sun, absent the usual protection the window and curtain provided.

Shaken by sight of such a familiar place unmade, Sophie stepped carefully through the store, crushed glass crackling underfoot. Once she reached the counter, she found the door to the stock room ajar.

"Madame Lalonde?" she whispered over the pounding sound of her heart, but no answer came. She moved to the door and pushed it back carefully. "Madame—?"

Before she could open the door fully, it struck something on the stockroom floor. The once lively proprietor lay there, a single slit across her throat, opened like a second mouth, spilling blood. Madame Lalonde's eyes stared to the sky and to the heaven of which she'd spoken.

Sophie's stomach convulsed. She rushed back into the shop, nausea causing her to retch. She grabbed a cloth from the counter to wipe her face clean, and tried to regain her composure. There would be time to mourn Madame Lalonde later, she told herself. Now, she needed to focus on finding Jean-Claude.

She stepped toward the front of the shop, fighting to clear her mind. Through the broken storefront window, she had a clear view of old part of town and the hillside behind it. Lévèque was at the temple, she thought. He had to be.

Driven by a renewed concern for his safety, she stepped out of the shop and into the road. Three steps out, she heard, "Halt!"

Sophie spun, panicked, toward the source of the voice—a Nazi soldier who stood only feet away.

He raised a black pistol and spoke in rough, rudimentary French. "Where are you go?"

Fear made her mouth turn dry. "I...I'm looking for my friend."

The soldier, a man of average height and wide forearms, curled his lip. "Perhaps your friend in there." He waived his pistol over his shoulder toward a truck that had escaped Sophie's view from the *fromagerie*. "You look?"

When Sophie didn't reply, the soldier took a step back and pointed his pistol again toward the vehicle, this time more emphatically. "There!"

With no apparent choice, she forced her unsteady legs to obey.

The carrier was as big as two tractors, large enough to carry a dozen soldiers, its metal frame covered with a dark canvas that bore the Nazi swastika. At the rear of the truck stood another soldier—a hulking man, nearly a foot taller than the first, a rifle hanging from his shoulder. His cap sat low on his brow, obscuring the look in his eyes, but from his sneer she surmised this soldier enjoyed his job.

"Inside," the large man said, and shoved her between the shoulders toward the carrier.

She stumbled, but grabbed the frame of the truck to keep from falling. She faced the canopied compartment and lifted the canvas door aside with an uncertain hand.

In the dim compartment, seated inside, were not the Nazi soldiers she'd expected, but local men and women, people like Sophie taken from the village. They were huddled in groups, some embracing one another, others crying. Though hard to discern faces, she saw an elderly woman, the woman closest to her, clutching a rosary.

Sophie whirled back to the shorter soldier with the pistol standing below her. "My friend's not in there."

The soldier scowled and struck her across the cheek. "In!" he barked. "Now."

The sting in her face called for attention, but she resisted the urge to touch it. She didn't wish to give the Nazi the satisfaction of her reaction. Instead, she turned away, back to the frightened prisoners. It was clear she had no options. She was one of them now.

She sat on the truck's cold metal seat next to the woman with the rosary who was now praying. The canvas door flapped closed, bringing back the darkness that insisted on keeping her from Lévèque.

The truck rattled to a start and lurched forward. As her eyes adjusted to the muted light of the compartment, a sense of doom grew in her bones. They rolled through the town center, and with each turn, the woman seated next to her whimpered and sniffed. Others cried and sobbed, but no one dared to speak. Crying and fear, she thought, were not going to save Lévèque.

She stood and reached for the canvas door, intent on jumping.

"Don't!" whispered a young woman who leapt through the darkness to grab her arm. It was Héloise. "If you jump, they'll kill you."

Sophie felt a moment's comfort to see a face she recognized. "There are only two of them," she answered. "We can jump before they've realized we've gone."

Héloise did not loosen her grip. "My father—" she stuttered uncharacteristically, "he tried that an hour ago. They shot him in the street."

The truck pitched as it hit a pothole, forcing Sophie and Héloise to sit once again, now beside each other.

The news of Monsieur Van Hoden was horrible, and Sophie wanted to put her arm around Héloise, tell her everything would be all right, but she knew she could promise no such thing. "Is Céline with you?" she asked, fearful of the answer.

"No," Héloise said. "She hid in the shop. They didn't find her." There was relief in Héloise's voice, a relief Sophie shared.

"Where are they taking us?"

"The vineyard." The butcher's daughter frowned. "My father taught us some German. "I heard those pigs say they've taken over the whole Lemaire château."

Learning the Germans had captured the home of Ville de Lemaire's richest family gave Sophie pause. The château would be an excellent stronghold. The grandest home in town, it hovered over the village, visible from every corner. The Germans would see it as a good place from which to exert their control. Judging by the size of the place, it could easily house the entire company of Nazis and the villagers they'd captured.

"Why bring us there?"

"To kill us," answered a young, weeping woman. Her outburst caused a few others to cry as well.

"Killing us would be merciful," Héloise hissed unsympathetically, "but they could've done that here in the village." She turned back to Sophie. "I think they have other plans."

Sophie's eyes, now more adjusted to the darkness, scanned the faces of the others in the truck: two elderly men, seven young ladies, and three old women, including Madame Geneviève from the *chocolaterie*. Their fear was palpable.

"We have to stop them," Sophie blurted. She couldn't understand how these people could sit there and let themselves be taken.

"Don't you understand?" said the weepy woman. "Most of the young men are off with *l'Armée*. There's no one left to fight. All we can do is cooperate."

"And pray," added the old woman with the rosary.

"No one left to fight?" Sophie scoffed. "There's us." She recalled her conversation with Maurice, seemingly a lifetime ago, when she realized she shared this fate with the gravedigger. Those who no one thought could fight were left behind.

The truck slowed and stopped. "We can't be there yet," said Madame Geneviève. "Why are they stopping?"

"To collect others," answered Héloise.

Sure enough, after a few moments, the flap opened and another young woman climbed inside with her elderly father. So it went for nearly an hour.

In all, fifteen women and five old men were crammed into the carrier like goats to market.

The sounds of other vehicles climbing and descending the hill beside them added to Sophie's fear. The Nazis were starting a collection.

With each shift of the carrier's transmission, with each movement up the hillside road, the canvas door let in glimpses of sunlight, moments of hope, reminders that freedom lay just outside, and yet a world away. At last, the truck's engine rattled and stopped. They'd arrived at the château.

The sounds of the truck's front doors opening and closing were followed by the gravelly steps of the soldiers. The two Nazis who'd collected them opened the door.

"Out, dogs," said the shorter of the two, unmistakably the higher ranking one. His French was coarse.

A farm girl with milky skin rose first and stepped forward. A gray-haired man went next, and then the old praying woman. Sophie rose and followed those before her, stepping onto the truck's rear runner.

The old woman attempted to step down, but lost her balance. Sophie reached to help, but before she could grab the woman, her captor grabbed Sophie's elbow and held her back, allowing the old woman to fall to the road.

Sophie instinctively jerked her arm free from the soldier's clutch. "Why did you stop me?" she railed. "I could have helped her."

Without pause, the soldier slapped Sophie across the same cheek where he'd struck her before. "There is no help for the weak."

Warmth rose in Sophie's face, but she was uncertain if it was from pain or anger. "It's not a weakness to be old."

The soldier fixed on her without flinching. "*Nein,*" he replied. "It's a weakness to help."

The old woman rose haltingly from the ground, blood on her knees. Her rosary had broken and beads dropped off the string that had held them, one by one, falling with the woman's tears.

After witnessing Sophie's conflict with the soldier, none of the others seemed willing to offer aid.

"Let us go," she said. "We have nothing. We can't help you." She hoped without reason that the young soldier, younger than she, would have a merciful impulse.

The others, including Héloise, looked to him, waiting for his reaction. Before he could answer, an officer, taller and more imposing, stepped over, his hand on the holster of his sidearm.

"*Was ist los?*"

"This skinny girl." The young soldier replied in French, plainly for the benefit of his prisoners. "She says we should let them go."

The officer glared at Sophie, hand still on his holster. "Let you go?" he asked. His French flowed more easily than his junior soldier's and he smelled of cigarettes.

"Yes," said Sophie, trying to sound brave like Esther when she'd pleaded with the Persian king for the Jews' freedom. "Let us go."

The officer glanced to the upstairs window of the looming château and then back to Sophie. "I think, instead, I will take you to *Hauptmann* Reichmann." He looked over her body like a man assessing the worth of a horse. "You're just the type of girl he's asked for."

The officer nodded to his subordinate, conveying the order.

Just the type of girl he'd asked for? Sophie felt her knees go weak. She spun back to Héloise whose face was no longer inscrutable.

She looked afraid.

Chapter 19

The Lemaire Château

The depth of Sophie's dread was compounded by the enormity of the Lemaire château that shadowed over her. The opulent home was as grand as the Loire Valley palaces she'd toured when she was a girl.

She entered the foyer and noticed the portraits of well-appointed people hanging high on the walls. Two gilded staircases spiraled upward from the room, seemingly into the sky, brightened by the glass chandeliers that hung overhead. The Germans had spared this place the destruction they'd wrought on the rest of the village.

The world of the Lemaire home would have seemed wondrous and pleasing to Sophie on any other day. Today, it only underscored her feelings of incongruity; nothing was happening as it should.

"*Schnell.* Upstairs."

The soldier that had brought her through the vaulting doors prodded her out of her reverie, forced her like an unruly child up the far staircase toward the Lemaire sleeping rooms. She worried, under the control of the Nazis, in the privacy of such rooms, unnamable things might be done to her.

German soldiers walked freely throughout the château, which, owing to their presence, seemed more like a military facility than an ancestral home. The soldiers only paid Sophie passing attention as she was led, to her relief, past the hallway of bedrooms.

The soldier ended his prodding at a large library, twice the size of Sophie's entire home in Avoine. He pushed her through the door.

The library was cut in two by the rays of the afternoon sun. Bookcases rose along the room's perimeter, floor to ceiling, carrying brass rails and rolling ladders to allow access to the thousands of books that graced their shelves.

A portrait of a girl in a blue dress hung on the wall between the bookcases. The painted girl smiled down at Sophie, reminding her of Lévèque's painting and all she had left to fight for.

"What have you brought me?" A male voice called from the shadows and spoke flawless French, though with a German accent.

Sophie squinted between the beams of sunlight and saw a man she presumed was Hauptmann Reichmann alone at a large wooden desk. He leaned back on his chair, a paper map unfurled in his lap, his shiny black boots set firmly on a desk blotter.

"*Herr Hauptmann*," replied the soldier. He shoved Sophie forward like a prized pig at a fair. "I have a girl, tall and thin, just as you requested. She believes she should be free."

The senior officer slowly withdrew his boots from the blotter and let the chair squeal along the polished floor until it came to rest on all four legs. "Free?"

He placed the map on the desk, rose from his seat, and walked like a spider, out of the shadows and into the sun, revealing his exceptional height. As he neared, Sophie saw the deep marks and pocks that spotted his face. She thought he was old, but could see now it was simply his muddled flesh that gave the impression of age. He was likely in his thirties. What little hair Reichmann had was slicked back with pungent-smelling pomade. His pointy teeth glistened when he spoke to his officer.

"You may leave us."

The junior officer enthusiastically raised his palm toward the ceiling in the Nazi salute Sophie had seen in newsreels.

"*Sieg Heil*," the officer blurted, then smacked the heels of his boots together and left.

Reichmann circled Sophie, inspecting her. She kept still, like a schoolgirl who'd come across a stray dog. She avoided looking in his eyes.

"Freedom," he said, stopping to face her, "is an interesting thing. You may think it's your right, *Fräulein*, but it isn't. It's a privilege."

Reichmann reached toward her face. She turned away, fearful she'd be slapped again. Instead, the Hauptmann clutched her chin in his skeletal fingers and turned her face.

"You're bruised," he said examining her cheek. "Who did this to you?"

"One of your men," she spat.

He let go of her face, which still stung from where the soldier had struck her.

"A man unworthy of his uniform. A gentleman knows better than to harm a lady."

She kept silent, unwilling to be swayed by this man's words.

"Freedom is a gift," Reichmann went on. "A gift only I can give—" he stared at her intently, "and I have not given it."

"What do you want from me?" she whispered.

"Obedience," Reichmann snapped. "Obedience to the Führer."

The word "Führer" made her shudder. "Why have you brought us here?"

The Hauptmann turned and strolled to one of the windows. He pushed aside a curtain, appearing to gather his words even as he looked to the road below. "Each of us has a use," he said coldly, "a purpose." He stared through the spotless glass. "Come closer."

Sophie didn't move.

The Hauptmann turned back to her, a beam from the window traveling across his face and its imperfections, like a ray of sunlight bathing a muddy road.

"Please." Reichmann smiled. "I won't bite."

She acquiesced, but with each step, felt her skin grow colder.

Once she arrived at his side, Reichmann pointed to the villagers corralled in front of the château. "There. You see that man, the one with the leather apron? Do you know him?"

She moved closer to the window and saw Monsieur Valene being marched to the barn. "Yes."

"What does that man do?"

"He's the blacksmith of the village." She recalled Monsieur Valene's son, Claude, had left, like her father, to fight the war.

"That man *was* the blacksmith of your village. Now, he's the blacksmith to the Führer. You see? I've promoted him. He now serves a greater purpose."

The coolness she felt on her skin crawled deeper into her flesh.

"So it shall be with all the townspeople, including you." Reichmann boasted. "You'll all be promoted to serve."

He smiled as though she were a child hearing an important lesson. "My men and I—" he sighed "—we're simply soldiers on our way through the countryside." Reichmann's warm, vinegary breath swirled in her nostrils and she tried not to inhale. "Our horses need water, shoes—items our new blacksmith can surely provide." He leaned in closer. "Of course, my men also need rest, sustenance, and...companionship."

Her stomach fell as he let the word echo through the library. When only the ghost of his pronouncement remained, he added with unmistakable pride, "It's not a small thing to command a company like mine, you know."

The Hauptmann's immodest tone revealed the truth of him. He employed fear as an equestrian uses a spur: to goad his charges into behaving as he wished them to behave. He was calculating like a banker, speaking of people as if they could be added together, subtracted apart, and accounted for like so much loose change. He wanted Sophie, on that she was clear, but first it was important to him that she admire him.

He leaned closer. "Do you understand?"

Sophie turned away from his putrid breath, knowing the gesture might offend him, but more afraid he'd see the revulsion she felt cross her face.

He leaned back from her when she didn't answer and then asked, "What do *you* do in the village?"

"I care for my grandmother," she replied matter-of-factly, adopting the plain tone Héloïse had proven effective in keeping people off balance.

"I see." Reichmann returned to the desk. "I imagine you cook for her, too. Are you useful in the kitchen?"

Sophie stayed at the window, watching soldiers lead villagers to the guest quarters, the château, and the farmhouse.

"She says I'm useful, yes."

"Then I shall presume your grandmother is a wise woman and trust her. Can I trust you as well?"

Sophie turned back from the window, puzzled. "Trust me?"

"You spoke of freedom." He raised an eyebrow. "This is your goal?"

"Yes."

"Then you should know your freedom will come only through your service to the Führer—a service pledged through me."

Reichmann grinned, visibly pleased that he could place himself in the same sentence as his beloved Führer. Sophie wanted nothing more than to slap the smile off his face as his soldiers had slapped her.

"You shall begin in the kitchen," he declared. "After that," he narrowed his eyes, "we shall see." Reichmann paused, allowing the weight of his commandments to sink in.

She hid her disgust, unwilling to give a moment's reaction for him to prey upon.

"When I tell you your service is complete," he continued, "you'll have earned your freedom."

He eyed her as if trying to see something from a distance. His lustful look was the same one Sophie had seen at the Taverne Bleue, the look given by the men who'd stared at her companion, Colette, as she'd danced. Sophie understood the service Reichmann desired wouldn't end in the kitchen.

"May I trust you, Fräulein?" He was a man used to getting his way. "Do we have an understanding?"

He beamed his confidence, glowing in the shine of his pomade, the polish of his boots, the sharp cut of his decorated uniform, the cunning in his gaze...Yet, all Sophie longed for was her disheveled artist with the paint in his hair, the stains on his shoes, and the clouds in his eyes.

"Yes," she replied. "We have an understanding."

"Very good." Reichmann grinned, his pocks squeezing together. "Very good, indeed."

His tone implied she'd passed some sort of test with him, but if he trusted her, he wasn't nearly as clever as he thought himself to be.

"Tonight," he announced, "your work will begin with dinner."

Sophie needed time to create a plan, to figure her options, to plan her escape. "All right." She smiled, knowing her performance as a pliable tool had to be believable, not overly enthusiastic.

"You shall serve my officers a banquet," the Hauptmann proclaimed. "A celebration of their hard work. It isn't often, at times like these, a man can enjoy a hot meal, cooked in a fine kitchen. Can you see that this is done?"

"How many am I feeding?"

"Thirty," he boasted, "and my officers should be treated like kings."

"Thirty?" Sophie hesitated. Thirty meals was a tall order for a single person. She was used to cooking for her father, for her grandmother, maybe a few houseguests...but thirty?

The Hauptmann eased closer, placed his hand on the center of her back. He crawled his fingers up her spine, lingered at her bra, but then continued to her shoulder. "Do not fear, Fräulein. Others will help."

She called upon all her strength not to flinch or draw away. Instead, she gave another smile, but only a slight one. Taking a page from Colette's book, she wished to use this man's own lust, his own vanity, against him. Reichmann would never believe Sophie desired him, but his trust might be maintained if he believed she could tolerate him.

"Others," she nodded, pretending to see the wisdom of his plan.

"Of course, my dear. I've thought of everything." He squeezed her shoulder and turned her toward the door. He stepped past her. "Come with me."

As she followed, she spied Reichmann's map on the desk and slowed to steal a closer look. It was a detailed drawing of the entire region, with a red ink line, presumably his route, boldly drawn across it. She noticed the line rose high above Ville de Lemaire, and that a star had been drawn on Belouis-en-l'Aisne, twenty kilometers north. The line continued to Paris.

"Does my map interest you?" the Hauptmann remarked, catching Sophie in her contemplation. He sounded more amused than angry.

Her heart raced at being caught. "Belouis-en-l'Aisne," she replied as calmly as she could. "You've placed a star there."

"Yes," Reichmann replied. "Your village."

"This village is Ville de Lemaire," she corrected. "Belouis-en-l'Aisne is north."

Reichmann's confidence appeared to fall away along with his arrogant smile. He pursed his lips and pulled the edges of his waistcoat to straighten his uniform. It was clear this information was not welcome news, though he struggled to keep her from noticing.

"A temporary respite in your lovely village," he said with haste. "An intentional detour."

It was obvious the Hauptmann had led his company off course, a mistake made by a man unaccustomed to admitting mistakes. She wondered what this error would cost him…but feared more what it would cost Ville de Lemaire.

"Come," he said, a new urgency in his voice. "There's work to be done."

They made their way back down the long staircase in silence. Reichmann remained tense, no doubt working out a plan for dealing with the unwanted information she'd given him, a fortunate distraction from the attention he had been placing on her.

Sophie, in the meantime, marveled in horror at how her circumstances, the entire village's circumstances, were the result of one man's miscalculation, the error of an overconfident Nazi Hauptmann—a pitiful man who'd separated her from the ones she loved. Fate, she could see, was cruel. Or, perhaps the entire world was cruel like Colette had said Paris was: "Eager to give, but willing to take; strong and generous, but at times, heartless."

Sophie wasn't like Colette, wasn't sure she could become heartless as Colette had done, just to ward off a world that was unfair. Nevertheless, she knew her time to act would come, and when it did, she'd have to be ready.

Reichmann led her through a series of halls and past a grand dining room on the main floor. Once they arrived at the kitchen, the Hauptmann resumed conversation.

"Remember," Reichmann said, "everyone has a purpose. Yours is to oversee the work of the others and to insure tonight's meal is extraordinary. I believe the former occupants of this house have left the kitchen well-stocked."

Sophie was tempted to ask what he'd done with the "former occupants" but figured it was self-explanatory. The kings she was to serve had supplanted the former royals. Reichmann expected his men to be hailed as conquerors. There were no questions to be asked.

Like everything else in the château, the kitchen was enormous, with three iron stovetops above three equally large ovens. Painted cabinets fitted with ivory handles encircled the room, and along the far wall stood two hulking iceboxes.

A solid wood preparation table with a pair of deep sinks sat in the center of the room, and overhead a series of copper rails hung, carrying metal pots, slotted spoons, whisks and utensils of every sort. More pots and pans lay nested in one another, placed on shelves beneath the countertops. It was a chef's heaven.

The space was immaculate with one exception. On the floor, past the far end of the large table, sat a heap of clothes.

Before she could ask Reichmann about the clothes, the far kitchen door swung open and a line of women, naked save their undergarments and shoes, entered. They shivered, their arms noticeably goosefleshed, their heads hung low.

"Meet your staff," Reichmann declared, unmoved by the palpable fear that rose from the group.

An officer, barrel-chested and blond, entered behind the procession of women. He was thick-necked and had the corpuscled, red nose of a man used to drinking or persistent cold. His brow was furrowed like half-kneaded bread over his dark, focused eyes. He was not a happy man.

Next to the officer, to Sophie's surprise, stood Héloise, carrying folded servant's uniforms stacked high in her bare arms. She too looked unhappy in her undergarments, but Sophie was relieved to see she appeared unharmed.

"Halt!" called the officer, and the women stopped, huddled in front of the pantry.

Reichmann cleared his throat, catching the attention of the officer, who'd not yet noticed his presence. The man saluted. "Herr Hauptmann."

"Lieutenant Drescher." The Hauptmann nodded to Drescher, accepting the salute. "I see you've gathered proper attire for the occasion."

Drescher pushed Héloise forward to distribute the uniforms to the silent women. Héloise set the few remaining clothes on the table and the women began to dress for their duty.

Reichmann smiled at Sophie and motioned for her to join the others. She silently complied, but froze when she recognized the small-frame of an older woman struggling to don her new servant's attire.

It was her grandmother.

Chapter 20

The Kitchen

P anic washed over Sophie as she stood in the kitchen of the stolen château. Until now, her only comforting thought in this Nazi stronghold was of her grandmother, safely secreted out of harm's way, back at Lévèque's. Now, it seemed the Germans had taken that, too.

When she met her grandmother's gaze, the old woman looked away. It was clear she didn't wish to convey their familiarity to their Nazi captors. She was visibly shaken, missing her cane, working hard to appear stronger than she was. Still, part of Sophie was comforted to see her grand-mère, to have her close.

"Fräulein?" Reichmann interrupted her reverie and pointed at the servant's clothing on the counter. "Your uniform." He seemed eager to see Sophie undress.

"Of course." Sophie took a garment from the table and turned away from Reichmann to change. She couldn't be the shy girl behind a screen at Madame Lefavre's maison now. She had to be confident and unafraid.

She bit her lip and held her breath. As she peeled away her blouse and skirt, she felt the Hauptmann's eyes upon her.

She folded her clothes and set them aside, slipped her arms through the sleeves of the uniform, and reached to affix the hooks that lined the back.

Seeing her struggle, Reichmann stepped forward. "Let me help you," he whispered.

He faced her, pressed his sticky cheek to hers, and reached around her like a spider gathering a bee in his silk, pressing himself upon her. With slow precision, he connected each hook to a hoop, enveloping Sophie in her new attire.

"There." When the last hook had taken, the Hauptmann hovered at her neck and inhaled her like a spring breeze. "Lovely," he breathed. "Quite... lovely."

Sophie stood frozen with contempt and fear. She knew he was savoring her scent—the aroma of lavender and honey—the gift she'd received from Madame Lefavre, the scent she'd worn to please Jean-Claude, not him.

Reichmann's breaths became rhythmic with his lustful embrace. The bile rose in her throat and when she coughed, the Hauptmann seemed to remember they were not alone.

He cleared his throat and stepped back. "Lieutenant Drescher." He turned to his subordinate. "These ladies now comprise our kitchen staff." He maintained his flawless French. "They are to remain under your supervision."

"*Wie du befehl*, Herr Hauptmann." Dresher's tone was unenthusiastic.

"No one is to leave the kitchen," Reichmann added, facing the women to address them all. "No one is to use a knife without the lieutenant's expressed permission, and unnecessary conversations should be avoided." He scanned their faces. "If anyone violates these rules, the entire group will be...punished."

The women exchanged nervous glances, the weight of the Hauptmann's pronouncement falling on them like dirt shoveled onto a casket. Even Héloise appeared unsettled.

"This one—" Reichmann turned his cratered face back to Sophie and smiled. "She is my *chef de cuisine*." He spun back to Drescher. "Take extra care with her."

Drescher stared at her, appearing to notice Sophie for the first time, an adversary for the Hauptmann's favor. He nodded to the Hauptmann as if he understood Reichmann's words in the same way Sophie did: no matter what Drescher had planned for the others, she belonged to the Hauptmann.

"We'll leave the menu to her." Reichmann eyed Sophie. "If the meal is to my liking, you'll be rewarded. If I do not"—he licked his lips—"there will be consequences."

Sophie shuddered. It was clear there would be consequences no matter how the meal turned out.

"Dinner is at seven." Reichmann lowered his voice. "Germans are never late." He strode toward the kitchen door, but halted before stepping through. "Lieutenant, one last thing...You may wish to limit the number of ladies that enter the pantry."

Drescher smirked. "*Jawohl.*"

With that, the Hauptmann gave Sophie a wink, pushed through the kitchen door, and disappeared into the depths of the château.

She took a breath, happy to be rid of Reichmann, if only for the moment.

"You, there," Drescher called to Sophie in harsh, unpracticed French. "You heard the Hauptmann. Choose the meal."

She felt the stare of her grandmother and the others. Their fate had been placed in Sophie's hands.

Before responding, she took an apron from a hook on the wall and tied it around her waist. She pushed her hair behind her ear and tried to add some confidence to her voice. "I must see what food is here," she explained, "before I choose the meal."

Drescher sneered. "Proceed."

In the first icebox, she found several chickens, plucked, but not cleaned. In the other, she found a few dozen eggs, pitchers of milk, and some large chops of beef. In her home, and in her grandmother's, beef and milk would never be served together, but she knew better than to cook like a Jew tonight.

A basket of apples sat on the table near her grandmother. On the counter beneath the window, catching the waning sun, sat a small bowl of pears and next to it a handbasket with field greens, rosemary sprigs, brown onions, leeks, and potatoes.

She mentally cataloged the items and turned to the door beside her—the one that lead to the pantry, whose access the Hauptmann had wished to limit. Without a word, she turned from the pantry to Drescher. He replied with a smile and motioned with his head, indicating she had permission to enter.

Murmurs rose from the women, transmitting quiet warnings to Sophie. She drew a breath and opened the door.

The dark pantry was enormous, its walls lined with shelves that ran into the shadows, a shelving rack in the room's center. An acrid smell, like the scent of gunpowder, tickled her nose, confusing her. Squinting for a light, she spotted a string hanging by the door and gave it a tug.

The room illuminated and she froze. In the back of the pantry, stacked like sacks of flour, lay the bodies of two women and one man—the Lemaire kitchen servants. The male servant still held a knife in his half-opened hand. Apparently, the real kitchen servants had resisted.

Blood ran down their faces, single bullet holes in their foreheads, their eyes wide as if in warning. Resistance would not be tolerated.

She covered her mouth to keep from crying out. The sight of them evoked the image of Madame Lalonde at the *fromagerie* and Sophie's nausea returned. This time, however, she held firm, not allowing herself to grow sick. Instead, she thought of Jean-Claude. She still needed to find him, to confess her love, to break her curse. She thought of her grandmother just outside the door and recalled Reichmann's words. Individual choices would determine the fate of them all. She had to stay focused, not on the gruesome death in the pantry, but on the hope for life ahead.

She cleared her mind and scanned the pantry. A jar of white sugar sat on the shelf, flanked by two bags of flour and a bowl of raisins from the Lemaire vineyards. These will do, she thought.

She lifted her apron and gathered the items upon it. Once she had what she needed, she forced herself to turn back to the dead servants. Under her breath, she promised to remember their sacrifice, to try and make it count for something. She then reached for the string, took a final breath, and darkened the light. It was time to get to work.

When Sophie returned to the kitchen, Drescher eyed her with anticipation, no doubt trying to perceive the affect the dead servants had upon her. However, she refused to give him the satisfaction, keeping her look stoic and indiscernible.

"Did you find what you wanted?" the lieutenant asked.

"I found what I expected," she retorted. She raised her head as if to tell her fellow captives that they too would need to be brave.

She unloaded the items from her apron onto the preparation table and announced, "Tonight, we'll serve roast chicken with poached pears, salted potatoes, and creamed peas."

The women exchanged looks as if, for the first time, they realized they would be cooking.

Sophie continued, feigning a confidence she hoped her shaking voice would not betray. "We'll also serve beef with leeks and greens from the field."

Drescher squinted. "You've forgotten something."

"I have?"

"Dessert. Germans adore dessert."

"Of course," said Sophie, working to maintain her composure. "For dessert—" she glanced to her grandmother who grabbed an apple from the counter and raised it toward her. "Tarte aux pommes." Sophie faced Drescher. "Just for you, lieutenant. A dessert fit for a king."

The officer gave a crooked sneer. "Very well. Proceed."

Though he seemed satisfied with the menu, Drescher continued to be unpleasant. He dragged a stool over to the kitchen door where he perched himself to keep a watchful eye on his hostages. He murmured to himself in German as he observed.

Héloise carried the bowl of pears past him toward Sophie and slowed as she passed her. "He doesn't like his assignment," Héloise whispered, "and he doesn't like you."

"Good," Sophie replied. "I don't like him, either."

Turning to the task at hand, Sophie helped the other women clean the chickens, peel the onions and potatoes, light the stoves, and prepare the pans. For all their work, Drescher allowed only two small paring knives to be shared between them, having removed all other knives from the room.

Sophie worked her way toward her grandmother, who'd begun peeling apples for the tarte aux pommes. Under the guise of assisting with the duty, Sophie whispered, "Why aren't you at Lévèque's, Grand-mère?"

"I guess we're too alike," her grandmother replied. "Can't remain still when people we love are at risk." She offered an awkward smile. "My child, there's something you must know. I've seen Lévèque and Felipe, here at the château."

Sophie nearly screamed in delight. "Where?"

"Outside. Hiding behind the trees."

"You!" Drescher's voice bellowed.

Sophie stiffened and stepped back from her grandmother, fearful she'd lingered too long in conversation. "Yes, Lieutenant?"

"What are you talking about?"

"We…we need a larger knife."

"The knives you have are fine."

In spite of the danger, Sophie felt it was time to make a stand. "Paring knives are fine for the fruit," she gestured toward her grandmother and Héloise, "but they won't cut your Hauptmann's beef. Perhaps you'll tell him you've decided his officers don't deserve the finely prepared meal he requested."

The other women looked up from their tasks, noticeably alarmed at Sophie's opposition.

Drescher gritted his teeth. "I *am* one of his officers."

"Of course," said Sophie. "Then, you understand." She placed a hand on her hip. "We need a different knife."

The lieutenant squinted at her unhappily. After a moment, he held out his hand. "Come then. Give them here."

The women handed Sophie their paring knives, which she turned over to Drescher. "We'll need the butcher knife," she explained. "It's the one—"

"I know which one it is." Drescher snatched Sophie's wrist and squeezed it. "If any of you tries something foolish, the rest will suffer."

She withdrew her hand abruptly. "We have too much work to do for that."

Drescher narrowed his eyes. "Yes, you do."

With the paring knives in hand, he stomped out of the kitchen, cursing again in German.

Just then, at the window, a man's familiar shadow moved haltingly past.

"My child," her grandmother pointed to the window, "he's here."

Sophie rushed over, pushed the curtain aside, and unlatched the window into the late afternoon air. Lévèque was edging along the château, working to keep out of sight, following Felipe. Both were dirty, their hair disheveled, their shirts clinging to them with sweat. They were the finest thing Sophie had ever seen.

"Jean-Claude," she whispered.

"Sophie?" Lévèque turned back.

"I'm here." She kept her voice low. "At the window."

Lévèque appeared to focus on her voice, raced over, and placed his hand on her cheek, just as he'd done when he'd drafted her portrait. Without a word, he pulled her close and kissed her.

She closed her eyes and, for an instant, the world disappeared. She imagined herself back in his studio, back where there were no Nazis, no murder—only him, only her.

The artist seemed to understand there wasn't time and drew away. "Come with us," he whispered. "You must escape."

"I can't. My grandmother is here and so are others." She gave a quick look over her shoulder to the kitchen and was relieved to see two women at the door where Drescher had gone. They nodded to her. All was still clear. "If I'm gone when the guard returns, they'll be killed."

"If you stay..." Lévèque stammered. "You must find a way to escape. All of you."

Sophie had only to recall the servants in the pantry to understand his point. How could she escape? How could she defeat so many armed men? Lévèque expected too much.

Her heart ached for him, as handsome and disheveled as he'd been when she'd first seen him in the street, dumping his paints into the gutters.

Then, it hit her...a desperate measure, but perhaps a necessary one.

"I have an idea," she said, "but we must act quickly."

"Of course."

"Your paint." She trembled at the dangerous plan forming in her mind. "The solution you make to keep the color, the one that kills the rats?"

"Yes. Arsenic butter."

She drew a breath. "Does it have the same effect on men?"

A grave look befell Lévèque as he gathered her plan. "Yes."

"Then, please, Jean-Claude. It may be our only hope."

The artist lowered his head. "I used the last of it for your painting."

Sophie swallowed hard at yet another cruel twist of fate. Lévèque's finest work, his tribute to her, took what now seemed her last chance to be with him, her one hope for survival.

"No," said Felipe, moving closer. He seemed taller now, more grown than when Sophie had first seen him. "Monsieur Sarque, the man who sells me the solution, keeps dozens of jars at his home." Felipe pointed south. "He's just down the road."

"Sophie," urged Lévèque. "What you suggest—"

"How much of this butter would I need?" she pleaded. "Quickly!"

"How many men are there?"

"Thirty." The number, spoken aloud, emphasized the gravity of her plan, the implications of her suggestion.

"Sophie…"

"There's no time for debate. How many jars?"

Lévèque's clouded eyes moved back and forth, calculating. "At least two. Maybe three."

"Then, Felipe, get four."

"Four jars?" Felipe's eyes widened.

"This plan has to work," said Sophie, unsure if she was trying to convince Lévèque or herself.

"I'll help," he offered. "I'll go with Felipe."

"You'll only slow him down. Just hide. I have an hour at most."

The artist gave a reluctant nod, for the first time revealing a frustration with his own blindness.

Her grandmother limped over and squeezed Sophie's elbow, urgent whispers rising from the kitchen. "He's coming back, child. Now."

Sophie leaned out the window. "Stay safe, *mon chéri*. One hour." She kissed Lévèque on the cheek, her heart pumping fiercely, though she wasn't sure if it was from fear or love.

With one final look, Sophie pulled the window closed and faced the kitchen. Just as she turned, the door flew open and Drescher strode in. He was still mumbling, but now clutched the butcher knife, swinging it dangerously as he stomped over.

He stood next to Sophie. "Here," he barked, pointing the knife in her face. "I'm nobody's servant. Remember that."

His breath smelled of alcohol, and she realized he'd used his absence from the kitchen to serve his own needs. Now, he seemed angrier and more miserable than before.

Sophie accepted the knife, taking it by the handle. "Thank you."

"Make it fast," he snapped. In spite of the drink on his breath, his focus remained clear.

She moved to the table and Drescher stayed with her, shadowing her movements. She reached for the shallow pans that carried the uncut chops of beef, covered with a bloody cheesecloth. She pulled away the cloth and set it in the sink, reminded of the horrible death she'd seen that day.

With Drescher over her shoulder, she cut the first chop into reasonable portions. She repeated her task until she had cut all the chops equally. She then wiped the bloody blade with a wet towel and rinsed her sticky fingers in the sink.

"Don't like blood on your hands, eh?" Drescher smirked.

"I lack your appetite," Sophie replied, understanding too well the irony of her words. If her dark plan was to work, she would indeed have blood on her hands, and the thought chilled her. The curse of her life, the death and despair she'd seemed destined to bring, now appeared to be the thing she required.

She lifted the knife by the handle and offered it back to Drescher. "That should do."

"Good," said Drescher, snatching away the butcher knife. He turned on his boot and sauntered out, clearly pleased with himself or, perhaps, buoyant from the alcohol.

Once the lieutenant disappeared back through the kitchen door, Héloise hastened toward Sophie, frowning.

"What you said to your friends at the window—you think you can poison all the Hauptmann's men?"

"Enough of them so we can escape," said Sophie. "The meal is for his officers, the men in charge of this whole thing. With them gone, we may have a chance."

Several of the other women paused their mixing and frying to listen to Héloise and Sophie.

"Your plan is insane," Héloise scoffed. "If you fail, you'll get us all killed."

"They'll kill us anyway," said Sophie. "Don't you see? We have to act."

"You're out of your mind."

Sophie locked eyes with the butcher's daughter. "Out of my mind, maybe, but I see no other choice."

The kitchen had grown silent, save the hiss of the stove and the sizzle of the buttered leeks, caramelizing in a pan.

Héloise raised her head in defiance. "Perhaps I should tell the lieutenant what you have planned."

"Tell me what?" Drescher's voice echoed from the open kitchen door, halting Sophie's heart. He entered slowly, the kitchen door swinging closed behind him, the two paring knives gleaming in his fist. "Tell me," he repeated.

The women at the stove pretended to continue their work but shot knowing glances to one another. Sophie's grandmother covered her mouth.

When neither Sophie nor Héloise replied, Drescher circled the kitchen and stepped next to Héloise. "You were saying this girl has a plan?" His eyes fixed on Sophie.

"Yes." Héloise gave Sophie a dark look. "A terrible plan I do not agree with."

Sophie's throat tightened. She frowned a warning to Héloise who turned away from her to face Drescher.

"Tell me your plan." The lieutenant worked his thick brow and held the paring knives close to Sophie's face.

Sophie straightened her back, trying not to show her alarm, noticing her grandmother shifting uncomfortably by the counter as if readying for some sort of action.

"It's your meal," Héloise said.

Drescher flexed his fingers around the handles of the knives, his gaze still upon Sophie. "Yes?"

"This woman plans to add raisins to the poached pears, and I think that would ruin them."

Drescher turned to Héloise, his mouth agape. "Raisins?"

She crossed her arms and looked him in the eye, drawing his focus away from Sophie. "I say, better to put them in her precious tarte aux pommes."

The lieutenant shot incredulous looks to both women. "*Gottfluch!* This is your argument? Raisins?" He stabbed the paring knives with a violent thrust into the wooden table, causing the others to jump. "*Idioten!*"

"Raisins change the taste of everything," Héloise added.

"Do what you please," barked Drescher, stomping back to his post at the stool, "and stop your *gottverlassen* squabbling."

Héloise narrowed her eyes at Sophie. "It seems you've prevailed."

"So it seems," Sophie replied, unable to hide the relief in her voice.

"Just be sure the meal turns out as well as you've planned." The butcher's daughter returned to the sink to rinse the field greens.

Sophie glanced to her grandmother who wiped her brow with a towel and clung to the counter. The old woman was strong, but the stress of this captivity was taking its toll.

With the beef and chickens in the ovens, the vegetables cut, potatoes boiling, and desserts baking, Sophie walked around the kitchen under Drescher's watchful eye to supervise the captives' work.

In spite of the tantalizing smells of caramelized leeks and sizzling beef, her mouth remained dry, the insides of her cheeks raw from where she had been chewing them. She wished she'd had Madame Lefavre's wisdom or Colette's strength to navigate this predicament.

Still, Sophie understood her calling was different. She was Esther. Like her Jewish ancestor, her circumstances demanded bravery beyond self-assuredness, action in spite of fear, sacrifice that could mean death.

She didn't need doubtful Héloise to remind her that when the night was through, either she'd be dead or she'd have caused the death of others, Nazis or captives. For some to survive, some had to die. Life required death.

It seemed, even when the circumstances were grim, all things still came in twos.

Sophie dabbed her beaded brow with the corner of her apron, trying to ignore the heat of the stoves and the fear that coursed through her veins. It wouldn't be long before the meal was complete, and yet there was still no sign of Felipe and Lévèque.

Focus, she thought. I must focus.

She turned her attention to Drescher and found him still murmuring, arguing with himself in German. It was clear this assignment lacked the bravado to which he'd been accustomed. The creases in his face seemed wrought by stress, the broken blood vessels in his nose speaking of his fondness for drink. For her plan to work, she'd have to find a way to administer the meal's lethal ingredient without drawing Drescher's attention. She'd already used the knives as an excuse to distract him once. Now, she had to get more creative—and there wasn't much time.

Instinctively, she moved to the window and opened it to the early evening air, allowing the cool breeze to wash across her warm face.

"You, there!" Drescher hopped off the stool and charged to Sophie's side. If the drink had affected him, he was hiding it well. "What are you doing?"

Sophie turned to him, adopting the confident posture of a seasoned chef. "We need to set the tarte aux pommes in the window to cool," she explained. "It keeps the dessert from falling."

He squinted at her. "You ask permission first, Fräulein."

"Permission not to ruin your dessert?" Sophie replied, with more nerve than she intended.

Drescher was not amused. With a single, swift move, he pulled the gun from his hip and strode beside her. He stuck the barrel to Sophie's temple. The women in the kitchen gasped.

"Don't...mock...me." Drescher's French was suddenly clear, slow, and precise.

She leaned away from the pistol, trying to stay calm. The confidence she'd hoped to convey had come across as arrogance. She'd overplayed her part.

"The Hauptmann may fancy you," he said through clenched teeth, "but he has no patience for the pompous French and neither do I."

"Please, Lieutenant." Sophie swallowed. "I...I only want the tarte to please the Hauptmann."

Drescher held the pistol firmly. "What about pleasing me?"

"—and you," she whispered. "Of course, you."

Drescher's hot stare lingered in the silent kitchen.

Then, as suddenly as his anger had risen, it vanished. He withdrew his pistol and stuffed it back into its holster, as though he were pocketing a Reichsmark.

"Your tarte better be perfect, Fräulein...for me." With a smirk, Drescher strode away.

Sophie rubbed her temple, recalling what her grandmother had told her about Hitler, and why he hated Jews.

A man in need of a target always finds one.

It seemed Drescher was like Hitler in that way. He was a man needing a target, and he'd chosen Sophie. Nevertheless, the danger she'd put herself in was worth it. She'd accomplished her goal: she'd opened the window.

An egg timer sounded out like the cry of the dead, drawing the attention of the women back to their duties. They took the beef and chickens from the ovens, put the creamed peas into a tureen, and set the gravy to simmer. Bottles of the Lemaire champagne were fetched from the wine rack and pitchers of water were filled. It was nearly time.

Sophie pushed her trembling hands into a pair of thick, padded oven mitts and lifted the tarte aux pommes from the oven to the window to cool. It was just then, through the evening air, she heard the call of a bird—but not quite a bird. This bird had a shrill and inharmonious whistle.

It was Lévèque. His tenor was unmistakable, though his aptitude for art did not translate to music. She grinned, happy, if just for a moment, at the knowledge that her love was near.

She set the dish on the sill and ventured a glance to the oak tree outside. There she spied Felipe who, after a furtive look around, held the small apothecary jars of arsenic butter up high for her to see, two in each hand, unlikely treasures on an awful day.

Beside him, Lévèque smiled an impractical, confident smile, staring at a place just to the left of the window where Sophie stood. These two heroes seemed like boys, children playing a game. She captured the moment like a portrait in her mind.

Her reverie was cut short, however, when her grandmother stepped over, blocking Drescher's view of her at the window.

With an artificial voice reminiscent of Madame Lefavre's grand pronouncements, her grandmother addressed the lieutenant directly. "Monsieur Lieutenant, perhaps you would like to sample the glorious beef?"

Her grandmother's tone told her this was her own cue to get ready.

"Yes," Drescher replied. "I would like that."

Her grand-mère led the lieutenant away, to the stove on the other side of the kitchen. The women all seemed to understand what was happening and began to crowd behind Sophie, nonchalantly busying themselves at the table, obscuring Drescher's view of her. They rattled utensils and dishes, creating ambient noise, allowing Sophie to wave Felipe to the window.

He dashed over, Lévèque at his side.

"Quickly," Sophie whispered. "The jars."

Felipe passed each jar through the window, over the steaming tarte, into Sophie's hands. The arsenic hardly looked like the butter she imagined. Instead, it was translucent like water, moving like syrup in the small jars. She pocketed the poison in her apron and the jars clinked as she moved.

"Be careful," the artist whispered, and reached to take her hand. His grip was unsteady, his eyes moist. "I...I love you."

At the word "love," a rush of warmth flowed through her like the summer stream of the river back home. She feared she'd fall where she stood, but she didn't need to stand. She was flying. Her grandmother was right. Lévèque loved her.

She'd heard the words, and yet, if her plan didn't work, they might be the last words she would ever hear from Jean-Claude Lévèque. She took a breath. "I love you too."

Part of her wanted to leap out the window, join him in a long embrace, and kiss him with the abandon she felt in her heart. Yet this impulse was halted by a nagging sense of duty. She was being torn, pulled apart by hope and despair. Sophie was on a path—one that would not allow her to indulge in Lévèque's love any longer.

The artist seemed to sense what she was feeling and hung his head.

She reached forward, held his face in her hands. "Adieu, my love. Adieu."

She kissed his head and turned from him, turned from the window to face the kitchen—to face her destiny, whatever it may be.

Pockets filled with poison, the true weight of her task washed over her. Love outside the window and death in the kitchen. Her time had come.

Chapter 21

A Meal for Kings

Sophie moved her attention to the preparation table, to her grandmother, who presided over the steaming beef. Drescher lifted a morsel from the pan to his eager lips, a drip of gravy falling onto his lapel. He chewed, ecstasy crossing his face, his eyes closing from the pleasure of the food. He licked his lips and opened his eyes as though returning from a dream.

"This will do," he offered, giving no verbal approval to the cooks for their labor. "Prepare the food to serve."

Drescher placed his hands behind his back and began to circle the large kitchen, giving one last inspection to the food before it was to be shared with his fellow officers.

He gave a glance to the window and Sophie feared the lieutenant had spotted the artist dashing away. However, Drescher continued to circle the kitchen, appearing eager for his meal.

Sophie worked to clear her mind of Jean-Claude's face, his lips, his words. She could afford no distractions now. Careful not to face the window again, she moved to a cabinet to gather some serving trays and table linen. When she moved, however, the jars knocked against one another in her pockets.

As if on cue, Héloise began to stack dinner plates, the clinking porcelain obscuring the indiscreet sounds of the arsenic jars. Sophie sighed her relief and used the moment to stuff a linen napkin into each pocket to stifle further noise. She had to get rid of this poison quickly.

Madame Geneviève, the chocolatier, gathered silverware, drawing the watchful eye of Drescher. Emma, a girl Sophie knew to be the florist's daughter, uncorked the champagne and put the opened bottles on a wheeled cart. She then filled several baskets with breads. Madame Geneviève helped Emma garnish the chicken with rosemary sprigs. It was time to serve.

"May we set the table, Lieutenant?" Sophie asked.

"Yes." He pushed open the door to the dining room and stood like a sentry, shifting his view between the kitchen and the dining hall. He had two rooms to secure now.

On Sophie's look, Héloise lifted her stack of dishes and wiggled past the lieutenant, steering clear of him as she made her way through the door.

The women with the silverware followed Héloise, trailed by others with water goblets, candlesticks, and napkins. They winced each time they passed the lieutenant with platters of crudités and gravy boats. Each time they drew close, he smirked, their discomfort prompting some perverse pleasure.

Sophie had been watching from her post by the sink, eager for her moment to administer the final ingredient to the food. Would it be best to add the poison to as many of the dishes as possible, or would that only diminish the arsenic butter's effect? Would it be better to saturate a single item, or would that prove problematic if some officers were to skip that particular dish? Sophie realized she had one chance to get this right—and she still needed Drescher out of the way.

"Lieutenant," Sophie called to Drescher. "Would you care to call your fellow officers?"

"Finally," Drescher said with exasperation.

Sophie watched him step through the door, now eager for her opportunity to act. Yet, instead of leaving the kitchen altogether, the lieutenant stopped, leaned his head into the dining room and called out to an unseen soldier. He turned back a moment later. "They're coming, and they're hungry."

Sophie swallowed in fear. She had to get Drescher out of view or all their work would be for naught. Her plan would be doomed and Reichmann would be readying his appalling gratitude.

Suddenly, she heard a gentle, familiar cough. At the opposite end of the kitchen, her grandmother stood, looking directly at her. She raised an eyebrow as if to convey something, but Sophie didn't understand.

She cocked her head inquisitively, but the old woman simply gave a reassuring nod. She then lifted her head and cried aloud, "Aagghh!" and then fell to the floor.

A group of others rushed to her grandmother's side. Madame Geneviève called to Drescher, "*Mon Dieu!* Monsieur, Lieutenant! Come quickly. This woman is ill."

"*Was ist los?*" replied Drescher from the door, annoyed.

Two of the women took hand towels and began to fan Sophie's grandmother where she lay unmoving on the floor.

"Please, monsieur! Come quickly!" Héloise called, hands on her hips. She too proved a convincing actress.

Sophie watched Drescher struggle between investigating the problem in the kitchen and watching the dining room.

"*Idioten!*" he spat. He let the kitchen door swing closed and marched to the gathering of women on the other side of the preparation table. "Stupid cows."

Drescher cursed the group of women who fussed over the fallen actress and Sophie made her selection. She ran the water in the sink to obscure the pop of her opening jars, and administered the clear liquid—one jar, then another.

"Step back!" Drescher barked. "Pick her up. If she can't work, she's no use to me." He fingered his holster.

Sophie's pulse banged like a military drum, calling out a warning for her grand-mère's safety—a warning she had to ignore. Instead, she let the liquid death flow from her jar, inspired by the risk her grandmother was taking. She too had a risk to take, and she had to stay focused.

"I—I'm fine, monsieur," Sophie's grandmother replied. Sophie looked up to see her grandmother pushing herself up onto one elbow. "The heat—" her grandmother waved to the air around her, "the heat of the kitchen must have overcome me."

Two of the larger women took her grandmother's hand and struggled to help her up, just as Sophie completed her work. She wrapped all four empty jars with the linen napkins and dropped them quietly into the waste bin beneath the sink. The plan was in motion.

"Get up. Get up," growled the lieutenant.

Sophie took a breath and looked back to her grandmother. "Madame," she called, rinsing her hands in the running water. "Perhaps you can get some air by helping me serve the food."

"Yes," said her grandmother. She pushed her fingers through her gray bob as she stood. "I think that would help."

Drescher cleared his throat. "Enough! Move. All of you. The officers are waiting."

The women peered at Sophie, no doubt wondering if they'd bought her enough time. She replied with a smile, settling her pulse. She drew a breath and directed each woman to take the remaining food to the dining room. "Dinner is served."

Drescher returned to the door and pushed it open to the rumble of German conversation and men's laughter. The soldiers had begun seating themselves. The moment for Sophie's final act had arrived.

One by one, the servant women carried through the dishes they'd prepared. First went the bowls of field greens and the baskets of breads. Next went the roasted chicken and potatoes, followed by the trays of beef with caramelized leeks, tureens of sautéed peas in cream sauce, the poached pears complete with raisins, and a selection of cheeses. The last in the parade of delicacies was the tarte aux pommes, carried by Héloise using the padded oven mitts.

Sophie's grandmother followed next, pushing the cart of Lemaire champagne, and Sophie ended the procession carrying a large silver tray of empty champagne flutes.

She paused at the door, as if preparing for God's judgment. She wanted to say a Jewish prayer, but struggled to think of an appropriate one, just as she'd struggled when Maurice had asked her to pray in Hebrew for his dead cousin Narina. To Sophie's great embarrassment, all she could recall at that time was the Hebrew prayer for bread. It seemed even back then, somewhere in her mind, food and mortality were linked.

"Go on," Drescher hissed in her ear. "Now."

Sophie raised her chin and stepped into the dining room, but what she saw nearly made her drop her tray. Seated at the table, next to each officer was a young woman from the village, hostage escorts the men had selected to join them in their meal.

The escorts all looked frightened. Most were just girls, barely teenagers, dressed in fancy ball gowns that clearly did not belong to them, ill-fitting and inappropriate for dinner.

The officers seemed as hungry for their companions as they were for their meal, a few of them groping the girls' arms, stroking their cheeks. One girl, a fair-skinned brunette whom she only knew as the postman's fifteen-year-old daughter, was crying. Sophie gritted her teeth, held her tray steady, and tried to remain calm.

Héloise spun to face her, desperation on her face. These extra guests were not part of the plan. She knew Héloise was asking the same thing all the kitchen women were probably asking themselves. Would Sophie have to kill these innocent young women just to rid the town of their captors?

At the head of the table, presiding over the meal, sat Hauptmann Reichmann. Perhaps from the horrified look on Sophie's face at the sight of the escorts, he said, "Do not fear, my dear. You've made plenty of food. I suspect few of these young ladies will each much anyway."

He beamed with pride, the candlelight twinkling off the pomade in his thinning hair. Evidently, he'd made peace with his mistake of bringing his company too far south to Ville de Lemaire. Like everything else, he'd found some way to rationalize his actions, calculate his next steps.

He stared at Sophie the way she figured cobras stared at their prey, mesmerized both by his hunger and the thought of his own satisfaction.

"Very well," Sophie replied.

Drescher rounded the table and took a seat among his fellow officers, next to a short-haired blond girl whom they'd selected for him. The lieutenant smiled, happy for the first time since Sophie had laid eyes on him. His kitchen duty was officially over.

Still unsettled by the appearance of the hostages, Héloise and the others tentatively set their dishes on the grand table and took their places around the perimeter of the room.

Sophie swallowed hard and approached the table, placing before each soldier a crystal champagne flute. Her grandmother followed close behind, filling the flutes with the Lemaire champagne. In spite of the delectable aromas of the food swirling around the room, Sophie felt nauseous.

Once she'd reached the last soldier, set the last glass, she stood back from the table and held the empty silver tray at her side. Her grandmother finished pouring and left the emptied champagne bottles on the wheeled cart. She joined Sophie in the corner of the room and stood quietly.

With the food on the table and the glasses full, the Hauptmann stood and opened his hand toward her. "Come, my dear. Join me."

Reichmann moved an empty chair from the corner of the room next to his. "Join me in the wonderful meal you've prepared." He widened his grin, full of pointed teeth.

At her side, she heard her grandmother stifle a cry, but Sophie kept her gaze on the Hauptmann. "I...I mustn't, monsieur."

"Of course, you must," replied Reichmann. "It's a German tradition. We honor the cook. She must sample her food before her guests are permitted to dine."

Sophie had never heard of this tradition, but figured it was Reichmann's clever way of assuring the safety of his food. It seemed he'd calculated her correctly after all.

Each of the women from the kitchen shared a look of fear, turning away from her as she tried to meet their eyes.

The soldiers, however, stared at Sophie, looking perplexed by the attention Reichmann was giving her.

"Come now," the Hauptmann called. "Don't be shy."

Sophie handed the empty tray to her grandmother, willed her eyes to say, "I love you," to say, "It will be all right," and offered a reassuring smile. She then turned to Reichmann, to accept what she had wrought.

"Here," said the Hauptmann, offering Sophie a silver fork and then taking his seat. "Which shall you sample first?"

Sophie sat, took a long breath, and said, "I leave the choice to you, monsieur."

"Very good!" Reichmann declared, indicating she'd chosen the only sensible option. She suddenly felt him slip his hand beneath the table onto her thigh. He leaned to her and whispered, "Very good."

Sophie curled her toes in revulsion at the uncomfortable attention given her. His breath still smelled like vinegar.

Reichmann turned and evaluated the bounty of food, his hand remaining connected to her leg. "There," he pointed. "The beef."

At Reichmann's command, one soldier handed the dish of beef to another, sending it down the table. Once it reached Sophie, she donned a smile, took a beef tip with her fork and placed it in her mouth. She chewed, gathered her confidence, and after swallowing, said, "Very nice, if I may say so."

Reichmann burst out in high-pitched laughter. "Yes, my dear, you may say so." He looked to the faces of his officers, as though his prized pet had just performed some impressive trick and he longed for signs of their amusement.

The men nodded to each other, good soldiers as they were.

The Hauptmann pointed to the peas. "Another."

She worked to free her face of any expression. If Reichmann was observing her to find some reaction, she would give him none. She closed her eyes and chewed the peas, savoring their flavor, their texture, just as Lévèque had taught her to focus on sounds, by closing off all other senses but the ones she desired the most. She pretended not to feel the bony fingers of the Hauptmann on her thigh. Instead she thought upon Lévèque, the man who had taught her so much.

"Well?" asked Reichmann.

She opened her eyes. "You'll love these, too."

"Ha!" He gave her thigh a squeeze.

Sophie held her tongue, sent herself further into the aromas, escaping into the meal.

Next came the potatoes and then the pears. With each bite Reichmann watched her, and with each bite she fought to escape his burning gaze, ignore his lecherous touch. It felt as if Reichmann were undressing her, peeling her like an onion, removing a garment with each dish she sampled. The feeling repulsed her, but only momentarily. She had a job to do.

So it went until Sophie had tasted every dish except the dessert.

"What's that?" Reichmann extended his elongated finger, indicating the tarte. "Are those apples?"

She opened her eyes and spied the tarte, caramelized slices of apple splayed like a fan on the flakey crust. "My most famous dish," she said, raising her head. "My grandmother's recipe. Tarte aux pommes."

Reichmann's smile animated the pock marks in his cheeks. "My favorite," he said.

Once the dish arrived, Sophie again dug in her fork, but rather than eating it immediately as she had done with the other dishes, she offered the bite playfully, instead, to Reichmann.

The soldiers looked astonished as the smile waned from the Hauptmann's face. Sophie had challenged Reichmann in front of his men, toyed with the toymaker.

She watched him stare at the morsel on her fork, then at his men. All the while, she held it steady.

From the corner of her eye, she saw Lieutenant Drescher grow angry, his white-knuckled fists gripping his fork and knife. In that moment, she was certain Drescher regretted not having shot her in the kitchen when he'd had the chance.

Reichmann removed his hand from her thigh and grasped Sophie by the wrist. "Please, Fräulein," he hissed through his teeth, his amusement at her now gone. "I'm a gentleman. Ladies first."

Sophie smiled. He was no gentleman, but she was satisfied with her symbolic victory, even if it had only lasted a moment.

"Very well," she replied.

Risk, reward. Life, death. Choices, consequences. All things in twos. She closed her eyes once more. Then, with the same zest she had given to eating her favorite dish her entire life, Sophie took the bite.

"Delicious."

She knew she was being precocious in a way that would have made Colette proud, but her feigned confidence was a tool, used to mask her persistent fear. It was fear Reichmann wanted. It was what he required of her and all his hostages. But she was determined to give him nothing. He and the Germans already taken too much.

Reichmann stood once again, this time lifting his champagne glass. The officers also stood.

"France is now part of our glorious Deutschland," Reichmann announced, "a bold step on our noble journey. All around, forces like ours enter this territory, even as I speak. Join me, gentlemen," he then looked to the women, "and the rest of you…in celebrating our beloved Deutschland. To the Führer! *Sieg Heil!*"

"*Sieg Heil!*" the soldiers replied in unison, and drank to their Hauptmann's toast. The young escorts shifted in their bulky dresses, looking to one another, none of them certain what to do or say.

"*Essen sie gut!*" bellowed Reichmann. "À votre santé! To your health. You've earned it."

Reichmann sat and nodded his permission, allowing them to send the dishes and tureens around the table.

The soldiers conversed in German, jovial and relaxed, serving themselves the food, eating voraciously. Some even served spoonfuls to their consorts.

A few of the young women ate the food eagerly, as if they believed this was their last meal on earth.

Sophie's fellow cooks grew tense, clearly uncertain where she'd placed the poison or what it would do to those who consumed it. Héloise covered her mouth with her hand. Madame Geneviève turned away. Sophie's grandmother chewed her lip, her cheeks moist with tears. All Sophie could do was watch the soldiers and wonder how long the poison would take.

Reichmann chewed a piece of beef, gleeful. He licked the sauce off his lips and leaned over to Sophie. "It seems my faith in you was well placed," he whispered. "The meal is a success, and you shall be rewarded." He moved his hand beneath the table back to her thigh. "Tonight will be glorious."

Sophie thought if the meal were truly a success, Reichmann would be in no position to offer any reward. She said nothing and remained stone-faced, masking her loathing and her eagerness for this grim night to end.

However, as the minutes passed, she became more and more concerned. Each man consumed his meal with no visible effect.

Just when she started to fear the arsenic had failed, plans took a sudden change.

From somewhere in the depths of the Lemaire home, angry voices in French and German rose in volume. The officers at the table turned, looking over their shoulders with concern to the door of the private dining room that separated them from the rest of the home.

Reichmann stopped eating and called out to the source of the noise in the adjoining great room. "*Was ist los?*"

Two German guards burst into the dining hall. Sophie jumped to her feet and let out an audible cry.

The guards each held a captive—Felipe and Lévèque.

Blood ran down the artist's chin from his lower lip. His hands appeared bound with twine, his wrists red and raw. His clothes were filthy and torn, as though he'd been dragged through the dirt, and his long hair was in disarray. He faced the dining room, the clouds in his blind eyes reflecting the chandelier light. Despite his condition, he turned at the sound of Sophie's cry and offered her an unexpected, confident smile.

Felipe, however, did not appear quite so confident. Slack-shouldered and sullen, the boy seemed defeated. His right cheek was bruised and his eyes lacked their previous fire. His hands, like Lévèque's, were bound behind his back.

The two guards who'd brought them in clutched Lévèque and Felipe by the arms. Like hunters returning victorious with their game, they offered them up to Reichmann.

"*Wir haben sie hinter dem schloss gefunden,* Herr Hauptmann," snapped the guard holding Felipe.

Unwittingly, Sophie grabbed the Hauptmann's arm. "Please! Don't hurt them!"

Reichmann rose from the table and turned to Sophie. "You know these men?"

She fixed on the artist as she fought to hold back her tears, fought the urge to rush to his side.

The Hauptmann's eyes darted between Sophie and Lévèque, seeming to trace the invisible thread that connected them. He then squinted at the artist.

"This man, is he blind?" Reichmann scowled. "He's important to you?" He sounded incredulous.

Sophie stiffened and didn't reply, uncertain how her answer might affect the situation.

The Hauptmann's features darkened. It was now Reichmann who seemed repulsed by Sophie. "This man is flawed," he explained, pointing at Lévèque. "He's not worthy of love."

"What could you know about love?" Sophie spat. "You're nothing but a hateful man, a fool lost in the wrong village." She regretted her words the moment she spoke them.

The Hauptmann reached to his hip, withdrew his sidearm and Sophie braced herself to be struck across the face again.

Instead he aimed at Lévèque.

"Such people are not fit for the glorious future."

Instinctively, Sophie lunged for the pistol, but it was too late. Reichmann fired a shot.

An instant after the crack of the gun, Lévèque slumped forward out of his guard's grasp and onto the floor.

"No!" Sophie cried.

She jumped from Reichmann, through the gun smoke, and around the table toward Lévèque.

The cooks and consorts cried out as well. Some dove under the dining table and others froze, horrified by the raw violence.

Amid the cries and confusion, Sophie knelt by Jean-Claude. His linen shirt was now spotted with red, a large stain growing at his side.

"Sophie," he whispered.

"Don't speak. Save your strength."

She snatched a corner of her apron and tore a piece of it, pressing it to his wound. Impulsively, she pulled him closer in her embrace and kissed him.

In spite of his condition, his lips felt strong, his touch reassuring. She could have convinced herself that everything was fine, but she tasted his blood on her trembling lips.

"I'm sorry," she whispered. "This is my fault."

She knew if she'd stayed in the basement, had listened to Jean-Claude, all of them would be safe. Instead, they'd all come for her. Now, Lévèque, Felipe, and even her grandmother were paying a horrible price. The goat girl of Avoine had unleashed her curse and doomed them all.

She pressed the apron fabric harder against his side. "I'm so sorry," she repeated. "My dreams bring death. You were right at the start. I'm just a foolish girl."

"No, my love," Lévèque protested. "You're not a fool."

Reichmann stepped over, crouched over them, a cold loathing forming in his eyes, as if their intimacy caused him offense. Again, he raised his pistol.

"This man is like an injured animal," he seethed. "The humane thing to do is to put him out of his misery." The Hauptmann again took aim.

"No!" Sophie cried. She released Jean-Claude's hand, and turned to face Reichmann, shielding Lévèque with her body.

But no shot came. Instead of pulling the trigger, confusion washed over Reichmann's pocked-marked face and his eyes flew wide. He convulsed with a sudden lurch.

"*Was ist——?*" He lurched again, this time making a horrible gulping noise.

The arsenic butter had finally found its mark.

Lévèque appeared to read the sounds of the moment and again took Sophie's hand. "It's working."

Reichmann seized again, looking surprised that his body was not cooperating with his will. "No!" He staggered back, let off a wild shot, which struck Lévèque's guard in the chest, sending the soldier staggering back to the wall and then down to the floor, dead.

Felipe, suddenly filled again with his youthful fire, took advantage of the pandemonium to pull free from his own captor, who had panicked at the sight of his fellow guard being shot by their Hauptmann. With a strength Sophie would never have expected from a fifteen-year-old boy, he stamped on the guard's shin with a horrible crunch and sent the man down. He then elbowed the guard in the head, until the man fell unconscious.

The screams began anew, and one of the young consorts fainted.

The Hauptmann dropped his gun, clutched his stomach, and fell to his knees, his wide-eyed gaze colliding with Sophie's. He knew what was happening. He'd miscalculated her.

"What——" he swallowed, "have you done?"

"It's what *you've* done! You—not me!" Tears stung Sophie's eyes. "Your drink to victory was a drink to your own death. The Lemaire's have had their revenge."

Other officers began to grasp their own throats in horror, convulsing, panic gripping their faces as the arsenic took hold of them.

Some of the hostage women jumped away, crawled away, or hid from their falling captors, crying. Though afraid, the hostages appeared unharmed. They had not drunk the champagne.

Lieutenant Drescher stood and scanned the faces of his fellow officers as they began to shudder and gurgle, one after the other, each in the throes of death, white foam spilling from their mouths.

A chill filled the room as the soldiers and consorts finally realized what was occurring, and who was responsible.

"No!" Reichmann's horrid cries disappeared in a gurgle of spittle, his skeletal fingers grasping his throat. After a haunting, guttural rattle, he stiffened and stopped moving, his brief, horrible reign coming to a fortuitous end.

Lieutenant Drescher howled like an angry beast, foam forming on his own lips. He labored past the table, toward Sophie and Lévèque, his fury helping him fight the effects of the poison like a practiced drunk wards off drunkenness.

Sophie clutched Lévèque as Drescher moved for his gun, a last act of desperation.

Before he could reach Sophie, however, Héloise leapt forward, a serrated knife in hand, and thrust the blade deep into Drescher's belly.

His mouth opened but no sound escaped.

"That," the butcher's daughter said fiercely, "is for my father."

The lieutenant struggled to remove the knife, but instead fell forward to the floor, beside Lévèque.

One after the other, each officer acquiesced to their poisoned champagne, some groaning and falling forward onto the table, some vomiting and dropping off their chairs. With each opportunity, their hostage consorts ran back to the kitchen to escape the horrible wave of death.

"Help the others," Sophie said to Héloise who nodded and returned to the consorts. "All into the kitchen. Don't let anyone run into the château."

"What's happening?" whispered Lévèque. His voice was weak, his eyes half-closed.

"We're leaving. Now."

Sophie crawled away from Lévèque's side to grab the knife from the Drescher's body. She cut Felipe's bindings. "Quickly," she snapped. "Help the others out of here, through the kitchen window. Go!"

Felipe needed no further direction. He raced to help Héloise lead the remaining hostages and cooks to safety. "Quietly!" he hissed. "Out of here."

Sophie heard the sounds of other soldiers yelling from the depths of the chateau and knew they'd come to investigate the sounds of the shots and cries from the dining hall. She took the leg of a broken chair and used it to secure the door leading to the great room. It wouldn't last, she thought, but it might buy them some time.

She raced back to Lévèque and examined his wound. The white apron fabric, which she'd pressed against him, was now saturated with his blood. As she removed it, he moaned in pain.

"Steady…" she said, though she wasn't sure if her reassurances were for her own sake or Lévèque's.

She untied her apron, applied the fresh fabric to his wound, and attempted to lift him.

Sophie's grandmother shuffled forward, against the flow of running hostages, stepping with obvious discomfort over fallen soldiers to reach her side.

"Let me help," she offered.

"I can stand on my own," Lévèque said, blinking in an apparent attempt to stay conscious. "It's not bad." When he tried to move, he winced and fell back to the floor.

Sophie showed her grandmother her hand, slick and red from holding Lévèque. She swallowed her fear and looked back to the artist. "Jean-Claude," she said as calmly as she could. "You're bleeding. You've been shot."

He reached to his side, felt his moist shirt, and rubbed the blood between his fingertips.

Sophie looked to her grandmother. "You go, Grand-mère. I'll stay."

"No!" Lévèque protested with a sudden burst of energy. "Just go without me."

"Nonsense!" blurted Sophie's grandmother. "No more heroes today. We all go together."

Sophie braced her knees and, with her grandmother's help, lifted Lévèque off the floor. He squeezed his eyes shut and cringed.

They hoisted his arms over their shoulders and carried him, half-walking, out of the dining room, through the swinging door, into the kitchen.

"Felipe!" called Sophie.

The orphan boy helped the last hostage through the kitchen window and strode over to help Sophie and her grandmother. Together, they managed to lift Lévèque carefully through, into the cool evening air, out to the hands of the waiting cooks and consorts.

"Gently!" hissed Madame Geneviève from beside the window. "Quietly!" She seemed more composed than she'd been only an hour before.

234

Emma, the florist's daughter, and five other women from the kitchen stepped up to the window and locked arms to carry Lévèque away from the château. Sophie and Felipe helped Sophie's grandmother through, and then followed quickly behind.

The night had fallen and brought with it a frosty breeze. Sophie ignored the chill, raced away from the oppressive château, and rushed to join the others who were carrying Lévèque into the hills.

"Stay in the shadows," she called ahead. "We're not safe yet."

She again pressed her apron to Lévèque's wound, noticing with horror how much blood he continued to lose. With her free hand, she stroked his hair. "I'm here, *mon chéri*. I'm here."

A series of gunshots rang out from the depths of the château, followed by angry calls in German.

"Faster!" snapped Madame Geneviève. "We must find safety."

The group of former hostages crowded together as one and shuffled into the darkness, carrying the injured Lévèque, their fear palpable.

Sophie kept her hands firmly on Jean-Claude, unwilling to part from him even for a moment. She sang "Au Clair de la Lune" in his ear, just as her father used to do when she was scared.

"Where's Héloise?" her grandmother asked, limping over to Sophie's side, struggling without her cane.

"She ran in the other direction," answered the florist's daughter, motioning with her head.

"Is she all right?" Sophie felt a sudden panic.

"Yes," the girl smiled. "Héloise can take care of herself."

Sophie nodded. She knew Héloise was strong and wouldn't rest so long as her sister, Céline, was in danger.

The remaining members of the kitchen crew stayed together, moving swiftly toward the surrounding hills. Gunshots and frantic voices in German and French could be heard rising and falling behind them, the sounds of the chaos they'd wrought now riding the breeze.

Madame Geneviève stopped walking, closed her eyes, and tilted her ear to the sky.

"Why are we stopping?" asked Sophie.

Madame Geneviève opened her eyes. "They've found their officers."

"You speak German?"

"Yes." She squinted again, straining to hear more. "They're confused. They don't know what to do with their leaders dead."

Lévèque moaned, his eyes now shut in pain.

"Please," said Sophie. "We must keep going."

Madame Geneviève nodded and the crowd resumed their escape, now more eagerly. The rattle of machine-gun fire occasionally cut the silence, reminding them of the danger, urging the group to move. Just as they crested the hill, a loud explosion ripped through the night.

Sophie spun back to see, in the distance below, in front of the château, a troop carrier explode in a ball of fire. Smoke and debris rose into the sky. Small silhouettes of soldiers ran in all directions to escape the fiery destruction. More angry calls in German echoed back and forth across the grounds.

"What's happened?" asked Sophie.

Madame Geneviève smiled, still listening to the darkness. "The others from the village…they're fighting back."

Sophie looked back down the path, realizing the turmoil she had sparked had replaced the dark order imposed by their German invaders.

A rebellion had begun.

Chapter 22

Half-Moon Night

The odor of smoke and gasoline carried in the air, the putrid scents of the destruction they'd left behind—smells that only urged the cooks and consorts faster down the trail, away from the château. Sophie pressed Lévèque's wound as if, by her will alone, she could force his blood to slow. Though he didn't speak, she saw his face clench from pain. He was fighting to live.

"We're on our way," said her grand-mère, limping to keep up. "We'll call on Monsieur Fournier."

"Monsieur Fournier?" Emma frowned. She looked at Lévèque and then back to Sophie, lowering her voice. "Fournier is a horse doctor, five kilometers away."

"He'll have to do," commanded Madame Geneviève. She smiled at Sophie. "We stay together and help each other. We owe you that much."

Uncomfortable with the thought that she was owed anything, Sophie didn't reply. All that mattered now was Lévèque.

She looked to the sky, desperate to see a full moon—Jean-Claude's moon, the one that filled her with hope. The one that brought them together and gave him sight. However, tonight the moon was only half-full, as if it too felt incomplete with the artist in peril.

"Blue," Lévèque rasped, gaining momentary consciousness. His eyes were half-open, his ashen face angled toward the road.

Sophie followed his blind gaze to the glow of the trail, bathed in moonlight blue. It was the same color Lévèque had used in his recent masterpiece, the blue he saw in her.

"Quiet," she whispered. She placed her finger on his lips and felt how cold they had become. "Save your strength."

The quiet reassurance she was trying to instill was shattered when the long bleat of an approaching automobile's horn pierced the quiet and sent panic through the group.

"Off the road!" her grandmother cried.

Sophie's heart tightened, yet before they could carry the artist out of sight, the source of the horn—a dark German truck—roared around the bend. A German personnel carrier, like the one she'd ridden to the château, barreled toward them, Nazi flags waving from its fenders.

Some of the women let out a scream and ran to the hills, tripping on their dresses as they fled. The car skidded to a halt next to Sophie and the others who carried Jean-Claude, enveloping them a cloud of dust, stopping them in their tracks.

Sophie lost her breath.

The driver's door flew open, and to their surprise, Héloise appeared.

"Get in!"

"Héloise? I thought—"

"Get in!" she repeated. "Hurry!"

Needing no further encouragement, Sophie and the others lifted Lévèque to the back of the carrier. The cooks and consorts who'd run away raced back from the foothills seeking the safety of the troop carrier.

Emma climbed in first, found a woolen blanket, and laid it on the floor of the truck's interior. "He can lie here," she offered.

They placed Lévèque on the blanket, his head listing to one side. Once he was resting, Sophie sat beside him and took his hand. Hold tight, she thought. Hold tight.

Her grandmother stepped forward and knelt at Sophie's side. "We'll be there soon, child," she whispered, rubbing Sophie's back. "He'll be fine."

Sophie forced a smile. She could always tell when her grandmother was lying.

Felipe again lent a hand, helping the rest of the group into the truck before taking his seat.

Madame Geneviève tied open the canvas door to let the moonlight shine into the carrier. "I won't travel in darkness again," she declared, then sat next to Felipe.

"Hang on," Héloïse called from the driver's seat. She cranked the gearshift into drive and stomped the gas, plunging them all into the night.

Sophie looked to the small grated window that separated her from the driver's cab. "When did you learn to drive?"

"I watched my father in our delivery truck," Héloïse explained.

Sophie didn't want to ask how many times Héloïse had actually taken the wheel.

"I thought you'd gone after Céline," Sophie said over the rumble of the engine. "No one would have blamed you."

"Céline is safe," Héloïse pronounced. "You are not."

Sophie was unsure how Héloïse knew of Céline's safety, and was equally unsure how to express her feelings of gratitude.

She turned back to Lévèque. "Stay with me," she commanded.

They soon approached a small house, standing a hundred meters off the road in a clutch of walnut trees. Lights shone through the windows, giving Sophie hope that the horse doctor, Fournier, was home.

Héloïse pressed the horn to announce their arrival. When the carrier pulled to a stop, Sophie wasted no time. She stood from Lévèque's side, leapt from the carrier, and raced between the trees to the house. She pounded on the door until it opened to reveal a plump man with round glasses and rosy cheeks. He looked annoyed, but his look turned to shock and his mouth fell open when he saw the Nazi truck behind her.

"Monsieur Fournier?" she said breathlessly.

"Y-yes."

"You must help. A man's been shot."

The doctor nodded away his amazed look, though it was clear he hadn't yet made sense of what was happening. "A man?"

"Please! He's dying!"

"Of course, of course," Fournier opened the door, "bring him in."

Sophie spun back to the carrier, but the women were already on their way, carrying Lévèque in the woolen blanket.

She stepped forward to stroke his hair. "You'll be fine," she whispered, echoing her grandmother's promise, yet still uncertain of her words. The artist's eyes remained closed.

The group maneuvered Lévèque through the doorway and entered the warm house. A slight woman, who Sophie assumed was Madame Fournier, stood from the couch, framed by the glow of the crackling hearth. Her eyes grew wide at the sight of the procession before her, women dressed in ball gowns and maid's uniforms, carrying a bleeding man.

"In the dining room," the doctor called from the hallway. "Lay him on the table." He dashed to the back of his house.

Felipe took a spot by the hearth, chewing his finger. He no longer looked like the young man who felled a Nazi guard and helped save a few dozen women, but more like an orphan boy, lost and confused.

The women placed Lévèque on the dining table and stepped back, giving Sophie space to approach.

With a trembling hand, she reached to Lévèque's cheek, desperate for a connection. His skin seemed gray and blood had dried on his lips. His breathing seemed thin, and the blanket beneath him dripped with crimson.

"Live," she pleaded, wishing she had her Chai to invoke her prayer. "You must live."

To her surprise, Lévèque's eyes fluttered and then opened. With obvious effort, he turned his head to face her. "Sophie," he whispered, his voice not quite his own. "Are we home?"

"Not yet," her tears spilled onto her cheeks, "but we're safe."

He coughed with alarming intensity and then whispered, "Today...you were wonderful."

"How can you say that? Nothing today was wonderful."

"You...stopped the darkness." His smile was crooked, his eyes only hardly open. "You're...an artist. Don't you see?"

"Jean-Claude..."

Her heart swelled, overloaded with too many emotions. She became aware of her grandmother crying behind her.

Lévèque feebly reached for Sophie's hand. Unlike the first time he touched her, he now felt cold. He took a long, labored breath and closed his eyes, his head falling to its side.

"Jean-Claude?"

The artist didn't answer.

"Please, mademoiselle. Stand back." Fournier had returned carrying a black leather bag overflowing with medical supplies. He pushed forward, but Sophie refused to let go of Lévèque's hand. "Please," Fournier repeated. "I must have room."

Sophie's grandmother gently pulled Sophie by the arm. "Let the doctor do what we came for," she instructed. "For Monsieur Lévèque."

Sophie released Jean-Claude's hand and let her grandmother lead her toward the crowd of women that stood nearby.

"Sit here," offered Madame Fournier, now more composed. She made space on the couch. "Rest."

Sophie sat, but felt lost in some dead space between fear and despair. Just like the night's moon, part of her had grown dark.

The house fell silent save the sobs and sniffles of the women traumatized by the day's events, and the industrious sounds of Monsieur Fournier, rummaging through his bag for whatever salvation he kept there.

The former hostages shared the few wooden chairs in the house, others stood tentatively around the room. Each held a stare that told of the day's desperation, each grieving for their own loss and sacrifice, or perhaps sharing in Sophie's.

She squeezed her eyes shut and leaned onto her grandmother's shoulder, trying to halt the flow of her tears and wish away this nightmare.

She attempted, once again, to reach out with her thoughts, this time to find Lévèque in the darkness. To her dismay, she found nothing but silence.

Fear rose within her like the Loire in a storm, until she thought she'd drown in it—fear that Jean-Claude might succumb, that the Germans might win after all, that her horrid curse would finally take everything.

Yet Sophie was determined to halt the fear, to stop the darkness as Lévèque had said she'd already done. She imagined the moon, but not the half-moon that hung now in the night sky. Rather, she imagined the magical moon of Lévèque's canvas, the moon that had urged her to be her better self and draw upon some hidden strength the artist thought she had.

She fell quiet for what seemed like hours, focused on the light of the moon in her mind, until her silent contemplation was broken by her grandmother's soft voice. "My darling?"

Sophie opened her eyes and saw her grandmother's grim face, saw the doctor standing beside her.

Fournier looked weary, his features drawn from exhaustion. How much time had passed? He wiped his glasses and cleared his throat. "I've removed the bullet and repaired the wound," he explained, "but I'm afraid your friend has lost a lot of blood. Perhaps too much."

No one spoke.

Fournier repositioned his glasses on his face. "If we were in a hospital, if I had the supplies, the equipment, I could try a transfusion..." he sighed, but then shook his head, his silence speaking for him.

A lump formed in Sophie's throat. "What can I do?"

The doctor looked back toward the table where Lévèque remained. "I've given him something for his pain and to ward off infection. What happens next is out of my hands." He turned back to Sophie, desperation in his eyes, amplified by his lenses. "Mademoiselle, I'm a veterinarian. I know dogs and horses."

Sophie raised her head. "Monsieur, I asked what I can do."

The portly veterinarian took her hand. "It doesn't look good for your friend. I'm very sorry."

Sophie pulled her hand back. "No!" she cried. "You don't know anything. You don't know Jean-Claude." She wanted to explain Lévèque's stubbornness, the depth of his feelings, the magic of his art and his spirit, his strength and vision in spite of his blindness. Surely these traits would help him live.

She rushed to the table, to Lévèque's side.

His shirt had been removed and a knit blanket placed over him as if he were simply sleeping. A bath towel, rolled into a pillow, held his motionless head. His eyes were closed, his skin still gray. She lifted the blanket to see the wound at his flank, now clean, but crudely stitched with black cotton thread like the hem of a dress. She blanched as though the wound were her own, lowered the blanket, leaned in, and kissed him.

Still, he didn't move.

She took his hand, tears forming again on her cheeks, her lips trembling in spite of her attempt to keep them still.

The others in the room approached and circled the table where Lévèque lay. Madame Geneviève reached for Emma's hand, and then Emma reached for another woman's. Soon, they had all joined hands, lowered their heads, and closed their eyes in silent prayer.

Back by the hearth, Felipe lowered himself to the floor, clutched himself around the knees and cried.

Héloïse stood from a chair in the corner of the room where she'd been watching, took Sophie's grandmother by the arm, and led her to Sophie.

"He won't die because you won't let him," Héloïse proclaimed defiantly.

Sophie's grandmother stuck out her chest, adopting Héloïse's forcefulness. "He won't die because if he does, I'll kill him."

Sophie couldn't smile. She'd simply lost the strength.

"What should I do?" she whispered, turning to her grandmother. "Tell me. Tell me and I'll do it."

"You'll do what you taught me to do." Her grandmother fixed her eyes on Sophie. "You'll do what you taught us all to do."

The women around the table opened their eyes.

"You'll hope."

The word "hope" struck her, warmed Sophie's blood, rang in her head like the sound of truth. Wasn't this how she'd always fought her curse, by clutching on to hope? It was why she wanted to escape to Paris in the first place, driven by a hope that she could change herself and, thus, her fate. It was hope she had for Maurice and Madame Lefavre, and hope she still held for her father.

Hope was what she now needed for Lévèque. This is where it has to end, she thought. This is where her curse must be defeated. She no longer wished to be the bringer of death. She wished to be the bringer of hope.

She lowered her lids and, rather than fight the darkness, she let it overtake her. She dropped to her knees at Lévèque's side, forgetting everyone else in the room. She held his hand and released all senses but one—her connection to him.

The image of his moon rose in her mind, but this time it did not call to her. Rather, its power infused her, became her; and she became the moon, whole, complete, confident, and assured. She wasn't Madame Lefavre. She wasn't Colette. She wasn't even Esther, the hero of the Jews. She was Sophie, Sophie en Bleu. Lévèque's Sophie. The embodiment of hope, driven by love, Chai Sophie, Blue Sophie, Moon Sophie, she would prevail, and no power on Earth would stop her.

Chapter 23

The Third Thing

The aroma of kosher lamb, garlic, and *haricots verts* wafted out of the kitchen and through the farmhouse, chasing away the midsummer scents of the Loire. Gravy bubbled on the stove and bread browned in the oven. Sophie breathed in the scents. It was good to be home, after enduring the trek from Ville de Lemaire back to Avoine.

"Where do you want this?" Céline asked, holding up the kosher wine Sophie had asked her to retrieve from the pantry.

"The table, please." Sophie was glad Céline seemed to have satisfied her curiosity with Jewish things.

Food, particularly kosher food, was harder to come by now that the war was in full bloom and provisions were rationed. War had a way of making everything more difficult, but tonight was going to be different. Sophie would see to it.

The front door burst open and Héloise strode in, a strand of hair flying wildly out of place. The cool, salty smell of the Loire River followed her through the door.

"Goats are a nuisance," Héloise declared, slamming the door shut behind her.

"You're a butcher," chided Sophie. "I thought you could handle a few goats. That's why I accepted them back from Monsieur Marcoux."

"Animals are easier to manage when they're dead," Héloise smirked, "and I'm ready to kill them."

Sophie's grandmother hobbled in from the hallway, pressing on her new, polished cane, interrupting the girls' banter.

"Is it time?"

Sophie looked to the kitchen clock. "*Mon Dieu!* Five minutes!" She wiped her hands on her apron and tossed it on the counter. "Watch the gravy, grand-mère?"

"Of course, child. Go!"

The Van Hoden girls smiled to one another, caught up in the excitement.

Sophie sprinted past them to the door, threw it open and ran out of the house. She jumped off the porch, foregoing the stairs like she used to do as a girl, feeling like she had wings. She flew over the muddy field to the main road, her heart soaring at the sound of the approaching car. It was right on time.

The sky was clear of planes this morning and the air was cool. In spite of the war, in that moment, the world seemed at peace.

The taxi halted at her feet. The driver opened his door, smiled to Sophie and tipped his hat, then scurried to assist his passenger.

The passenger—a man, thin and pale—stepped out. He wore a soldier's uniform adorned with medals, his hair cut short, his hat tilted on his head. His left sleeve was folded and pinned to his shoulder where he'd lost his arm.

As he stood, he seemed strong in spite of his diminished stature. A smile transformed his face when he saw her.

"Papa!" Sophie cried. She threw her arms around him and hugged him like she was squeezing the juice from a grape, the familiar roughness of his cheek pressing against hers. He was leaner than he'd been ten months ago, less muscular. Still, it was him, here with her, alive—and she never wanted to let go.

"*Ma belle fille,*" her father said, emotion stealing his voice. He touched her cheek, tears forming in his eyes.

Sophie clutched his single hand and pressed it to her lips, looked into his eyes, and captured the moment as a portrait she'd have forever. "There are a lot of people waiting to see you." She smiled.

"Let them wait," he replied.

After a moment, the taxi driver stepped forward and set her father's suitcase at the side of the road next to them.

"Au revoir, monsieur," the man whispered, clearly trying not to interrupt their reunion.

"But, your payment." Her father wiped his arm across his moist eyes, and reached into his pocket to pay the driver.

"No, no." The driver waived his hand at the roll of franc notes her father held. "You're a hero of France, monsieur. It's my honor." He bowed, pinched the brim of his hat, climbed back into his taxi, and left.

"You *are* a hero," Sophie repeated.

Her father returned his money to his pocket and hung his head. "Sophie, I never meant to put you in danger." He reached for her and gripped her hand. "I should never have sent you to your grandmother's."

"Of course you should have," she snapped. "I already told you in my letter. You couldn't have known what the Germans would do. Even they didn't know they were in Ville de Lemaire."

"It's my job to protect you." His face fell, stricken with guilt. "What you endured—the things you had to do—grown men, soldiers, fail at such things, but you..."

"Papa." She squeezed his hand and commanded his look. "I protect myself. You did everything you should've done and so did I. Please, this is a happy day. Don't think about anything else."

"You *can* protect yourself," he said. "That much is clear." He chuckled. "You know, the story made its way to the hospital: 'The Girl Who Saved Ville de Lemaire.' I doubted it could be true. This war is full of tales. Still, I wondered if you had met this girl." He shook his head. "I'm such a fool not to have realized it was you."

Sophie drew a breath, sending away the dark thoughts she had now put behind her, and looked her father in the eye. "I did what you would have done." She reached to his shoulder, to the folded sleeve affixed to his uniform. She secured the pin, which had come loose during their embrace. "You've sacrificed more than I have."

She recalled her grandmother's story of how her father had met her mother, how he'd hurt that arm, falling from the barn loft into her mother's lap.

"Well," he laughed, "at least my shoulder won't bother me anymore." He smiled at her and then reached for his suitcase. "Now, let's meet those people you said are waiting."

At the doorstep her father immediately raised his head. He closed his eyes sniffed the air. "Lamb?"

"Of course," Sophie beamed. "Kosher. Your favorite." She opened the door, glancing at the shining mezuzah, still there to protect them.

They had hardly entered when Sophie's grandmother stepped forward, dropped her cane, and threw her arms around her son.

"Gérard!"

The tears began anew. Even Céline and Héloise, whom Sophie once thought incapable of feeling anything, let go their tears, reminding Sophie that some in France had lost more than she had.

Her grandmother released her father from her frantic embrace and stared at him, silenced by overwhelming emotion, allowing the house to grow quiet save the bubbling sounds from the kitchen.

Just then, a long creak echoed from Sophie's bedroom door, breaking the silence. A beam of sunset light shone from the hallway behind Jean-Claude as he emerged. His square jaw and confident features belied his tentative movements. He walked stiffly and relied on a cane much like Sophie's grandmother. His long hair was combed back, his face freshly shaven, and his clothes clean and crisp. He smiled with content.

Sophie rushed to his side.

"Jean-Claude, you should be sleeping. You know what the doctor said."

He rolled his clouded eyes. "Maybe you're not the only stubborn one in the house." Lévèque smiled. "Besides, I know a party when I hear one."

Sophie led the artist to her father.

"Papa, this is Jean-Claude. The man I wrote you about. My fiancé."

Héloise and Céline leaned forward in a clear attempt to read Sophie's father's face for a reaction, eager for a scandal.

To their obvious disappointment, he grinned, reached out, and took Jean-Claude's hand.

"I see she coddles you like she coddles me."

"Oui, monsieur, she does," Lévèque answered, "but I've learned not to argue with her. She's quite formidable."

Her father burst out laughing. "Then you know her well."

"And love her deeply, monsieur."

Sophie's father stared at Jean-Claude, his hand still grasping the artist's. "I can see that you do."

Watching her father clutch hands with Lévèque made Sophie's heart soar. This was the moment she'd worked for, the one she thought impossible. It was the moment the Germans had seemed determined to deny her, the one her curse seemed designed to stop, and yet was the moment that now seemed destined to occur.

She had her father's blessing to pursue the life she had chosen. It wasn't at La Sorbonne as she once thought it would be. It was with the brilliant artist who saw her, not as the goat girl, but as a woman with art in her heart—a heart she'd pledged to him.

"Ahem," coughed Héloise. She raised an eyebrow.

"Oh," Sophie called apologetically. "Papa, these are my friends, Héloise and Céline."

The girls offered a polite curtsy. "Bonjour, monsieur," said Héloise.

"Bonjour, mesdemoiselles," her father replied with a grin. "Sophie told me about your bravery, and I'm sure she's told you you're welcome to stay here however long you'd like."

"Merci, Monsieur Claveaux," answered Héloise, "but Monsieur Maurice is letting us stay at his house, here in Avoine."

"Maurice?" Sophie's father squinted in confusion.

"Maurice is married now," explained Sophie, "to Madame Lefavre. He's living with her at his cousin Narina's house, leaving his house in Avoine open. He's quite happy."

"Happy? Are we talking about Maurice, the gravedigger?"

Sophie laughed. "It's a long story."

Her father smirked. "Don't tell me you're part of that story too."

Suddenly, Felipe flew in through the open front door, panting and sweating. "Is he here yet?" The boy put a hand on his knee to catch his breath.

"This is him!" chortled Sophie, clasping her father's hand in hers.

Felipe looked up at her father, stood erect, and saluted. "*Enchanté, monsieur.*"

"*Enchanté?*" Sophie's father looked at her, perplexed.

"This is Felipe," laughed Sophie. "Madame Lefavre is teaching him to be a gentleman. He's been staying with Maurice to help fix up Narina's house."

"Did he run all the way here?"

"Only the last two hundred meters," grumbled a voice behind them.

Sophie turned back to the door to see Maurice standing at the foot of the steps. His eyes were bright and uncharacteristically playful. His arm was hooped at the elbow of the spectacularly dressed Madame Lefavre.

Madame wore an ornate, floral summer dress matching the broad hat, which rested on her delicate coiffure. She looked like the cover of a Parisian fashion magazine.

"Madame! You're here!" Sophie embraced Madame Lefavre, exchanging kisses on both cheeks.

"Of course, my dear, of course. I wouldn't miss this day if Maurice's life depended on it." She gave her new husband a playful elbow to the gut.

"Hey!" Maurice laughed. He reached forward and shook Sophie's father's hand. "Happy to see you home, Gérard."

"I'm happy to see you…happy," her father replied with a grin.

Madame Lefavre ascended the steps and offered her hand to Sophie's father. "Josephine," she announced. "Maurice's wife."

"Gérard," her father replied. He politely took Madame's hand and kissed it.

"You see?" said Madame, turning to Felipe. "This is a gentleman."

Felipe shook his head. "Always lessons."

"Careful, boy," said Maurice, "or I'll have you running another two hundred meters."

"Why did you have to run?" asked Sophie.

"Maurice thought it was suitable punishment for Felipe's faux pas," explained Madame.

"Faux pas?"

Felipe frowned. "I asked how old Monsieur Maurice was."

"Not too old to teach you a thing or two, that's for sure!" Maurice grumbled jokingly.

"The meal is growing cold," announced Sophie's grandmother, finding her voice. "Let's eat."

Sophie closed the door and watched the members of her new, large family take their seats. She thought of the last time she'd served lamb at this table, before her adventure had begun. She'd lamented the loss of her dream to study in Paris, fearing her life was over. Now, she saw her life had just begun.

Art didn't rest solely within the halls of the university, but within her, and within her love, Jean-Claude. Art was made of dreams, the stuff of life. It surrounded her and pulled her forward. It would always be a part of her. The Germans couldn't stop that even as they took more of France for themselves.

Once Sophie had served the meal, the others waited politely as her father said the brucha and then leaned over his plate to sniff the food. He looked up to the group, cocked his head, and smiled puckishly. "Is it safe to eat?" he joked.

The group giggled awkwardly, and then let loose in uproarious laughter.

"That's not funny," said Sophie, her eyes wide. She turned to Lévèque. "Jean-Claude. Tell him that's not funny."

Lévèque smirked. "Yes...of course." he said, barely containing his own laughter. "It's not funny." He turned to Sophie's father, his blind eyes looking over the plate. "The food is safe, monsieur." Sophie nodded in affirmation until Lévèque added, "Still, I'd be careful of your drink."

Again the group roared.

"I'm serious." Sophie thumped her hand on the table, causing the silverware to bounce and the room to fall silent. She scanned everyone's face, looking for an ally, but they all snickered, seeming ready to split open.

Her father lifted his napkin to obscure his smile, but that only made the group howl anew, this time even more loudly.

Sophie shot an angry look at her father, but to see him so undone by joy forced her to smile too, if only a little. "Okay," she begged. "Enough."

Soon, the laughter and teasing subsided and the food made the rounds. Héloise (with the help of Sophie's grandmother) proceeded to retell Sophie's father the whole story of Sophie's bravery. Though he'd already heard the basics, they spared him no detail, telling of the painful sacrifices they'd seen, including that of poor Monsieur Van Hoden, and of the ultimate retreat of Reichmann's company from Ville de Lemaire, thanks to Sophie and her kitchen comrades.

Inspired by the rebellion at the château, the village, they'd learned, had resisted their invaders and driven the remainder of Reichmann's troop out of Ville de Lemaire. Though much of northern France was now occupied, hosting her German invaders as guests, places like Ville de Lemaire continued to resist. And talk of resistance now spread throughout the country. France's fate was far from written.

"My sister chained me to the radiator beneath the shop," blurted Céline, appearing eager to contribute her own story of sacrifice. "She said that's what saved me, but it was humiliating."

"It *is* what saved you," snapped Héloise. "You can't be trusted to sit still or to keep quiet. I had no choice."

"Well, it wasn't very nice." Céline folded her arms.

"Your sister's a hero, Céline," offered Sophie. "If she hadn't brought the truck that night, Jean-Claude might be dead."

Jean-Claude smiled. "It's true, and I'm grateful." He reached to clutch Sophie's hand. "Very grateful."

Héloise looked over the table to Sophie. "We're all lucky in our friends."

"Yes," she grinned. "We are."

Jean-Claude raised his glass of wine to the room and stood with some help from Sophie. "To friends," he proclaimed.

They each raised their glasses. "Friends!"

They toasted and drank heartily, told their tales, and found cause for more laughter.

Madame Lefavre spoke of her latest letter from Colette. Business for her protégé was booming, although the Lefavre Maison had moved to London, the last destination for young allied soldiers before deploying to the field. This kept Colette and the others busier than ever in their "patriotic duties."

"Everyone returns to Paris," Colette had written, and Sophie still hoped it was true.

"That Colette is strong," Madame announced. "Strong enough to get through this. Beautiful and powerful. All things in twos."

Sophie looked to the man she loved and then to the father she adored— both men she'd almost lost. She scanned the living room, looking to a place just above the hearth, where Lévèque had hung her picture "Sophie en Bleu," his masterpiece.

His painting had captured more than Sophie's smiling image; it had captured her life. Small, seemingly random brushstrokes, each recalled a decision, a moment, an action, a point of fortune. Each was unfocused and appeared unintentional when taken alone, but each was important in its contribution to the larger picture. Like the artist's paint strokes, every step in Sophie's journey had led her here.

On the opposite wall, facing her portrait, hung Lévèque's moon, as full as her heart now felt. Its bright aura captured a piece of the real moon's own shine, reminding Sophie of her first night with Jean-Claude. That was the night she learned to see beyond sight, to see beyond herself—lessons La Sorbonne could never teach.

It felt that here in Avoine, all was in its place. Nevertheless, France was still in jeopardy. The war wasn't over, and Sophie knew, as long as there were families like hers, willing to take risks, to dream new dreams, France stood a chance of surviving.

Where there was fear, there could be joy. Where there was risk, there could be reward. Where once there was despair, there could be endless, boundless love.

These contrasts seemed to support Madame Lefavre's belief that all things came in twos. However, Sophie now understood, Madame had been wrong, or at least not altogether right. All things in two still required a third thing— the thing that bound them together; the thing that had carried Sophie, and even Madame Lefavre herself, to happiness; the thing that linked all "twos" together.

Hope.

About the Author

As an active business writer, blogger, screenwriter, and novelist, Herb Williams-Dalgart has been recognized by several national and regional writing competitions for developing rich, memorable stories; interesting, layered characters; and exciting, fresh dialogue across many genres.

The grandson of a World War II veteran after whom he was named, Herb maintains a great respect for and fascination with "the greatest generation." Many of his works, including his debut novel, *The French Girl's War*, draw from the tapestry of this war-torn era to find stories that seek to capture the heart, humor, drama, and sacrifice of the time.

Herb is a graduate of UC Santa Barbara with a degree in English and an emphasis in creative writing. He holds a certificate in screenwriting from UCLA's Writers' Program, spent a year at England's Birmingham University, and studied at the Shakespeare Institute in Stratford-upon-Avon.

When not writing blog posts, fiction, or screenplays, Herb loves to travel and to spend time with his family at their home in southern California.

Visit him at www.herbthewriter.com.

Made in the USA
Charleston, SC
29 June 2014